I0831529

Titha Mae and the Dawn of Celtica

written and illustrated by

Jon B. Dalvy

Author's Note: ***Celtica*** is pronounced with a hard C, or K sound, as is the academic pronunciation of Celtic; i.e. Keltic-ah. Onward, then!

Hardcover, Series Edition
Book Two of the Titha Mae Series,
Following ***The Ballad of Titha Mae***

BOOK TWO OF THE TITHA MAE SERIES

"To my three brothers: The stoic, the bard, and the lion-hearted."

Contents

TIME HAS BROKEN

CHAPTER ONE
Posture & Decorum

"**You want me to** ***what?*****"** Titha scoffed, her brow bent and firmly furrowed.

"Curtsy, please, and then extend your hand for the greeting of a gent'luna," the unbearably shrill voice of Mrs. Mint replied, her frame highlighted by a bright green dress as gaudy as her tone. "Just as your sister is, Miss Mae. See now how Gilly's entire arm is extended into a perfectly straight line? Simply place your fingers together—like so—and then bend your wrist as far down as it'll point, and—Miss Mae what in Gaela's name are you doing?"

Titha turned 'round. "I found a worm," she replied, the tiny thing squirming between her fingers.

Gilly couldn't help but laugh, a snort escaping in between. Mrs. Mint, however, let out a squeal that would curl the hairs of a wolf. Her plump throat lumped into two knots: one for frustration and another of pure, nightmarish disgust. She gasped before speaking.

“Put that… that—”

“Invertebrateà,” Titha interrupted.

“—Repulsive creature back where it came from!” Mint finished, glaring.

“Can’t. The soil is too dry here. That’s why he’s mad,” Titha clarified without a hint of sarcasm.

“I assure you the insect is not mad ”

“—Invertebrateà,” Titha interrupted again.

“Please do not interrupt me when I am speaking, Miss Mae! Now, put down the—inv—invertra—*thing*—so we may continue with a lesson of actual importance.”

Titha shook her head, forcing her toes into the ground to find a more suitable spot for her new wiggling friend. She looked to the darker, moss-covered earth behind Gilly and spotted their baby sister mushing her toes into the pete, too.

“Try here. It’s squishy,” the tiny Luna pointed, copying Titha’s every move.

“It’s perfect, Beebee,” Titha smiled. “This little guy’s gonna be much happier now, thanks to you.”

“You welcome, worm,” Beebbee waved, her tiny hand fluttering as Titha released the creature to be on his way in life.

Their tutor was not amused. “Master Begonia Bee, please do not encourage your sister’s… *choices…* in life,” Mrs. Mint scoffed. She glared over at Gilly, who took the not-so-subtle hint before rolling her eyes.

“We actually need to know this stuff, you two. Focus, please,” she said, a smirk still on her face.

Mint took a deep breath, pulling a handkerchief from

betwixt her bosom to wipe the dirt from Titha's hands. Titha immediately jerked her fingers as far from the lacey silk as she could.

"Absolutely not!" she cried out. "Dirt is way cleaner than where that rag just came from."

Beebee burst into laughter, breaking her tiny sense of composure.

"Why, I never!" Mint scoffed, her indigo cheeks turning to a bright Summer's red. "I assure you that my bosom is of the utmost cleanliness! Of all the things to say to a lady of the forest, Miss Mae! I know you prefer to spend your time with the—those *brutish* humans—but make no mistake, you are a Lunish wola! You will learn to act like one and you will prepare yourself for the eventuality that a gent'luna boy will come calling. I pray when one finally does you will have gained, by then, some semblance of proper decorum!"

"Or posture," Gilly added, smacking the slouch out of Titha's back. She took the rag from Mrs. Mint's hand and forcibly wiped the mud from her little sister's fingernails and knuckles. Doing so just revealed more; a layer of caked dirt that was practically permanent. Gilly scrunched her face, handing the formerly dainty handkerchief back to their teacher.

"Thank you, Master Gillian," Mrs. Mint hesitated. "Let us try this... one last time." She took a deep breath and requested Titha's hands, placing one on the young Luna's hip while extending the other until Titha thought her elbow was going to snap from straightness. "Now please," Mint continued, "Place your fingers together, slightly fanning their tips like the graceful wings of a swan, and then point them down and out, like so. There! Now you are prepared to receive the kiss of a true gent'lu—"

"Yeah that's not happening," Titha jerked away.

"*Enough*!" Mrs. Mint screeched, finally snapping. "I will not stand here to be interrupted and—and— constantly *devalued* by such an ungrateful—"

"Woah, okay, there's no need for name-calling!" Titha blurted. "I'm just no perfect prim'proper like you, okay? Have no desire to be. At all. That's not the end of the world, is it?"

Mrs. Mint didn't reply. Instead her expression went blank. She then turned (quite dramatically) to gather her belongings from the edge of the Meadow.

"Wait, I wasn't trying to be mean. I am sorry, Mrs. Mint. I am! I was just explaining myself!"

Still no response came as their tutor snatched up a stack of leaflets.

"Great..." Titha sighed.

Mint huffed a mighty huff, stomping t'ward the Grand Steps that led to the girls' home atop Mt. Meri. A small, portly porcupine scrunched forth from the bushes to greet their tutor as she stormed away.

"Your highly-respected services are no longer required, Reginald. There will be no needlepoint for the Mae sisters this Night, nor any other!"

With that Mrs. Mint's chin rose, a sharp "harrumph" leaving her lips as she marched straight up to Roostwood.

"Perfect, she's going to tell father," Gilly scolded. "That's the second tutor this Spring! What has gotten into you?"

"You're in trouble now," Beebee added. She picked clovers for Reginald to try and cheer him up as her siblings stared daggers into one another.

"Second tutor down. That firmly plants the blame on *you*. Not on Mint. Not on Mr. Crabgrass and his 'terrifying face'. You."

"Okay he was a creep and you've definitely said the same. Father said to let him know how our lessons were going and, well, I continue to let him know."

"This is clearly not the way to do that!"

"Mint's the one that stormed off, not me! All I said was we're different and this isn't the end of the world. Trust me."

"Maybe this *is* the world to her, Titha. Have you stopped to consider that?"

"Well that's just sad."

"Do you hear yourself when you say things like that?" Gilly scolded. "The blame is on you, Titha. For both tutors. You're the problem."

Mint reached the halfway point of the Great Stairs before the sound of her footsteps ceased, replaced by a sort of hapless flailing. Their tutor slipped, fell, then let out a squeal that evolved into a blood-curdling scream as she landed, alone. The girls flinched.

"Father's going to kill you," Gilly pointed. "If she doesn't first."

"And *I'm* the dramatic one," Titha frowned. She looked down to the velveteen dress covering everything but her toes, and then Reginald the porcupine, then sighed. "Sorry, Reg," she offered. "It's not your fault, little buddy." The stout porcupine smiled faintly, then pouted as he returned to the bushes.

"Bye I love you!" Beebee waved.

"Father holds Mint's studies in high regard, Titha," Gilly said, refusing to change the subject. "You need to catch up to her and apologize before she reaches the top. And you need to start taking our customs and our history seriously."

"I put on this stupid dress and stood here while she demeaned us for a whole evening, didn't I? I love our customs!" Titha replied. "Just not the ones that require me to *curtsy* for boys or let them *speak first in all proper settings*. What does that even mean?" Titha rolled her eyes.

"It means that boys talk first when smart things happen," Beebee answered.

"Hear that?" Titha added. "And that doesn't bother you? That this sort of garbage is being put into our baby sister's head?"

"No," Gilly responded firmly. "Because I not only *love* our customs, I *respect* them."

"Well in that case! If only I wereth as perfect as thou!" Titha scoffed, mumbling off into an exaggerated impression of her much taller sister. "Some of us would prefer to speak'eth before thoust is'eth spoken to," she forced under her breath, pulling at the tight dress she could not wait to replace with her tunic and pants.

"What was that?" Gilly yelled.

"Nothing, dear sister! Nothing at'all."

The Meadow turned eerily quiet. As the girls picked up their lesson's worth of discarded parchments, Titha's mind began to wander. She stopped, looking around the still, quiet and boringly-familiar landscape. Things had returned to exactly where they were one forest-year ago; before the Festival of Dawn, Vulduun's betrayal, and the eventual Breaking of the Horizon.

She frowned into the dark.

"Titha!" her father's voice boomed loud and clear from atop the mountain, breaking the silence.

"That's my cue," she responded. "And in record time. Mint sure is fast for such a stubby ol' geezer. Sorry for ruining your lesson, Gillian."

"Are you?" her older sister replied, shuffling leaflets with one hand, Beebee cradled in the opposite arm. "I'm not the wola you need to apologize to."

"You're right. Beebee, since I actually care what you think, I am sorry for ruining your lesson."

Beebee snorted, parting her long locks so she could see out of them. Titha snagged a vine to tie up her baby sister's hair, placing it in a knot atop her head just like her own.

"I meant Mrs. Mint, smart'mouth," Gilly replied, unamused. "You know, I really thought that everything you did—everything you went through out in the world would've matured you a bit," she said. "But I guess not."

"I'm just not the righteous, sparkling noble lady of Ythengrey, sis. That's you," Titha scoffed. "So as much as I'd love to stand here and be lectured for another full cycle of the Moon, I have to save that honor for father."

She turned from her sisters and headed for the steps. Beebee climbed down from Gilly's embrace, starting to walk with Titha, but the eldest held her firm. Beebee's bottom lip quivered as she began to cry for her other sister. Gilly picked her up again, even if she was almost too big to carry now.

"This behavior doesn't just affect you," she said pointedly as Beebee squirmed.

Titha lowered her head and kept walking.

Above them, the Meadow's clearing housed a crescent Moon surrounded by bright stars. Such a slender, sharpened shape usually answered Titha's question of "why am I so upset?". Lunas lived by the Moon's light, and the harsher its shape, the fainter the glow. Like most, she much preferred a fuller Moon, missing the wide, pale face that would sometimes reveal the smile of her mother. Thea would understand what she was going through. Gilly did not. Her older sister was so much like their mother in some ways, but empathy was not one, nor Gilly's strong-suit when it came to her middle sibling. At all.

Titha made her climb of shame up the many, many steps to Roostwood. She morphed her face into the exact expression she knew their father would be wearing when the doors opened. And as they did, sure enough, there he sat; brows'a'furrowed. Theole slouched forward in his grand silver throne amid the quiet halls of their home.

"I just finished a most interesting chat with one Calluna Mint," he decreed.

"Whatever about?" Titha responded cheekily.

"A particularly disrespectful pupil that also happens to be my daughter," he added with a bit more irritation in his baritone. "That is, before she began rambling on about something called an invalidate—or I believe that to be the term. She muttered incessantly, and I could barely make out a word after that. It was most odd. Then she ran off!" He dropped the leaflets from his hand, pounding his fist onto the log'top table beside his throne. "You have *broken* Mrs. Mint, Titha Mae!"

"The word is invertebrateà," Titha responded without a hint of doubt.

"What in Gaela's name is an invertebrateà?" Theole

grumbled. "It better be important, young lady!"

"It means without vertebrà. Like, you know, something that doesn't have a backbone. Nech taught me. From his research. It's a new word. Very important. I'm helping him classify animals and their body parts, father. It's really amazing work! Something I'm deeply passionate about, too, as you know—"

"That's enough." Theole let loose an angry sigh. "Two tutors, Titha. Not one. Two. I am not sure what has gotten into you this Spring, sproutling, but treating your elders with disrespect is not how I raised you, nor is it something I will ever have any daughter of mine accused of again. Are we clear?"

"Why should I respect her if she has no respect for me?" Titha asked.

"Do not talk back to me! This is precisely what I mean! You will learn to hold your tongue!"

"Father I am serious! She's constantly spouting incredibly off-putting remarks about everything we've worked for—and especially Sigrid and the Vikingmen. You should hear what she calls them, and *I'm* the one not being a lady?" Titha replied.

"Titha, please—"

"—And every single time it leads into some rant about Celtica and the sanctity of our forest. Then the Men, and their cows, and their hogs, and the horses and dogs, and the dogs *really* don't deserve any hate because, let's face it they're just the cutest things Men have ever given the world and she—she spends more time on *this* than our lessons! I see her gossiping with the other tutors before, during, and long after our prim and proper 'teachings'! She is bad news, father. Why should I respect her if she acts like that? Why is she even teaching us if she can't keep her awful opinions to herself? She has absolutely zero respect for everything we've worked so hard to—"

"*Enough*!" Theole commanded, his yell echoing through the halls. "Lower your voice, young lady, and do not raise it again. I am fully aware of Mrs. Mint's beliefs, but she is entitled to her opinions as are we all."

"But her opinions are wrong…"

"That is something you must learn to live with, little one. We inhabit a wider, connected world now, and not everyone will think, act, or live as we do. This is something you adore, correct?"

"Yeah."

"Then you must learn to be the bigger person and appreciate these differences in all peoples, not just those who think like you. Titha, my daughter, there is so much left for you to learn. Stop. Think. Breathe. You—*we* must not judge those around us so harshly. Instead, we must inhabit the change we wish to see in the world."

"I know…"

"Carry yourself that way, then, would you?"

"Yes sir…"

"Thank you. Now, as for your tutor. Her sternly black-and-white view of Gaela aside, Mrs. Mint is a brilliant socialite. Her studies of our culture and customs are unrivaled and invaluable, and I will only have the brightest of teachers for my daughters."

"See, that's the thing, father. Just before she stormed off she was trying to make me learn how to curtsy and extend my hand properly to be kissed by boys. Like I—is that a life skill I need right now? Or *ever*?"

"It's called manners, Titha."

"Oh, it gets better. She followed this with a stern order that we are never to speak to a boy unless spoken to first."

"She said what, now, hmm?" Theole replied, taken a'back.

"You heard me."

"That... seems a far reach from posture and décorum, I would say."

"That's all I've been trying to say! Where is she digging up these rules? It's like she's become obsessed with the past all of a sudden. Not the 'yesterday' past, either—I'm talking the *way-back* past. I get the value of good posture and standing up straight and walking the path of our ancestors, but I'll croak before I start bowing when boys enter the room. She told us to do that, too! Can you believe that nonsense? Again, no offense to our ancestors, which I love, but if I live by anything they taught us I'm not doing it for a boy. I'm doing it for me."

"As you should, my child. As you should," Theole frowned. "However, as persuasive as you have become, I am not foolish enough to think the fault lies solely on your tutor's choice in curriculum. Titha... I know this past forest-year has been, for lack of a better word—*boring*—for you, but you must understand there is great value in knowing our customs. And ever wiser are those who not only *acknowledge* history, but *respect* it as well. Never forget that."

"Yes, father," she replied sincerely.

"I will have a discussion with Calluna. Firstly to find out if she will even return, and secondly to be sure your lessons focus much more on preserving our culture and less on... boys. But you must promise me you will show her mutual respect. Unwavering mutual respect. Understood?"

"Understood," Titha complied, her back perfectly straight.

"Good. Now that we have that settled, what do you have prepared for the Festival this next full Moon?" Theole shuffled through the leaflets beside him, clearly pleased with his daughter's strength of character despite the situation.

"About that..." Titha replied coyly.

Theole slumped. "What is it now?"

"Maple and I have been putting together a little performance, you could say, right? A play about everything that happened last year. It's pretty epic. But Maple told her father and he said she can't do it, so now she won't do it. He says your idea for a Festival of Celtica is wrong, and he won't have any daughter of his performing in it for the whole forest to see. She said that he says that we should never be celebrating anything that, uhm, 'validates the Vikingmen'. Which is just real dumb. Sounded to me like he's been drinking whatever high-and-mighty-water Mint is gulping down lately."

"He told her this?" Theole responded, taken by surprise. "That seems rather harsh, does it not? From a friend? Has all our progress this past cycle of seasons meant nothing to him? Would he prefer we still celebrate the treacherous Vulduun and his Festival of Dawn come the longest Day of the year, hmm? Would he have us ring in Summer's warmth with such foul memories instead?"

"We must respect the opinions of others, father, remember? Especially our elders."

"Pish'posh! Melvinnious and I fought side by side *before and through* the Ever-war! His support should be unwavering! What would he have me celebrate instead? What would he suggest that I, one of his oldest allies and the Watcher of our people, do instead, *hmm*?"

"Mr. Maple suggested in place of a Celtican festival that, maybe, we have one to celebrate… The Grand Silver Owl."

"I did not expect you to have an answer for that," Theole replied, "which was foolish of me. Not nearly as foolish as such an absurd suggestion as celebrating the Grand Silver… *me*! We will do no such thing!" He seemed greatly disturbed by this suggestion; by the thought of himself as some sort of divine entity to be celebrated in the same ways as the Drakes of Old. "I am no deity," he said, "I am the Watcher. I was appointed a task—to keep our people safe—and that is what I shall do for the remainder of my time. Tell the young Maple when she sees her father next to tell him that spreading such nonsense will earn him no closer friendship of mine. Better yet, I will tell Melvinnious myself! The wrinkled fool."

"Geez, now who needs to calm down?" Titha responded. "Are you okay, father?"

"I am sorry, my child," Theole spoke softly. "It is just that Sigrid and I have discussed this exact subject several times over these past Moons; the very nature of our *being* seems in conflict with what we want for our world, and for Celtica. It is most concerning to me. To us. Do you think that other Lunas feel this way? Tell me, daughter, do many others share the opinions of the Mints and Maples?"

"Clover does," Titha added, "but he never talks to anyone but Gilly, so I wouldn't worry about him."

"I see," Theole laughed. "Perhaps if I keep my concerns to the adults of Yythengrey my worries will be less numerous. Keep an ear out for me, sprout, and do not perpetuate this rubbish. Bigotry thrives on attention, so we must give it none. Agreed?"

"Agreed," she smiled, finally stepping up for a hug. "For

what it's worth, I can't wait for the first Festival of Celtica," she added. "I love it out there."

"I know you do, my dearest. As would Thea, your mother. 'Tis a good thing, too, for if not for her such a festival would not bear such a name—and if not for you it would not bear such an existence! But try not to become any prouder of yourself for this than you already are, please."

"No promises," Titha smiled, hopping down from her father's throne. "Speaking of Celtica, how is Nech *still* not back? Wait! Ooh! Can I go fetch him? Please?"

"I planned to send a Crow, but I find it very hard to say no to that face when it smiles so." Theole rustled the knotted hair atop his still young, yet quickly-maturing middle child's head. "He is quite late, isn't he? Most unusual for him."

"Definitely," Titha nodded. She then jumped onto her father once more, embracing him.

"What is this for?" he grinned.

"I just love you," she said, continuing to hug him.

"I just love you, too, sprout. More than the Moon and—"

"—All her Stars combined," they finished. He tightened the vine around her hair bun.

"Go forth, my daughter. Do what must be done! Fetch the Goblin Squire!" he decreed, playing into her thirst for adventure.

She bounded for the doors of Roostwood much happier than when she entered them. Stopping just short of her exit, she let loose a whistle that pierced through the doors' cracks and into Yythengrey below.

"Ten, nine, eight, seven," she counted, "six, five, four, three… two… two and a half… two and a quarter? Yeah, two and a quarter…"

Finally the entrance burst open, her mighty steed present at last. Only it wasn't a steed, of course, but her bounding Bear-brother, Paw. He was a'light with purpose just as he was any time Titha let loose their 'go-time' whistle. The big black bear leaned forward with his nose down.

"Boop," Titha pipped as she pressed her nose against his. "Hello, sweet brother. We have a mission!" she exclaimed triumphantly. "Find Nechalec, my Bear-kin! Use that oversized nose and make haste!"

Paw's stump of a tail waggled amid a massive posterior as he prepared to take off.

"Wait!" Titha shouted. "I've got to get out of this ridiculous dress first and into my pants. Feathersword awaits, as well! Hasty, hasty…"

Paw groaned at his Luna-sister's bravado, taking her instead up the north wing to her chambers so she could change in preparation for their next grand, and sorely-awaited, adventure.

CHAPTER TWO
Budding Beauts

Down in the Meadow, Gilly and Beebee tended to the buds that would soon become new giant flowerbeds for their kin. Summer was right around the corner, and the enormous white Moonflowers would soon return to their ancestral home by Gilly's hands. Behind her, Beebee sloshed around a watering tulip as large as herself, plopping it down after every use so she could pat the seedlings on their tops and give them a pep talk.

"When will they be big?" she asked, barely able to contain her excitement.

"Hopefully by the end of the Festival, Weebee," Gilly replied. "Keep talking to them, too. They'll grow faster."

"You can do it, baby flowers!" Beebee yelled into the ground. As she did, another tiny sprout sprung from the soil, a single leaf in tow. Her smile spread across her entire face as she squealed.

"Even better if you sing to them, little one," Gilly added,

shaking her head at how impossibly cute her baby sister was in everything she did.

"I can sing to them?" Beebee clasped her hands together, wrinkling her nose. "Should I do it now?"

"Now is great," Gilly smiled.

"Okay," Beebee squeaked as she swayed, her little lavender dress'ends flowing like petals. Taking an impressively-deep breath, Beebee leaned down, her rosy round cheeks poised to deliver every melodious word to the budlings with gusto:

Daenu's waters, are clean and clear
Her shining river, Her mighty tears
Flow through our mountains, flow through our hearts
Through giving droplets, all new life starts

No tears of Hers, are tears of sadness
No tears of Hers, bring gloom or strife
'Bring only mercy, 'bring only light
To all who dwell here, in Moonlit Night

No tears of Hers, shall e'r be wasted
No tears of Daenu flow in vain
Flow ever on now, within our heartland
For all who dwell here, in Moonlit Night

For all who dwell here, in Moonlit Night…

Gilly wiped several tears from her eyes, trying to hide her weeping.

"Don't cry, big sister! It's a happy song!" Beebee reassured her. But it was too late, Gilly was full-on blubbering beneath both hands covering her mouth.

"I'm fine," she mumbled. "You're just the sweetest thing and that was beautiful, okay? Don't tell Titha I cried, please. Or anyone."

"Like him?" she snorted.

"Hi," a quaint, smooth voice responded.

"Oh no, oh Gaela... Oh Gods, oh Gods why," Gilly panicked to herself, frantically wiping the tears from her face. Before her stood Clover, a Lunish boy of her exact seventeen-forest-years in age, and one she'd come to know quite well. He was, in her and many other's young eyes, as handsome as the Duskridge ever made 'em.

"Am I interrupting something?" Clover asked, brushing his short silvery hair to the side.

"Yes!" Gilly blurted, hiccupping herself into a silence. "I mean... no. Just me looking an absolute mess, is all. You don't, though."

"I don't... what?"

"Look a mess."

"Oh. Thanks," he smiled.

"She thinks you're miiiiiighty hand-i-some," Beebee stated matter-o-factly as she waddled between them. "She can draw your face *exactly*, too. Wanna see?"

"Begonia Bee!" Gilly screeched, mortified. "Of course I can't draw your face. Why would I have it memorized? That would be super creepy and *so*-not-me. Right?"

"Right," Clover laughed. "I'll let you get back to it. Just wanted to see if everything was alright since your lessons didn't go so well."

"Ah, you heard that?" Gilly asked.

"Well, no, but I saw Mint on her way out of the forest. And she did not look happy. She, ah, looked less happy than usual, I mean. She's the worst, right?"

They shared a laugh, Gilly sideswiping her bangs to get a better look at his dimples. As she did, his expression slightly changed.

"Anyway, shouldn't be an issue for much longer," Clover added as he looked away. "Her tantrums, I mean."

"What? Oh, no, is she quitting for good this time?"

"You could say that," he replied, fidgeting with his tunic. "Well, definitely. Probably. Oh, hey! Are we still on for later?"

"Yes—" Gilly blurted again without thinking. "Yeah, yup. Yes. Let's be. Let's be that. I'll see you then for that?"

"Okay," Clover smiled. "We can talk more about Mint and her awfulness then. If you can keep a secret, that is. Can you?" he asked, looking directly into her eyes, or what felt like—to her—her very soul.

"I can. I can keep those…" she mumbled.

"Great…"

Clover smiled to one side, and Gilly's world started to swirl. Just as the trees began to sway and the leaves turned to hearts, an unbearably pervasive holler cut through the dense forest.

"What *is* that?" Clover jumped back, startled.

"Take a guess," Gilly scoffed. She counted on her fingers, then pointed to the air right when another set of 'wahoos' broke out into the Night.

"Here she comes!" Beebee exclaimed, her little fists clenched with excitement.

"Titha Mae?" Clover asked.

"Titha Mae…" Gilly gritted her teeth. "Impeccable timing, as always…"

Out from the tree line shot Paw with his Luna-sister astride; Titha's riled-up haw'ing rattling Clover as it pounded the pointed ears of all nearby.

"No, no, no!" Gilly shouted. "This is a rough-housing-free-zone, twerp! These seedlings are incredibly fragile! Titha Lilly Mae, stop! *Paw*!"

Titha couldn't hear a word Gilly was saying, nor did she want to. She would never harm the future Moonflowers but relished any chance to rile up her infinitely-rile'able sister. She pulled on Paw's fur, guiding his bounding footsteps around the flowerbeds, much to the entertainment of Beebee. Gilly's gums were still flapping, her hands holding her silver hair from obstructing the endless orders spewing forth. Clover was… polite about it all.

"Can't talk now, sis," Titha yelled over Gilly. She jumped down from Paw, playfully pulling on his ear before flinging her arms open to greet Beebee. "Oh hi, Clover," she quipped.

"Hi Titha," he replied.

"You two dating yet?" she asked before *WHACK*, Gilly planted a firm five fingers on the back of her head. Titha grunted, turning to her sister with fists clenched. Clover stepped between them, pushing the riled girls apart.

"Please, ladies—please!" he shouted.

Beebee hopped into her sister's view. "Titha, Titha! Are you on a mission?" she asked, her little arms balled up in excitement.

"You know it, Weebee!" Titha replied, shoving Clover into Gilly. They both blushed.

"Take me with you, please," Beebee requested. "I want to see Hickory."

"Who is Hickory?" Gilly asked as she straightened her already-impossibly-straight hair.

"*My* boyfriend," Beebee replied.

"*Your* boyfriend?" Titha laughed. "Is everyone dating someone around here but me?"

"Everyone but you? Please!" Gilly added, "And where's Audun, hmm? I though he was supposed to meet us here after lessons."

"Audun is not my boyfriend, sticklegs," Titha spat back. "He's like two forest-years younger than me, or like… a lot… in his time, however that works. So no thanks."

"Not to mention he's human?" Gilly cocked her eyebrows.

"Pffft, please! I've seen how you look at Rainer, too," Titha laughed. "Mister tall, freckle'y, and handsome Vikingman atop your noble white steed! Please sweep me away from my princess-like duties, I am so eager to be your wiiife!" She let loose another laugh (as she truly amused herself deeply), then snorted to a stop before making eye contact with Clover. "No offense," she added.

Gilly smacked the hairbun atop Titha's head. "Third one

lands on your mouth," she quipped.

"Only if you want to lose that hand!" Titha barked, pointing to her now properly-smithed weapon, Feathersword, that brandished her hip.

"Hush, hush, hush," Beebee interrupted, much more concerned with the adventure a'foot. "Hickory is a Luna, not a man-boy, so can I go see him now please?"

"Aren't you just the most perfect'est of the Mae sisters?" Titha laughed. "I have to go find Nech first, but we can't keep any boyfriend of Miss Begonia Bee Mae waiting, can we?" She plopped her still-tiny sister atop Paw, who reached around to snatch her for some nuzzling of his own. "After we find ol' wrinkly, your boyfriend is next, Beebs. Deal?"

"Okay!" Beebee squeaked.

"Please stop encouraging her," Gilly groaned. "She's four."

"I'm four-and-a-half, lady," Beebee croaked, attemptting to hold up four-and-a-half fingers.

Titha chuckled as she threw herself atop Paw. She readied her little sister betwixt her straddle, patting her Bear-brother on the noggin. Smiling, she looked back at Gilly.

"C'mon, sis," Titha smirked. "You know you wanna' come."

Gilly rolled her eyes. "Won't they be asleep? The Goblins and the Vikingmen? It's Midnight."

"Nope! Sigrid has been awake watching the Auroras every night this week. It's been absolutely gorgeous!" Titha replied. "I bet Audun is sketching them for her now, and Nech is babbling on about something that has him late for his meeting with father. Oh, and I'm sure it's a family affair, as usual, and

Rainer is there, too. You know, if any of that interests you in any way."

Gilly attempted, very poorly, to look uninterested before her teenaged-mind bounced back to Clover, who stood still behind her. He blinked, bemused.

"I'll see you later?" she asked him. "I mean, only if you still want to, you know. Or come with us now? The Aurora really is something."

"I'll have to pass, but thanks," he replied, looking to Paw, who let loose a snarl at the youngster. "I've... got to catch up with some family before I can be free for later. So I'll see you at low'Moon?"

"Suit yourself, cutie-pie!" Titha yelled.

Gilly couldn't help but laugh at that one. "See you then," she grinned, setting her watering tulip down to hop atop Paw, who now held all three Mae sisters with ease. The girls waved bye to Clover as he walked back toward the Meadow.

"Let's go, twerp," Gilly commanded. "But I'm only doing this to see the emerald Aurora in an open sky."

"Whatever you need to tell yourself," Titha laughed. "From one boy to the next, and you think I'm the one that's going to give father a heart attack. And you, little miss—better hold on tight, Weebee!" she added, pulling upward on the tuffs behind Paw's ears as the sisters gripped to one another. "Show 'em how it's done, fuzzybutt!"

The black bear whipped his head 'round and roared, taking off down the tree-hall path, and off the Mae sisters went; Celtica bound.

Many things had remained the same in their Luna lives, but what awaited outside their Wood Gate was a world entirely unimaginable to those that came before them; to those who once held the light of Day and its kin in the same disdain as the fires of Death itself.

It truly was, in Titha's words, "quite the time to be alive."

CHAPTER THREE
Celtica Rising

Celtica was a sight to behold. The Mae sisters bounded across once-barren fields, Paw kicking up dust in the Moonlight as they traversed the land between Yythengrey and Autumnhill. What was once a wild, forgotten pathway of wheat and rocks was now a sprawling trading post during Night or Day—brimming with the smells of otherworldly foods and the sounds of craftsmen of many races. Titha never tired of Celtica's splendor, and how could she? The trinkets, treats, and aromas changed nightly. Goods both fine and splendid made their way from the worlds of Day to her Night-kin for the first time in her people's lives. Vikingmen brought their smithing and smelting of thick weaponry and armor amid massive stone firepits, which the girls found most chaotically fascinating. Lunas crafted the finest garments of silk, velvet, and cotton beneath newly sprouted tree canopies, where young Vikings came to try on garments the likes of which they'd never seen nor felt. Even the occasional Goblin's corner stand popped up, each chock-full of mince pies (Paw's personal favorite, though they might not've been had he known what was in them). The occasional scuffle and scoff accompanied a Goblin's kart if they happened to set up in front of a Gnomish tavern, but this was understandable. Each brimmed with beverages, brews, and savory dishes, regardless, always attempting to top the others. There's no harm to be found in a little lively competition! Such a colorful tapestry of cultures, fineries, peoples and their traditions inspired greatness in each race; and it showed.

"Ah, a good Night to you, Ladies of Yythengrey!" one particularly boisterous vendor yelled out. "Welcome back to Celtica this fine Spring's eve!" the gangly Luna added. He bowed forward with an immaculate silver hair-do he kept swirled straight up, placing one hand out and the other onto the finest flower-laden apron one could ever hope to see.

"Good Night, Mister Ponderosa," the sisters replied in tandem.

"What's tonight's special?" Titha asked.

"Only the most stupendous, most fabulously scrumptious frosted portobello cake you'll have in your Luna lives! Care for a slice?" Ponderosa replied, the curl of his thin silver moustache only rivaled by his smile. Paw didn't wait for his sister's response, slumping to a halt with his big nose smack-dab against the icing on the edge of the cake.

"Now please, Master Paw—" Ponderosa spat, stuttering. "We mustn't be so hasty! One must s-s-s-savor a mushroom cake such as this! Why, this—this is Peony Ponderosa's finest recipe yet!" he finished, speaking of himself.

Such words meant absolutely nothing to Paw. Before Ponderosa could pull the delicious display back it disappeared with one big sweep of a pink tongue. Titha laughed, holding her little sister who did the same. Beebee clapped and cackled, their Bear-brother creating a most adorably-sloppy display. Gilly, who was never one to enjoy a good mishap, cringed at the sounds of the bear slurping and swallowing away.

"I'm really sorry about this," Gilly offered, thumbing a few stones in her pocket. "This ought to cover the whole cake." She flipped her shiniest riverstone to Ponderosa, whose expression immediately changed.

"Thank you, Lady Gillian!" he pleaded, his hands clasped to the beautiful piece of currency. "You have your mother's generosity, rest her spirit."

"Unless you're her sister," Titha responded with a smirk. She patted Paw's side, which was undoubtedly a bit "fuzzier" than it had been in years past, thanks to Celtica's abundance of such sweet treats. "Thanks for feeding the beast!"

"Feed him more!" Beebee yelled, leaning over to ruffle Paw's cheeks as the bear happily agreed.

"I think we've caused Mr. 'Rosa enough trouble for one Night, wee one," Titha replied. "Besides, we're on a mission, remember? *Hyah*!"

Titha yipped, swinging her ankles into their Bear-brother's sides, sending him into a bounding frenzy, if only to frazzle the unprepared Gilly astride behind her. Ponderosa waved, his pointed indigo hands sending the Mae sisters off into the center of Celtica.

Before them the pathways narrowed between cobblestone chalets and wooden lodges as they reached the middle of the settlement. Within Celtica's heart stood an incredible monument raised of earth and stone, built by the Vikingmen as a sort of peace offering for the dawn of Celtica. It was structured almost exactly like the former tower of Skaldhall; the titanic citadel that once stretched straight up into the sky housing their precious Sunstone. There was one striking difference, however; the Tower of Celtica housed no such glowing Eternal Stone, but looked as if it should; like the spirits of those who built it longed for the Light of the Drakes and their Gods to return to them.

In place of a familiar glow, new banners hung from its pointed top. Three enormous, tapestries of a rich, billowing green flowed down from the top of the Tower, each baring the identical insignia of Celtica: The Tree of Life, Igdrasil, flanked by an owl and the Moon to the left—and the Sun and an eagle on the right. These were the crests of Theole and Sigrid, respectively, and were placed upon the banner as signs of both their founding influence and their continued reign.

Around the tower, workers of both Lunish and Viking descent hammered a'top wooden framing, as Celtica was still very much a work-in-progress. The past year had been colorful in the new city—a stark contrast to they grey beauty of her home—and Titha genuinely felt better for it. She saw the best in its successes: in its vibrant vendors like Mister Ponderosa, or the incredible copper bracelet Bjor, Sigrid's blacksmith, gave to her that she would never be parted with.

Though such splendor was not without struggle and hard work. Her young green eyes had seen much the past forest-year; sharp memories of petty disputes between her people and the Vikingmen kept with her like splinters of the mind. Not everyone was in support of such "mingling", as it was called, and not all hearts had held the lessons of the journeys of Titha Mae and the Companions. For wherever the light of harmony shines shadows of doubt linger. Whenever progress prospers, bigotry rears its ugly head. Every dozen persons thrilled with the existence of Celtica produced one who wished to see it *burn*.

The Breaking of the Horizon was not without its costs; the least of which the absence of the Eternal Stones and joining of societies under a unified banner.

Titha furrowed her brow as these dark thoughts took hold, something she had perfected in her father's tutelage. Just as she was about to tug on her older sister's dress, a familiar voice called to her from beside the Tower.

"Titha!" the young caller exclaimed. Out from the Tower's Moonshadow rode Audun astride his trusty hound, Haldor; each bearing a matching grin.

"Hey girls!" he shouted. "I've been looking all over for you!"

"For us? *You* were supposed to meet us in the Meadow!" Titha yelled back.

"Yeah!" Beebee added, "You lied!"

"I know, I know—I'm sorry—but you've really gotta see this!" he exclaimed, his little hands pointing behind the tower. The sisters and Paw rode over to Haldor's stride, rounding the courtyard at the foot of the Tower. Behind it, the Night sky opened—unobstructed by huts, stands, and trees.

And *there they were.* Painted across the heavens like the brushstrokes of a goddess: The *Aurora Borealis.* The girls were awestruck… not a word escaped their purple lips. Audun smiled as he beheld his dear friends' astonishment, turning to join them.

The Vikingmen called this phenomenon their Northern Lights, or the *Path of the Gods.* Lunas knew it as the Merrilight, as they were told by her that it was a gift from their Duskmother, Meriduun. They were much less attuned to its majesty given their penchant for tree-covered canopies, but no creature could deny the splendor of this particular display, as whatever name was used to describe their beauty paled in comparison to said beauty itself. Such a colorful display was unlike anything else witnessed in the natural world. The Aurora billowed across a deep blanket of midnight stars, its translucence ebbing and flowing like ribbons of every glorious shade of green imaginable. Emerald, to be more precise. They had been this way for the past week, and Audun had grown quite attached to them. He was not alone in this—as his mother, the mighty Sigrid Shieldmaiden, had taken up great interest in their hue, direction, and consistency.

"It is a pattern," Sigrid spoke, her melodic voice rolling in tandem with the colors of the sky. Titha lit up at the sound. She had been so mesmerized with the Aurora she hadn't noticed Audun's before them. While the faces of those around her were all painted with smiles and awe, the Shieldmaiden of Autumnhill stood stoic in comparison, yet concerned. Audun sat astride Haldor to her left, resuming his frantic scribbling with colored pigments—effortlessly recording the night and its Aurora. As he drew, a familiar long, pointed yellow nose rose up over Haldor's side to the paper, studying every stroke the young boy made. Here was Nech beside his Vikingfolk and Luna friends, far later now for a meeting with Theole than he had ever been on any occasion before.

"Good, good!" the old Craglin decreed. "You have the skill of a true talent! A marvelous Scribe's apprentice!" Nech continued, thrilled with Audun's work. "I dare say the artistry you display surpasses even your skill with the written word! If I were not so sure of my own abilities, I would be green with envy! Green as this Night's heavenly Aurora Borealis, indeed."

Audun didn't flinch, his focus unwavering. He made one final stroke with light green chalk across the black parchment. "There," he spoke confidently. "I think that should do it!" He handed the drawing up to his mother, who took it eagerly.

"It is most beautiful, my son," she smiled, running her hands through his curled auburn hair. "And truly accurate. Just as it is in the sky, and in my dreams."

"Your dreams, you say?" Nech perked up.

"Look, Nech, here," Sigrid pointed quickly, changing the subject to the bottom left corner of the art. "The Lights. They point again—making an arrow sweeping northeast over the Horizon." She traced her finger upward, then downward, following their path all the way to the bottom right corner of Audun's art.

"Indeed, they do," Nech replied, his spindly finger tapping a sharp chin. "Surely it is to mean something grandiose… but what?"

Before he had a chance to spout what was sure to be a brilliant theory, Paw bounded through the darkness over to the Scribe; all three Mae sisters still astride after finishing their first round of Auroroa-watching. The bear planted one big, wet lick up the side of Nech's wrinkly yellow face as the Craglin cackled jovially.

"Masters!" he cried, "Your timing is simply impeccable, as always."

"Yours isn't!" Titha replied from atop Paw.

"Whatever do you mean?" His eyes narrowed, then snapped wide open like beetles taking flight. "Oh! Oh! Gracious me! Your father awaits my arrival! Yes, yes, there your Mistress Moon sits high in the Midnight sky as I dawdle on below with drawings and fanciful thoughts. Blast it all if I am still not accustomed to this Night'time scheduling after these past seasons. Time, it would seem, is escaping me more and more!"

Titha laughed, dismounting her brother as she helped

Beebee slide down. "That's why we're here, pal. Better get your butt up the Grand Steps!"

"Immediately!" Nech screeched.

Paw rolled his eyes, grunting as he plopped the entirety of his weight onto the ground. Then, and only then, did Gilly step off the bear. She was a windswept wreck.

Sigrid stepped forward to greet the girls, bending to the ground with her arms spread wide. Titha jumped into her hero's embrace, Beebee along with; the two of them elated. Sigrid's presence was always blissful for them, and the feeling was very mutual. Gilly was not so warm with the Shieldmaiden. A tinge of resentment tainted their would-be relationship. The oldest Mae sister was heartily aware of her sisters' need for a mother figure, and their father's long absence of a ruling equal. Gilly would not entertain such thoughts and clung ever-tighter to the memory of her mother in Sigrid's presence.

Sigrid, though, could never be faulted for a lack of trying. She stepped to Gilly, offering a warm yet reserved smile.

"Your hair looks nice like this, eldest," she stated.

"... Like what?" Gilly was caught off guard. Was she being made fun of? Still queasy from Paw's nonsensical bounding, she reached up to feel her scalp.

Sigrid reached out, sweeping a few strands behind Gilly's ear. "It looks very full and free. A fitting visage for a natural beauty such as yourself," she spoke sincerely.

"Oh *Gaela*, does it?" Gilly panicked, scowling over at Paw so hard he could feel it. She scrambled to straighten her precious hair, looking to-and-fro as she did.

"Do you wish for me to fetch Rainer?" Sigrid asked, observing her bird-like peeping and primping.

Gilly harrumphed, rolling her eyes as she let loose of her locks. "Why does everyone keep asking me that?" she mumbled, stomping off.

Frustration turned her gaze back to the sky as it often did. There her beloved Moon held high and bright, despite its sharpness of late. Forever a constant, it was. The Aurora billowed on around Her, its hundred shades of green lending a luminous emerald glow to the crescent Moon. A small, bony figure about half her height stumbled into her, his pep'full backward stepping abruptly ending.

"Sincerest apologies, Lady Mae!" Nech decreed, composing himself. She barely noticed him. "Are you alright, Master Gillian?" he asked.

"I'm fine, thank you Nech," she responded solemnly, her gaze locked upon the Moon. "I'm fine."

The other Companions chatted on merrily, as if they did not see each other on an almost-Nightly basis. Their unbreakable bond held as mightily as ever.

"As much as I hate to leave this most splendid viewing, I truly must be off," Nech decreed, gathering a few scrolls and one rather thick tome from the dry grass. He looked to Gilly once more, following her gaze and noticing the Moon's position in the sky. "Bah!" he scoffed, panicking. "Bless my bones it is far past Midnight now!" he cried. "Have I grown so careless? What have I become!?"

Sigrid cocked an eyebrow at her friend's statement. "A moment, Nech…" she called. Holding to her serious demeanor she pulled him in close, speaking with the hush of guarded secrets.

"Do you not find this odd, my wise friend?" she asked.

"Do you not feel it, too? Or do you just speak carelessly of it? That the very Time of existence—the passing of it we live and breathe—has somehow *broken*? I hesitate to say such things, but... Do you not think that Time itself may be off, and not you?"

Nech's nose pointed to the ground, his heavy eyes filled with thought. Sigrid brushed her wolves'fur cape back, placing a hand upon her fallen husband's axe. Thinking of Angvar's sacrifice against Vulduun, the absence of the Elder Stones, the Elk Kings, the Breaking of the Horizon, Igdrasil, and everything in-between, she breathed in deep. "All legends of Gaela tell of the Nightfolk dwelling in a forest all their own, where Time passes slowly and peacefully. Does it not intrigue you that this vast difference in Time has begun to... fade? Do you not see the same age in yourself here as you do in Yythengrey day after day? Do Theole's daughters not seem to age alongside my beloved sons now?"

Nech stopped, his usual chipper demeanor vanishing, giving way to gloom. "I think it may be best if you accompanied me to Roostwood this Night, Shieldmaiden. And if I may be so bold, we mustn't go shouting such revelations into the darkness of Night. Not here in Celtica. But what you speak of is... Theole has feared the same for quite some time.

Sigrid stood shocked. Titha, never letting an interesting conversation escape her, listened on with one sharp ear perked over Paw.

"And I was not made aware of this? Or to attend such council from the start? Where was I when such a revelation was decreed?" Sigrid demanded.

"You know Master Theole," Nech sighed. "He wishes to have his talking points perfect before holding any sort of official court. Especially with you, Shieldmaiden, for he respects no other more than you."

"You're lying," she smirked, raising a blonde eyebrow to the Craglin, smacking his small back. "Which means you are up to something. To Roostwood then, sly Goblin. I am indeed coming with you."

CHAPTER FOUR

Revelations of Time

"**Any second now I will be sending out the Crows,**" Theole huffed. "This is most unusual and, if I am being honest, rather irritating!"

He paced back and forth in front of his throne, the plopping of enormous feet echoing throughout the chamber. Upon his right shoulder perched a very familiar falcon. Maya, of the Peregrine Order, was to hold council tonight as well, and had flown in all the way from Cragoa to advise the Watcher.

"This is unlike them both, I will admit," Maya added, her beak crooked with concern. "Nech has his flaws, but tardiness has never been among them. Nor does Titha Mae do *anything* slowly. I'll fetch them, no sense in sending out your band of slowfeathers."

"I'll have you stop insulting my crows, Maya," Theole frowned. "They are a part of the very fabric of Yythengrey—But fine. Go."

Maya smiled slyly, wiggling her backside in preparation for flight. Just as her talons left Theole's deep blue robes, the doors of Roostwood flung open. Two Cedarguards held the entry outside as Nech walked in, absolutely exhausted.

"We must find... me a Bear-brother for those... unbearably steep steps," he wheezed, "though I would settle for an Opossum or Beaver-brother... Any beast of burden at all... *whew*!" He stopped, leaning over to catch his breath. "Please forgive my tardiness, Master Theole, but here... here I am."

"You're late," Maya squawked.

"Bless my—Maya!" Nech blurted, thrilled but surprised to see his oldest comrade.

"I called on her attendance," Theole interjected. "Take a seat and catch your breath, my friend. We have much to discuss before—"

Theole stopped mid-sentence as a most familiar silhouette crossed through the closing doors. "I will be joining this council," the figure decreed gracefully, wolves'fur flowing.

"Si-Sigrid!" Theole stuttered, immediately shuffling his robes in order. "What are you doing here at this hour of Night?"

"You are up to something, are you not, Watcher? I see Maya is to join as well. Good! It shall be a full hall. Light the hearth. Warm evenings to you, Peregrine."

"And you, Shieldmaiden," Maya replied, scoffing at Theole's panicked state. "Relax, sire," she whispered into his pointed ear. "She's only a human."

"I am in my roost'robes!" he shushed back to her, reaching for a wool sash and gown atop his throne, throwing its greys and browns over his relaxed attire. His deep respect for Sigrid would

never waver, let alone be tainted by such inappropriate attire.

"This is a most pleasant surprise, Shieldmaiden," he added, fastening the sash around the thick woolen-gown, his indigo face now a deep shade of purple. He grabbed Nech's vest below him. "Did I not say we were to convene *before* presenting such revelations to Sigrid?"

"Y-yes-of-course, sire!" Nech replied, scrambling amidst the grip of Theole's enormous hand. "But forgive me for saying that the Shieldmaiden does not need our permission nor blessing to come and go as she—*ack*!"

"I know that, you craggy old codger!" Theole barked before letting loose of his friend, straightening the Craglin's intricate vest; still very much embarrassed. He turned to Sigrid, fluffing his beard and clearing his throat. "You must forgive my attire, for I have done all I can. Let us convene in the study, Companions. There we will continue. And despite my appearance I am glad you have joined us, Shieldmaiden. We have a matter of dire importance to attend to that, in hindsight, should not wait any longer."

Sigrid nodded, walking behind Theole as the four great minds headed for Roostwood's south'wing.

Deep within its wooden corridors and round rooms rested a dusty library of sorts; a long-vacant study once belonging to a Luna no longer welcome in these halls.

The Companions traversed their passage silently, each running scenarios through their heads as to how such a meeting would play out. As they walked, a large shadow followed outside. Every window they passed was darkened shortly after by a lumbering presence, one blacker than the Night behind it. As Theole crossed the entrance to the study, he caught a glimpse of what appeared to be black fur shimmering in the large round window to the back of the room.

"Retreat!" a voice whispered outside Roostwood. "Get down or they'll spot us!"

The shadow revealed itself to be nothing more than the youngest three Companions hiding behind the very black (and very wide) posterior of Paw. Titha tried pushing her Bear-brother's head down into the grass, but the stout beast wouldn't budge. His chestnut eyes peeped into the study, curiosity lighting their hazel centers. Beside him climbed two more pairs of eyes—a set of shimmering green joined by warm amber. The younglings squabbled and shuffled as their parents and advisors settled into tall, thin chairs situated around a large round wooden table inside. It looked magnificent, even from outside. Titha recognized it from her childhood, its wide top carved from the once-proud trunk of a tree as the rest of it remained firmly rooted into the ground of the study.

"Move, Titha!" Audun shouted. "Your knee is in my back!"

"Pipe down, dogbreath," she spat back at him. "Humans are so loud. You're going to blow our cover!"

"And Paw's giant nose on the glass isn't?" he responded, Paw's hot breath wisping fog onto the pane.

"Just hush, will you?" Titha whispered. "We've got to hear this. Your mother was so concerned, which means it's *actually* important."

"Nech was, too. Did you hear what they said about us being in the same time now forever? Or growing up the same, or something—"

"I'd like to hear what they're saying *right now*, squirt!

Shush!" She reached over, placing her hand on his mouth. Audun licked it without hesitation. Titha jerked back, half smiling and half disgusted as she wiped it on her tunic. "You spend too much time with Haldor," she laughed. Taking Audun's cheek, she placed his head up against the cold glass, both children resting their chins atop Paw as the elders began their council.

Theole outstretched his hands, clearing dusty tomes and leaflets from the massive table. Guarding the others with raised sleeves, he blew forth onto the surface, sending dust swirling into the moonlit room. Before them rested an intricately carved surface—a fully detailed map of Westlyn and their homelands as they were before the dawn of Celtica. The etched locales stretched from where the Northfjord joined the Horizon's Sea in the north, all the way down to unnamed lands in the south before the lands disappeared altogether. Nech and Maya had never seen the southern expanses mapped out before—shock clear on their faces. Theole motioned to Yythengrey on the map, his hand brushing the final layer of dust off Duskridge.

"For as long as our lands have been, by the grace or foul of the Great Drakes, Time has stood apart in the Duskridge Mountains and the west beyond. The reaches of our land were once dormant and peaceful under the wings of Meriduun's influence. For a full Eon we remained isolated; hidden in the safety of the Duskmother's bosom as our lives ebbed and flowed slower than the tumultuous times outside our forest halls. Even on, after her tragedy, Vulduun upheld her mist—her wish. But I fear this has all been undone. Nothing is as it was before the Breaking of the Horizon and the passing of the Last Drake, and it shall never be so again.

With Vulduun's defeat at our Companion's hands—and wings—Meriduun's shroud and therefore Time itself, has begun to unravel.

Slowly, but steadily, the past year has seen the rebuilding of Yythengrey at nearly the same rate as the growth of Celtica outside our tree-halls. This has been the utmost of joys for us; the joining of our peoples and cultures in a truce the likes of which the First Eon could never have imagined, let alone witnessed. Yet now, as we live out the infantile seasons of the Second Eon... *Time*, as it were, *has broken*."

Theole stopped, running his pointer finger to the Barren Fields between Yythengrey and Autumnhill. A dim light akin to that of the Moon's beams filled his fingertip before he pressed down onto the wooden stump. As he did, the hearth behind them abruptly ignited with a Moon-like blue flame. The glow remained in his fingertip, and he began etching a distinct marking into the table where Celtica now stood.

"I have deliberated much on how to bring this news to you, Sigrid," he continued, his finger still burning shapes into the map. "I do not fear for my people, nor yours, as I *feel* no difference nor haste of life. I experience each Night and Day the same as I have these many past forest-years—and see the same in my kin. It is not mortality or decay I fear for us, as all Lunas are mortal in the end. No... it is Celtica I fear for."

"You are right to be concerned," Sigrid interjected, finally breaking her intent silence. "Not all in our midst will be thrilled with such a prospect! Lunas will surely revolt over this news—they will blame the Vikingfolk for bringing such an age upon them, and they will blame us, the Companions, for setting it in motion and in stone!"

"But, perhaps, if we explain it properly," Nech added, his finger pointed, "surely the wiser of our peoples will see that this is, if nothing else, a true sign of the joining of worlds and the end of the chaotic magicks of old!"

"Simpletons care nothing for the truth unless it benefits them," Maya scoffed. "It will start with riots—then raiding—and we will watch as Celtica is torn from the earth."

"But if they are made to listen?" Nech responded. "It cannot escape their thoughts, nor ours, that keeping the worlds of Night and Day separate within the ancient, deceptive cloak of a deceased Dragon was only in the best interest *of* said Dragon, not us mortal'folk, can it? To live to see such walls crumble is a blessing, surely?"

"I agree, my friend," Theole spoke, "For the sake of progress and peace, it is a blessing, indeed. Yet try as I might, I have found no way to make this revelation clearer to those it will concern the most... Though I feel no different myself, and see no acceleration of time with my own eyes, I feel as if others will fear for a shortening of their very lives."

"Would they be wrong to?" Sigrid asked. "I mean this sincerely. If I understand what you are saying, then all that has happened is that the fog of an age-old illusion has been lifted, yes? Our peoples will still live out their days the very same as before, but now at the same pace as the rest of the world, correct? Our peoples will now be *unbound* from the controlling magic of our fallen Drakes and free to witness Gaela as she truly is. But illusion or not, the *simple* explanation will leave fear in their hearts, not doubt… For this will place a mortal sort of existence firmly into their minds. And this is what truly concerns me." She sat firm, placing balled fists onto the table's cold surface. "Though the silence of my Companions concerns me greater. It is clear now that we have all feared the same, yet failed to speak up to one another! If we are to survive this as we entered it, then we must bring our truths forward in the same spirit—as *one*—whatever they may be."

"You are right, and on behalf of Nech and I our sincerest apologies are in order," Theole nodded, bowing his head. "Though the damage has already been done. We have waited too long. Whispers have taken hold, and what is viewed as progress by some is felt as the very-end-of-all-things to others."

"Change, especially of this magnitude, is never easy to swallow," Maya added solemnly. "This feels akin to Ugar's uprising in our Cragoa," she motioned to Nech, who knew what she meant all too well. His hands ran themselves along the scars of his arms. Old eyes met the table, and he sat silently—a rarity anywhere, let alone council. Maya's heart sank. She turned back to her Companions.

"I hate to always be the bearer of bad news," she continued, "But we have witnessed such unwelcomed change before. And we have watched it eat civilization *alive*."

"What are they saying? I can't hear anything now that they got all whisperey!" Audun asked.

"A lot of real bad stuff," Titha responded, who's pointed ear remained pressed against the frosty glass. "They're being real' dramatic. That, or Celtica is in some form of actual danger. I think." She scratched behind Paw's ear as worrisome thoughts seeped in. "It's all because of what we did, the Companions. We saved our people, but we also seem to have broken Time in the Duskridge—or upset the way things used to be, rather."

"That sounds… bad. We should go before we get caught," Audun pipped, suddenly in a hurry.

Titha rolled her eyes, grabbing the furl a'top his shirt. "We're not going anywhere—I want to hear this! Don't you?"

"Our parents are going to kill us, and even if they don't, I don't think I want to hear anymore. It's really late for me anyway and I want to go home."

"Fine, go! I'll tell you all the unbelievable and amazing secrets of our lifetime tomorrow." She turned back to the window. "Always end up doing everything myself around here."

"… I can stay a bit longer if you're going to be like that," Audun added.

"Oh good!" Titha whispered hard, immediately grabbing his fur-laden hat and mushing the left side of his face up against the window.

"Ow, Titha!" he scoffed, wiggling as he laughed. "Too hard! You are *really* strong for a girl!"

This, of course, only made her push harder. Too hard, in fact. *Crrrreak* the window went.

"Titha stop! Let go you banshee!" Audun shouted. The windowpane creaked again, its hold in the bark'laden wall loosening and loosening for no reason other than Titha Mae did *not at all* like being called names.

Each elder's head whipped 'round to the sound, their eyes locked onto a pale squealing face pressed up against the glass.

"*Banshee*?" Titha barked back, squishing Audun's cheek playfully. "Which is it, buster? Am I a little fragile girl or a big mean banshee? Hmm?" she laughed as she tickled him, his laughs shaking the glass vigorously.

Crrrrrreeak went the window again as it trembled. But just before Titha was able to quell her own merriment with a well-timed "uh oh", Paw leapt to her side smiling, wishing to get in on the fun. Only he missed and hit the glass.

CRASH! The windowpane shot out of its holding and into the study—shattering into a million pieces. Audun's bottom flipped up as he rolled face first into the opening, landing on a pile of books atop a massive shelf.

Sigrid's eyes shot to the commotion and her hand to her axe's hilt. Theole, ever-watchful, was already on his feet, pointed ears flared. He whipped his woolen'cloak 'round, waving his hands in the air as every ounce of Moonlight in the room swirled to his palms. With a bright flash and thund'rous clap his staff materialized in his hands, pointed directly at the intruder(s).

Audun's eyes went as wide as Paw's backside. He opened his mouth to scream but no words came out. So he smiled, gulped, then waved silently. Behind him Paw immediately ducked from the window, ears splayed, revealing two green eyes as wide as Audun's.

"Oops."

"*Titha Lilly Mae*!" Theole shouted.

Nech, hands on his chest, removed himself from his seat to fetch something to clean the glass shards from the middle of the floor. Sigrid rushed to her son, checking him for cuts and kissing his forehead.

"I'm fine, mother, I'm fine," Audun replied, brushing himself off. "We were, uhm, we were just playing outside, when this big gust of wind just came and, and *whoosh*! There went that window!"

"Lies are not becoming on a young man," Sigrid frowned. "Go sit down."

Theole clapped his hands together, the staff disappearing into a violent spark betwixt his palms.

"Do not think I have forgotten you, Paw!" he shouted out the window. "Down to the Meadow with you immediately, cub, or it's stool-cauldron-duty for life! Shoo!"

The aged Luna's brow was as furrowed as ever, but he could not help the half-smirk that accompanied his grumbling. Oh, the curiosity of his daughter, and the trouble she weaved. Especially for her friends. With one huge step toward the window his arms lunged through the round hole, grabbing his middle daughter by the scruff of her violet tunic. He pulled her in before she could escape astride Paw.

"Just the bear is to leave, not you," he frowned. "How much did you hear?"

"All of it…" she replied coyly.

"How much did you comprehend?"

"All of it…"

"How much of it are you going to repeat outside this room?"

"None of it..."

Theole, exhausted once again by his daughter's impeccably predictable mischief, checked her for scrapes, finding one on her leg.

"Always covered by bruise or abrasion, my wild'child." His expression then changed as he recalled pulling her through the windowsill. "Did I do that? This one, here? Are you alright, my darling? By Gaela I am so sorry!"

"No, father, I fell on the steps on the way up here. It's okay!"

"I am sorry for my sternness either way—No—*No I am not*! Titha Mae, you have chosen perhaps the most dire of our councils ever held to eavesdrop upon! Where is your self control? I am wasting my time putting you through etiquette lessons, let alone teaching you *manners* myself if this is how you are constantly to behave! Do you not respect the word of your father? There is a time and a place for foolery and the secrets of your elders are not yours to take as you please!"

He stopped himself, reminding his old soul the importance of his role as a father first, then Watcher second, and most of all everything his middle daughter had been through the past seasons. She was still young, sure: just shy of twelve forest-years. But who among them was worthier to wield such knowledge than the little Luna who risked everything so they could even hold such councils? Would he even be here to hold council if not for her? Probably not. Definitely not. A long sigh escaped his parched lips.

"Come sit down, my child, and I'll tend to your wounds, and explain everything. You are still in trouble, but this is, for the moment, vastly more important."

Theole began—but found there was no need to explain most. Titha hadn't missed a single word that Audun hadn't talked over, which thankfully was less than usual. In some way they were both prepared for this talk; for these revelations. Many things young ears wished not to hear flowed through the alleyways of Celtica. Whispers of change festered in Celtican Night. Glimpses of their affects could be found in the dank, bleak corners of the settlement; foul whispers from seedy folk who carried messages from pointed to round ears, and vice versa. "The Watcher aims to be human!" some spoke. "The Shieldmaiden wishes to become immortal!" others murmured, clearly void of any real information or facts, other than that change was a'foot. Yet their hushed aim was not in truth; it was in deception. In breeding conflict.

Titha could feel the difference in what she overheard tonight, though. The importance of it. Much moreso than any field-bound whispers. Paying mind to blubbering troublemakers wasn't to her liking, nor was meaningless gossip and, well, people who had nothing better to do than spread said grimy gossip were never worth her time (or anyone elses, for that matter). "Shady'speak..." she thought to herself, shaking her head. But if her perilous journey the year prior had taught her anything, it was that everything happens for a reason, and nothing was ever gained from inaction. Or apathy, rather.

Her father returned to his seat beside Nech, who sat across from Sigrid. Maya perched atop her own chair. Silence sat heavy.

"So what are you going to do about it?" Titha asked the elders, breaking the tension. "Time breaking, and all?"

"We hadn't made it that far, young lady," Maya responded. "We were just getting to it before your bear pushed a human child through the window."

"Hi Maya," Audun spoke up, waving meekly once more.

"Hello, little one," she smiled back, taking a deep breath.

"You really should get those windows looked at, father," Titha fiddled. "Lords know how old this place is. Paw pushed Audun's little butt right through."

"Titha, please," Theole palmed his forehead. "Language. And we are not here to discuss the structural integrity of Cypress' stu—"

Theole stopped himself. He hadn't uttered that name in many Moons. *Cypress*. With his mention it became apparent to Titha why she wasn't overtly familiar with this room. Come to think of it, this was a rounded corner of Roostwood she'd never stepped foot in but maybe once before. It was Cypress' study: his main quarters for both strategy and reflection. And a lot more made sense to her now.

Cypress was always a true paradox to Titha: warm yet stern, inviting yet secretive, loving yet harsh and rigid. Looking around the room she spotted many of his old affects, and much of her childhood outside of that study came flooding back.

"Gracious me," Nech stammered, attempting to liven the room. "With Titha and Audun present, why if we are not all in the same room once more. The Companions of Westlyn."

Sigrid smiled, her eyes meeting Theole's, then Maya's. The Peregrine grimaced atop her chair and stared into the blue flames of the fireplace.

"Despite these circumstances, it is good to see you all again," she spoke sincerely.

'All' stood out to Titha. Her young eyes scanned the study and sure enough, every Companion save their beasts stood amongst them with newfound knowledge that a journey they long assumed 'over' was still actively unfolding. Behind beloved friends and family the blue fire smoldered to a standstill, black coal sizzling. Titha stared into it as a strong feeling of purpose washed over her.

A faint clamor stirred in the back of her mind. Wind? No, too sharp. The coals were all but mute, too, so it wasn't the hearth, either. It sounded distant, like memories. Voices.

"My lor…"

Faint words shot down the south'wing hall, bouncing into the study and breaking her concentration.

"My Lor…" they called again.

"My lord!" the words rang out, finally true to the Companions' ears. Titha perked from the fire to the pitter-patter of armor-clad footsteps rounding the doorway. The racket revealed itself as Sprucewill, current Captain of the Cedarguard.

"What is it, Captain?" Theole commanded.

"My Lord—and my Shieldmaiden—it is Celtica, sires," Sprucewill clarified, out of breath. "A great and terrible disturbance at the Tower! Riots have begun! Calluna—Calluna Mint has—"

"What of her?" Titha pipped in, cutting the guard off.

"Quiet!" Theole barked. "Calm yourself, my friend. What could possi—"

"—Please, sire, heed my words!" the Captain wheezed. "She is—is unhinged! Calluna Mint has raised a large crowd, and she calls for—no, I cannot say! We fear it may grow unruly!"

"Unruly? Calluna? That is most unlikely!" Theole scoffed. "She is a scholarly lady of both culture and deep principle!"

Sigrid looked to Nech and Maya. The Shieldmaiden could see the fear in Sprucewill's eyes. Clear as Day. She stood calmly, sweeping her flowing blonde locks aside and placed a gentle hand upon the Captain's shoulder.

"Breathe," she spoke softly. "Now tell me, my friend, all that you can of what has transpired."

Sprucewill stared into Sigrid's ice blue eyes, finally catching his breath. "Calluna Mint, my lady, alone and enraged, stands atop a stony crop in the Tower gardens feverishly spitting foul words and calls to action, to rally and to arms. Several of my Cedarguards have attempted to quell her, but she has cast each of us aside! No Houndsmen will touch her for fear of starting a full-blown riot. It is like nothing I have ever seen in wola, lumen, or *anyone* in my life. The strength of a wild beast, she has!"

Theole was still in disbelief. "Are we speaking of the same lady, the same Calluna Mint?" he asked sternly. "Captain, I urge you to calm yourself and think of any factors that may be altering your perception of these events. Her family has resided in this forest for as long as it has bared saplings!"

"I only tell you what I know to be true, sire, as I have seen it with my own eyes!" Sprucewill grabbed his shackled leg armor, showing a brazen tear and dent. "She did *this*, sire! With her *bare hands*! Please, your people need you both! Urgently! Her words have stirred many and she shows no signs of ceasing."

"We have been gone for only an hour," Sigrid remarked

in shock.

"Or has it been longer?" Titha replied, remembering all she had heard.

No one had an answer. The elders only looked to each other with grave concern.

"A fire one tiny spark can make," Sigrid offered before raising her hair into a knot behind her head. "No need to look for further council, my friends. It sounds as if our greatest fears have come calling for us."

Theole stood silent, in shock still.

"Onward, then," she added in his place.

"As you wish, Shieldmaiden," Nech replied.

"I will fly ahead to scout the situation," Maya offered.

Titha looked to Audun, her eyes sharp as talons. "I knew it," she croaked. "I knew that prissy prim-n'-proper Mint was no good!"

"Really?" Audun asked. "She is that awful?"

"You heard Sprucewill! She's wicked, if you ask me. Never has anything nice to say about anyone in Celtica, especially when it comes to your kin. Boy, does she hate Vikingmen. It was only a matter of time before she—"

"—Snapped?" Theole barked to his daughter, startling her. "And what in Gaela's name could have caused *that,* Titha Mae?"

Titha stood shook.

"Good! Silence. Not another word! Stay put and keep Audun safe. He is under *your* protection."

"Yes, father."

Sigrid began to usher Theole out the door, Nech and

Maya already on their way out. As they left the study, the younglings sat quiet for a moment. Any other boy would've assumed Titha was doing what she was told, but he knew better. Looking to her ears, he watched them twitch as if they were counting. Which they were. Footsteps, to be precise. *Two, three.... Twenty-six, thirty-eight...*

Slam! The doors of Roostwood finally shut behind their parents. *Click—CLACK*! Shut tight, they were. That was the cue! Titha popped to her feet.

"Ready?" she asked without hesitation.

"Ready..." Audun warbled.

Off they went, running out of Roostwood and down the Grand Steps, then into the Meadow as the Emerald Aurora danced on above. Titha let out a blistering whistle and her Bear-brother lept from the bushes.

Paw stuck to the outskirts of the thoroughfare, dodging the usual hustle and bustle of Midnight Lunas with Titha and Audun astride. As they neared the eastern tree'wall, a familiar set of silhouettes caught their eye.

"Gilly, Beebee!" Titha cried out, "And hi again, Clover. What are you still doing out here? You three know what's happening right now, don't you?"

"Yup," Beebee lit up. "Father's busy so I am on Gilly's date now, too," she grinned.

"No, goober, in Celtica! We've got to get out there! Mint's lost it completely! Audun and I just heard it all straight from Sprucewill!"

"Told you," Clover spoke softly to Gilly. He looked hard into her eyes, then stood to leave. She sat still, as if deep thoughts rooted her firmly to the ground.

"I'd better find my parents," he continued. "Thanks for a great time. And for listening," he spoke softly, dusting off his maroon pants.

"Anytime," Gilly replied, still planted in the grass.

"Up with you too, wola! We are not missing this! Calluna McStubby Mint has finally gone nuts! Mae sisters, unite!" Titha trumpeted, her finger pointed into the sky. But Gilly still didn't budge.

"Lords did he finally kiss you or something?" she poked Gilly. "Get up, sticklegs! Let's go!"

"Fine," Gilly retorted, unamused as usual.

Audun, ever the gentleman, offered his hands down to her and Beebee, and with a tug upward the eldest and youngest Maes joined the fray for what was surely to be *the* spectacle of Spring's eve.

CHAPTER FIVE
Figures of Speech

"You are officially on a diet!" Titha barked to Paw as he finally reached Celtica. He growled, roaring a few Bearish retorts at her, mightily displeased.

"I don't care how many of us are riding a'top you, that was pitiful!" Titha sparred back, patting his fluffed-up side.

Paw grumbled, throwing his huge front paws into the trail's dirt, sliding them to an awful stop.

"What are you doing?" she screeched. "We cannot miss this! I won't take away any of your treats—I was just kidding!"

Paw shook his head 'no' and grunted, pointing his snout directly ahead. Before them, four mighty hooves cycled furiously in the dusty field as a white mained horse bellowed forth.

"Oh joy," Titha scoffed. She turned to her sisters straddled behind her. Gilly's face was stark red.

"Why are your cheeks red again?" Beebee asked. "Are we going on a date with him, too?"

Gilly's entire body shook with disgust. "No!" she shouted. "And enough about dates and boyfriends!"

The horse's hooves drudged up another wave of earth as she halted Paw and his companions. The Mae sisters coughed as they waved dust and pure shock from their faces.

"Good morning, ladies!" Rainer cried out from atop his beautiful horse Kelliah, her white mane glistening forth from every inch not covered by leather armor.

"Out of the way, pretty'boy!" Titha shouted.

"That's *Jarl* pretty'boy to you, young lady," Rainer laughed. "Your father said you would be here—and so I am here to stop you from any prep—er'... preposter... ah'... preposterous plans you may have!"

"Move, Rainer," Gilly retorted. "We don't have time for your ineptitude."

"He said you would say that, too. Lords alive, I need to teach you Lunas some smaller words." He shook his head, making eye contact with a tiny peach hand gripping the side of Gilly's torso. "Cannot let you pass, Mae sisters. Sorry! Orders of the Masters—also known as our parents. And me. Now where is my little brother? His Jarl demands his presence!"

Paw raised his head, frowning as high as he could in an attempt to match Kelliah's gaze. The mare bowed her nose, hardening her brow. She wasn't budging.

"I see," Rainer patted the stubble on his chin. "If this is the way it shall be, then your Jarl of Autumnhill will personally guard this entrance to Celtica. The situation is too dangerous, I'm afraid, and I'll not have you endanger yourselves, Audun, or the bear," Rainer boasted.

Titha laughed once and loud. The obviously forced 'hah'

was followed by a trail of laughter, much to the young Jarl's chagrin.

"Too dangerous?" she chuckled. "Listen here, pal—your little brother and I traveled across every inch of the known lands, bested a Dragon, and saved civilization with nothing more than a feather, a crusty scribe, and a *bird,* so I think I can handle Minty McStubbins and her angry words, okay?"

"Is that her full name?" Rainer asked.

"No, you moron! Now move!" Titha drove her ankles into Paw. He leaped forward, but Kelliah neighed a mighty neigh, cycling her hooves ferociously before him. She was met with nothing more than a whimper from the enormous cub.

"Stand down, girls! Audun!" he shouted. "I see you, you little sneak."

An amber pair of peepers finally poked out from behind Gilly's back.

"Come here, brother," Rainer commanded.

Audun didn't fight his command. "Sorry, girls," he pouted as he shuffled off Paw and to Kelliah. Rainer extended his long, muscly arm, flinging his pint-sized brother up onto his saddle.

"I am fully aware of the exploits you two younglings have under your belts, Titha Mae. I was there, if you remember. Simply doing my duty as Jarl, of course."

"Wait, are you the Jarl?" Gilly groaned. "I don't think I knew that! Could you say it one more time for us, please?"

Rainer slicked his brown hair back, an awkward laugh stumbling from his jaw.

"Oh, you," he bumbled, caught up in his own machismo.

"I… look here, ladies, and… bear. Past heroic acts and forever being in your debt aside, if you would just heed the example of Audun and unwind, then we could enjoy ourselves while our parents do the dirty work for once!"

"Where's the fun in that?" Titha asked.

"I don't answer to you," Gilly interrupted, scolding Rainer over her sister. "So give me one good reason why I shouldn't just keep walking."

"I can think of several reasons," Rainer spoke with a shine. He hopped down from Kelliah, slowly waltzing toward Gilly with beefed-up swagger. "We are both the eldest, are we not? I am, as you know, Jarl of Autumnhill—and you, Lady Gillian Rose Mae—are sworn to take your father's place as fellow leader of these vast lands. We would surely benefit from *getting along* with one another, don't you think?" Rainer decreed, his trademark smirk smeared across his face as he tried desperately to charm her.

"I've been *getting along* just fine without you so far, but thanks," Gilly replied, her face half hidden.

"Is that so?"

"*Beyond* so. Now move."

"Come now, Gillian!" he spurted back. "Did I do something to offend you? I am simply trying to do what is right. Events of tonight aside, I—I truly wish to know you better. For our people's sake!"

"I'm sure all the time you've spent with every blonde in Celtica is for the good of the people, too."

Titha let out a full-bellied laugh behind her sister. Beebee didn't get it.

"That was… that was just rude!" Rainer barked, taken

aback. Kelliah neighed, stomping a hoof into the ground. "Fine. I get it. Don't give me the time of Day or Night. It's because I am human, isn't it?"

"*Hah*!" Gilly scoffed loudly. "You are an arrogant, boastful, *loudmouthed* cretin so *unbelievably* full of yourself that you assume *race* is the *only* reason a lady would *ever* not be interested in you!" She marched right up to his comfy seat atop Kelliah, her finger pointed like a spear. "I have *plenty* more words I'd use to describe you and I promise that *human* is the *least* offensive among them!"

Rainer and Kelliah stood as still as statues with matching blank expressions. Gilly poked her finger forward. They both flinched. She turned and flipped her flowing silver locks, sending them smacking across Kelliah's muzzle.

"It's okay, muscles," Titha added as her sister stormed off. "Try flowers, she *loves* flowers."

"Right," Rainer whispered to no one. Kelliah shook her head as if she was getting rid of a sneeze. "Well, if I ever have the need, I shall fetch her some. For now, I'd say I have done quite well without."

"Well? You? With what?" Titha replied.

"Stalling you, of course," he said with a smile.

"Why you vile, lying *horsesnake*!" Gilly retorted, her fire reignited. "You expect me to believe that you… you are *that* clever!? Don't you have more important things to do, boy-Jarl? What could Mrs. Calluna-Posture-and-Decorum-Mint be up to that could *possibly* warrant keeping us so far away from her?"

"The days of decorum are over!" Mrs. Mint shouted through Celtica, her voice shrill as a flock of herons (and as loud, too). Her knuckles were bone white and contorted as she gripped a piece of silver Lunish armor, its shape bent within her grasp. Behind her the waxing Moon was setting astride the impressive nighttime silhouette of the Tower of Celtica. It was well into the darkest hours of morning now.

"There will be no rest for the children of Night or Day, for the oppressive rule of the Great Avians has bound us together not only in the blasphemous debauchery of Celtica… but in the unbreakable shackles of mortality!" she continued, her voice utterly horrible.

"Please, Calluna, we simply want to speak with you peacefully!" Theole shouted above the crowd of Vikingmen, Lunas, Goblins, and all folk of Celtica. "We wish to address your concerns properly! No others need come to harm."

"No harm shall ever match that which you and the Viking harlot have brought upon our kind!" Mint's voice grew great and terrible, and her next words were spoken as if her own soul had left her body and a far fouler one entered to speak:

"Death to the Avians!" Mint trumpeted into the crowd, her voice like violent thunder. It echoed through every corridor of Celtica, right up to the western side where the Mae sisters overheard in utter disbelief.

"What was that!?" Titha cried out. "That couldn't have

been Mint."

"Did she just shout 'death to the Avians'?" Gilly asked, taken a'back.

"She absolutely did," Titha replied, astonished.

"Uh oh," Beebee hiccuped.

"And this is the same Calluna Mint who's best friends with a porcupine?" Gilly added, wide-eyed.

"Yup."

"I know you think she's crazy but... but she can't be *this* crazy..." Gilly whispered before looking to Rainer. "Still think we should stay put?"

Rainer's expression sunk. Audun turned to look up to his brother.

"We have to go now," he said. "Look at all those people!" Audun couldn't believe such foul things could ever come from a Luna. Yet Mint echoed her ghastly phrase once more, and the young Companions shivered.

"Rainer!" Audun stilted. "Our parents might be in trouble!"

And trouble they were in, indeed.

Mint threw more mangled armor into the crowd, landing a Viking spectator on his backside. The black-haired bear-of-a-man looked to his shoulder, removing his hand to spot his own blood. Astounded, he looked to his Shieldmaiden. Sigrid's eyes were wide with shock. She drew her axe, flipping it once before gripping it with all the strength of a Cave Giant, her shield removed from her back in the opposite hand, as well.

"Stand down!" Theole asked of her, horrified. "I will handle this!"

Another Cedarguard rushed the rocky outcrop as his Watcher motioned commands, but Mint would have none of it. She swept her right hand down, backhanding the guard to the grass with the strength of a feral boar. As his silver armor ricocheted off the soil, Paw, The Mae Sisters, and the Sons of Angvar made their entrance. Titha looked to Gilly, eyebrow cocked.

"She's gone mental!" Titha roared. "Full-blown insane! Stop hurting your own people, you *wench*!"

Mint's ears perked, and like a wolf through a flock of sheep her eyes parted the crowd and landed directly upon her former pupil.

"Death to the Avians… And DEATH TO ALL THEIR KIN!"

Titha's skin went cold.

But Mint wasn't done. She trumpeted again, louder this time. Her voice was unlike anything Titha had heard before; like ten screams leaving one mouth.

"Death to the Avians! Death to their Kin! And Death to all Vikingmen!"

Screams broke out as the spectators swelled into opposing shouts of their own. Feet of every race and color trampled and stomped, shoving the Mae sisters back.

"Okay never mind—time to go!" Titha shouted, grabbing her sister's arm. But it was too late. The panic had surrounded them.

"Is what she has said the truth?" a young voice cried out over the screams. "Are we to die sooner?" A Luna demanded. "Have we become like the humans? Mere mortals?"

"We have *always been mortals*!" Theole spat, rumbling with impatience. "Calm yourselves, my Lunas. Please!" His eyes began to glow as his fingertips bristled with the ancient power swelling inside him. Sigrid grabbed his arm, flinging her axe's blade into the ground. "No, Theole," she commanded. "The Grand Owl will only make matters much, much worse."

"See now! As he wishes to oppress me for speaking the truth!" Calluna spat into the crowd, motioning to Theole. *"Look as his eyes glow with the hatred of an Ancient Avian! While we are all to walk the hours, days, and years of mere MEN now, my Lunish folk! And it is them you have to thank for it!"*

The once-docile tutor grew even more violent with these words, her hands trembling as she turned to Sigrid. *"Burn her!"* she screeched. *"Capture the Avian Witch and turn her into the very ash she wishes upon our peop– "*

The air popped, and then all was silent. Mint coughed, then froze—jolting backward as if struck by lightning.

As screams settled and eyes peeled themselves back open it was revealed: A spear piercing Mint's torso like a stake, bolting her to the rock she stood upon.

It was a Viking spear.

Calluna Mint took one more breath as she grasped the weapon with one hand and pointed to Sigrid with the other.

"Burn her."

Her arms fell to her sides as she exhaled, never to take another breath.

Titha's hands clenched to her mouth. Gilly squeezed

Beebee into her, shielding her from the horrid sight.

An elder Luna rushed to Mint's aid, grabbing her cold hands and chanting her name, but nothing came of it.

"She's dead!" he whimpered.

"A Viking spear!" another voice shot out from the crowd, wasting no time. "A Man has done the deed! A *Man* has taken Lunish life!"

Fear and panic doubled. Celtica began to shove and separate itself: Lunas to the West and Vikingmen to the East, with the garish site in the Tower gardens between them. The air circled chants and threats. Yet as the crowd split, one round figure stayed put. Amidst the chaos he didn't budge, firmly planted in the panic. A blank stare painted his face, unable to break gaze from the horrible silhouette atop the once beautiful rocks of Celtica's gardens.

"It was him!" a familiar young Lunish voice shouted again, this time stepping forth from the mob to point directly at the still man. "Get him!" the Luna shouted, his eyes filled with purpose.

Titha knew that voice. She knew it well enough to finally break from her state of shock.

"Is that Clover?" she spoke, trying to spot the source of the words. "There's no way. Gilly? Is that him?"

"It is…" her sister replied, hesitantly.

"Forget him!" Audun cried out from astride his brother's horse. "Who is the man there in the middle? Did he do it? That must be his spear! Right, Rainer?"

Rainer didn't think. Instead, his brother's words spurred him into action, and he drove his heels into Kelliah, steering her toward the culprit. In an instant they were upon him, and Rainer did what he did best: apprehend.

The stranger squirmed and screamed, obviously panicked and in shock. His face was round and plain with only a hint of black peach'fuzz for a beard, and his clothes were quaint, dark... muddy. Rainer was not immediately familiar with his face, which struck the young Jarl deep. Yet there was no time to assess further, as each finger in the crowd pointed harder and harder, the eyes of his people and every single Luna demanding swift justice.

"Did anyone see him do it?" Rainer shouted as he scanned the crowd for his Houndsmen. "Did anyone, Viking, Luna, or Goblin, see this Man strike Mint down?"

Houndsmen guarding the front of the crowd shook their heads 'no'. So did the Cedarguard.

"Maya! I know you are here somewhere. Did your Peregrine eyes see nothing?"

"The discord was too great, Jarl," she squawked from atop Nech's shoulder in the gardens. "I could not see."

"So no one saw this Man do the deed?" Rainer commanded as he halted tying the stranger's wrists. "No one saw *anything*?"

"I certainly did!" the young Luna shouted once more. It *was* Clover. He stepped forth.

"There he is again!" Titha shouted to Gilly.

"You saw him, Luna?" Rainer asked of Clover.

"I did!" Clover retorted.

The girls were stunned. They had never seen Clover so purposeful.

"This man killed Calluna Mint! He took a Lunish life and

now we should take his! He should be executed!" Clover cried, spurring gasps in the crowd.

"I... I should not... I did not!" the stranger finally mumbled, his voice weak. "Please, Jarl Rainer, Sire! I would... I would never!" His round cheeks were bloodshot, but his gaze stood firm on Rainer, terrified.

"His eyes hold terror, but not deceit," Rainer spoke. "Are you sure of what you speak, Luna boy? *Murder* is a strong word, as is *execution*."

"How could I not be? The eyes of a Luna are never to be doubted," Clover decreed.

"He's lying!" the round stranger yelled, his voice finally peaking. "He is *lying* to you!"

"That's just what a murderous killmonger like you would say! You murdered my tutor! Murderer! *Murderer!*" Clover shrieked.

Rainer could sense the tension rising once more and motioned for Clover to tone it down. Voices catted and chattered frantically around them all.

"I saw it, too!" another Luna shouted.

"And I! That strange Man did the deed!"

"Alright, alright!" Rainer roared. "I will handle this, citizens of Celtica! If you saw anything—and I mean *anything*—come with me and deliver your truths. Now. Your Jarl and Shieldmaiden will hold trial in Autumnhill for this gruesome act at once. But please, if you are not to be of help, then do not make this tragic situation worse. Return to your homes and do as you would on any other Day. We will handle this, you have my word." He pulled the stranger from the ground by his bindings and turned to Clover.

"You," Rainer pointed. "Come with me."

The crowd grew silent, all eyes on Rainer, Clover, and the strange Man.

The Sun began to rise behind them as they left for trial. Its red first-light illuminated the ghastly silhouette of Calluna Mint, marred as she lay motionless; staked to the center of Celtica.

Titha approached the outcrop slowly, hands clutched. Her young mind whirled as the Sunrise conjured memories from one year ago, each just as, if not more, foul. She did not like Mrs. Mint, not one bit, but… did she deserve this? Did she deserve to die? Did *anyone* deserve such a terrible fate?

What was to happen to her?

Titha's bare feet walked to her father out of instinct, and he did not scold her for leaving the forest, nor anything else. Instead he held her, shielding her eyes from the sight. Nech approached slowly, bowing in sorrow. Behind them, Sigrid motioned to the remaining Houndsmen to retrieve Mint from the rock, but Theole outstretched his hand.

"Please," he stated. "It should be her people."

Sigrid nodded, sighing. Death was no stranger to her or her kin, she thought. Not like it was to most Lunas. She offered what condolences she had, but not many words came.

Theole asked Nech to walk with his children as he took to the outcrop to be met with another dead Luna on his hands; his watch.

With a deep breath, the bright power within him manifested in his hands, and he vanquished the spear from Mint's body. Only the damning end remained, staked into the rock. Theole cradled Calluna above it as best he could. The Watcher tore his own sash from his shoulders, shrouding the fallen Luna. His kin. A former friend.

Mint's final words of hate meant nothing in this moment. To hold a fallen Luna was to hold sorrow itself. Nothing could tarnish that.

"To the Meadow..." Theole spoke somberly. "Gather our people, her friends and family foremost. Everything else is to wait. For now we are to hold the first Luneralle of the year. Let us hope it is the last."

His people shadowed their Watcher as he left for Ythengrey, their heads bowed over the body of Calluna Mint for the last journey she would ever take out of Celtica. Nech swaddled Beebee as Titha clung tight to Gilly. The sisters turned back to get one more look at the Sunrise, its radiance fighting the Tower of Celtica for dominance in the sky.

There Sigrid stood, Audun by her side. Slowly she traversed the rocky outcrop, waving to a people she had come to love and respect as her own. She had failed them in letting this atrocious act come to pass, she thought. Deeply failed.

The sky brightened behind her youngest son as she examined what remained of the spear. Morning rose as a welcomed ally, its warmth reinvigorating both vision and spirit.

"We will need this for the trial," she spoke softly, running her finger along the wooden shaft of the weapon.

"Those markings, mother," Audun spoke up as his eyes met the spear's intricate patterns. "They look Viking... but I've never seen them before."

"Neither have I, my son."

Grasping its end, she attempted to pull the spear from the

rock. Nothing. It would not budge! She frowned, snarling under her breath. No Daughter of Autumnhill would be bested by some stick in a pebble! The Shieldmaiden flung her wolves'fur cloak from her shoulders, cracked her knuckles—and yanked the spear with all her might, thrusting every muscle in her body upward. With one more mighty thrust with her arms and legs, knees unbending, the spear loosened, tilted, then finally—*CLANK*! It broke free! Audun smiled, in awe of his mother as he so often was.

She raised it slowly into the Sunlight, its bladed-end unfazed by the rock. Though as she tilted its axis, the weapon let loose a blinding reflection that almost knocked them both back.

"This blade… It is not made of bone," she spoke. "Nor does it gleam of copper, iron or any metal the races of Gaela have crafted before."

"It looks like stone," Audun thought, mesmerized. "Is it mineral stone? It's so dark…"

"—And bears such strange markings," Sigrid observed. The blade was completely foreign to their eyes. Ancient, yet new. Strange, yet Viking. Present, yet otherworldly.

Great concern washed over her as the slick feel of the blade began to affect her mind's eye. Slowly its smooth carvings conjured flashes of the horrid nightmares she'd been plagued with the past seasons.

"Mother, are you alright?" Audun asked as her face ran ghostly pale.

She was not, and the flashing visions grew darker, more severe. Swiftly she desired to have her precious young son as far away from this violent scene, and the object sparking her dreams, as possible.

"Go and fetch Nech for me, my son," she spoke sternly. "Ask him to meet me before the trial. Tell him it is of the utmost importance."

"Yes, mother," Audun frowned. He turned for Autumnhill, but Sigrid remained locked onto the stone blade.

"What… *are* you?"

CHAPTER SIX
Fates Not Chosen

The trial of Mint's murder was to begin at high noon, when the Sun reached its peak. Morning still embraced Autumnhill, the mist and dew just beginning to fade. Rainer stood strong atop the steps of Skaldhall, his family's ancestral home. He looked for his father's face in the Sunrise as he did every morning; he could use Angvar's red-bearded smile now more than any other day in his life thus far. He kept a pleasant face, however, ushering in the Lawmasters as they prepared for a most interesting hearing. All Vikings were to be present, not just those holding the oral tradition of their laws. For a Viking trial was a matter that concerned every soul within their walls, and none were left unaccounted for.

As the last few boots scuffed through Skaldhall's doors, Sigrid approached from town. Slowly she walked, heavy thoughts hindering her steps.

"You remember you can fly, don't you, mother?" Rainer called out from atop the steps, smiling.

She grinned in tandem, quickening her pace a bit as she carried half the spear that murdered Calluna Mint.

"Not very well, my eldest," she finally replied, climbing the stone steps. "Nor should those who wield great power wield it for the mundane. We cannot get too comfortable in such skins, can we?"

"I certainly would," he boasted, beyond proud to be the eldest son of the Glorious Red Eagle.

"You only think that now, Rainer," she replied. "Lust for power is the seed of the tyrannical. And tyrants the Angvarssons are not."

"Right, mother," he bowed.

She lifted his strong chin, brushing the short beard he refused to shave. "My son," she spoke softly, "My radiant Jarl. I am so proud of you. Never think for a moment that I am not. And your father stands proud above us."

She took his hand raising it to hers and placed the half-spear into his grasp. "You are ready for this," she offered.

"Ready for what?" Rainer replied.

"To lead our people through this most important thing. This most important trial."

"Mother—surely you are staying?"

"I cannot," she replied, pushing the weapon into his possession. "There is something I must do."

"A task that is more important than this?" Rainer laughed, but his mother stood stone-faced. "You're serious?" he asked, his joy vanishing. "What is going on? What are you not telling me? You are expected inside!"

"No, *you* are. And you are more than capable. Our people

look to *your* protection in Autumnhill. They respect your reserve and your guidance, my eldest. Confidence is a tool greater than any weapon. You have it, and you must use it now. Go in. With you my love goes."

"That's not good enough!" Rainer cried out, the entrance doors slamming shut behind him. "Tell me why you are leaving, mother. As your Jarl I... I deserve to know why you would abandon your people—abandon me—in this hour of need!"

"Do not wield that word against me!" she commanded. "You know what I must do! But you stand as stubborn as your father before me! Too stubborn to break free of this needless self-doubt and recall all that has plagued me this past year. Do you not remember my dreams, my son?"

"You do not speak of what ails you often, mother. We spoke of that in *Winter*. Not a word since. Not when you pace the halls at night, not when you forget to tend to the gardens, and not when you spend weeks staring into the night sky."

"I... I am sorry, and you are right. I do not wish to place my own burdens upon my children. It is not a mother's place—" She paused as another crowd made their way up the stairs, spotting a familiar set of yellow ears at the tail-end. Nech approached, Maya perched atop his shoulder, with Audun shortly behind.

"Look alive," Maya whispered into Nech's ear. "Her mightiness awaits."

"Oh pish posh, you cranky bird!" Nech replied, scolding her. "You must get over your hatred of eagles, 'lest Audun hear you! The Shieldmaiden is the finest human I have ever met. Much more than the Red Eagle, is she. Much more, indeed."

"You must say that to all the Shieldmaidens," Sigrid

smiled, placing a hand on Nech's other shoulder as the rest of the crowd passed by, followed by Audun.

"My word! Shieldmaiden! You must forgive anything you heard my comrade saying. She has a most detestable bias against eagles. I was simply explaining to her that—"

"There is no need, my friend," Sigrid added. "A moment, please. Wait here."

"As you wish, Shieldmaiden," Nech bowed.

Sigrid bent down, her youngest son before her. "No hug for your mother?" she asked Audun.

"You're leaving, aren't you?" he replied with a frown.

"Yes, dearheart. How did you know?"

"The knapsack. Extra daggers. Father's axe. The undercloak. Your eyebrows. Drawings of the Aurora. Figured those weren't all for nothing, mother."

Sigrid laughed as she pulled her son's intricate parchments from her provisions.

"See how I have bound them? They are of utmost importance to me. I could not embark on this journey without the brilliance of my sons. My Jarl and my Scribe. I need you both to be strong for me until I return. Can you do that?"

"Yes..." Audun responded, fighting a quivering lip. "But why do you have to go? Why now?"

Rainer stepped forward, taking Audun's hand. "We need to know the part you are not telling us."

"And you deserve to know," she replied. "We do not have much time. I can hear the restlessness within Skaldhall. But listen to me: your brother's sketches, Maya's council, Nech's mappings, have all been of great value, but I have also used them as excuses to prolong my leaving. I can hesitate no longer. The Emerald Aurora these past Moons is the one from my dreams. I am sure of it. Your mother has not simply been restless in her dreams. I have been plagued by… visions."

"Of what?" Rainer asked, clutching Audun's hand.

"The days to come… and a fate I fear most of all…" Sigrid looked to the sky, her eyes glossing over:

"When I sleep the visions come to me. The same fire and death and destruction of Vulduun's Treachery one year ago. I see Autumnhill burning… the trees of Yythengrey raised to ash… and Celtica is erased violently from existence. But it is not the Great Drakes over the flames. It is The Great Avians, twisted and black we've become; our talons wet with the flesh of those we swore to protect. Yet every time I see it, when the turmoil reaches its peak, a ribbon of green cuts through the madness like a shooting star, leaving behind it the glorious Emerald Aurora. It shines a path over the Horizon. In the dream, I always choose to follow it. And when I reach the end, the burning stops. Though this past morning, as I gripped the stone blade that took Calluna Mint's life, the visions overtook me once more. I relived my dreams, but this time… I hesitated. I found myself curious, for the first time, what would happen if I turned the other direction: away from the Aurora and into the madness. In one moment of weakness I looked back. I turned from the path I felt to be right… and found myself amidst Ragnarok, the very end of all things, as I held the stone blade. But I was unable to fight with it… unable to aid or speak or even move. Instead, I was made to watch and to suffer as all I love burned before me. I was shown my darkest fears. Shown what happens if I do choose to stay. If I continue to turn from the Aurora and delay my destiny. I cannot let such things—any of this vision—come to pass. It is a most terrifying truth, my sons, of this I am certain, and I must follow to where it leads; to the end of the Emerald Aurora. There is no other way."

"But to what end?" Rainer asked. "How long will you be gone? You do not even know what awaits you at the end of your path!"

"I am sorry I do not have more answers for you, I truly am," his mother answered, deeply torn. "The dream reveals only the path, not the solution. Yet whatever lies at the end of the Aurora's pointed glow... I must go to it. For the alternative is a fate worse than death, and I will not become the Black Avian I have foreseen. I will not allow it."

"Mother you would never hurt—"

"Greater Men and greater Drakes have fallen to the madness, my son," she interrupted. "This you know all too well. But our fates are our own, I believe. These visions have presented me with a choice, and I must choose before it is too late."

Rainer said nothing, a lump holding in his words. Sigrid turned to Nech, whose hand held his chin in deep thought. Maya perched upon his shoulder, silent.

"I am glad you are both here," Sigrid said. "We do not see eye to eye, falcon, this you have made clear, but the journey I am to undertake is one that requires an eye for the North which I do not possess. Will you help me?"

"Help you what?" Maya squawked.

Nech smacked her.

"What?" Maya retorted. "She has told us nothing yet asks for help! I need to know what I'm getting into, and if I can even be of service."

"The Auroras!" Nech decreed. "She is to follow them and needs your eyes and mind. She is a warrior in need of a navigator! For goodness sake, Maya."

"Yes, my friend," Sigrid bowed. "Time is of the essence,

too. If I am to navigate the harsh waters beyond our Northfjord I will certainly need your expertise."

"Navigate the Fjord—Sigrid, dear," Maya laid on thick. "Do you plan to sail this journey from your docks, crammed into a longboat, rowing tirelessly, fighting wave and ice alike, only to meet frozen wastelands you cannot traverse in a flute of wood? This is how you aim to follow the Northern Lights? The ones in the *sky*?"

"... Yes," Sigrid spoke, stone-cold.

"Absolutely not," Maya answered.

"Maya!" Nech scolded.

"Oh, hear me out, alright? Look, Shieldmaiden, I understand your hesitation to embrace something as radical as... becoming a giant eagle... and trust me—the less you embrace such a form the more I'll like you—but—whether you asked for it or not, you're an *Avian* now. And Avians do not sail. They *fly*."

Theole stepped down from the Meadow's middle mound, a pile of thick, dry brush behind him. Atop it rested Calluna Mint's Moonflower bed, the very flower that had grown with her since she was born, cradling her through her entire life just as all flowerbeds did for their Lunas. Dim rays of morning Sunlight pierced the foliage, the forest still pale from its thick canopy. Slowly, as the crickets chirped in the grass, fireflies began to flash their luminescence, lighting the Duskridge in tandem. In groups they would glow, creating a symphony of lights around the memorial. The forest understood what a Luneralle was—and did all it could to make it beautiful.

Elders placed Mint's precious belongings beside her as she lay shrouded and motionless in death. Her parchments, leaflets, studies of posture & decorum dating back centuries, along with a quill pen, inkwell, and anything else she held dear in life. As her effects were settled, a final covering of beautiful silk was placed over her, filled with the intricate knot-work of Lunish art. Theole bowed his head and turned to the brushpile. Whirling his hands, he summoned a spark, lighting a blue flame beneath her Moonflower.

Mothers took the hands of their daughters as fathers and sons stepped forth to lift Calluna's burial cradle. Tears fell in the silence, all heads bowed. The blue flame grew higher and higher behind them, Mint's Moonflower gone forever. The cold light lit their walk as generations of lumen who knew her as a stern but wise tutor walked her to a place she would never return from. Bear-brothers followed, preparing themselves to move heavy stones. As they disappeared into grey forest, mothers and daughters stayed behind to tend the ashes of her Moonflower until its last blue ember snuffed out.

"How can something so beautiful be so sad?" Titha asked, wiping a tear. The fireflies still sparked about. She leaned into Paw, nuzzling into his neck as Gilly did the same to the other side.

"There is much beauty in sorrow," Theole replied, wiping another tear from his daughter's face. "And we must remember that. We must remember to honor all that was good and bright and beautiful about Calluna Mint—"

"But she said so many horrible things," Titha replied. "How, father? She was terrifying in the end… and she… she never liked me, or Celtica. She wanted to rip everything we love apart! She just wanted everything to stay as it had been. Forever 'safe'… *Trapped.*"

"What if she was right?" Gilly interjected. "Do we not owe it to that half—no—*all* of our people, regardless of their beliefs, the right to choose? What if all Luna's don't wish to live in the 'normal' of the world outside?" She looked to Beebee, who rested upon Paw's head. "And what if, for all that she believed, Calluna is lost now? There's no way she'll be at rest with the trees and moss, not with all that she said—all she wished to change. Surely, she will be just as restless in death. Is that fair?"

Theole bowed. It was time to follow the Lumen into the forest.

"Come with me, girls," he spoke softly. "There is something you need to see."

Theole turned his back from their people, his long feet leading to a path barely trodden. It was a road those bearing the body of Calluna Mint had to clear before them, as it had not been used in seasons.

As Titha followed, her eyes squinted in the Sunlight. She focused on trees she had never seen before; a hallway of her forest home she'd not once laid green eyes upon. She looked back to her sisters, but Gilly's expression had not changed, not even with the wonderment she, too, felt within.

Each tree became more knotted than the one before. Taller, wiser, and older they stood. Titha could hear the enormous shoulders of Bear-brothers breaking through branches ahead of them, all the way through the brush until the path led uphill, and the canopy broke out into a circle much like the Meadow's. Beebee's eyes grew wide, as did her sisters'.

Before them, in the middle of the opening, stood a grand mound atop the hill, a sod and earthen structure the likes of which they'd never seen. Wrapping its front were beautiful white riverstones that glistened in the morning Sun, each interlocked perfectly—all the way from the clover-filled ground up to the grass-laden top. In its center rested a single, enormous and oblong boulder. Titha's eyes met it. It was the entrance stone; ancient and unmovable. Its oval shape bared many etchings and spirals, bur each led to its center, where it bore a symbol she swore she had seen before, but could not place:

As they stood in awe, the lumen gave way to their Bear-brothers. Paw separated from his Luna-sisters, planting one more wet lick up the side of Titha's face before joining his kin. Together they grunted, growled and snorted as they threw massive backs into the entrance stone. Theole shot a single spark into the air, and the bears pushed in unison, moving the stone one inch at a time.

"I often ask myself the same question you have for me, my daughter: *Was Calluna right*?" Theole said to Gilly, breaking the silence. "Were Calluna and those a'kin to her *correct* to want to keep the old ways sacred and our lives, our Time, separate? Untouched?"

The bears continued to push as lumen broke away from Mint's burial cradle. Only the eldest among them were to carry her inside the mound.

"And whenever I find myself asking this difficult question again," Theole continued, "I come here."

CRAANG. The entrance stone hit its mark, and the darkness of the mound's mouth laid open.

There was nothing *but* darkness within. Titha stared into the black. It did not feel to her as if it led somewhere, like a Druidune or an intriguing cave. It felt cold. Empty. Foreign.

"What is this place?" Gilly asked, her sisters speechless. "It looks ancient."

"It is, eldest. As is the song of its keeping. You may recall the lyrics of 'The Fomorrigan'?"

The girls stood silent, entranced with the silent emptiness of the chamber.

"No? The one my grandfather composed?" Theole asked with a frown. "Ah. Well. I should not be surprised, in truth. We have left much of our old ways behind… much of the *Other Gods*… remain in shadows still… even after Meriduun's passing."

"You're not going to start singing, are you?" Gilly croaked, earning a wiggle from Beebee.

"No, my eldest," Theole smiled. "I am not." His smile faded as old, worn lilac eyes returned to the tomb before them. "I do not feel like singing, my daughters. Not in the least. Though the song of this tomb, as it was told, was—*is* of great importance. This was a tomb built for the Fomorrigan: Herald of the Afterlife—Vanguard to Eternity. It was here we brought to her those who left us too soon," he replied. "Some viewed it as a portal, if you will, one for those bound for her care in Oathera—the Otherworld of yon; each of their journeys unfinished in this world, our Gaela."

"The Otherworld…" Titha muttered, entranced. "There's something we never talk about anymore."

Her father bowed his head. "Indeed," he offered heavily. "Some things are better left to the past."

"What are they doing?" Gillian interjected. She watched as several elders prepped a round, earthen vessel before walking it into the darkness of the tomb.

"When we burn the Moonflowers of our dead, here in this tomb lies their final destination, too," Theole answered. "The ashes are placed into the cauldron within the tomb's center. This is an offering to her, to the Fomorrigan of song. My grandfather Dagdus once told me, much as I tell you now, that we Lunas were offered —no, *promised*—that in return for our fallen and the fertile ashes of their beds, that those who left us too soon would be granted a *purpose* in the Afterlife, instead of facing the haunting expanses of death alone. It is a tomb that has grown much more burdened these last few seasons of late. Moreso than any since the height of the Ever-war." He stopped, bowing his head before the overpowering sight, resting his hand on one of many timeworn standing stones that circled the grounds. "I only hope that this promise, made clear to dear Grandfather Dagdus, does not lie dormant and forgotten."

"Do you think this is where Calluna would want to spend her afterlife?" Titha asked coldly. She shivered as the emptiness of the tomb stared back at her.

"If Calluna were still alive she would curse me something terrible for bringing three young wolas to such a foreboding, heavy place to begin with," Theole replied. He lifted Beebee to him, gently bouncing her as she nodded off. "But you are ready for this, my two eldest daughters. And in truth, I think Calluna would be honored to reside here in this historic, hallowed place. Yes… here, with our fierce ancestors: those lost in battle, to strife, and who sacrificed themselves for the good of all Lunas. May the Fomorrigan grant her purpose in the Otherworld, too."

"You keep saying 'Fomorrigan' as if we know her," Gilly scolded impatiently. "I'm here to honor our fallen tutor, not some forgotten spirit."

Theole swooped to his daughter, engulfing her in a hushing cloud of shadow, as if to keep her words form echoing into the tomb. The girls both flinched, their eyes wide. All fell silent as Theole prevented further harsh words from his daughters.

"You're afraid," Titha inhaled through his hand.

"Afraid?" Theole scoffed.

"Yes!" she retorted. "Of this place."

"Not afraid. Respectful. *Respectful* of the tomb my grandfather built, and the Old Tales our ancestors told. Enough of their beliefs have come to truth and light for us to *not* hold them in great respect. As you both should. Beebee will as well, when she is old enough."

"In order for any of us to do that, we would need to know these tales and legends in full," Gilly said as she shook her head beside Titha, who leaned into her.

"Have I not brought you here to enlighten you so?" Theole replied. "I need not remind you, Gillian, how strict—how *cold and vengeful*—Meriduun became in her twilight. There was to be *no* mention of *any* deities, nor Gods nor Goddesses, not even her own kin, unless they were *her*. Our *Duskmother*. Our One and Only God."

"I remember," Gilly answered, harsh memories storming within.

"Was she really that terrible in the end?" Titha pipped in.

"Yes, my dear," Theole shuddered. "And the resurgence of this tomb into our lives serves as evidence. Every Luna we lost during the Treachery of the Great Drakes is now buried here. *Every single body* that perished during the Ever-war lies within, for they were all taken too soon. Those not fortunate enough to fulfill their long Nights with Gaela; those not granted a natural death, where their roots return to the soil and their flesh feed the grasses… rest here, instead. It looks ancient to your eyes, my daughters, because it has laid untouched for generations, unused until Vulduun's Ever-war forced this cairn back into our ways. This is where our greatest sorrows lie; past and present. And it is the keeper of my greatest failures."

His voice began to weaken as he lowered himself to the ground for a sit.

"I get it," Gilly spoke up after a brief silence. "I understand Calluna's... hesitance. Her violence I don't, but... I can't help but think that... If we join the rest of the world, and their Time, this tomb will be much fuller and at a much faster pace, will it not?"

Her father was unsure how to answer. He leaned forward, rocking Beebee as he brushed his toes and fingers into the old green grasses.

"Cypress felt that way, too, if you remember. He and Calluna shared many viewpoints—many friends. And they would have gladly kept us cut off from the rest of Gaela's world forever. I cannot say you are wrong, my child, but I can assure you that there are things you have not yet come to understand. That Time is but a fleeting concept we perceive. It is not absolute, like the waters or earth or sky. It is an illusion. A concept. And sometimes, a trap."

From the tomb the elders finally emerged before them, each empty handed. No Calluna, nor clay pot holding her Moonflower's ashes, returned from it and its depths; only those who shepherded her to her final destination. Titha's hands began to tingle, and in this moment she understood. She understood perminance. She understood consequence. And she understood the importance of *life*.

Theole reached for her, rubbing her back as some of the most respected Lunas to ever grace the Duskridge walked past. "Calluna's tragedy has shown me how deep the concern, and the *hatred* of the outside world truly runs," he said to his daughters, nodding to each passerby. "Cypress would have been among those to send Calluna into this tomb, too, if he were loyal still. He—*they*—felt so strongly that the traditions of our people were worth more than the lives of those outside our walls that he was willing to turn his back on everything and everyone he loved. So, whenever I feel even the slightest tinge of regret… or when I hear his voice in the edges of my mind reminding me he may have been 'right', that 'perhaps we should have continued to shun the world and silence the calls for help that echoed outside our Wood Gate'… I come here. I sit, and I wait for something. Anything. A sign. A whisper from the wind. A glisten from the Moon or a thrush's song. But nothing ever comes… and no one ever returns. That silence, my daughters, is what reminds me that Cypress is *wrong*. That *I* was wrong. We all were."

"What do you mean, father?" Titha asked, her growing concern robbing her of the Sun's low warmth.

"Tell me what you remember of my teachings. Of the beauty of Life, and our connection to Gaela through death," he requested.

"… That those who are granted a natural death from Gaela, our Mother Nature, become one with her again," Titha answered politely.

"Yes… and it is a most *beautiful* thing to me. To think of those we've lost forever singing with the leaves, swimming as the salmon and otter do, flying on a robin's wing, or running as Bear-kin between bramble and trees… This, to me, is as it should be. To be birthed from the soil then return unto it again. It comforts me in the face of Death. To know that this incredible shell, this hallowed husk of a body returns to whence it came. But the very existence of the Fomorrigan, the Other Gods, and the offerings we make to her cauldron within… tell of a different path, a different Death for those taken too soon. And we have known, and felt this, in the mists and shadow that cross our lands. The

Otherworld is just that; mist and shadow, a world kin to ours yet not our own. It is where lost souls are kept, never to return. An *oblivion,* as our Great Drakes came to threaten it. But shortsighted are we mortals in our ability to see past Death. To see the other side. For all we are aware, the soil is where the soul returns to be reborn. The soil is where the soul resides. And we become one with Her again. With Gaela."

Titha looked to the Tri-Spiral on the entrance stone, it's never-ending curl seeming to move in tandem with her father's words as he went on. "Do you believe that, father?" she asked, her mind so heavy it could sink a boat.

"I do not think any to ever live will have the right or wrong answer to such questions. But understand this, my daughter: the fleeting nature of life, and the finite light of mortality, to me, is what makes life so very precious, and so very worth conserving."

"Always worth fighting for," Titha added.

"Exactly, my dear. Exactly that. So as we settled into our forests and withdrew from the ways of the world outside and its wars, this Oathera we speak of, the fabled Otherword of our ancestors, beckoned our people less and less, until our great tombs and cairns such as this one, became relics; frozen in a time long forgotten. But Oathera's mists have not forgotten us. They, and their masters, await those whose odysseys were not finished in this life. Though I, and your mother—"

"What about her?" Gilly jolted.

"She..." Theole's eyes lit up with memories of his beloved. "Your mother... well, she respected these tales more than any I have ever known. As if, somehow, she *knew* Oathera. Not just *of* it. She *knew* it..." Theole looked to his children, their faces heavy. "Whatever we choose to believe now, as the world renews such rapid change before our eyes, I hold one thing to be *absolutely* true: If there truly is a place inOathera for the dead, an oblivion-esque Otherworld for them and their afterlife, then none have ever returned from it… No matter how many Days or Nights one has spent in waiting…"

His tired gaze drifted back to the tomb's opening, and a thousand nights spent waiting—each for a sign from his beloved—sauntered through his mind's eye.

"People will believe what they want to," Gilly said, breaking her father's thoughts. "Whether it is cauldrons and Goddesses or buds and soil. But Mint didn't die to answer any of those questions, did she? She died because of bigots. Because a bunch of near-sided twits can't handle a shared tower and trading port."

Theole rose to his feet. He began to pace, knotting his hands together as his thoughts wandered deeper into days when those he missed were still alive.

"We are in agreeance there, Gillian. To shut ourselves off is to bring about our own end!" he cried out. "None will ever forget the sight of our home burning, the screams of our kin, or the faces of those who were taken from us because we *chose*, my daughters. Before Celtica, we *chose* the old, comfortable ways above a dying world. This mound, this ancient corridor would lie *half* as full if we had but heeded others before it was too late. Alas, we chose not to listen instead. We chose a *wall* over *words*. Closing our people off—choosing to hate and fear has led to nothing but blood and ash. Wherever those two meet, Death follows. And I will never be their cause again."

Gilly rustled through the grass to place her hands on her

father's. "Vulduun was their cause, and Meriduun before him. Not you."

"We can only place blame elsewhere for so long before it comes back to haunt us. This we have seen with our own eyes." Theole stood tall before his girls; his young women. He brushed Gilly's cheek, looking into her violet eyes.

"Our duty, as leaders, is not to do what is fair, but what is right." He took Beebee from her arms, cradling his youngest. "The safe and easy solutions are always the strongest of temptations. But *true* strength comes to those who can lead a righteous path without falling unto the easy. In this moment, though, I want you to hear me not as your Watcher. For I will always be that second. First, I am your *father*. And I will always, for as long as I breathe, take the Duskridge down whatever path keeps you three, and all our kin, the farthest from harm. In our world of today, it is open arms. It is *Celtica*."

Gilly collapsed into Theole, followed by Titha, who nuzzled her face far into Beebee's dozy demeanor. There they rested together, their family; their world.

The lumen elders had all returned home at this point; the Bear-brothers staying behind to re-seal the tomb. Mint's cradle was at rest inside its walls. She was in her final resting place now.

As the Bear-brothers returned the entrance stone to its post, Titha stopped. A strange feeling shot up her spine, and goosebumps up each limb. As she watched the empty darkness of the cairn disappear into morning sunlight, a freezing, wisping breeze shot through the last little crack, gently embracing her. With one last push from the Bear-brothers the tomb was shut, and the breeze disappeared.

"Is mother in there?" she asked, the wind's soft whisper

familiar to her. "I… we always think of her as part of Mother Nature… but she died in battle, right? She died saving us. So she… Is she… in there?"

"No, sprout, no," Theole responded gently. "She was not buried here. Nor was your mother *lost* in battle. She was right where she wanted to be when the end came. It… it is hard to explain. She left us in such a way that… We were unable to bury her."

"There was nothing left of her to bury," Gilly added somberly.

"Gillian!" Theole scolded, covering Beebee's ears. "Hold your tongue, young wola. That is not true. It is also part of why I brought you here. I knew this would all be… well, *troubling*, at the least. Perhaps beyond what you were prepared for. Therefore, I have brought something. *Some things*. Each long overdue."

He placed Beebee back into Gilly's arms and leaned to his side, fishing what sounded like heavy silver trinkets from his pocketed sash.

"It has been years since your mother left us now, yet I have still not found myself ready to pass on this knowledge… to truly accept she is gone from Gaela forever, as are so many others now. Calluna's tragedy, however, has also shown me that I mustn't continue to wait for a tomorrow that may never come. Therefore, *ahem*, I believe it is time you each were given… these."

Theole pulled a clenched fist from his pocket, opening it before his eldest daughter.

"For you, Gillian Rose Mae, your mother's ring."

The gorgeous, knotted silver gleamed in the speckled forest, and in its center shone a light amethyst bearing a spiral just like one of the branches of the Tri-Spiral on the tomb's entrance stone.

"Thea wore that ring her entire life," Theole added. "It was on her hand the day I met her, the day you were born, and until the day she left us. Now it is yours, my child. I see so much of your mother in you, Gillian; her poise, her grace, her beautiful, unbreakable spirit, but above all her absolute embodiment of justice and truth. This ring was of the utmost importance to her, and she looked to it whenever we spoke of home. I hope that now you will do the same."

Gilly slipped the ring onto her finger. It fit perfectly, sitting on her hand exactly as she remembered it gracing her mother's. A warm smile covered her face.

"When your time comes to lead; whenever you must make a difficult decision, or feel as if you've lost your way, look to this stone—this ring—and think of her. Think of your home, your people, the love you hold for them, the love she held for *you*—and you will know what to do."

He reached back into his pocket, pulling forth a glistening torc bracelet made of equally fine silver; its length twisted 'round like vines up a tree. Each end bore a piece of amethyst without any symbols upon them. Wrapped with it was a beautiful necklace of the most delicate chain. Upon it dangled an amethyst with a spiral almost identical to the ring's.

"For you, Begonia Bee Mae, my tiny princess, your mother's necklace. I know you do not remember her in sight, but this amethyst holds the infinite love she radiated for you, as she was wearing it when you were born. I'll never forget her face the first time you opened your eyes to meet hers. '*My perfect flower*,' she whispered, and you smiled up at her. You were everything to her, Begonia Bee, and still are."

He placed the necklace over her neck slowly, nuzzling his nose into her.

"Is the bracelet for me?" Titha asked, looking to the torc in her father's hands.

"It is not," he smiled.

"Oh. That's okay, father. I don't need anything. I still remember her perfectly."

"My sweet Titha Mae," Theole whimpered. "Do you honestly think I would leave you without? This is a torc," he explained, "A type of bracelet our people have made for each other since the beginning. This one is comprised of two strands of Duskridge silver—one representing your mother, and the other myself—twisted together for eternity, making one perfect bond. If it is alright with you, I would like to wear it—because this other, last treasure, is for you." He pulled another item from his pocket.

Titha absolutely lit up, her eyes darting to his sash as his worn fingers pulled the most gorgeous silver circlet she'd ever seen. It was thin and graceful, yet brimmed with power. It bore another spiral amethyst in its crest, just as the items given to her sisters. It was flawless.

"For my brave warrior," Theole decreed as he placed the circlet upon his daughter's head, its crest resting perfectly on Titha's forehead. "My fearless Lilly... My champion."

Titha grasped her father's hands as he finished adorning the circlet, and every emotion she had ever felt whisped through her young veins.

"Your mother wore this only when she was called upon for *war*, my daughter. It graced her final days in this world. She was a true defender, gifted with a spear and shield, something you have inherited every bit of. But she was cautious, always, Titha Mae, and never sought trouble where it was not. Remember that. I pass on this circlet to you in hopes that you will do the same; that you will only wear its stone when the time calls, and in turn only rush to battle when all other options have failed."

"I promise, father," she spoke softly, her voice hoarse under the pressure of the magnificent silver circlet. She touched the amethyst gem in its center. "I promise you, too, mother." As she felt the spiral in the amethyst, she looked to the entrance stone. "This is how I know that symbol!" she spoke. "Mother's things..." Seeing it on a tomb and feeling one of its spirals on her at the same time, however, proved too much, and Titha Mae fell into longing for her mother.

Paw came bounding from his kin, plomping himself down before Titha and pressing his face into her. She squeezed her arms around his throat as he took a big breath and sighed for her.

"What is this symbol?" Gilly asked their father. She had stood silent in deep thought, but was growing a bit miffed. Frustrated that they didn't know more.

"It is an ancient emblem," Theole spoke slowly. "It, too, is of Old Grandfather Dagdus' design. Ask me again when we are home, and I will pull the parchments for you, my daughter. For they have not been touched in many, many Moons."

"So mother wore these spirals," Gilly questioned, "ones that only exist here at this tomb and on her own belongings, and this is all you can tell us?"

"He just told us a great deal," Titha frowned.

"Not enough," Gilly returned, her sister's retort only serving to make her more upset. "This ring. The necklace. That circlet, and this tomb. Now. Here. After all that has happened to our family, to our people, and to our mother, this is all you can tell us? This is all mother wished for us to know? In all the time you spent with her, you never thought to ask her *more*?"

CHAPTER SEVEN

The Hunt Begins

Sigrid walked Celtica's main road at high noon, the Sun beating down on her wolv'sfur. It was an empty sight. Tents were left unattended, only those choosing to live as if nothing had ever happened remained—being, of course, mostly Goblins. One Goblin in particular, though, was beyond flustered to be there in that moment and time.

"I am still not sure if I am best suited for such an, how should I say, *air-bound* assignment, my Shieldmaiden," Nech clamored, tripping over his own provisions as he struggled to straighten them. "And if I may be so bold, I do not recall being asked! Oh, my sincerest apologies, Sire, that slipped out of my wrinkled mouth and indeed *was* too bold. I am but a bundle of nerves at the moment—a bundle of nerves serving as your faithful servant!"

"Relax, my friend," Sigrid smiled. "You are of utmost importance to me. Maya and I cannot read my son's drawings, nor your maps, if we are in flight. You are to be our cartographer, and our thumbs. It is much appreciated."

"Oh, heavens this is to be such a mess… My sincerest apologies, again, in advance. I only hope not to prove a burden on any or all proceedings. If I do—"

"If? Try *when,*" Maya smirked as she preened her feathers in preparation for their flight.

Nech fiddled his thumbs as he imagined reading important documents astride the back of a giant bird… He was fumbling with them already, there, firmly planted on sturdy ground.

"Besides, if I'm going on this wild goose chase, so are you," Maya scoffed, readying herself as she looked to the Sun's position over the horizon. "The shadows resting on the Fell Mountains tell me we head Northeast if we are to follow Audun's sketchings. Once over their peaks we can raise our elevation to chart a true course."

"I am in your hands, Maya, and in your debt. Ready to follow your every command," Sigrid decreed.

"I don't have hands, and in a moment neither shall you, so let's get used to that as soon as possible. That'll be my first command, yes?" she returned, eyes already rolling. "If we are to make this trip, you need to start thinking like… *ugh*… an Eagle—and *now*—not after it's too late. How do I put this… Everything north of your fjords and mountain-walled homeland is much less warm hearths and frothy ales and much, much more… just prepare for anything that has eyes wanting to either eat you or strip you of everything you're worth. And in my experience, things that fly, things *without* hands, are much less likely to fall prey to either."

"Phenomenal news!" Nech cried out, accidentally crumpling the map.

As Maya finished speaking, sure enough, Sigrid's very fingertips gave way to a sparkling amber energy, one as old as Time itself. Her hands spread into wings; gloriously-long primary feathers of red and gold taking to the sky. Massive talons gripped the dry earth as a sharp amber beak ripped into the wind, letting loose a fierce cry that would shatter the ears of the lesser. The Glorious Red Eagle had returned.

"There she is," Maya scoffed at the sight. "You look… less handsy. Good. Good. Now, we may begin."

Off the trio went, the rest of Daylight spent ensuring they covered as much ground as possible.

As Day ended, all three flowerbeds sat open in the center of Roostwood, their petals wide and shining in the Moon's first light as it competed with the Sunset. The girls' quarters mixed with beautiful shades of Moon and Sun swirling down through the open ceiling.

Titha rubbed her eyes, exhausted. She rolled over in her flower, flinching with an "ouch!" as she found her mother's circlet with her hip. It had not left her side since her father bestowed it upon her. She held it up, the Tri-Spiral amethyst shimmering. In its reflection she could see, to her surprise, that Gilly was awake. Her baby sister's delightful morning chirping, however, was absent.

"Where's Weebee?" she asked.

"She has springly, springee, sprung-sprout-time tonight, whatever that ridiculous sounding class is named. Father is walking her down," Gilly responded. She saw the circlet in Titha's hand and her own fingers wandered to her mother's ring.

"The trial will be nearly over by now," she spoke softly, looking up to the positions of the Sun and Moon, which was even thinner now, it's waxing crescent giving way to its dark side.

Titha looked up with her. She slid the circlet onto her head as she stared into the crescent above.

"I don't think I got any good sleep," she said, fastening her white hair into a messy bun. "I can't get Mint out of my head. What she said… how she said it… the sight of her on that rock in Celtica. Not to mention the spear and—"

"Clover…" Gilly added.

"Really, Gills?"

"You wouldn't understand," Gilly replied, her eyes heavy.

"You're right, I definitely do not understand," Titha replied. "Does it make *any* sense to you that he was so eager to place himself in the middle of a murder? Have you *ever* seen him do anything other than flip his hair during lessons or stand in the back row of the sprout-choir? Or just, you know, generally *not* try to be the center of attention?"

"I know," Gilly agreed. "He has seemed really… *energized* of late."

"Yes! Full of some sort of off-putting purpose. Maybe he really did see the human stranger do it. Do the deed with the spear. I just didn't know he had that sort of *caring* in him. But stranger things have happened," Titha added, taking off her mother's circlet and staring into the amethyst. "Look at this circlet," she continued, rotating it. "It's amazing. Mother was amazing. *So amazing*. She would never have let this happen. She would've stopped that spear, or Mint, really, before she ever got that far with such a hateful speech. She certainly wouldn't be laying on her backside like a slug talking about it. She'd be at the center of everything, doing whatever she could to *help*."

"She was incredible…"

"And I feel entirely un-incredible slugging it up here!" Titha floundered, finally stirring out of her Moonflower. "I'm going down there."

"To Skaldhall? To what? Watch a bunch of Men decide whether or not to torch the stranger? He did it, Titha. There's no question. Rainer will sentence him, and this will all be over soon. You'd just be in the way."

"Maybe, but none of that brings Mint back. I can't get the Cairn out of my mind. The coldness of its entrance—or exit, whatever it is. Hateful or not, Calluna was our people. A 'flower that will never blossom again' as mother used to say. This trial *means* something, Gilly. I have to see it. I have to see how it ends."

"No you don't, you just can't stand not being in the middle of everything for once," Gilly scolded, jumping up in her flowerbed. "This has nothing to do with you!"

"It has everything to do with me—*us*, I mean! Wh-why am I even arguing with you? All you ever do is say no. Have fun doing nothing tonight! Bye."

Before Gilly heard her sister's feet hit the ground she knew what was to happen. "Titha Lilly Mae I swear to Gaela if you whistle—"

Titha let loose a whistle that would 'waken dead trees, and sure enough Paw came bounding down the halls of Roostwood from his own slumber, his hair knotted from a rude awakening.

"Fetch Feathersword and prepare for travel, brother boy!" Titha decreed, placing her mother's circlet in her pouch. As she did, she pulled out a scribbled leaflet and slapped it onto her wooden nightstand beside her flowerbed.

"Titha listen to me, I am in charge while father is out, okay? And you are not leaving my sight! We are to stay here and—Paw if you touch me I will bite your stupid adorable face. Paw. *PAW*!" The fluffball picked her up by the bottoms of her sleepgown, hovering her over her flowerbed like a dragonfly before dropping her onto the mossy floor.

"Go get dressed, boss-lady," Titha commanded, already sliding into her pants and tunic. "Come with me and I never leave your sight, right? You can pretend you're in charge and taa'daa! We both win!"

"This feels nothing like winning," she mumbled, her face still pressed into the moss-covered ground.

After much arguing and surprisingly-less-slapping than usual, the two oldest Mae sisters got fully dressed and took off astride Paw.

The Sun had almost completely retreated, and as they exited Roostwood Gilly's thoughts returned to Clover. "Perhaps heading down isn't the worst idea," she thought. His part in all this, after all, would be revealed down there, not up here. Her frown remained, though, as it was never in her best interest to let Titha know she may be... *right*.

And 'right' Titha felt. She could feel the air stirring outside Ythengrey as she gripped Feathersword's hilt. What awaited them? Would this stranger have already answered for Mint's fate? Would Sigrid be the one to end him? If so, would Audun faint again? Would Gillian be able to choose between staring at Clover or Rainer? Uncontainable curiosity ruled her once more, and she loved every second of it.

Audun sat atop the steps of Skaldhall as he scratched beneath Haldor's chin, both staring at the gorgeous blanket of stars above. Not a single soul walked the dark streets of Autumnhill. Everyone was behind them, enclosed in their ancient ancestral home, yelling and screaming and pointing.

"Politics," he thought, harrumphing as he patted Haldor's head. Another bout of 'debate' broke out behind the stone walls, and Haldor flopped himself down onto the front stoop, grumbling.

"You said it, buddy," Audun sighed. "I think I'd rather take an arrow to the knee than ever put up with that mess. Do they do anything other than yell at each other? I think that is all politics is now. Yelling."

Haldor looked up, as if he was about to answer plain.

Instead, his curly muzzle shot straight toward town. A familiar, barreling outline made its way through the streets of Autumnhill.

"Titha! Paw! Hey!" Audun yelled. No response.

"Girls! Hey! Up here!" ...Still nothing.

"Are they moving?" he asked Haldor. "Are they moving at all? Or, oh, Paw has gotten slow."

Down on the dusty dirt roads Paw lumbered like a one-ton turtle, his body about to give out from fur-bound exhaustion. Finally, a voice made its way back to Audun.

"Can you fetch him some water, please?" Titha shouted. Audun waved with a "no need!", pointing his friends to the north of the stairs where the horses' troughs sat. He skipped down the many steps to meet them, Haldor in tow.

Paw took to the trough like... well, like an obtuse thirsty bear would take to any source of water. Titha almost couldn't hear herself to ask a question over all the slurping. "You did great, fuzzybutt," she patted him. "But you're still going on a diet."

"Morning, Gilly," Audun greeted. "Not to be rude, but why are you here?"

"Because I was cursed with her, then that slurping thing, and life hates me, in that order," she scoffed back.

"Did we miss it? Is it over? What's the stranger's name? Where's he from? Is your mother inside? Of course she is, I bet she's doing all the important talking, right? *Ooh* I bet she's wearing her 'I'm in charge here' cloak, you know the one I mean? The one with the gold trim? Gah, gotta get one of those someday—" Titha rapid-fired.

"No... No. She, uhm, she left. She's with Nech and Maya. She had to follow the Aurora."

"*What*?" Titha croaked.

"It was time, she said. Couldn't wait any longer. This has not been a fun day."

"Wow," Titha replied, "That stinks! I'm sorry… Are you okay?"

"I'll be fine, thank you. It is just hard—when she leaves, I mean. With father gone now. When she's gone, too, I worry about her."

"We know the feeling," she reassured him. "Aha! No wonder the crows were so chatty this past Day," Titha chirped, completely changing expression. "I hardly slept at all, either way, but *Gaela* were those chatterbeaks noisy with father. This makes sense, though, doesn't it? So much is happening all at once. Things are changing again, Audun. Can you feel it?"

"Ugh you are *so* over-dramatic," Gilly quipped, slouching onto Paw. "It's too early for this much drama. Someone give me a bedddd."

"Why aren't you up there inside?" Titha asked Audun. "How could you possibly miss any of this?"

"Rainer sent me out. It started getting pretty nasty in th—"

As Audun spoke Skaldhall's doors flung open above the steps, crashing into the stones that housed them.

"That's why," he added, scratching Haldor.

But this time was different. Dozens of Vikingmen shot out into the evening, each screaming and red-faced. The Houndsmen soon followed, weapons raised. Haldor stared straight up the stairs as commotion overtook the high ground, his back end poised between his master and the danger. He led the young Companions backward, shoving them away from the possibility of violence spilling down the steps.

"Stop them!" a familiar voice cried out amid the chaos above. "Stop them at once!"

It was Rainer! The young Jarl burst forth from the kerfuffle, knocking aside his own soldiers whose speed was not up to his standards. But the discord was too great, and he became trapped in another never-ending wave of Man-wrestling-Man, occasional Luna-witness- grappling-Man, and especially Man-punching-Man, as a Viking never resisted a good fight.

Without warning a smoky blast rocked the hall inside, and even more screams broke out. Strange shades of black and purple began to whirl above the cries of panic and anger.

"Toward Southtown!" a Houndsman called out. "They are breaking for it!"

Like badgers, two figures shot from the panic, one round and one thin; both hooded in cloaks as black as the Darkside of the Moon. Nearby citizens jumped for the escaping figures at the edge of Skaldhall's awning, but shadows moved with the fleeing. They seemed untouchable.

Making way for the southern side of the steps, the skinny figure's hood flung back.

"Clover?" Titha whispered. Her eyes focused on the silver-haired boy, catching a glimpse of his unmistakably gentle features as he ran down the southern side of the steps. "Gilly, that's Clover! And he looks mighty shady!" she yelled, appalled.

"No it's not," Gilly retorted. "Stop projecting your drama onto this mess and let's get out of here! I knew we shouldn't have come down."

Another shadowy blast rocked Skaldhall. This one sent debris flying over the heads of the crowd spilling out the doors.

"Gilly, *that* is Clover! Right there! Don't act like you don't have the *back* of his head memorized, too!" Titha grabbed her sister's neck, pointing her violet eyes directly at the culprit just before he managed to pull his hood back up. Her jaw dropped.

"What... is he... doing... in a cloak? To father. I'm going to tell father!"

"Great idea! You go tell father, Paw and I will go after the hoods!"

"Ohhhhh no, no, no, no, no, twerp, nice try, but you are not running off this time. We're *all* going to father together. Now!"

"Uhm, girls?" Audun shouted above the chaos. "Whatever you are going to do, make it faster. Gilly's boyfriend is getting away."

Clover jumped from the final step, his bare indigo feet crunching the dry grasses. His cohort landed with a heavy *THUD*, black leather boots kicking up dust as he took off behind Clover. The younglings watched as he quickly outpaced everyone, including the young Luna, breaking into a stride no one would've guessed such a figure was capable of. He could not be caught, not even by those emerging from the southside of town to help.

"If we don't do something they're going to escape! Where's Rainer? Jarl!" Audun shouted.

He looked back for his brother, whose face was currently being punched by a rather brawny and unbelievably angry bearded Man. Skaldhall was now hosting a full-out, raucous brawl, with Rainer trapped in the middle attempting to restore any sort of order.

"Let me go! Is no one going to stop them!?" a Houndsman shouted out, furious and mortified. "They escape us as we punch each-oth—" *THWACK.*

"Catch those murderers!" one of the elder Luna witnesses shouted out.

"Murderers?" Titha whispered, sharp green eyes still focused on Clover's fleeing silhouette. "*Murderers*? Oh no…"

Gilly grabbed her, squeezing her arm as tight as she could. "Listen to me now, little sister. I absolutely forbid you to run off into something you have no business in! They're calling Clover a murderer! They are shouting *murderer* at the stranger *and* Clover!"

Titha whistled for Paw, yanking her wrist from Gilly's grasp.

"There are two kinds of people, sis," Titha shouted, "Those who run away from the swarm, and those who run into it, stings and all!"

"Don't you quote mother to me right now, Titha Mae! We—*you* are not going anywhere near anyone others are shouting 'murderer' at! This is not the time for one of your escapades! This is serious!"

"Blah blah blah—also a mother quote!" Titha chirped, grabbing Paw's scruff. "*That* is Clover, in a black cloak, right there, running away from a place that is currently exploding! An exploding place that *was* housing the trial for a *dead wola*, Gillian. Mint is *dead*, remember? Dead. She is gone now. Forever. Like mother."

"I know what dead means, Titha!"

"Then you agree we have to find out what is going on here before anyone else gets killed. I won't let anyone else die. Will you?"

"Let the guards handle this!" Gilly screamed.

"They're too busy punching each other! The murderers are getting away! None of these humans can see in the dark, anyway! But we can! Again, why am I arguing with you? *Paw*!" She dug her heels into her Bear-brother and leaned forward, and he began to walk southward.

Gilly's fists clenched as she growled, teeth grinding. "This is absolutely out of the question! Paw, stop! Father will be furious!"

"With you, surely," Titha laughed, "You're in charge here, remember?"

"I do think it is better to do something than— than nothing," Audun murmured as he mounted Haldor. "Just... just my thoughts."

"Loosen up and look alive, sis!" Titha shouted as the boys began to trot into a stride. "Besides, it's just Clover, right? What could possibly go wrong?" she shouted, and the beasts were off into the darkness.

"What are you doing!?" Gilly panicked astride. "I still never agreed to *thiiiissss*!"

She ducked into her little sister's back as Paw barreled off southward. Titha's green eyes took in the Moon and starlight as she guided Paw around corners of stone huts and wooden barrels. He leaped and dodged through city corridors as Gilly held on for dear life, choking back what was surely to be a swift vomit.

"There, I see them!" Titha shouted into the Night, the crescent Moon now bright above them. "They're headed straight down the alleyway! We're catching up—but *wow* they're fast!"

"They are headed for the South Wall!" Audun shouted up

from Haldor behind them. "They'll never make it over! We'll catch them there!"

Haldor accepted his master's challenge, lowering his neck with a snarl as he greatly outpaced Paw. The much thinner, much more limber wolfhound skirted past the girls, drenched in grey curls and pure determination. He was, after all, born from a line bred to hunt. And the hunt was on.

The South Wall fast approached, and the cloaked figures gave way to its imposing stature. Clover lowered his hood to clear his vision, using flawless Luna night'sight to comb the bottom of the wall. He spotted was he was looking for, and took off, not waiting for his larger partner. Just as he did, a maw of sharp canine teeth snatched the very tip of his cloak, snagging it then yanking him back. Clover flew onto his arse, the scrap of fabric dissolving into a cloud of black smoke, disappearing from Haldor's grasp. This only angered the hound more, and he pounced forth, Paw fast approaching from behind. But they were too late—Clover slipped like a ferret across the dry ground and down into a hole beneath the South Wall—and he was gone.

The much, much larger cloaked figure paused, looking to Haldor and Paw. Flinching, it made the plunge, and just barely squeezed through with another poof of smoke. Haldor wasted no time, shooting head-first down into the burrow, Audun ducking with one hand on his hat in turn. Paw scuffed and scammored his front paws, stopping before the opening. He grunted.

"I told you! Diet! It's happening!" Titha shouted, smacking his side as she looked to the hole. "Get your butt in there, we're not losing them!"

Paw grumbled a few Bearish words.

"I don't care! Whoever is in that cloak was no small guy!

Now go! You okay back there, Gills?"

Gillian mumbled something that sounded an awful lot like keeping her supper down.

"It'll be just like digging under tree'stumps back home, fuzzybutt—Now come on!" Titha yelled.

Paw roared in protest, but Titha wasn't having it and yanked backward on his round ears until he his groaning turned into motion. Paw crammed his massive shoulders into the opening, his back legs wiggling for dear life. Titha and Gilly slid backward off him.

"I think I'm going to be sick," Gilly murmured.

"Push now, throw-up later—" Titha yelled as she shoved her Bear-brother's enormous backside as hard as she could. With one more hefty shove of her own and zero help from Gilly, *SHLUMP!* Paw fumbled into the burrow with Titha after him.

"I hate you—*hiccup*—oh no—" Gilly grabbed her mouth.

"Don't you even!" Titha screamed from directly below her sister as she got up. "Swallow it and come on!" But Gilly didn't budge. She was in the middle of the biggest decision she'd ever made in her near 18 forest-years o' life.

"It's now or never!" Titha shouted at her.

"I am fully aware!" Gillian screamed back, clenching her stomach. She looked behind her, smoke pouring from the open doors above Skaldhall as the world of Men completely failed to contain their trial.

"Alright fine, I'll tell you all about it when I get back with Clover's dumb face strapped to a plank!" Titha's voice grew faint as she began making her way through the tunnel. "Wait up, Audun!" she shouted into the deep.

"Strapped to a what!?" Gilly cried out. "We don't even know if he actually *did* anything—I mean—*Ugh*!"

Her gaze turned from Skaldhall to the crescent Moon above, then back down to the hole as she stood alone. She took one step forward, then hesitated. She did so again, running scenarios in her head before—*sllllip*—she second-guessed her footing and froze, falling face first into the dirt-filled tunnel, screaming internally.

Titha laughed hard from the middle of the tunnel. "Didn't know what you were getting into, did you, sis? Look at you all dirty back there. Proud of you!"

"I'm the eldest," Gilly shouted, brushing her silken dress off. "I'm the one who gets to be proud, not you. And I'm just here to stop you!"

"From all the way back there? Good luck!"

"Titha come on, stop! You cannot do this to father and Beebee—they'll be worried sick!"

"No they won't. I left a note!"

"Don't you lie to me!" Gilly snorted as she stumbled through mounds of dirt.

"I did!"

"When? When could you have possibly had time to leave him a note before scampering off like the ungrateful shrew you are?"

"I keep them prepped in my pouch," Titha laughed hard, as she found this particular little habit of hers quite ingenious. "When he sees this one he'll just think we're off relocating homeless frogs—Or did I leave him the newborn bunnies one? Anyway, if you'd stop whining and pick up the pace, we could be back in time for supper! All the notes I make say I'll be back for supper."

"Lords you just think you are so clever, don't you?" Gilly groaned, still tending to her green dress.

"It's pretty great, admit it!" Titha chuckled at herself again as she nudged Paw along the tunnel. "Going to be a long trip if you don't lighten up a bit!"

As they traveled the shaft, a faint light showed at the other end, barely lit by starlight. Paw stuck his head down, grunting what surely translated to 'hurry up'! He groaned and pouted as he helped his sisters climb out, guiding them ahead as Haldor made haste after the culprits. Paw was not happy that his friend was so far ahead.

The trial's culprits, however, were even farther ahead. Clover's cloaked visage was well into the night, but not out of sight just yet. He scurried about, shuffling to keep himself shrouded as if no one had spotted him, taking off into the land outside Autumnhill. His bare indigo feet slapped as he ran, Haldor's keen ears following each *plat*, and his even keener nose locked onto the boy's unique scent. Audun leaned forward in silence, as if he had become one with his hound's gifts for the hunt.

The sisters mounted Paw as he began to gallop, their eyes adjusting to a landscape much like the one that gave birth to Celtica. An advantage, this was, as it meant no forest, wall, nor town stood before them. Nothing hindered the hunters *or* the hunted now.

Clover was far faster than he had any reason to be, and whatever he was 'drinking'—as Titha quipped—to gain such unfathomable speed was absolutely being shared in double doses with his rotund comrade, as the larger rogue had them all outpaced. But he could not outrun a wolfhound forever, and Haldor knew it.

Audun ducked his entire body even further into his best pal, one hand still on his leather hat as not to lose it. Though with Sigrid gone, would it really matter? It only got in his way, and he only wore it because she liked for him to. With that thought, though, he wouldn't let it go. If it was precious to her it was precious to him.

He gripped tighter into Haldor's curls with his right hand, helping his trusty hound manage their weight as they dodged small boulders and longer outcrops of dry brush. They narrowed in on the two shadowed-figures, each straight ahead. Just enough distance separated them that Haldor knew he could finally pounce, but only for one target. Whether out of instinct or bias, he went for the Luna. *SKGRAM!* Direct hit. Clover went down hard, sliding into the dirt.

Paw and the girls were just behind. Clover fumbled and flailed like (again) a ferret, terrified of the hound snarling over him. As Paw closed in, Gilly wasted no time. She jumped down from him, wiping spit from her face and flinging her hair back as she cocked her left fist. *THWACK!* She planted a firm punch straight across Clover's jaw. Turned out he squealed like a ferret, too.

"Tell us what's going on!" she yelled in his face, pulling her fist back again. "*Talk!*"

"Woah!" Audun gasped.

"Hah! That's my sister!" Titha cried out. "Punch him again!" she called out. "No, wait! Don't do that yet! Hold him instead, we're going after the big one—the stranger!" She kicked her heels into Paw.

"You're not fast enough!" Audun yelled back. "Stay here with your sister, we'll snatch him!"

"You can't see out here at night like I can!" Titha argued, their wits locked. But by the time they could make up their minds, there was no one left to snatch. The enormous culprit had vanished!

"Where did he go!?" Titha cried out. "No one just vanishes!" She grasped Feathersword at her waist.

"He does," Clover murmured from below Gilly's hold. "He can do many things! Which is why you must let him go, and me with him!"

"And you think *I'm* dramatic," Titha rolled her eyes to Gilly. "Listen here, pal," she threatened, looking down to Clover from atop Paw. "My sister only ever has that look in her eyes when she really feels like breaking something, 'kay? And right now the closest something to break is your pretty face. So start talking!"

"No!" Clover shouted, panicking. "Go home! Get out of here! You don't understand what's going on, you two—Let me go and go home to your father!"

"Not a chance, cupcake," Titha barked, turning to Gilly, who pulled her fist back.

"Who was that and how did he just vanish?" Gilly demanded. "You need to explain yourself *now*."

"Gillian, please, this isn't the same as it was!"

"What does he mean?" Titha added. "Tell us something we don't know, or the bear gets a turn at holding you down next."

"No don't! Please no, I'm not your enemy, I promise. I have no choice in all this, okay? Just keep Paw and that—that *wolf-thing* back and let me go! Please! I have to get to the Ruins! I have to go back or he'll kill—"

"What ruins? And who will? I can't believe you, Clover! I can't believe any of this!" Gilly cried out.

"Nothing! No ruins! I said nothing!"

"Oh, please! You better fess up or I'm going to *ruin* a face I'd really rather not! Or maybe I'll let *him*—" she growled, pointing to Haldor as Audun made punching motions astride.

"You honestly think I did this, Gilly?" Clover whimpered desperately, "Huh? That I murdered our teacher? Or anyone, for that matter? I was just there to help, okay? You are in way over your heads!"

"So are you," Gilly replied, "Which is exactly why I will have you sent straight to the Watcher for a little trial of our own!"

As she tightened her grip, Clover's cloak began to smoke in her hands, giving way to what little shadows the Moon was producing.

"I'm sorry, girls," he shuttered. "He won't let that happen! I… I have to get back to the Ruins or he'll… he'll…"

"He's vanishing!" Audun cried out.

The cloak's front *poofed* into thin air, leaving only a hooded cape and an ashen-cloud of ink-like black betwixt Gilly's grasp. Clover scrambled backward, hopping to his feet. Haldor growled, leaping forward, but the mist of Clover's cloak simply wisped around his jaws as they snapped. Clover stood cloakless before them, just a scared boy in the Night.

"*Traitor*!" Titha cried out.

"Oh no, Titha Mae…" Clover groaned, pulling his hood over two eyes full of sadness. His own form began to smoke and ink into the wind. "I am sorry, but I have no choice in this... *There are far worse things to fear in this world than Dragons...*"

With those words he faded into the black mist. Or so it appeared. Titha's keen eyes scoured the night in disbelief, and mere seconds later she spotted a far off shape darting about in the distance.

"Follow that blur!" she shouted. Paw and Haldor took off without hesitation. As they bounded forth, the Nighttime air began to swirl and crack; a great black cloud manifesting with spurts of lightning crossing and crashing amidst its whirl. In it, a horrible beast blacker than the night around it, with glowing eyes and a long, crooked onyx beak, unfurled. Atop it, another figure emerged slowly... It was the much larger stranger! His hood shot around, and as it did Titha and Audun fully expected to see the face of the culprit from Celtica, but they did not. Instead, a cold, emotionless pit with two blank white eyes stared straight back at them. A tremendous fear washed over Titha, but Paw did not give way. He flinched it off, while to his right Haldor sprinted immediately toward the rogues. The mighty hound leaped once more, snagging Clover's heel and bringing him crashing through the dirt before he could mount the giant shadow'beast. A nasty *SQUAWK* left the creature's beak before them, and its cloaked master clapped his hands together, sending a deep mist into the air before Clover. The young Luna scrambled through it, kicking the ashen cloud and dust into Haldor's eyes. With a desperate flail Clover mounted the creature's back, and the trio of villains shot off into the darkness of the South upon wings of solid black.

CHAPTER EIGHT

Cardinal Destinies

"If you cannot see them then they are gone, Titha!" Audun shouted, Haldor slowing down. "I'm useless at Night… If neither of you see them then they are gone for good. That thing they're riding is too fast, and the beasts have been running forever. They need rest. They need food and water!"

"Hello? So do I," Gilly growled, her stomach in knots.

"Curse these barren, useless lands!" Titha cried out dramatically as she scanned the Night. "I know we're hungry, thirsty, tired, and everything else, but we've got to keep moving. We can't let them get away! They'll just hurt more people. Or worse."

"Titha—we'll just be wandering aimlessly if we go any further," Gilly moaned. "We need to turn back and tell father what we know, and if we do it now we'll be back for supper just like your stupid note supposedly says."

"No, no, no, and yes it does say that but again, no. I refuse to give up. A Luna is dead, maybe at the hands of your boyfriend, and no one else thinks this is important enough to keep heading South? I can't believe I am still trying to convince you of what is at stake, here! So say we do turn back, hm? Say we do give up and just let them run off to murder more people. We haven't seen another soul come after them, right? So it's up to us. Or they just get off free; free forever to take life as they see fit."

"We. Are not. Qualified! End of story!" Gilly screamed.

"That's where you're wrong, stringbean. We know where we're going. Clover and his cloaked friend have been headed in a straight line this entire time ever since they fled Skaldhall. Straight south. Right, Audun?"

"Yes, but—" Audun pipped in.

"—And we know they're headed toward a place with Ruins, right?"

"Well, yes, Clover mumbled something about 'making it back to the Ruins'," he agreed again.

"But none of that means anything if the *murderers murder us*! Or, I don't know, we *starve to death*!" Gilly shouted.

"Oh my lords, lady!" Titha groaned. "It's been like two hours! Get a grip! Or chew on some grass!"

Audun pulled his parchment satchel around. Gilly lit up, thinking he was about to pull out food. He did not.

"Rainer wanted to use my map for the trial," he added, unrolling it from his pouch as Haldor slowly marched on. "So luckily I have it still. Let me check and see if there are any ruins directly south of us..." His mind wandered into words and symbols as he scanned his Map of the First Eon, copied directly from Nech's on a much calmer night.

"...You've had a map this entire time?" Gilly snipped.

"Well, yeah, but it's not really something you need when you're chasing a target, so—aha! There!" he shouted, pointing his finger firmly onto a location directly southward of them. "The Ruins... of... B? Ruins of B! ...*B*? That doesn't seem right... Oh no!" He shouted, flinging the map above him. "It's ripped! My map is ripped! Those boorish oafs must've torn it during the trial!"

"Boorish oafs!" Titha laughed. "I like that! Hey, maybe it's the Ruins of B-oorish oafs!"

"Very funny," Audun mocked as he thumbed the ripped portion at the bottom of the map. "This thing is important to me, okay?"

"I know, I know, I'm sorry, I'm not making fun. And we'd be lost without it, and you, most definitely."

"Yes you would. It is just a small bit that is missing, thankfully." He lifted the map to show Titha. "I can fix it when we get back home and I can reference Nech's master tome. For now, we can still see the Ruins themselves on here, and they're directly south of us. So we just... keep down the Fields and into... huh."

"Huh what?" Gillian interjected.

"There's not much down here," Audun pondered. "Guess I've never really noticed how undetailed the southwestern corner of the Map of the First Eon is."

"Let me see this thing," Gillian mumbled as she grabbed the parchment. The northwest of the map felt very familiar to her; Audun's sketches of Yythengrey, Autumnhill, and the newer addition of Celtica in-between all just as they should be. Yet as she perused down to the bottom corner, a strange sense of deja-vu washed over her. The same area of a different map danced within her mind, one far more detailed. One she had seen somewhere else entirely, but now could not place.

"There's nothing down here because someone didn't want there to be," she spoke slowly. "I've seen this area before, just more complete. A lot more complete."

"But why would anyone do that?" Audun asked. "Maps aren't made for any other reason than to be complete."

The rest of the young Companions leaned into the piece, all five faces fixated on what they could not see. Titha traced downward with her finger, her eyes growing wider as the detail grew sparser. She withdrew her hand so she could see the entirety of where these supposed Ruins resided:

"Unless there's something worth hiding..."

Far up into the North, a much different quest consumed Sigrid. She flew upon great red wings, shades of gold glistening off her feathered crest as the evening's vivid sunset unfolded. Nech clenched to her neck as tightly as possible, appreciating her steady stream of flight as they watched Maya dart and dive frantically.

"I do not know how she does that," Sigrid spoke, her amber beak cutting through swift air.

"A great many years of experience, my Shieldmaiden!" Nech answered loudly, always impressed with his swift friend.

"It would be dishonest of me to say I wish you could do the same!" he added, his old hands clenched to the Glorious Red Eagle for dear life.

"I loathe flying," Sigrid answered sincerely. "I do not wish to do what she does any more than you wish to fall from me doing it. Though I do feel that more skill with my Avian wings would permit for less attitude from Maya."

"Pay her no mind in that regard, Sire. She wields great respect for you. She just wishes you had taken a different form, is all, I believe. Perhaps a duck, methinks. Or a crane, yes? A more agreeable Avian that does not directly stoke the darkest corners of her past."

"She is aware this was no choice of mine, correct? I did not choose this fate."

"Oh absolutely. But, if I may—though it is not my story to tell, nor would I ever recommend letting her know you are privy to such information—I believe it is in your best interest to know that: in her youth... Maya's parents and siblings were slaughtered by eagles... before her eyes. She hides it well from most, but it is what led her into the Peregrine Order, and absolutely what birthed a lifetime loathing of your kind."

"My kind? I am no Eagle," Sigrid decreed.

"I beg your pardon, Sire, but you are Lord of *all* Eagles now. Certainly those that now roost a'top Skaldhall think as much."

As they spoke Maya circled back. The Fell Mountains northernmost peaks were finally behind them, and she could now see the lands of the Horizon clearly before them.

"We need to heed eastward," Maya screeched, her gaze unbreaking. "Compare the map to Audun's Aurora, Nech. See if a northeastern course over the Snowy Lands will set us right."

"Your eyes never fail, my dear!" Nech shouted, his hands desperately gripping the map. "North-eastward the winds must take us if we are to reach the Aurora's arrowed-end! But do you mean to fly us directly over Frorora?"

"I would not advise this, either, Maya," Sigrid added loudly. "My kin have a long and troubled history with those born of frost."

"I am aware of the tales of our lands, Shieldmaiden. More than most. But there is no other way. Frorora stretches into the Snowly Lands, far beyond their glacial fortress, and we must cross such unforgiving skies if we are to reach our desired destination."

"Is there any possibility the Frororans will let us advance without discord, flying projectiles, and other things that may... hasten our mortality?" Nech asked nervously.

"Only if we remain unseen," Sigrid spoke sternly. "And in

my current form I do not see that being a possibility."

"Leave that to me," Maya replied. "See the icy rivers ahead? Flying low and fast through their canyons will allow us to pass swiftly and undetected. Their channels swell with tunneling currents, perfect for gliding. It is the only way we were able to chart these lands much nearer to our youth. And when I say we, I mean myself as Nech kept an annoyingly safe distance."

"I must confess I did quite the hurried job, as well," Nech added, " As neither of us were terribly keen for an icy impalement care of the locals…"

"*Now* he admits it!" Maya squawked. "Let's hope you sketched at least a decent enough rendering to keep us headed Northeast while navigating the canyons below or this will all have been for not."

"Oh dear…" Nech mumbled to himself. "You have become awful quiet, Shieldmaiden. Are you alright? What would you have us do?"

"Yes. Though…. No. I am not. I am not confident in my ability to navigate such a narrow flight-space."

"You're going to learn today!" Maya screeched, grinning. "Follow my lead, and we'll make it through. Ready?"

"Not in the least."

"The currents make it easy. You'll be fine. Now… dive!" Maya gave the Shieldmaiden no quarter for deciding, perhaps wisely so. She shot down through a misty cloud into the landscape below them, folding her wings in as she propelled herself to unfathomable speeds. Sigrid cocked her head back.

"Is she serious?" she asked.

Nech gulped, digging himself into her feathers and the straps he had fastened to her torso.

"I… am afraid so. Well… as the Craglins in the East say… tally ho'…"

"Tally ho'…" Sigrid replied, and down she dove, her mass allowing for a significant amount of unexpected gain. The winds swept her feathers, clouds dissolving into nothing as she rocketed through them. A slight smile began to grace her beak. Then, a laugh escaped. Before long she was diving at an immense speed and laughing the entire way, absolutely thrilled.

"This is amazing!" she shouted, closing her eyes as she felt the sharp embrace of gulfing air.

"I… am so… glad you… think… so… sire!" Nech squealed, his eyes squinched shut; the wrinkes on his face flapping wildly in the wind. Maya's tiny brown and white form began to show itself below them, and Sigrid laughed again.

"We are gaining on her!" she shouted. "Amazing! We are… we are gaining fast! Perhaps too fast!" Her smile disappeared as the glacial rivers and canyons below began to approach at alarming speed, as did Maya's backside. The Peregrine could hear them approaching behind, and she turned 'round. Her eyes shot open as she gasped.

"Slow down, Sigrid!" she screamed as loud as she possibly could. "Sigrid! Spread your wings and pull up! You're too heavy, you need to even out! *Sigrid*!" But she had to turn around herself. Maya slowly spread her wings, evening her stream and arcing gracefully into the canyon below them.

Sigrid heeded her advice, but much less gracefully. Her enormous wingspan shot open, catching every bit of wind below them, sending her into a severe halt.

"Hold on, Nech!" she shouted, scrambling. "*Hold on!*"

Flapping furiously, she steadied herself and began to

descend into the canyon. Her downy underside felt the immense cold drafting up from the river below them, its waters barely unfrozen as they carried massive chunks of ice downstream. The extreme chill heightened her nerves even more, and she continued to flap, massive gusts building around her.

"Glide, Shieldmaiden!" Maya shouted back, now flying steadily in front of them. "Stop flapping like a chicken and glide like a falcon! Look to me!"

"I cannot! I will fall!" Sigrid replied, mortified of the icy chasm below.

"You will not!' You must trust me! The draft in this canyon is immense. It will carry you, you just have to let it and glide! Trust me!"

Sigrid heeded, but had much trouble letting go of such a foreign fear. With one large inhale, she closed her eyes, stiffening her wings straight out. Slowly but surely… it worked!

"There you are!" Maya screeched happily. "Now get ready for this turn! Ready?" she spoke, arcing right.

But Sigrid's eyes were still closed. She exhaled, letting the streams carry her bulk.

"Sire?" Nech gargled, looking over her pointed head. "Perhaps we should turn?"

"What?" Sigrid answered, still focused on the glide.

"Turn, Shieldmaiden! *TURN! Before –* "

SSCRAASH! Sigrid barreled straight into a snowbank on the far side of the canyon, frost and ice exploding into the air. Maya screeched, turning sharply to double back. She landed atop the site, frantically scanning with her eyes as a small avalanche made its way down toward the river.

"Sigrid!" she cried out. "Nech! Sigrid!" But no answer came. Making her way to the top, she pecked and clawed for any sign of her Companions. As the tumbling snow settled, a swift, enormous beak poked out of the frost'bank, still smiling.

"That was unexpected," the Great Eagle grinned as she mumbled through snow.

"Typical," Maya scoffed. "Is Nech alright?"

A hand shot up through the loose snow atop Sigrid. She had cradled him to shield him from the alarming albeit soft crash landing.

"I am okay, my dear! If not a bit queasy," Nech decreed as Sigrid plucked him from the snow.

"Good. Failure to listen aside, Sigrid's little tumble has turned out to be a blessing," Maya spoke stoically.

"Why is that?" Sigrid asked.

"Straight ahead. That is most certainly a new development," Maya pointed with her wing outstretched. "And it is no bridge of Man nor Goblin."

"Oh gracious," Nech spoke, his old eyes meeting the sight. Before them, though still covered by cold distance, was an enormous arched bridge crafted from the most beautiful ice.

"An impressive bout of frozen architecture, indeed!" Nech wowed. He fumbled among the snow for his belongings, stepping into sturdier footing alongside Sigrid and Maya as he pulled his map from his satchel.

"Is it Frororan in nature, I wonder? That would not bode well for our current course. No, not at all. Let me see here... oh my," he hesitated. "It would seem this bridge's position aligns perfectly with the main paths leading outside Frorora. Oh dear."

"Should we be surprised?" Maya asked. "That map is older than most. We may have laid quick eyes on the Snowy Lands—but we are certainly strangers here. Are you sure?"

"I am sure, my friend. Look here—" Nech pointed, his frown deepening.

"Do we pass under it?" Sigrid asked, sitting like a massive statue of an Eagle from a bygone era.

"Perhaps we can? It looks empty from afar," Nech pondered.

"As do all *ambushes* before they happen," Maya retorted.

"None know of our travels," Sigrid clarified. "I told but my sons and the two of you. We should indeed have discretion on our side. Let us approach and assess, yes?"

"It does seem to be quite far off into the canyon," Nech decreed, "Giving us ample time to devise a plan of passage. I see no other option, do you, Maya?"

"I suppose not."

"Onward, then!" Nech cried out, gathering his things. "Look, there. A shallowed road following the river just ahead. Oh, how nice it will be to handle parchment whilst on my own two feet."

"I share this sentiment," Sigrid nodded. "A moment, if you don't mind." She wrapped her body in shimmering red wings as her head careened back. As her shoulders arched and an exhale left her beak, Sigrid regressed into the Shieldmaiden of Autumnhill, her crest of golden amber feathers giving way to flowing blonde locks, and her blood-hued feathers molting into armor and wolves'fur. "Much better…"

"On that, Shieldmaiden, we both agree," Maya responded, staring back at the ice-bridge. "I will admit, a rest off-wing would benefit me as well."

"That's the spirit!" Nech boasted, patting his shoulder free of snow. "We may even find time and place for a fire. My old bones grow dreadfully stiff in this cold." He rubbed his hands together as his oldest comrade flapped to her usual perch atop his shoulder.

"I still have an absolutely terrible feeling about this... Where Frororans dwell, bad things follow," Maya added. "May Craga protect us."

Down the snowbank to the bottom of the glacial canyon they went, their new path lit by Moon and starlight above. What awaited them, however, was anyone's worst guess.

CHAPTER NINE

Thunder on the Hills

"I hope mother's okay," Audun said as he cupped fresh flowing water into his hands. A cloudy sky churned on above as the Young Companions settled down for a well earned rest, one full of thirst quenching and beast resting.

"She is," Titha replied, bent down beside Audun with her sister. "She can handle anything."

Haldor sat to their right on the bank of the Great Daenu River, its life-giving waters tumbling southward out of Ythengrey and into the Barren Fields they now inhabited. Paw slouched to their left, his entire face in the river as he guzzled, occasionally watching for a trout or salmon. He would've taken a minnow at this point. Anything that wasn't a rock, really.

"This all used to be forest. Much like our own," Gilly spoke into the Night air. She looked back behind them away from the river. "I was young, maybe only Beebee's age when it was, but I remember these lands before Meriduun burned them into oblivion. We used to be so much more connected to the Great River."

"Do you remember Meriduun? The real her. Before she turned," Titha asked.

"Sometimes I see glimpses," Gilly pondered. "In the Moon, or a heavy morning mist. But we were so young... Meriduun and mother passed just days after Beebee's birth. Ugh, Beebee. Poor thing. She is going to be worried sick about us, you know. When we don't show up for supper she's going to know something's wrong."

"She is the smartest one of the lot," Titha smiled. "That little lady's going to be trouble. Mark my words. You think *I'm* a handful? When she's our age? I pity anyone that gets in her way."

"Our age?" Gilly rolled her eyes. "You really are in a hurry to grow up, aren't you? I am five forest-years older than you, stumps, and trust you me, it only gets harder. Slow down a bit and enjoy your frog catching days before they're gone. One day those frogs will be boys and it's all downhill from there."

"To be fair, I think the three of us have experienced more in our young days than most," Audun added somberly. "Especially you girls. I wonder how old you *really* are."

"Twelve and seventeen," Titha scolded. "Just because time 'passes slower' in the Duskridge doesn't mean we're like your grandmas or something. It's just a matter of perspective. To me, it all feels the same out here as it always has at home. It does to Gilly, too, but she won't admit it—so what's the difference?" She plopped down into the mud beside Paw. For the first time, the fervent commotion surrounding Celtica—and the passionate last words of Calluna Mint—felt personal.

"The *difference* is you live in your own little bubble," Gilly responded. "This is not just some trivial joke to our people, Titha. This is real. It is life or death."

"Only if you look at it in a negative way, which is your specialty. I would much rather join the natural world than be trapped in one tiny place forever, forced to live by rules we never even asked for, going 'round and 'round, on and on in the same circle of a forest until we're stretched so thin tha—"

"—Oh please! So you felt trapped as a child? When mother and father and you and I used to plant endless flowerbeds together and chase otters up the streams and lay awake staring into the golden rays breaking through the treetops for Days on end—you felt stretched and miserable? Bloody poppycock! Of course you didn't!"

"You said it yourself, wola. We were tiny! What had we seen? What did we know? What were we *allowed* to know? Anything? At all? What had we *done*, Gilly? What had we done besides the same flower-tending and bear-romping over and over and over again? Huh? How could you possibly understand? The past four hours is the most you've ever seen of anything outside the same patch of land you were born to."

"That doesn't make me *wrong*, Titha. It makes me *different* than you. *Ugh* you think you are so worldly and know all the things, but you don't! You are just a child! You're a spoiled little father's girl who did something amazing *one time*, then let it all go to her head instead of using it to *grow up*. Grow up, Titha Mae. *Grow. U—"*

Titha growled, which evolved into a full-bellied roar,

before flailing from the mud onto her sister. She tackled Gilly down into the pit, smacks and fists a'flying.

"Girls!" Audun shouted from a distance, being wise enough not to get between them. "Paw, do something!" he shouted louder, but the big bear just shrugged. He rolled his chestnut eyes as if this was their normal. Which it was.

"Should've... left you... at home... you cry-baby!" Titha screeched, wrestling herself away from Gilly's grasp. "You think I'm doing this for me? Huh? Our teacher is dead and no one cares! No one else is coming! The murderers run free, one of which is *your boyfriend*, and you think I'm out here in the middle of nowhere because I want *attention*?"

"Of course you are!" Gilly screamed, pushing Titha back down onto the mudbank. "That's all you *ever* want!"

"There's no one out here, idiot!" Titha yelled furiously. "Who is out here to give me attention? *Audun?*"

"Hey!" he yelled back, frowning.

"Sorry, didn't mean it! Love you!" Titha smiled before *SPLOSH*, Gillian tossed her aside into the luke-warm river.

"You want us all to think you're some big strong warrior," Gilly shouted, fists muddied and clenched. "You walk around the Meadow like you're our anointed hero, like we should all thank our lucky stars that you were ever born to save us all from Dragons and Ogres and Demons! But you had help. You were with Nech. Right? You two *children* were with Nech and Maya; Two experienced, *adult* explorers that had done what you were doing a *thousand times* before! This is *not that*, okay? *You* are not that. *You* are a spoiled little brat so full of herself that you won't even listen to your own *father* when he tells you to stay—"

"—Oh—shut—*UP*!" Titha screamed. "Ever since mother

died you have done nothing but complain! I am sick of it! I am sick of *you. I am sick of you without her!* So go home. Go home and live your forever until you rot, *and you can be just like her."*

Gillian stood silent. Paw's ears flattened, and Audun leaned to Haldor, shocked.

"Gilly I'm sorry, I... that was too far," Titha whimpered. "I really didn't mean that. I'm sorry."

"Forget it," she murmured, throwing the mud in her hand to the ground. She walked past Audun and Haldor silently, back toward the grasses.

"Where are you going?" Audun asked.

"Where do you think?"

"Gilly you can't just wander off into the fields by yourself!" Titha yelled, chasing after her. "Not without us! Not without Paw and Haldor to protect—"

She grabbed Gilly's wrist, but her sister flung herself around, slapping her arm away.

"Do not touch me," she cried.

"Gilly please, please don't go," Titha warbled through sudden tears. "I didn't mean it, you know I didn't mean it! I just got so mad and—"

"Whatever, Titha. I don't care anymore."

"That's fine, I get it now and I won't ever mention this again, okay?" She tried to step into Gilly's view, but she wouldn't have it. "Gills, really, I didn't mean—"

"—It's not that," Gilly paused, finally turning to her little sister, revealing eyes swelling with guilt.

"Then what is it?"

"I can't say."

"Sure you can. You can tell me."

"Not this," Gilly began to sob, her hands on her face.

"Gilly what is it? What's wrong? You're starting to scare me..."

"Clo—ver," she hiccuped, lumps juggling in her throat as crocodile tears fell like rain.

"What about him? Gilly what is it?"

"He told me..." she gasped, "he told me he was going to do something!"

"To Calluna?"

"He didn't—tell me he—he didn't say what, he just—he just said he was going to do something to help 'fix it all' and that it—it had to be done but I—I didn't do... Anything! I—I didn't tell anyone and I—I didn't know what to do!"

Gillian screamed into her tears as she collapsed onto Titha, her body convulsing within deep sobbing. Not knowing entirely how to react, Titha stood still for a moment before choosing to clutch Gilly tightly. She was, however, unable to help the Theole-esque furrowing of her own brow.

"There's no way you could've known," she reassured Gilly.

"Of course not!" Gilly screeched, "That's why I—I punched his stupid, gorgeous, beautiful face when we finally caught him and—and I should've punched it a hundred more times, but I felt—I felt like it was *my* fault for not telling anyone in the first place so I—"

"Gillian listen to me," Titha spoke softly as she grabbed her sister's shoulders. "Listen to me! This is not your fault! Absolutely none of this could be your fault, okay?"

"But I did nothing, Titha!" Gilly jerked back. "I did exactly what you tell me I do all the time—*nothing*! I knew something was not right and I did *nothing about it* and now Mint's *dead*! Mint's dead and *you*—you just run off *risking your own life*, and—trying to fix something I could've done something about and I'm trying to make *you* feel bad for it!"

"That explains why you came with us..." Audun mumbled.

"Audun!" Titha shouted before taking a moment, a breath, and then her sister's hand. "Look, sis, half the things that come out of my mouth are just leftover thoughts, okay? Don't ever listen to a word I say unless I'm making this exact face—"

She scrunched her features into an unbelievably exaggerated serious-face, and for the first time in what felt like years Gillian laughed.

"You didn't make anyone do anything," Titha declared. "And not in our wildest dreams would we ever have pegged that freckle-faced sprite for a killer."

Gillian laughed again, wiping snot and tears from her rosy face.

"I still don't think he did it," Audun added, cuddled into Haldor, "so you can feel a bit less guilty, Gillian."

"Thanks, I think," Gillian replied, still trying to recover from her meltdown. "But what do you mean?"

"I mean that the whole time we had him pinned down he kept crying about 'him' and 'it' and whoever *did* do it. We are not just chasing one person, right? The stranger from Celtica—none of us knew his face in the courtroom, not even Rainer. And Rainer knows everyone now, as Mr. Mighty Jarl. So the stranger *did* do it. That is what Clover was yelling all along, right? That this strange man murdered Calluna Mint. Rainer thinks the Stranger was telling the truth, that he did not do it. But I think he did. I think it was him."

"Right, but Clover was involved regardless," Titha replied. "He helped make it happen, instead of helping stop it. He made a choice, and he chose the wrong side. Aren't you just as curious to know why he would be involved, and what would cause him to be involved with such a horrible thing?"

"I suppose so..."

"Well I absolutely am. I want to know why. Why would he even consider helping such a thing happen? What could possibly be worth that? I don't understand. But I don't have to, because I know I want to do whatever I can to stop it from happening again. I won't let him cause the death of another of our kin. And now he's out there somewhere, running into unknown lands toward whatever is going to cause others to die. Unless they're found and stopped, anyone could be next."

"Next for what?" Gillian asked, her eyes as wide as apples.

A massive clap of thunder rocked the sky. Gilly screamed for dear life, squeaming out of her skin as lightning shot through the clouds. Audun's face went pale.

"I don't think we... we will have to wait to find out... because... girls... girls?" Audun stuttered, teeth clamoring. "Hood... hooded cloak... hooded cloaked thing... hooded cloaked thing is here, not there... here!"

"Very funny, Audun," Titha smirked as she stepped from Gilly to scrub fish'bits from Paw's face. "That is what we call thunder, Lunas and gentlemen. Nothing to be—"

Lightning and thunder cracked once more, revealing a

tall, slender figure cloaked in a strange fabric.

"Oh," Titha blurted. "Paw... *Paw*!" she followed, flinging his face to the phantom-esque shape. Haldor shot around in turn, shaking his head at the sight before lowering himself into a full snarl. Paw whipped to his side, spitting a trout tail from his mouth. The cloaked mass outstretched his hands, revealing a long, thick, knotted staff. Whether this was in peace or for attack Titha did not wait to find out. "Get 'em!" she shouted, and off the boys went.

Haldor lunged first, his toothy maw fully extended. With one fell swoop of the hooked staff the phantom twirled Haldor in the air, then slammed him head first into the ground, bringing his weapon full circle. Paw took a pass next but was met with the blunt end of the instrument, which sent the rest of the half-eaten trout in his mouth flying like a boomerang 'til it landed directly in front of Gilly. She moaned, then held her mouth as she gagged.

"Who are you?" Titha shouted out, low thunder rumbling behind her voice.

"I would ask ye the same first!" the rogue responded, standing tall like a statue, a knocked-out beast to each side. Lightning struck again, revealing two huge ram's horns protruding from a tattered green hood. Audun lit up.

"It has horns..." he whispered to the sisters. "It—it has horns! This... This him... this him has horns!"

"That supposed to mean something?" Titha murmured. "Who are you?" She followed confidently. "We haven't seen anyone else out here but the murderers we're after, and if you... are them... then—"

Calamitous, bumbling thunder interrupted what was sure to be a hearty threat.

"These are *my* lands, lass!" the roguish figure clapped back, his voice raspy and weathered with a thick accent they'd never heard before. "Which means *you* answer to *me*."

The beasts were still knocked out as the horned phantom approached. He walked through the dry grasses with thick *thuds*, each step knocking the soil with the sound of a hoof, not a foot. Audun stumbled back, bumping into Gilly who wrapped her arms around him. Titha didn't budge.

"I'll… answer to you when I know who you are!" she stammered. "And… when I know what it is you're… you're wanting!" She took a step toward her sister. "Stay back! You will not harm them" she shouted. With a great swing she brandished Feathersword, pointing it directly at the horned figure without so much as a flinch. "I'm warning you!"

"Are ye' daft?" the being responded, taken a'back as many often were with Titha Mae. He stepped closer, lightning striking again. With its brief illuminating stroke, the stranger received his first good look at the Young Companions.

"Fer Gaela's sake, yer' just a wee bairn. All of ye' are!" he scoffed, lowering his staff to point Titha's blade t'ward the ground. She quickly struck it back, raising her weapon once more.

"I don't know what a *bairn* is, pal, but if it means I have a sword and ain't afraid to use the pointy end, then a *bairn* I am!" she shouted, poking Feathersword forward as she held firm.

"Aye, put that wee-dagger away," the rogue groaned, withdrawing his staff. "I mean no harm to a child. *Bairn* means wee, lass. Wee like you. What are the likes of ye' doin' out here t'begin with, let alone by this very spot on teh bank?"

The clearer his voice became, the less threatening it

sounded. He finally removed his hood, revealing a bearded visage somewhere between a man and a goat with deep-set, wise eyes and hair that ran long, knotted and tousled; rusty in color.

"We're just fetching some water," Titha replied, still not loosening Feathersword. "We've come quite a way and we're parched."

"Aye, that much is obvious," he replied, his mouth wide. "But ye donnae know where yah happen to be sittin', or ye wouldn't be sittin' there. Certainly not a place many sit fer' long."

"Why?" Audun gulped.

The goat'ish stranger didn't speak, just pointed with his staff to a gigantic and deep four-toed pawprint almost as big as Paw's, but belonged to something else entirely. Gilly took one look and promptly began to faint.

"Dusklions," the rogue added, pulling his staff back to trace the tracks. "Enormous, long-fanged felines that stalk these lands. Heard screamin', I did, so I came to assess what was sure to be some poor soul's final moments and found the likes a' you. Yer lucky to be alive."

Gilly sank fully onto the ground.

"She alright, lad?" he asked Audun.

"This is her first adventure," he responded, now holding her. The stranger smirked. These wee ones were no threat to him or his own.

"Death waits here, lads. Best be movin' on."

"You're just going to leave us?" Audun cried out. "You knocked out our only protection!"

"Just a wee bump, I gave 'em. They'll wake soon. When they do, head back north where ye came from. Yer in the Deep

South now, lads. Tis no place fer… lemme get'a closer look at yeh…"

The goat-man leaned down to feel Gilly's forehead, as her skin was quite pale. His hands were large and rugged with a short light brown fur covering their tops.

"Don't touch her!" Titha screamed, flinging Feathersword so hard she sliced a bundle of locks straight from the fellow's head.

"Barmy lass! Put 'at thing away before ye maim somethin', ya wee dodger!" he scolded, yanking Titha's attacking hand away. "Well bless my horns!" he shouted as he got a look at the small indigo arm in his grasp. "A Luna, ye are! As is she! And you, a human! Two Luna lasses—wit' a Vikingboy! What in the name of all that be' holy is such a strange band doin' this far south? Best be mighty important!"

"It is," Titha forced. "And we're not too far, thanks. We just left this Dawn."

"Not too far, she says! Hah!" he laughed, stroking his short, wavy beard. "Yer a far cry from Yythengrey, lassie! That's fer' sure! A full Day's trip, it is. Ye' must've been hauling some serious arse! Yer' nearly in the Wick of it, little Luna."

"The wick of it?" Audun asked as he helped prop Gilly up.

"Aye, the Wick lies south of 'ere. Once the Daenu begins to breed 'er wetlands the fields spread all shallow and marsh'like creating the Wick. The border of my lands, it'is. And a right foul, gimp place it is, too. Bairns have no business 'ere. None do, to speak te' truth. That's not where yer' headed, now is it, lads? Tell me true."

"Headed? To the Wick? We had no idea such a place even

existed," Titha added, concerned for both her own ignorance and her ailing sister.

"It's not on my map," Audun responded as he fumbled with both his things and Gilly, almost dropping her.

"Audun! Careful!" Titha scolded. "I think my sister needs help. Can you help us?"

"I cannot," the strange being replied, looking her over. "Just a wee bit of a shock, she's had. She'll be fine."

"Right. The kindness of strangers," Titha replied. "Welp, thank you for scaring the fungus outta' us and pretty much nothing else—but we really should be off now so it's been real pleasant getting to know you, Mr. ... whatever you are."

"She simply needs rest, lass," he replied, "And to cool off. Tis almost Summer's time and the air settles thick down 'ere once Spring has sprung its last. Aye."

The younglings looked at him like he was crazy, still only understanding every third word out of his mouth.

The goat-man let loose a heavy sigh, looking to the provisions he traveled with. "Here," he offered, a stale crack of bread in hand. "Feed 'er this when she 'wakens. Get 'er fill'ed up. She looks like she needs all t'bread she can stomach, poor lass."

"Nope, that's just her," Titha replied as she took the loaf'piece. "She's my sweet stringbean."

He cocked an eyebrow, then reached to his green cloak and ripped a swatch from the bottom, handing it to Titha as well. It was old, so old in fact that she was rather insulted to be handed it. Yet upon further inspection... it was absolutely amazing! She examined it carefully, running it through her hands; it's heavy woolen length striped with a yellow, white, and olive checkered plaid. She'd never seen plaid before, and she was discovering that she absolutely adored it.

"Wet that in the river, lass, and place it on yer' stringbean's forehead."

Titha did just that, continuing to admire the interlocking patterns.

"She's not actually my—she's my sister," Titha snorted as she complied with the first sensible thing the stranger had said to them.

"Then tend to her well, lassie. She'll need her strength, as will you. Yer masters o' the Night in the Duskridge, wee Luna, but out here yer bottom of the foodchain."

"How comforting," she responded from the riverbank. "I hope you sleep well tonight in your safe home after leaving us with that nugget of wisdom."

Low thunder rumbled above them, though this time it seemed to take on a certain personality as it moved closer.

"Titha... that was a strange bit of thunderring," Audun spoke up.

"Because 'at was no thunder," the goat-man responded, rising to his hooves. Another rumble followed. "There it is again. Behind me, lads. Quickly."

"Thanks, but no thanks," Titha jabbed, placing the cold wet plaid on Gilly's forehead.

"Don't be daft, lass, this is no time for smart-mouthing!"

The hairy fellow swung his hooked staff forward, scanning the Night with it until he landed on a rustling spot in the grass by the bank.

Slowly a crouched, thick form revealed itself. Its growl was low and rumbling like the skies above them, and its eyes glowed yellow in the Moonlight amidst dusty, striped yellow fur.

"D-d-dd-dusklion," Audun stammered.

The goat-man spun his hooked staff, pointing its hardened bulk at the beast. "Now would be a wonderful time fer' yer beast-kin to awaken, lads," he spoke, a nervous tick in his voice.

"Oh *now* you want them bushy-tailed!" Titha scolded. "Perhaps you should've thought of that before whacking them both into a coma!" She took a deep breath, looking to Audun as they both propped Gilly up, who was now completely unconscious.

"Paw..." Titha whispered hard. "Paw! Get up, you roundbottomed, raccoon of a slouch!" No response. The Dusklion began to snarl and gnash its teeth in the distance, taking a bite out of the dark air as it moved toward their acquaintance's staff. He jabbed at it to keep its distance.

"Any time now, lads!" their unwitting yet cunning ally barked.

"Haldor, boy!" Audun jumped in, followed by a whistle. "Time to wake up, boy! Time to wake up *now*! Haldor? *HALDOR*!" he screamed, his voice piercing at a frequency only dogs would respond to—and with that the wolfhound shot to his feet as if he'd been poked in the backside by a hot iron.

The lion reared its head behind them, the hair on its neck standing up straight. Haldor took a few sniffs of the air, then turned to meet a creature he'd never seen before. His ears lowered as he showed his teeth, growling at an intensity matching the lion's. But he knew he could not take it alone. He shuffled his right foot, fishing for Paw's side—kicking the bear, then twice more, then a third time as hard as he possibly could.

"Grrrrooooounnnnt!" Paw roared out, rolling up onto his enormous side. He shook his head, heavily dazed. After his eyes focused, he too was met with a foreign, terrifying maw. The oversized black bear stumbled back in confusion, but his size was enough to scare the outnumbered Dusklion into submission. It lowered its tail between its legs and shuffled one step backward. Paw planted his feet in turn, taking one look at his sisters then back at the strange, enormous cat with its two long saberteeth, followed by a grunting, ferocious roar. He stood firm between his kin and their aggressor, and with one deep breath let loose another roar so mighty it shook the waters of the Daenu River. The cat hissed, then tucked its tail and ran.

"Haha!" Audun cried out, his fist shooting up. "Take that, you overgrown kitten!"

"We've got to work on your insults," Titha quipped, a hand on her chest as she caught her breath. Gilly finally came-to between them.

"What just happened? Are we yelling again?" she asked.

"Just a cat, sis. Go back to sleep. We've got you."

"Lynx or a bobcat? Never mind, I don't even care. I hate both."

"Neither," Titha smiled, happy for the break in tension. "We'll tell you all about it tomorrow."

"Please don't," Gilly slouched her full bodyweight onto Titha and Audun as they stumbled away from the riverbank. Soft rain began to fall from a still-bellowing sky, though the lightning had ceased.

"See that wasn't so bad!" Audun added triumphantly as he scratched Haldor's wet cheek. "You did so good, boy! Yes you did! My fearless pup!"

"Ah. That was a wee one, lad," the plaid clad goat-man decreed, still on guard. "A lioness' cub, no doubt. The big'ins have fangs the length of yer' arms, and donnae linger long enough to get ta' know ye. Yah never see 'em coming. Just perish into the night."

"Oh... Okay. I would rather not perish into the night," Audun whimpered, his curls now heavy with rain.

"Aye, we're in agreeance 'ere, lad. Therefore I must give congratulations to yer beast-kin, fer that was a mighty fine display. Well done. And thank ye both."

"You're welcome," Titha replied.

The goat-man outstretched a hand. With a smile she took it.

"That's a firm handshake, lass," he smirked. "Yer no normal wee one, are ye'?"

"That's what they tell me," she said with a grin. "I'm Titha Mae. This is my sister, Gillian, and my best friend, Audun."

"Mae, aye?" he responded. "So yer Theole's kin? The Watcher?"

"Great," she blurted, breaking their handshake. "Someday I'll meet someone who *doesn't* know my father."

"Not in Westlyn ye won't, lass. And yer father, he is?" He rubbed the end of one of his cracked, curved horns and let out a deep breath. "I cannot leave those a'kin to the Watcher out in the wilds to starve or t'be eaten. Aye... Imagine he wouldn't take kindly to that should our paths cross 'ere again." Another sigh left him.

"Would you leave children out here to die if they *weren't* the kin of someone you know?" Audun asked sincere.

"Got a mouth on this one, too, have we?" their acquaintance smirked. "Who's that make yer kin?"

"I don't even know your name, Mister… Goat. I'll tell you my title once we know yours."

"A wise strategy, lad," he chuckled, impressed with what he'd seen of these younglings so far. "And a fair request. But I am no goat, and my true title is one I donnae imagine yer young tongues can pronounce. T'yer Watcher, lads, I am Kernos. So to ye, Kernos I'll be," he responded.

"Audun," the youngster replied. "Now we are all acquainted."

"Aye, that we are, lad," Kernos grinned, before a sigh escaped his beard. "Look, weans, I cannot offer the daughters of Theole an' their friends much, but I can grant yer lot safe passage through my lands. Come, let's get yer sister a'top yer bear and off her flappers fer a while, then be off from this plot o'mud before that lion cub comes back with mum. Then ye can fess up to yer… peculiar traveling habits."

CHAPTER TEN

Frost & Flames

Sigrid marched on in the Moonlight, her thick leather and wolves'fur boots trudging through hard snow. Maya still sat atop Nech's shoulder, but Nech himself was astride Sigrid's back once more. This time, however, she was not a giant eagle. The old Craglin held his map to their front, looking it over as he compared notes with Maya, their position under the stars of great importance to both.

"It must connect the Snowy Lands to the foothills of the Snowy Fells, then," Nech said, pleased with himself.

The Frost-Bridge laid just before them, a massive structure of icy ingenuity. But its true purpose was a mystery.

"Goodness, Maya, a master of navigation you certainly are! Your prompt cut northeastward has us halfway to our destination. Once we cross under this bridge, that is. And if Audun's sketches of the Aurora are correct, in turn, then we are off to a wondrous start."

"They are," Sigrid smiled. "Look—" She aligned his artwork with Nech's Map of the First Eon laying it directly over, then held it up to the Moon's crescent light as they marched. "See? The trajectory of our taken path, it aligns perfectly with the first half of the Aurora. The second half is a pointed arrow leading to a spot still northeastward on the Horizon."

"That is odd, I must say," Nech noted, staring into the lapped parchments. "How fascinating! Has it always done that?"

"Done what?" Maya asked, examining alongside. Nech took Audun's Aurora, shifting it slightly so the corners of the papers matched exactly. Maya gasped. As their eyes followed the final point of the Aurora, it led them directly to the former cradle of life, the Tree herself; Igdrasil.

"How?" Sigrid shuttered. "How have we not seen this before?"

"Because we weren't looking for it," Maya answered. "This map is old. It is of the past. The First Eon is behind us… as is Igdrasil's splendor."

"Never did I think I would see its resting place again," Sigrid responded, flabbergasted.

"Exactly my point," Maya squawked. "Most eyes only see what we wish them to. Nothing more."

Nech perked up, his body swelling with awe. "Heavens above, if only Igdrasil were still there, waiting to greet us in all her splendor," he spoke, sadness tinging his voice. "It shall always ail me that I did not make it to her glorious valley with you and our beloved Titha Mae, my dear falcon. Let us hope we all make it to what she has left behind for us now. Perhaps, even in death, she holds answers for us."

Sigrid stepped to the side of their white path, taking them behind a snowbank for the moment. "Let us make it past this bridge first, then we will worry for our journey's prize," she spoke softly. The gentle yet impressive icy hues of the bridge sparkled back in Sigrid's eyes, magnifying their brilliance in the Moonlight. It was a beautiful sight, indeed, but rigid and foreboding. Harsh. Still. *Too* still, as was the air in the valley. She may have dismissed Maya's suspicions, but now that the Frost-bridge loomed directly overhead Sigrid began to feel she was wrong to do so. But the cover of Night was, at least, on their side.

"Having second thoughts now, are we, Shieldmaiden?" Maya whispered, her eyes locked onto the structure.

"If this were to go awry... let me state now that this would not be the first time a bridge was used to ambush me," Sigrid replied as she began to walk out from behind the snowbank to pass under the bridge. "But the same could be said for canyons, rivers, and mountains, too, so I have learned to take each one with caution."

She had a bit more to say on the matter, but wasn't going to let Maya win their little battle of wits. The brave Vikingwoman sealed her lips and grasped her axe's hilt, lowering her shoulders as she led their small party underneath the towering pillars and archway. Not a drip fell from the ice above, as the air was undoubtedly colder than the frost this far north.

With a final deep breath, they stepped out from underneath the other side of the titanic structure, safe and sound. Sigrid sighed, clasping her hands together as she rubbed them for warmth.

"See? Nothing to fear. Shall we count our blessings to the All'father?" She smiled. "I think so. And look: More has been provided for us. Let us make our way to that rocky overhang and set up camp for the night. I could use the warmth of a fire to rejuvenate my bones, as could we all."

"That sounds marvelous, indeed, my Shieldmaiden!" Nech agreed. "And though Maya will not admit it, I know she is in dire need of warmth, for the cold of Frorora vastly outweighs the cold of our native Cragoa."

"Let me remind you both that none of this was my idea," Maya mumbled, the breath from her beak very visible. "There's a reason our mappings of the lands near the Horizon are... s-s-simple," she shivered.

"Bless your feathers, my dear friend! We must get you toasty at once! It is vastly colder at this furthest depth of the canyon than either of us anticipated, isn't it? A return to the surface would be most welcome. Yes, yes, after a nice fire, indeed. Come! Come. We must make haste."

"A fire it is," Sigrid nodded, and forward they marched through the shallow snow to the cliffside just ahead, which proved perfect for a small encampment.

Never had warmth been so welcome, each vastly different set of appendages outstretched over the flames.

"This will have to do for now," Sigrid spoke. "We must conserve what kindling we have left for the return journey, and any fire greater than this will surely attract unwanted attention."

"It already has," a sinister voice replied, popping forth from the coals. With its sound the fire raged tenfold out of nowhere, and a large and imposing silhouette of burnt orange and black stepped forth, smiling as smoldering eyes crept into the Companions' souls.

"Ugar!" Nech shouted, flailing backward as their peaceful

refuge went to shambles: For there he stood, a towering arch-nemesis from their past, defeated by Rainer Angvarsson at the height of Vulduun's treachery. Sigrid, if her son was to be believed, thought him dead. Nech knew better, and now here was his proof burning before him. Ugar, the twisted, vile stooge of Vulduun, responsible for everything from Nech's exile to the fall of Cragoa, grinned before him once more.

"We meet at last, Shieldmaiden," Ugar declared, a wicked grin exposing his crooked, sharp teeth. "I expected to find you in less *pathetic* company."

"What do you want?" Sigrid asked directly. "Make your intentions known. We only wish to pass and be on our way. We are not within your Craglands. You hold no power in Frorora, and we bring no ill will."

"Oh, but you do. One far greater than the two traitors you harbor," he grinned, his incisors jagging together as he pointed to the satchel on her belt. As he did, something began to glow within it—something as foul and hot as the fire in which Ugar stood.

"What is that?" Maya questioned, gravely concerned; her eyes a'light with the glow escaping Sigrid's pouch.

"The blade!" Sigrid gasped. "What do you know of this weapon? Speak!" she demanded, flinging the stone spear'tip, the very one that killed Calluna Mint, from her bag. Her Companions knew nothing of her carrying it until now. It burned heartily before them.

"You know not even what you hold," Ugar growled. "*Vikings*... Any shiny trinket, even one baring as much darkness as this, is to be coveted and treasured. My master thanks you for predictability."

"Your master is dead," Maya hissed, flying to Nech.

"Always living in the past are you worm-ridden Scribes. Vulduun is but a faded relic of the First Eon. I serve the future now. And the future has a message for you."

The fire reached peak intensity as the stone blade in Sigrid's hand grew so hot it burned her hand. She hissed, dropping it into sizzling snow as the message left the flames before her in a foul, crackling voice:

The Aurora's end holds what you seek
There it lies cradled: The Stone of Life
Heed its call and bring it forth to me
Or suffer your nightmares eternal

The fire sizzled its last word, and Ugar stepped forward in the flames. "Such shock and disdain," he groaned. "Did you think you would be the only one to read the signs? The only one to see the greens of the Aurora's path and put such prophecies together? Predictable *and* arrogant."

"Who is your master?" Sigrid cried out, frightened, but doubly angry. "How do they know of my dreams? My visions? Who demands this cruel fate of me, demon? Speak!"

"Once you have found it, you will bring the Lifestone to us. In the Ruins of the South we await you. There—all your questions will be answered."

Ugar vanished into the smoke, and the embers turned to ash with a whirling inhail below.

"I am lackey to no one!" Sigrid shouted, her axe flying from its hilt as she sliced through thin air.

"This cannot be," Nech cried out. Before him, in a melted puddle of snow, laid the stone blade, still burning hot with the ferocity of the message. In its center, a seething symbol churned:

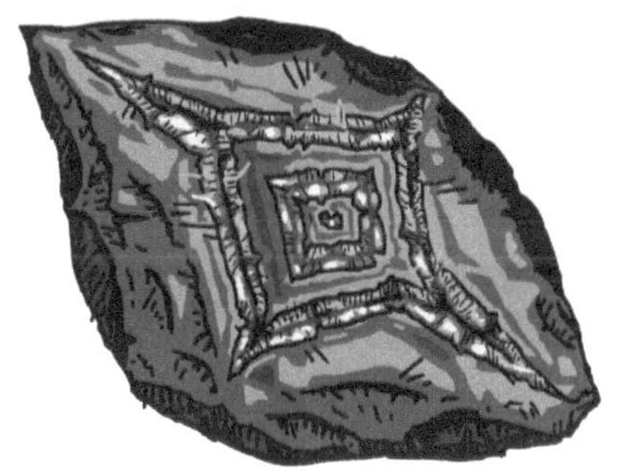

"And yet, here it is," Maya answered. "A runestone."

"Runestone?" Sigrid asked, blindsided. "No, this is the blade from the tip of the spear used to strike down Calluna Mint. It is no runestone! It is of human make. See? Its former wooden shaft held Viking carvings, as does the blade, here—" but as she pointed to it, all other markings disappeared, save the one now glowing with an orange as fierce as their once-raging fire. She gasped, stepping backward from its hot aura.

"Is it the one, my dear Peregrite?" Nech asked Maya, both staring into it.

"The symbol is the same," she answered, disappointed.

"What is this stone, truly?" Sigrid asked. "What do you know?"

"What you see before you is the only remaining runestone in Gaela," Maya spoke.

"To our knowledge, of course," Nech added. "You see, it bears a symbol Maya and I became familiar with early in our travels of Cragoa. This marking, the very one burning before you, represents our Goddess in her volcano form. It is an aerial view of her, of Mount Crag. This rune, carved exactly as so, has been found only in the most ancient places of our homeland, of which are few."

"And we have never seen its like anywhere else," Maya added from Nech's shoulder. "Only in Mydlan. I never thought I'd see it again. It is one of many artifacts Nech's council was entrusted with guarding. Before Ugar. And unfortunately, in this mess, I would fear this stone's involvement over that wretched imp."

"Such tremendous failure... This piece of history is one of many we left behind, try as we might. My constituents and I hid each artifact in desparation before our disbandment... before our calamitous exile and... slaughter. I personally hid this mighty runestone as deep beneath the bowels of Mt. Crag as I could manage. Truly, I hoped I would never see it again. But alas... Ugar has grown desperate and ruthless in the age after the Great Drakes... for it has been found!"

"Why did it bear Viking markings? Ones that would only have been made by Man, yet not in the makings of Autumnhill's craftsmen?" Sigrid asked, still in shock. "Does it not come from some other tribe of Man?"

"Because the spear was meant to be *seen* as Viking-made, Shieldmaiden," Maya spoke stoically. "Whoever crafted it only mimicked the symbols of your artisans, for they must not have been Man themselves... We were all meant to simply see the murder and *think* it was of humanity's doing; that it was *Man who slain the Luna.*"

"This is a most grievous turn of events," Nech rasped, his voice thin. "I shudder at further comprehending the many strands this web weaves! The resurfacing of Ugar, of the rune-stone—and this Stone of Life—all at once and tied to a mysterious new master of evil deeds? It is almost too much to process!"

The runestone finally ceased its burning below them. Nech took off his leather vest, wrapping his hand as to lift the stone slowly.

"Whoever now pulls upon that foul puppet's strings," he continued, speaking of Ugar, "Their identity may not yet be known, but their chief motive certainly has been revealed, has it not, my Companions? They wish to drive a sharp wedge, as sharp as this rune's bladed sides, between Humanity and Lunish'kind... They wish to see the two mightiest races of Westlyn spiral into the old ways of division and chaos... to reverse the Dawn of Celtica to quickly become its Dusk. Oh, what bigotry. What horror!"

"We cannot heed to their wishes. We will not!" Sigrid cried out. "It is *my* dreams this foul demon's message speaks of. It is my *very mind and soul they threaten* with this task! But I will not bend to their will, my friends. Never. We *will*, however, find this Stone of Life. Yes. We will follow the Aurora and find its prize, then take this Lifestone for our own, far away from these proposed 'Ruins in the South'. Instead it will be guarded by all the armies of Westlyn... and these villains shall come to us. They shall come to *their* doom. Not ours!"

"Ruins in the South…" Maya chimed in. "That is what the message relayed, yes?"

"Yes, Maya," Nech reassured her. "But that matters not! You heard the Shieldmaiden. We are never to go there, and I heartily agree with this alteration in plans!"

"Pipe down, Goblin, and think. Think for a second! What is the only major ruin we have ever charted in the South?"

"Why the Ruins of Byle, of course."

Maya waited for a response, but Nech stood unaffected still. She scoffed, rolling her eyes. "Byle, Nechalec. The Ruins of *Byle*! Is that not the most concerning piece of this puzzle to all? By a long shot?"

Sigrid and Nech paused, before his face went as pale as the snow.

"Byle… you do not think?" Nech asked feverishly. "Surely he is not capable! Such evil deeds and foul alliances could never spring from the soul of a Luna! Not even one as lost as he!"

"Speak plainly, goblin! Now is not the time for further riddles," Sigrid demanded.

"Byle… is Cypress," Maya answered for him.

"Cypress… Sylvanus… Byle…" Nech replied, his voice slow and heavy. "Formerly Squire to the Watcher and Commander of Ythengrey's Cedarguard—Since banished for rather—*bigoted* misgivings upon our return from the Breaking of the Horizon."

"I remember him well," Sigrid responded with loathing in her voice. "But these are *ruins* we speak of; ancient and forgotten. Just because they bear his family's name does not mean he is there residing in blame."

"I must agree wholeheartedly, Shieldmaiden," Nech added, unfolding his vest to reveal the now calm runestone. He handed it to Sigrid. "Cypress may have been banished from his homeland upon our return with Titha Mae as Companions, but I too suffered the same fate at the hands of those I once trusted in Cragoa. We are vastly different individuals, Cypress and I, but I dare say banishment has never driven me anywhere close to the depravity of senseless murder! No, no, never would I contemplate such a thing! Nor would Cypress, I believe. An honorable, dutiful Luna he was in his time. One our Titha Mae, and Watcher Theole, cherished. No, no, I simply do not believe him capable of any of this!"

"We did not know him, Nechalec, at all," Maya retorted. "Not-a-one of the three of us knew him beyond the *hate* we saw in his eyes as we returned with Titha to Yythengrey. And hate drives even the best of beings to foul deeds—"

Out of the thick air an icy arrow shot through the campfire's smoke, *THWAP*'ing into the ground between Nech's feet. He screamed like a banshee, Maya letting loose a panicked squawk as she flapped into the air—each of them violently shaken from deep thought. Sigrid tossed Nech behind her, drawing her shield up to guard her friends as she processed what just happened.

"The smoke!" she whispered. "We've lingered here too long, Companions, and our fire has been spotted! Nech, that arrow—from where does it hail?" He did not budge, instead choosing to shake behind her in safety. "Fool of a goblin!" she shouted, ducking to grab the projectile's flute. It was so cold to the touch it burned her fingertips. "Frororan!" she shouted, throwing it back into the snow. "We must leave—now!"

"I heartily concur!" Nech screamed out.

Sigrid swung her shield 'round, fastening it to her belongings as she flapped her wolves'fur cloak like massive wings. The air gave way to ancient, misty magic as a familiar amber glow shielded the Companions. One by one, thousands of rigid red feathers sprouted, and the Glorious Red Eagle returned to them. She flapped her wings, sending ash and snow swirling into the air, shrouding their narrow window of escape.

"This is our only chance, my friends! To me! To me!" Nech jumped onto his position atop her back, but Maya hesitated to join.

"Do not let pride cost you your life!" Sigrid scolded. "Frororans only miss once!"

Maya hissed, then flew up to Nech's side, digging her talons as far into Sigrid's belongings as she could. Once her Companions were secure, Sigrid swooped both enormous wings into a hurricane-like force of lift, and into the northern skies they shot; their focus now turned to this mysterious Stone of Life.

Due south in Autumnhill, the Shieldmaiden's eldest son struggled to contain their home. Her absence proved to be a weight neither he nor their proud people were prepared for. Pressure was getting the better of the young Jarl, sweat escaping his armor like water from cracks in a failing dam.

"Still no sign of the cloaked vermin," a Houndsman

recounted to Rainer. "We have searched the entirety of the city, the Fields south, and Celtica, my Jarl. Four times, even, but still… Nothing."

Rainer stood still, great thoughts burdening his hot head. His pride was thick, but the Night grew dire. He knew what he had to do, and it was time to give in.

"Because we cannot see into the night," he finally replied. "Send for the Watcher. Tell him we are in great need of his assistance—No," he stopped himself. "Guidance—tell him we are in great need of his *guidance.* That sounds more appropriate, does it not?"

"Y-yes, my Jarl," the Houndsman stammered.

"Be sure to say *guidance,* then. Right, that will do. Ask him if he will meet me at the Tower in Celtica. For guidance."

"As you wish, my Jarl," the Houndsman replied.

"And be sure to stress this is of the utmost importance. Explain our situation. He will understand."

"It will be done, my Jarl."

"Why are you still standing here?" Rainer yelled, smacking the back of stout leather armor, sending him scuttling off toward Celtica. Before the Jarl could catch his breath, an equally-winded Wiseman stumbled out of Skaldhall, arms a'flailing.

"My Jarl!" the elder cried out. "My Jarl, please, heed my words!"

"What is it, old man?" Rainer scoffed, beyond fatigued with the calamity of late.

"Another disastrous disappearance, mighty Jarl! Skaldhall's blacksmith, the great Bjor! His furnace still burns bright as his tools lay scattered below—but he is nowhere to be found!"

"Is he not simply taking a break?" Rainer waived. "I have no time for this. Bjor loves his honey'mead. Check the taverns."

"He resides not in his home, and no one has seen him since before the trial, my Jarl. His vanishment leaves us without three of our own! Some individuals less than vital, I grant you, but the pleas of the people grow evermore restless and with that Bjor's absence troubles our council greatly!"

"That will be all, Gaffer. Rest now. I will look into it once more pressing matters are resolved."

"Are you not to send the Houndsmen to search for him? For the townsfolk?" he clasped his wrinkled mouth. "Forgive me, Jarl, I speak too hastily."

"My men scour every corner of Autumnhill and the Barren Fields as we speak," Rainer leaned in, agitated. "The only two leads we have for the *murder of a Luna on shared soil* scurried off into the night like rats, eluding even my best scouts! The entire civilization and peace my mother has risked *everything* to build hangs by a single thread—and you want me to disband my men to search for a drunken blacksmith who forgot to tidy his workstation?"

Rainer stepped back, noticing how tight his fists had become. Inhaling, he looking to the Emerald Aurora that still bounced atop the dark Horizon. His mother was far better at this part of the job, and he longed for her steady voice.

"Do not doubt my drive," he continued, evening himself out. "I know you question my youth, as do all the Wisemen of Autumnhill, but I have traveled far and seen much in my short time, lest you forget all I have done for our people. And in my experience—which I do not think should be overlooked—these 'disappearances' you speak of are merely part of such chaotic events—part of the rabble. For now, we are to focus. Yes. Focus is the greatest ally in troubled times."

"The wise words of your mother," Gaffer replied, nodding.

"Yes. And whatever force has set this accursed Night into motion has us... outmatched. So I continue to follow her guidance as best I can in her absence. She would send for the Watcher, and so *I* have sent for the Watcher. There is nothing else I can do."

The Wiseman nodded, and off he waddled to be of service to their people.

"This all better be worth it, mother," Rainer whispered into the northern sky as clouds rolled in—their weight beginning to block Moon, stars, and Aurora. "For we need you now more than ever..."

CHAPTER ELEVEN
Horns & Hooves

Far off into the South, Titha and her Companions had seen just about all the Barren Fields had to offer. The air grew considerably warmer; warmer than any Night they'd yet experienced. A steady breeze washed over an increasing number of shrubs and viny plants as the amber tones of the Fields gave way to ivy and olive greens.

"It's so different down here," Audun observed, shuffling for a sheet of parchment and coal atop Haldor. "What do you call this place?"

"Lowlands, lad," Kernos replied, his eyes ever-scanning the lands ahead. "Though I suppose I've ne'er really thought too hard about it past that. Yer in the wilds now, and most of the wilds remain nameless. Tis part of what keeps 'em wild."

"Are these your lands, as well?" Audun asked, sketching a few of the strange plants.

"Aye, though I only guard them. I d'not own them. Land is not mine ta own. Either way, the edge we're nearin'. 'Tis the Wick below'ere. And I have to ask befar' we get but any closer to it: How'd ye lads end up bein' out here, wanderin' into the Deep South? 'Tis no place for weans," Kernos asked, his plaid wrappings and dusty brown cloak billowing in the low winds of his lands.

"The Luna we're after, my sister's boyfriend, the one I mentioned," Titha replied as she continued to hold the wet cloth over Gilly's still-sleeping visage, "He slipped through the South Wall of Autumnhill and darted off, after having gotten himself into a fair bit of trouble, then—"

"Aye, ye told me that part. I mean *how*? Truly? Yer father, last I knew him, dinnae let any of his folk wander the world at'tall. Let alone his own kin. And this far into the South? Rootin' fer Ruins? Aye, now there's a right troubling conundrum in his eyes, and mine. What are ye up to, lads?"

"The world above you is a much different place now," Titha answered sincerely. "Especially Ythengrey. We're not closed off like we once were. A lot has happened, because a lot has changed."

"Humans and Lunas trade and build and work together now," Audun added, fidgeting with one of his fine bags of Celtican make, switching parchments. "Even Goblins! It's pretty great."

"*Bah!* Yer *mad*, aye?" Kernos chortled, flabbergasted. "I suppose 'at means the Ever-war 'tis over? If yer races have time fer craftin' and shakin' hands and the like?"

"Done!" Audun gleefully responded, his nose buried in new sketches.

"Finished," Titha added, "And we should know," she grinned.

"That does explain a fair bit," Kernos nodded. "Many a'less foul trespassers on mine lands these past few seasons, aye, and a right bless'ed thing 'at is, too... The way of the wilds does line up right n' fair with yer story. I'll accept it."

Haldor's nose began to twitch, and his ears perked. The hair stood up on his back before he barked furiously into the east. Paw's nose picked up the scent in turn, then joined his friend's foray.

"What is it, boys?" Titha asked, "Lords help the cat if it's another Dusklion."

"Not a lion at'tall, lassie. Let'off, ye daft beasties! Let'off!"

Kernos waved his enormous crooked staff before them, as if he was guiding something. The lands below began to rumble, pebbles dancing in place as the shrubs and leaves quaked. Out of their eastern view shot dozens of large faunae, each shaggier than the last. Their massive, spiral-curved horns framed sleek, stone'willed faces as heavy hooves barreled down sloping foothills in the distance.

As the commotion grew, Gilly stirred for the first time in nearly an hour. "Is that... more storms?" she asked, groggy.

"Gills!" Titha and Audun screamed in turn.

"You're awake!" Titha continued, elated. "Oh thank Gaela!"

"Welcome back, stringbean," Kernos added.

Gilly rubbed one eye as she looked the cloaked stranger up and down. "... Who is this goat-man and why does he know me?" she frowned, sitting up to a pounding headache.

"It'd be wise fer ye to keep layin' low, lassie, and plug yer earholes. Aye, yer head'll throb at this," Kernos decreed over thundering hooves. "To me, my floc'clan! To me!" he willed, slowly lowering his staff to guide the incoming rabble.

"Did one of you kick him in the throat?" Gilly asked, understanding absolutely nothing of what she'd just been told.

"You get used to it. Right Paw?" Titha laughed, patting their Bear-brother. He groaned in disagreement.

"This is Kernos, sis. He is guiding us to the Ruins. To Clover," Titha continued. "He says the only place in Westlyn referred to as 'ruins' lies just south of here, so we've been on the right trail. Correct?"

"Aye, lass," Kernos yelled.

"What? Where are we? You mean you didn't turn around and take us home? Titha Lilly Mae! We—Paw! Stop! This is clearly out of our hands now! *Uugh,*" she groaned, flopping herself down onto Paw as she grabbed her head. "Will someone tell those cows to *keep it down*?"

"Not cows, lass" Kernos cried out over the intensifying rumble. "To me, yah stubborn arses!"

"You're a shepherd!" Audun cried out, excited to finally learn something of use about their mysterious new guide. He watched enthusiastically as Kernos herded his flock with nothing more than the motion of his staff. "And those are… goats?"

"Sheep, lad. *Sheep*!" Kernos decreed as they stampeded into view; a mightily impressive sight to behold (and hear, much to Gilly's dismay). "Bighorn sheep, they are. And all that's left of our dynasties."

"They're beautiful!" Titha cried out. "Are they friendly?"

"Friendly is the wrong word, lass. Peaceful? Aye, but their

folk are of a spry, hardy stock. Bighorns are made t' survive, ye understand. And they don't take kindly ta' strangers."

"You're perfect for each other, then," she spat. "Does that mean… *these* are your people?"

"No, no, lass. I am a Satyr."

Titha shook her head. "Never heard of one."

"Aye, tis a common reaction down 'ere. Not many of my ilk have there ever been, I'd wager. Let alone in the Lowlands ye call home. Just me and my bride fer now—no more—no less."

"Your bride's not… in *there*… is she?" Titha skirted, pointing to the flock of sheep.

"Yer off yer head!" Kernos cried out, trying not to laugh. "As I am a Satyr, the bride is a Faun. Two sides of the same coin; same ancient race, aye. At home, she is, tending t'our lovely hearth. Brigid and I'are the last of our kin. Have been for generations on. We tend 'ese lands as best we can, and with them comes the mighty Rams and their own brides, the Ewes. Shared these lands since, well, 'at's another story fer another time, lads."

"So your wife stays at home while you get to do all the fun stuff?" Titha snorted. "Sounds unfair. And an awful lot like our backwards Duskridge elders…"

"We take turns, yah wee sass'er. Shifts in shepherding. 'Tis a partnership, t'ru and t'ru, and the only way t'keep these strong-willed horns an' hooves from causin' their own demise." He turned about, waving the crooked end of his staff at her. "Though there's no shame in tending ta one's home, mind you, lassie. 'Tis the opposite! A full time, demandin' sort of fate, home-tendin' is. One ta take pride in, just as much as shepherding, or any o'er venture."

"That's the first thing you've said that makes any sense,"

Gilly blurted out. "I've been trying to tell her that for years." She rubbed her temples, finally sitting all the way up atop Paw. "That's all I want in life. Let others do the dirty work. Oh, a hearth sounds so lovely right now. Cozy fire. Roasting mushrooms. Berries. I want to go home. Take me *hooome…*"

"I'll get you home, sis, I promise," Titha replied. "But after we find Clover. He's coming back with us, Gilly. For what he did."

"And since we kind of have you to thank for that, please try to be more helpful and less contradictory," Audun quipped.

"Audun Houndstooth Angvarsson!" Titha snorted, slapping her knee. "That was beautiful."

"This all affects my people, too, you know," he replied sincerely, still staring Gilly down. "And me. They blasted my home. Hurt my people. So we take them down."

"Aye, 'tis prey worth pursuin', and a trial worth finishin', though bickerin' wonnae get ye any closer t'yer goal, lads. Only the will t' survive will do 'at," Kernos countered, his flock of mighty Bighorns finally settling in to graze. "And ye'll need all the will yer young minds can muster—fer certain death certainly awaits the unprepared. Alas, we've arrived."

The mist before them was so thick it was hardly noticeable if one wasn't searching for it. Just beyond the grazing sheep crept a land shrouded in fog so heavy the only thing it could not hide was its smell.

Paw and Haldor's constant nose rubbing now made sense to the less smell-inclined. As they neared, the pungent odor took on an almost physical form.

"What an awful stink!" Audun cried out, covering his nose with his amber tunic.

"Aye, a right foul stench the Wick puts out," Kernos replied from the edge of his herd. "The first o' many warnings it gives to any daft enough to wander into its mist. Makin' it past the odor only sets yer souls up fer the worser. All manner o' deserters and murky beasts linger in waitin' fer any dim enough t'continue. So I ask ye lads, heed its wall now, and heed my advice. How important is the lasses' boyfriend? The Wick is no place fer weans."

"Boyfriend?" Gilly screeched, frogging her sister's shoulder. "What did you tell him, you little witch?"

"Ssssh, rest now, Gillian," Titha pressed her sister's nose. "Not important."

"Do you know this place well?" Audun asked, a shiver running up his spine.

All eyes locked onto the mist; contemplating.

"Aye, though from a chapter in mine life I'd prefer to keep permanently shut."

"Too scary?" Audun asked as he watched the fogging mass swirl and churn.

"*I* was what to fear, lad... wanderin' its mists as a wee Satyr, snatchin' and tradin' all manner o' goods to and from any souls lost within. Many o'er forgotten folk remain in the trade, I'd wager, aye. Plenty o' raff left to pick the lost clean. Well, any lucky enough t'make it past the kelpies and their juttin' teeth, 'at is. Lost many a' consorts to the bogs. Snatched, they were! Gone in a flash o' mud an' blood, n'er ta be seen again."

"Oh..." Audun gulped.

"Aye. T'was my love fer mine bride, Brigid alone, that pulled me from the Wick's horrors. And fer her sweet betrothal I'll never set hoof back in such a wicked place 'er again."

"Not even if... we need you to?" Titha batted her eyelashes. Paw grunted and moaned, looking back at her with disapproval, but she dismounted anyway.

"Givin' up all I've worked t'be, build, an' protect fer the whims of a stranger tis'nt a fair bargain, lass. Not a word ye can conjure shall get mine arse beyond t'at wall o' mist."

"Thanks for making that crystal clear," Titha mumbled.

"Good. That's settled. So we can turn back!" Gilly replied over her sister.

"How in Gaela's name are we ever going to get to the ruins now?" Titha continued, oblivious.

"Can we go around it? We've done that before and it worked," Audun guessed, about to pull out his parchments and maps.

"Fer Gaela's sake!" Kernos cried out. "Yer deaf, the two of yeh'! Yer stringbean tis the only one wit' any sense between her pointed ears! Foolhardy weans... All I've said and ye still wish to wander in *there*? Blindly? With not but yer tunics and bears and... whatever this curled-wolf be? Daft! Deaf and daft, ye are!"

"Why would you lead us all this way if you don't want us to enter?" Audun scoffed. "You're wasting our time!"

"T'show ye fer yerseves, lad," Kernos scowled, pointing into the ghastly oblivion. "Tis not my place to guide yer fates, as yer eager lassie here pointed out. But I certainly can advise against'it. Which I am."

"Advise all you want," Titha retorted. "But we didn't come all this way to do what's easy. We came to do what's right."

"Aye and I've been tryin'a talk yins out of it fer nigh-on two hours, lass! 'Tis not courage ye display, 'tis *madness*! Any other young'ins would've turned tail fer home at just *one* o' the Wick's horrors I've recounted! Comfort. Safety! Do ye not care fer home, as yer sister does? Fer the worries of yer kin nor the fear in yer own hearts? I cannot let ye wander in there unattended, 'ere a'tall! Aye, I cannot let ye go in. And 'at's my final words."

"Oh so now you're stopping us?" Titha shouted. "Make up your mind, goat-man! Are you helping us or not? If you want to—great—but if not, I don't think you're in any position to hold us back. We just met, you've been kind of a jerk, and this is important to us. To our people, and we will see it through. We will bring those murderers back to trial, and make sure no one else dies at their hands. There is no turning back now *or* being stopped by someone we just met."

"And there's no gettin' further south in Westlyn but through the Wick, lass. *Think*. Heed mine words: Nothin' but death an' even fouler things await ye in there. Do what's best fer the kin you've brought into this same fate. Turn tail, lass."

Titha looked to Audun, then shook her head as she nudged Paw forward.

Kernos sighed deeply, bringing his knotted staff 'round.

"Donnae make me force ye back, lass," he commanded. "If I have to, aye, I shall."

"Is that a threat?" Titha growled, furrowing her brow.

"You've done it now," Audun interjected.

Kernos stamped a hoof into the earth, its great rumble overtaking the scene. "Back, Mae. I will not ask ye again!" He lowered his staff, holding its mighty weight like a club poised to strike.

Paw had no patience for those wielding weapons at his sisters and let loose a furious grunt to match Titha's immense displeasure.

"Home it is, then," Gilly sputtered, shaking her sister furiously. "Come on, sis, you heard the goat!"

Another great growl bumbled forth. Paw looked to Haldor, but his friend wasn't a'rumble.

Swiftly the Ewe'sheep began to swirl inward, their Ram guardians doing the opposite. Quickly the herd became a mobile fortress, one perfectly spiraled to protect their Ewes and lambs.

Kernos' staff flung away from Titha and into the Night, his breath held.

"Turn yer eyes to the west and back yer way t'wards mine herd," Kernos demanded, shattering their debate into splintering urgency.

"Nice try, pal," Titha retorted. "But I already told you—"

"—*Silence*!" Kernos spat sharply, his voice cutting right through Titha's defiance. "Do as I say, lads! *Now*!"

Another, more hateful roar burst from the fields, and Titha's ears perked.

"What… was that?" Gilly asked.

The Young Companions looked about, Paw and Haldor lowering their necks and gazes into the Western Fields. Several large Rams flanked them as they froze in place. Enormous horns and hooves engulfed the younglings in a protective wall. Then they understood.

"Dusklions?" Titha asked.

"Aye," Kernos spat. "They wonnae attack mine Rams as a herd. Lookin' t'pick one off, they are; the weak or sick, one at'ta'time."

"That is awful!" Audun replied.

"Tis nature's way, lad. Now quiet! Not another peep."

Kernos lowered his staff so that he wielded it like a battleaxe with two hands. Paw and Haldor both began to growl behind him, impatiently awaiting what they could not see, nor smell, thanks to the Wick's pungent aroma beside them.

"W-what's happening?" Gilly asked, tucked as far into Paw's fur as she could possibly be.

"Remember those cats I told you about earlier?"

"Vaguely, w-why?"

"They're less *cats*... and more gigantic murder lions with spears for fangs."

"Oh—Okay," Gilly murmured, shaking. "That's f-fine. Totally prepared for that. Better than going home, *right Titha*?"

"They are actually quite impressive," Titha responded before thinking. The obvious then occurred to her as she thumbed the hilt of Feathersword, her fingertips awaiting the danger to come. "We definitely should have gotten you a weapon..." she thought aloud, patting her sister with her left hand.

"Those are two very contradictory statements!" Gilly blurted, bumbling into a rowdy panic. "I'm ready to turn back *now*, Titha!"

"I'm having second thoughts, too," She gulped. "I will get you home, sis. I promise."

"Bite yer tongues, lads, or none o'us get ta go to any o'er homes," Kernos demanded, his harsh whisper only making Gilly's more frantic. "Mine Rams can hold off any lion so long as we keep 'em calm and focused. Donnae break that focus!"

"Don't listen to him—Get us out of here now, Paw!" Gilly

shrieked, preferring not to wait around to be eaten. "*Paw*! What are you doing? Are you deaf? Get us out of this horrid place! I command you! *Stupid bear, do you hear me*?"

Paw held firm with a low grunt. He knew there was no outrunning these beasts.

"Gills—Gilly—*Gillian Rose*!" Titha turned back to her sister as Paw grumbled for them both to shush. "We've made it through worse, okay? You're going to be fine! But right now you need to shut your mouth'hole, okay? Like, *completely*!"

She fully faced her sister, grabbing her shoulders. Gilly's hands shot up to push Titha off her, and a beautiful sheen jumped from her right hand.

"Here, see! Mother's ring!" Titha barked. "Think of her, Gillian. Think of her braveness. It courses through your veins—*our* veins! And we are *strong* together!"

Gilly nodded and gripped tight to the spiraled amethyst, and Titha pulled her mother's circlet from her provisions, placing it onto her head in turn; Moonlight bouncing from its prominent symbol.

Titha's pep-talk had worked for the moment. Gilly focused her panic onto the treasure, her hands shaking as she reduced her mumbling to a sort of hurried buzzing. That is, until three sets of neon yellow eyes broke through the Night and straight into her gaze. Then she lost it.

A blood-curdling scream the likes of which Kernos had never heard sliced through the thick air, and chaos broke out amongst the inner-herd. Ewes and young sheep baa'ed and bucked, knocking each other out of formation.

"To me, to me!" their shepherd shouted, but it was no use. The largest Rams stood their ground alongside their master, but the kin they guarded descended into pandemonium as a trio of Dusklions fully made themselves known in the Moonlight.

"Aye, lads. Now we defend ourselves."

The farthest Lion held a familiar face: it was the cub from the riverbank! He pounced first, his still-massive claws pinning a fleeing Ewe to the ground as horrible sounds escaped both beasts. The largest lion began to flank the Companions to their north, as the third held her ground from where they entered. After the cub finished its show of strength, he promptly leaped eastward; sheep's blood dripping from both fangs. As he dug his paws into the dry earth, Titha Mae and all those with her became trapped between ferocious beasts and the swirling border of the Wick.

Titha swung Feathersword from its Celtican hilt, the blade gleaming in the Moon's aura.

"There's no way this is how it ends…" she spoke to Paw, rubbing his cheek. "We've been through so much worse, haven't we, buddy?" Her weapon gleamed, as if it was present for the pep-talk, as well.

Gilly twirled the fingers nearest her mother's ring, teeth a'clanking as she looked to Audun behind.

Kernos lowered his plaid-covered chest, sweeping his billowing cloak behind him. The enormous lioness approached him, a harsh gleam in her eye suggesting she and the shepherd had met before. Kernos thumbed massive toothmarks in his staff as he examined the dusy stripes of her fur.

Without warning he let loose a shrill and very impressive whistle that could've been heard all the way back in Ythengrey. As he did, the lioness took the chance to leap, and outstretched her killer claws with a mighty roar. Kernos twirled his staff twice, throwing weight into its enormous crook'd end before *THWAP*'ing the bottom of the beast's enormous jaw. A great *clank* of teeth rattled the air, and she flipped backward onto her broad back. The shepherd brought his club back to him, twirling it continuously as not to lose his bludgeoning momentum.

The largest lion growled in anger at seeing his mate on her back, wasting no time in bounding toward vengeance. His fangs were by far the largest, and he bared them fully; black gums shining above them as he turned his upper body mid-air. Kernos ebbed to his left, his still-swirling staff swinging the opposite direction as *CLAFF*: it met the side of the male's muzzle, sending fur and a thick spatter of bloodied saliva into the Fields. The feral beast landed hard, licking the inside of his mouth before spitting a huge tooth into the dirt. Not only that, but Kernos had cracked his right fang. The enormous lion jumped to his feet, roaring in a frenzied rage. As he barreled forward, his mate flew through the air over him, both lions aiming claws and jaws for Kernos' neck. His staff jutted upward, sending the lioness careening backward again, but the bottom end of his weapon wasn't fast enough, and her mate nearly took the shepherd's head clean off.

Much to both of their surprise, Paw careened into the fray, digging his teeth deep into the side of the lion's neck; sending him flying from Kernos' face. Behind him, Haldor swatted at the cub, who now wore his own lblood as well, but still greatly outweighed the hound.

The lioness and her mate stood together, their gigantic heads hanging low as they plotted ripping Paw and his sisters astride limb from limb. The bear did not budge, holding firm between them and Kernos.

"Move, lads!" he screamed, horrified. "Ye donnae stand a chance against dusklions!"

They didn't budge. Titha pointed Feathersword straight over Paw's muzzle, its business end threatening the beasts.

Kernos smiled amidst the desperate moment. The Rams took notice behind him, looking to the Maes, then Audun and Haldor as they held off the cub, then to their own master, and stepped forth. The largest two baa'ed deeply before barreling directly from their flock toward the lion couple. This took the feral felines off guard, and for the first time since the battle broke out, they scuffled backward. Paw let loose a mighty roar as the Rams jumped to each side of him, arching into the air before pointing their massive horns directly down.

WHAM! Each enormous, bludgeoning crown of horns dented the earth, debris flying as the lions leaped backward just in time. The Rams cocked themselves back again, shaking their heads in readiness for round two. But the lions weren't backing down, especially as Haldor continued to swat their cub back, agitating them further.

The lioness darted north for her offspring, attempting to break up the line that threatened her and her mate. She jumped into the Night sky, roaring something awful. Yet as she reached her pinnacle, a new silhouette rushed in from the darkness. From the edge of battle shot another horned being cloaked in deep woolen plaid astride an Ewe larger than any present in the herd.

"Back, ye devils!" the feminine voice cried out, a bow aimed directly for the lioness.

THWIP! She let loose an arrow, striking the Lioness in the shoulder mid-air, a shrill call leaving her maw.

"Brigid, my bride!" Kernos cried out. "Aye yer in fer it

now, ya fleabagged dobbers!"

His great whistle had reached her sensitive ears, and Brigid wasted no time in her arrival; arrows a'flying. She let loose two more; one for the cub and one for its father. The first landed directly before said cub, scaring it off Haldor—the second flying straight past Titha and Gilly to hit the patriarchal lion in his thigh with a great *THUD*.

The male whipped his head around with fire in his eyes, grabbing one of the battling Rams by the throat before thrashing it to death. Kernos cried out, crashing his staff down onto the bridge of the lion's nose. It snorted blood, dropping the now lifeless Ram before dodging one of Paw's massive swipes with the bear's own formidable claws. As the lion landed to the left, he bounded back right, carrying his momentum forward as he mashed his teeth down onto Kernos' staff, tackling the shepherd into the ground. The lion pushed into the earth with all his great weight, gnashing his teeth into the staff, trying as he might to snap it in two. But it was of solid, ancient'make, and would not splinter. Angered by this, the lion threw it to the side, ripping it from Kernos' hands before sending one of his paws mashing down into the shepherd's chest.

"*Gyah*!" Kernos screamed, grabbing the lion's tusks with his hands. Titha, Gilly and Audun all called out to him as he fought the colossal cat. Another of Brigid's arrows loosed and hit the lion in the shoulder, but it was not enough. The beast dug his claws further into Kernos' chest, and with a roar flung him southward into the mist. Into the Wick.

"*No!*" Titha cried out astride Paw, her sister's arms strangling her torso. The father'lion turned to them, his claws' tips now dipped in shepherd's blood. He let loose a massive roar.

THWIP; another arrow landed, this one planting deep into his collar, ending his roar in a whimper. Brigid took aim at the female, who attempted surprising them as she lunged from the darkness. Brigid's Ewe stamped backward, aiming their shot, and the arrow landed true, right between the lioness' eyes.

The great male lion cried out something awful, his son following with a horrid bellow. Their lioness hit the dry ground with a massive *THUD;* dirt billowing as she slid across the Field, stopping just short of Brigid and her mighty sheep.

The lion'father cried out again, knocking Paw aside as he barreled for Brigid.

"Into the Wick!" Brigid cried out to the younglings. "In ye go now, an' I will follow! To my Kernos! To safety!"

Titha looked to her, stunned. Neither waivered.

"Off with yerself! While ye still can!" Brigid screamed. "Tis blood t'ey're after now! T'ey wonnae stop 'til we're all but shreds in teh soil!"

The fierce Faun fired another arrow into the lion'father, slowing his advance as his cub flanked her form behind. Her Ewe baa'ed before bucking its back legs into the youngster's jaw.

THWIP; another arrow pierced the male's front. Then another, and another. It wasn't stopping.

"Are ye thick in the horns, child? Away into the mist! *Go now!*"

Titha and Audun's eyes met, as did Paw and Haldor's.

"Do we go in?" Audun shouted.

The cub rose behind them, brushing soil from his maw before darting directly for them with a fearsome cry and blood on its fangs.

"We go in! We go in!" Audun cried, digging his heels into Haldor. The hound shot off for where the mist met the Fields.

Titha took one last look at the bloddied hillside behind them; her ears ringing from the chaos; wounds of mighty beasts still bleeding. Brigid signaled for her to follow Audun as she continued to protect their exit. But Brigid herself did not follow. Her focus was clearly, in that moment, on her precious flock. They were not to be slaughtered while she still drew breath.

"Is she abandoning us?" Gilly shouted.

"*No,*" Titha replied. "She is protecting her own."

Titha knew then that she had to do the very same. With a deep inhale, she looked to the Wick's edge where Audun awaited. Her hands flailed frantically as she motioned for him to go first; to remove himself from danger. The young Viking snatched his leather cap from his curls before nestling deep into Haldor's fur. He shut his eyes—held his breath—and with a massive leap of faith the hound and his master shot from certain death into the mist.

Titha watched as her precious friend disappeared into thick shadows and fog. She turned back for a moment: There, Brigid barreled between lions and Rams. The incredible Faun turned her bow, its string loaded with three arrows. When let loose, the trio of flutes landed hard into their target, and the lion'father screeched and clawed before finally retreating.

Victorious baas and bleets rung within the herd as the sheep checked for their young, but Brigid did not slow. The cub grew evermore vicious at the sight of his wounded father and shot for the Lunas. Brigid shouted and careened forward, and as she rounded the small bend she cut off the cub's path to Paw. She slapped his round butt hard, stunning him into a spurt. Titha and

Gilly gripped him tight as Paw dashed for the swirling hole in the Wick left by Audun and Haldor.

The last thing Titha saw was the cub lunging atop Brigid's Ewe, bloodthirsty and distraught. Then mist filled her eyesight, and the Wick took her: sister, Bear-brother, and all.

CHAPTER TWELVE

If Memory Serves

"Thank you for seeing me on such short notice, Watcher," Rainer spoke as the doors of Roostwood shut behind him. Two Cedarguards flanked him, nodding slightly to his presence. He puffed out his chest in return, lowering his brow and voice. "I apologize for the lateness of my arrival. Perhaps you would not have been left waiting if we had met in Celtica, as I asked," he crooned.

"How old are you?" Theole replied, looking the spry young Jarl over.

"My age is irrelevant when it comes to my title and authority as Jarl of Autumnhill," Rainer offered as if he'd rehearsed the words a hundred times. "We have much more important things to discuss—"

"Than the eye of my daughter?" Theole frowned. "I must admit, I am surprised," he added, hiding a smirk below his beard, "But she seems to be smitten with you."

"Gossip, that is. Gossip from faeries. I do not believe either of us is old enough to be concerned and—I do not wish to change the subject!" Rainer panicked, beyond unprepared to be discussing a daughter with a father.

"Why, I remember receiving word of your birth!" Theole laughed to himself. "Gillian was tending to the wounds of soldiers in the Ever-war before you could walk, my youthful friend. And to think she finds you—what did Beebee say—hand-i-some? Handsome? Hah! What an age we live in."

"Thank you, I think?" Rainer cocked back, confused. "Theole—Watcher, I mean—please. I come to you within frustrating circumstances. As important as Gillian is to us both—I—times are dire, and I need your help."

The young Jarl would not be swayed from his course. Theole's brow bent, and he caved, dropping his jovial front.

"The Sun begins his reign over our lands, and so ends another watchful Night," he spoke slowly. "I have but just eased the minds of my people, let alone myself, from the murder of Calluna Mint, Rainer. We laid a Luna citizen to rest this past Day. Not a warrior. Not an elder. Do you know the weight of this to my people? To me?"

"I stand before you in my fallen father's place, and not by choice," Rainer replied. "I know loss."

Theole leaned back. "I am sorry, Rainer. I am... forgive my wandering mind. It has been a horrid end to Spring. Summer and his solstice could not arrive more welcomed."

"I share your hardship, Watcher. The trial—"

"—Yes, of course, the trial. I have been so utterly consumed with our loss that I have not returned to our present.

Have you imprisoned those responsible? Oh good, this alone will bring joy to our peoples, having such vile Men in bonds. Your mother will be proud upon her return."

"That is what I hoped to discuss with you. The trial did... not go as planned. A fight—or several—broke out. Which is to be expected. But the last erupted in strange blasts of black smoke, and the Man our Wisemen deemed responsible... has escaped."

"Then you shall hunt him down, yes? No culprits hide within my Duskridge, Rainer. My eyes would behold them if they did. So they are at large! But as masters of the hills and fields, surely your Men do not require an old Luna and his Crows for your search?"

"The Man from Celtica was not the only one to flee, Watcher. With him fled a young Luna—"

Theole's fists shook as the parchment he held crumpled into nothing before Rainer could finish the word. "I may be tired and weary, child, but do not take me for ignorant. I spoke to your messenger, Rainer. He fed me the same, but I passed it up for folly. I will not hear such blasphemy from you, too!"

"You think I came all the way up here to lie to you?"

"*Lunas do not take Lunish life*!" Theole thundered, his voice terrifying as he rose to his feet. "I—I know this concept is foreign to you, young one, and believe you me I struggle Nightly to adjust to the ways of Men for the sake of our shared existence—but I will *not* suffer this falsehood so that you and your council may deflect blame for the *murder of Calluna Mint from your own hands!"*

Rainer adjusted his leather armor, jerking his breastplate downward. "This is beyond hard to swallow, Watcher. All of this is. But whether you accept it or not, from where I stand, as clear as Day, both a Man and a Luna were—*are* responsible for this crime. I did not come here to fight with you—"

"—Smart boy!" Theole decreed. "For there is no fight to be had! I placed a great deal of trust in your people to handle this trial, Rainer. A Man fell to the center of it all as our most-assured culprit, and as such it was only fair for justice to be served upon him by his own people! And yet here we are, a precious pupil of *mine own kin* lost forever to the blade of a *Vikingman*, and the standing Jarl of this new Eon cannot even manage to contain his sentencing!"

"... Forget it," Rainer sighed. "We will find them ourselves." He turned toward the doors, jaw locked. The Cedarguard stood before him. He looked to their eyes, their indigo faces filled with the same doubts and fears as those swirling within him. Swiftly, purpose rose to replace said doubts, and he turned back 'round.

"My mother speaks very highly of you" the Jarl decreed. "And I do not take her opinion lightly. I know the loss of one in the forest is different. I understand that. You live with the same kin, the same voices and faces for decades on end... and I watch Men die every day. But however long or short it may be, a life is a life. Mother taught me that. And if she were here, I have no doubt you would have already sent out scouts, or crows, or at least a *squirrel* to aid us in our search. You would not hesitate to send anyone or anything into the darkness of Night for her. Yet here we are, the culprits now firmly out of grasp, because you sit too proudly upon your silver throne to heed the calls of those you've sworn to protect as your own!"

In a flash of magick Theole's staff materialized, a great clap of blue booming through the chamber as he slammed it's end onto the ground.

"Perhaps the events of late have led me to reconsider that very vow, boy!" he cried out horribly. His Cedarguards gasped alongside Rainer. A weakness then took him amidst such an abuse of hateful power. "Perhaps... all of this... *Celtica* herself... has been in vain." Theole collapsed into his own sadness amidst a cold throne. "Perhaps we have failed."

From the northern hall a tiny pitter'patter came, and two beautiful yellow eyes bobbled up toward him.

"What's wrong father?" Beebee asked, running to his side. "Are you al'wight? I saw the blue again."

He shivered, scooping his youngest up into a tight embrace. Theole held her, and as she swaddled into his robes to comfort him he was slowly reminded of why he did everything and anything worth doing.

"*Much* weighs my mind, young Jarl... You must understand. But such is not your burden to bear. Nor is my misplaced anger. Truly, only a fool would expect the world we wish to build to be an easy one to keep."

"It is not," Rainer replied, still on guard.

"And it may never be. But it is one worth keeping." He hugged Beebee tightly again. "For her. For our young. For *all*, or we never would have made it thus far. Yes. I see it clearly once more."

"Tell Rainer you're sorry, father," Beebee pipped from within his robes. Theole half choked, half laughed at his daughter's wisdom.

"My daughter is right, Rainer. Please forgive me. Forgive my emotional state, and above all forgive my hostility." He smiled. "You shall have your scouts, Jarl. You shall have them and they shall serve you well. Guards!" he shouted, bringing the two at the doors to an abrupt alertness. "Are you up to the task?"

"These are your personal guards, Sire!" Rainer replied.

"Yes, and this matter is most urgent. I cannot stall Time, nor the reality it weaves, any longer… I have delayed it long enough. Off with you three, then, yes? Fetch our best and take all resources you require. I must be left to clear my mind. That much has been made embarrassingly obvious."

"Thank you, Watcher. Truly. We will have those responsible for this awful act returned. And together, we will oversee their fates. I appreciate your change of heart."

"You may thank my daughter. Nothing brings us back to what is important like the eyes of our young."

"Yes, and to that end, I must fetch Audun first before I can be on my way."

"Indeed. Off with you!"

"I—meant that as an inquiry. He is he not here with the girls?" Rainer asked.

"Nope," Beebee replied from her father's robes.

"And how would you know?" Theole asked her.

"Because Titha's not here, either. Nobody's here but us. Didn't you see this?" Beebee pulled a folded note out from her tiny dress pocket, unfurling it many times.

"Now how would I have seen it if you held it yourself, littl'est one? What is this?"

Theole smiled and grabbed the note, unraveling it the rest of the way to reveal a calculatedly-neat message:

Dear father,

I am currently relocating homeless frogs. This is very important work, as their homes were taken by weasels. Please do not look for me. I will be back before supper.

Your favorite,

Titha

Theole folded the note back hastily, concern taking him. "When did you last see your brother?" he asked Rainer.

"Mid-trial. I had him step outside as it grew unruly."

"And you have not seen him since?"

"No, but he is by far the better behaved of the two of us. I am sure he is fine."

"Foolish boy!" Theole thundered. "Do you forget with whom he is bonded? Responsible as Audun may be, he has proven inseparable from the most rambunctious Luna in a full Eon! They will be halfway to Eastlyn again by the time we find them!"

"Uh oh," Beebee whispered.

"Begonia Bee Mae! Where is Titha? Do not lie to your father!"

"I cannot lie because I donnot know anything," she replied, chin up.

Theole's eyes glowed as he fought back another round of

deep-rooted frustration. This time, however, it was tinged with a sense of life-or-death.

"If they gave chase to the—the *scum* responsible for this," Theole rumbled. "To fly upon the footsteps of, of—"

"—*Murderers*," Rainer gritted. "They are not so stupid!"

"Stupid, no. *Naïve*? Yes. There is no stopping Titha Mae from doing what she believes to be *right*. And once again, such drive places her in grave danger!"

Theole lifted Beebee to his chest, flinging his olive robe 'round them. "Guards! You no longer search for the culprits, but for our Titha Mae and Audun of Autumnhill! They will be a'foot with Paw and the boy's hound, Haldor, certainly. Pray she has not brought her older sister into this, but keep your eyes keen for Gillian Rose, as well. Now go!"

"What will you do, Watcher?" Rainer cried out as he turned for the doors.

"I cannot leave Begonia, nor will I bring her into harm's way. Neither can we abandon our peoples in such a time! Nech, your mother, any that we trust of our fellow Companions are afar. Titha has placed us, and herself, between a wolf and a cliff... We must trust in the skill of our best in the meantime."

"We cannot do nothing!" Rainer replied.

"I shall search every scrap of parchment in Roostwood to find some clue as to where these foul beings flee, and in turn where they may lead our young. Our lands are finite, my youthful friend, and evil is shortsighted. They will not have gone far. But know this: If our beloveds are not returned to us within the next half-Day, then we find a way to fetch them, and we fly together. Agreed?"

"Half-Day?" Rainer replied. "Theole, it has already been

past a half-day... The world outside churns on!"

Theole shuttered. Time, it would seem, had still failed to settle, its ancient tapestry desperately clinging to strands of the past. "We will do what must be done," he reassured Rainer.

The young Jarl nodded, then turned to exit Roostwood.

As the doors shut behind him, Theole rushed with Beebee to the Southwing. His mind churned, as did his stomach—for the absence of his daughters amid the fleeting of the old ways—was of the gravest concern. For the study he flew.

The old Watcher always found himself there during times of strife. Where the ancient library once brought him knowledge and comfort, however, it was stooped much further in grief of late; the grief of an estranged brotherly Luna. Cypress' voice echoed to him from each cover and scroll; a memory buried within every page or surface of his former study.

"What are we doing?" Beebee asked. Theole began ripping through papers, looking for something.

"Rainer's messenger told me the bad people fled into the south, Beebee. But in order to find them, and your hard-headed sister, I must know more than 'south'. I must know more..."

As he flung squire and scribe'ly work alike, more and more came rushing back to him. He could hear the luman who once stood as his closest confidante as clear as Night. Cypress' words, both good and bad, rung within his pointed ears, until it became unbearable. He fought it at first, until he finally found that which he sought. As he looked upon it, all will to stave off such loud memories vanished. Theole gave in, and like a magick far stronger than his will, the voice of the past overtook him:

"You will tell your daughters the truth and you will do it in a fashion in which they will understand!" Cypress demanded. His words echoed down the halls of the same study, unchanged, from their history together.

"Sometimes I believe you forget to whom you speak, old friend," Theole offered back. He could see himself in the memory; a particularly powerful one it was, from almost exactly a forest-year prior.

"Do not pull that fallacy with me here and now. Too much is at stake. Thea gave us much. But she did not give you a son. This is a fact our peoples have overlooked time and again simply for *trust* in you. If their great and wise Watcher tells them that *daughters* will carry on his legacy, then they are prepared to accept that truth. Because they *love* you, Theole. They *believe* in you. To the ends that they will sacrifice our long traditions by your words alone."

"And have I not earned that trust?" Theole asked. "Have I not reciprocated their compassion and their love?"

"You have done well by our people. By all of us, to the best of your means, my friend. You have preserved our way of life through unimaginable trials, and I am forever grateful. We all are. But now we stand on the cusp of great change once more. Change that will be, perhaps, even more blinding than what has come before. And if it is your *daughters* that are to lead the Duskridge into, and beyond, this change… if that is to be the way of things… then they must know the *truth*, Theole! They must know the history of their people… The truths of where we come from. Who we *are*. What we are *capable* of… What *they* are capable of!"

"*Enough*! I will not subject them to the failings of your bloodline, Cypress! Of a disgraced kingdom! I will not have the future leaders of our kin drowned in a past that offers nothing but the shadows of things that *should be forgotten*! How many times must we discuss this?"

"As many as it takes!"

"Then must we do this here and now? As the Festival of Dawn beckons us both? You force me to say words I do not wish to say, in a time in which we should both be merry!"

"There is no changing the past, my brother. No matter how hard you fight it, it is still who we are. Who we will *always be*. Our bloodlines are two of the three royal families. And the decisions we make—what *we* choose to pass on—will be all the future kin of said bloodlines come to know. I do not want our past *forgotten*. Do you? Improved upon, yes. But not forgotten. Not forever. Nor do I want our girls to suffer the fate of fallen leaders, doomed to repeat the mistakes of said past. *Do you*?"

....

Theole gasped, coming-to in the same spot. His hands felt inseparable from the tabletop. Beebee stood before him frantically smacking his bearded cheeks with tiny hands.

"Wake up!" she yelped, still pounding away at him. "Wake up, father, wake up!"

"I am awake, wee one. I am awake!" he replied, his eyes opening slowly as his youngest walked into his arms.

"What happened?" Beebee asked.

"A memory, my dear child. A strong one."

"Are you okay now?"

"Yes, yes, Begonia. Though, no, to be truthful, I am not. I

am deeply troubled. This memory that took me… it aligns with all the tragic events of late in a most concerning way." Theole stepped back, standing Beebee on the table as he rubbed his temples. "Move those scrolls for me, tiny bean," he asked.

"You didn't say please," Beebee replied. But she did what her father asked in exchange for his warm smile instead, revealing the map etchings on the table's surface. Theole followed them south, his mind painting a trajectory based on all Rainer and his messenger had told him—and all his mind had taken in from Cypress' library. Soon, his old eyes found the place he knew they would, but that he least wanted them to. A shiver took him as his fingers rubbed over the written words:

Ruins of Byle

"Cypress…" Theole whispered to himself, heartbroken. *"It cannot be you."*

CHAPTER THIRTEEN

Into the Wick of It

"Hold on as tight as you can—I've got you!" Titha screamed, her hands clamped to Audun's. His entire body from the waist down was stuck in a gurgling bog, and the same fate held Haldor.

Gilly reached with her long arms, plunging into the muck as she fished for his tunic or limbs; anything she could grab ahold of.

"Stay still!" she shouted, finally getting a grip on him. "We'll never get home with you stuck in here, boy!"

Together the sisters pulled, and in one fell swoop managed to free their young Companion from a horrible mess. Behind them, Paw fought to do the same for Haldor, who was still stuck in the same thorn-covered bog that had claimed his foothing before causing him to fling Audun into his current predicament.

The Viking'boy caught his breath, and promptly thanked both sisters for saving his life; even though the bog he was stuck in was only a few feet deep.

What a revolting place the Wick was, though. Swampy bogs made traveling in a straight line nearly impossible. Sharp, bristly undergrowth made for often stops to pull huge thorns from fur and belongings alike —usually with a whimper or foul word (or two). If there were a defining attribute for this place, aside from said thorns and swamps, it was undoubtedly the lack of anything beautiful.

Even Titha was hard-pressed to find something admirable about this newfound nature. She sat still for what felt like the first time in a season, still holding Audun's hand as he recovered, while his other hand searched his curly hair.

"Mother is going to be so upset," he thought aloud. "That's the third hat I've lost this year."

"I'm sure she'll be happy to have you back in one piece, hat or no hat," Gilly added, wiping the mud from Audun's face with the swatch of Kernos' green plaid. Titha looked to it, then back out into their wretched, fog-filled surroundings.

"Can you stand, Scribe?" Titha asked. "We've got to get moving. I'm hearing more chirps and croaks, which means we're finally further into this habitat. I hope, anyway. We're never going to find Kernos sitting around, right?"

"You're out of your mind!" Gilly exploded out of nowhere. "Look around you! Look at *him*! We are not going a step further into this place. We are turning back and we are going north—t'ward home—immediately."

"And let Kernos die in here? Alone? After what he did for us? I don't think so!" Titha shouted back, disgusted with the thought.

"That's just it, Titha, you *don't think*. You haven't *thought* since we left home! Our parents won't care how clever you think you are by leaving notes or saving a goat'man or whatever else you've done, if something happens to one of us! Father is going to… if father knew the danger you have put us through, do you think he would be proud of you right now?"

"I'm not doing this for anyone to be proud of me! This isn't about me, or you, or father, for that matter. This is about repaying a life-debt!"

"What does that even mean!?"

"Kernos saved our lives! Maybe you can live with yourself for the rest of yours if we leave him to die in this Gaela-forsaken place, but I can't. I won't. So we keep moving."

"To where?" Gilly screamed back. "Where do we go now, oh wise one? Farther into this fog? Or that fog? Because it all looks the same, and every part of this place is trying to kill us! For all we know we are going in circles! Kernos got himself out once, and he can do it again. Even if he's hurt, he has a far better chance of surviving this place than we do. You know that! So what is this *really* about?"

"That is unbelievably selfish," Titha growled. "You must not have seen or heard what I did, when a giant lion threw his bloodied body in here, or his bride asked us to help her beloved as she fought off more giant lions to *save our lives.* Where were you during all that? Thinking of your safe little flowerbed at home?"

"*I'm* selfish!?" Gilly spat back. "Is this crusade of yours worth the lives of those you love the most? Huh? Fulfilling your little adventure fantasy and saving some horn'ed stranger and getting to come home the hero again is worth Audun? Paw? Haldor? *Me*?"

"You're not listening to me."

"Oh I am listening intently, little sister. And all I hear is the same spoiled little girl who whined over her chores before she ran off and saved the world. You did save the world, Titha. You did. And for the thousandth time, *hooray* and thanks for that. But you learned *nothing* from it. If you can look us in the eyes and be okay with all that has happened tonight and not want to turn back —for us—then you haven't learned a single thing."

Titha flung mud from her hands, turning to Audun. She stared into his face, expecting his eyes to rise. But they did not meet hers.

"You feel the same?" she asked him.

"I… this place is terrible," he mumbled.

"That's not an answer…" she replied.

"I… think we should turn back, yes," he finally spoke up. "I really wish we could find Kernos but we have no idea where we're going—we aren't even chasing Clover anymore, are we? The murderers? Now we're in here for someone else entirely, and I… I think we lost this one. But don't be upset with me, okay? Please don't be mad. I still think you are a hero. And me too, I guess."

Titha gulped. Hearing him say such a thing, while he stood before her covered in bloody scrapes and foreign muck, was harder than any part of this journey. She stammered before wrapping her arms around him.

"He would follow you into oblivion," Gilly spoke softly. "But a true hero would never ask him to."

"A hero would never leave someone behind, to die

alone—or do *nothing* when they could do *something*, Gillian! Didn't we just discuss this? Didn't you have your chance to prevent Clover from helping this all happen?" Titha spurted, her voice rising. "Didn't Clover put himself in the middle of Mint's murder because you failed to say something, or tell someone, or *do anything at all*? I'm sorry, sis, but I can't do that. I won't do it. I've been through worse, I *have* learned a lot, and I will get us out of here. I promise. But we are finding Kernos—*and* Clover—first. Okay?"

The boys lumbered up behind them, each taking to licking the wounds of their respective kin. Paw gave one extra-wet slop to Titha's cheek in attempt to calm her down, then looked to Gilly, who would not make eye contact with him or their sister.

"I'm fine, thanks, please don't," Gilly pushed. "What about you, Paw? Want to leave this disgusting place?"

His head nodded so hard up and down that he lost his footing. Until Titha looked back at him, that is. Then he sat as straight as a tree's trunk with a head that could only shake side to side.

Titha looked to her Young Companions, but no matter how hard she tried, or thought, then tried again—she could not change her mind. "I can't, I'm sorry," she said. "I can't do it! I cannot give up on Kernos, or Clover, and neither should any of you."

"You're not giving up. You're living," Gilly replied. "Living to fight another Night. We're no good to them, Celtica, or anyone dead in a swamp."

"I would also like to live," Audun piped in, Haldor licking his scraped little hands.

"So would Kernos, guys! I cannot leave this place without

him. He would not leave without us. We can't split up, either, so we're going to have to work something out."

Everyone fell quiet, before Audun's small hands pipped up.

"What if... we travel in a straight line, as best we can," Audun calculated, "and if we do not find him on our way out, we will have at least left this place alive, knowing we did the best we could? I do not think there is anything else we can do, is there? We can not navigate this place. We have tried. Right, Titha?"

"You know he's right," Gilly added. "This is not where we die, little sister. Not in here. It's far too gross."

"Your idea makes sense, Audun. For Gilly. Can't have her dying in here—not before choosing between her many suiters. We cannot deprive the Duskridge of its first Watchress and her future prince..."

Gilly laughed, recognizing her sister's sarcasm as her way of agreeing with her. "At least we know one boy's off the table..."

"You should really give Rainer a chance in the future," Audun replied sincerely. "My brother really is a great young man."

"Yeah I was talking about Clover, you little ditz," Gilly groaned.

"Oh. Yes. Please don't like him anymore," Audun hicc-uped.

For a moment Gillian and Audun's joy outweighed their peril, and the Wick absorbed merriment for the first time in ages. But Titha couldn't shake her sense of duty to Kernos. She was determined to save him, as he had them, even if it meant leading her kin to believe she was willing to "leave". Which she was, again, absolutely not willing to do—as was made evident by her meticulous searching for hoof'prints in any moment when she could escape the eyes of her Companions.

It was not long, however, before Audun got to work, and she was able to keep her vision sharp for any sign of Kernos.

"I will need a bit to try and find our best path," Audun said. "I really should make a few drawings before we leave, too. This place may be awful, but it is unlike anywhere else we've been, isn't it, Titha?"

"In all the worst ways," she agreed, eyes preening the mushy ground. "You want to stop and draw this place? Here? Now?"

"The Wick isn't on any map we have ever seen. I want to record it for what it really is. Nech will be speechless when he sees what we have seen!"

"Doubtful," Gilly chortled. "He's incapable of silence."

"Get to it then please, good sir!" Titha replied. "Oh, and let me know if you see any of the things that have been chirping away, will you? I've been holding out for some frogs—perhaps a salamander or snake or two—but I have yet to see a singl—" She stopped mid-word, her pointed ears twitching as her green eyes scanned for a wisping in the mist. "What do we have here?" she added as her eyes caught a faint glow in the fog before them. The harder she stared, the clearer it became.

"Fire!" she screamed. "Look! Through there—it's faint but it's there! It has to be Kernos!"

"Or Brigid?" Gilly added, squinting.

The gang threw their belongings together excitedly, and Paw was already ahead making his way toward the flame. A good fire meant warmth, naps, and roasted salmon, and precisely nothing could stand between him and these bear-sized dreams.

As they moved toward the glow, the mist let up ever so slightly. Breathing became a tad easier, vision became clearer, and footing more assured. The ground beneath them went from squishy to solid, and before they knew it a cobblestone path made itself known. The Mae sisters looked to each other, overjoyed.

But Audun remained cautious, his strong Viking instincts treating any foreign stone path as the path of an enemy until proven otherwise. He raised his finger to his lips, shushing his fellows before mounting Haldor.

Titha nodded, scanning ahead. Her sharp eyes detected no movement, save for Paw's waddling. It was quiet. Nothing else stirred. No birds above nor insects below. Then, up ahead and to the left, something made itself known.

A stone hut! Shaped like half an egg protruding from the ground, its simple silhouette became one of many as the path widened, leading the Young Companions directly into what looked to be an abandoned village. Each hut had an opening in its front of the same shape. The structures themselves were overrun with further thorny bramble-vines, yet someone, or something, had cleared the doorways of their creeping.

At the far end of their walkway, the fog parted to light, and the glowing flame showed itself in full. It was a torch's flame.

"Someone is here," Audun spoke softly.

He knew, as did any Vikingman, that a lit torch meant life was not far away. Slowly they approached it, his hands frantically sketching the huts and their layout, then the torch itself.

"Audun!" Titha whispered. The nearer he drew to the

torch, the more nervous she became. "Audun!" she hushed again. Her friend was clearly entranced with discovery. But her ears were twitching. Hard.

"Make that a quick sketch and then a hasty departure," she spoke, moving closer to Paw. Her green eyes skittered to each side of their trappings. There was no sign of Kernos. Something wasn't right.

"You okay?" Gilly asked from behind.

"I'm getting that feeling again…"

"What feeling?" Gilly asked.

"Like we're being watched…"

Titha climbed her Bear-brother with all the pep and stealth of a squirrel, then tapped the top of his noggin twice (their signal for "stay on high alert"). Gilly rolled her violet eyes.

"I really hate when you get like this," she scolded, mocking the motions her sister made.

Audun was still entranced with his findings, and the torch's glow amid them. He looked about, but could discern little between the still-billowing, bulbous smog.

"Can't go two minutes without a dramatic outburst, can we?" Gilly snarked, furious she was giving into her sister's drama.

Titha shot a ferocious glare at her sister, signaling a hasty "shut up" along with.

"I get it! I'm coming! Quit it, already."

Titha's motioning grew frantic. She began swooping her arms toward her sister, but Gilly's pace didn't hasten.

"For the love of Gaela, twerp, *knock it off*!"

"*Knockings*?" a croaky voice belched out from the fog.

"What's to be knockings, *hmm*?"

Gilly stopped cold in her tracks. She looked to Titha; both sets of eyes wide as a full Moon, and neither of their mouths in motion. Slowly the lanky Luna turned 'round to the sound.

"Helloss," a stout little creature croaked from the nearest stone hut.

Gilly let out a scream the banshees themselves would envy.

"*aaaaAAAAH*!!" the ugly critter returned, before both stood frozen as they screamed in one another's faces.

Gilly fell backward, fumbling the rest of the way to Paw. Titha wasted no time in unsheathing Feathersword, aiming its silver at the stone doorway in which the little thing stood.

"*What* and *who* are you?" Titha cried out, the phrase second nature to her at this point.

"Pleases, pleasess!" it shouted back, hands together. "No hurtings! No slicings! I am simple peddlers! Simple, simple! Offering you goods on your travels through the Wicks, I am. Goods you need! Goods I can provide, *yesss*?"

"…No?" Titha stumbled. "Have you been in there this whole time? Why did you startle us like that?"

"An *excellent* question," Gilly shouted, her hand still on her chest.

"Apologieses, apologiesesss, childrens. Is a Wickish hello, methinks, yesss? No ones ever sees you comings in the Wicks, childrens, no… hmm hmmm!"

As it spoke, more like it stepped forth from the stone huts; each shorter and uglier than the last. *This* finally got Audun's attention.

"Wh-what is happening?" he mumbled out the side of his mouth as more little beings bobbled from their housings. "T-t-ti-time to g-go!"

"No, no! Goingss gets you nowheress!" the peddler replied, hopping frantically toward them, its merry little band in tow. She… it… or him… whatever it was, waddled like a duck and spoke with the same raspy tone. Its hair was thin and grey, as was its skin, giving it perfect 'Wickish' camouflage, as it would mutter. From head to toe it wore the tattered, mucky attire one would expect from any that called this putrid place 'home'.

"Lost! Lost your ways you haves, yes? Yess, lost and afraids, my dearies are. Lost in the Wicks! And the Wicks iss no places to be losts, *hmm*?"

"We're not lost," Titha barked from atop Paw. "We're… on the move," she reaffirmed, puffing up her shoulders. "On the hunt, in fact! Yes! On the hunt, we are. Obviously. And we have no time for idle chat!"

"*Idle chat*?" Gilly whispered.

"I heard Sigrid say it once. It felt appropriate," she shushed back. "I know you think I've learned nothing from adventuring but if I have learned *anything* it's to always appear tougher than you are!" She turned back to the peddlers, twirling Feathersword twice in show before sheathing it. "The hunter waits for no one, I'm afraid," she added, a cheesy grin smeared across her face. "So off we must go. But this has been… pleasant."

"Ahhhh!" the peddler replied gleefully. "Huntingss, you says, yesss?" It rubbed its hands together. "Yess, yess, we can helps with huntings, hmmhmm… "

"You hunting skins? Or *soulss*?" the shiftiest of the lot asked with a wide, grimy smile.

"That is, I believe, the creepiest thing anyone has ever asked me," Titha cocked back. She leaned down to Paw. "Do I answer that?"

He shook his mane "no" feverishly.

Another little fellow stepped forward, removing a heavy hood that looked to be stitched together from half-dead animal skins. His grey ears slipped from holes carved in each side before springing right back into place.

"Hey, youss," he ribbited. "Yous are a princess, yes, hmm? Princesses have many thingsss. They do, they do. Many things to be trading..."

"Hah!" Gilly snorted heftily. "Oh, I needed that."

"I beg your pardon?" Titha replied, smacking her sister with one hand as she buffed up her tunic with the other.

"I askss you simple questionses. Are you princessess?"

"Believe you me, you little... thing. She is no princess," Gilly responded for her sister.

"Oh... You looks like princesss. Shiny hairs. Shiny thingss. Princessess *always* have thingss to trade to peddlerss, yes? Always things to be trading for helpingsss."

"How many princesses come through here?" Audun asked sincerely before Titha waved him into an abrupt shush.

"I already told you we're not looking for help—" Titha chirped, standing her ground.

"—Unless you can guide us out of here?" Gilly interjected.

"Gilly! I am trying to keep us alive!"

"They obviously live in this sludge-heap and can show us a safe path out. We sho—"

"—They can also take us to another friendly little ambush where more gremlins jump out of horror-huts to tie us up and eat us alive! What else is there to eat in this pit but us? Have you seen any food? 'Cause I haven't!"

"You have a very overactive imagination," Gilly scolded.

"No, I have a very *strong memory* of what Kernos told us about this ridiculous place! Trust me on this one when I tell you our odds of survival are much higher if we try to make it out of here on our own over trusting a squad of murder-goblins."

"No goblinses here, shiny princesses. Only us, hmm? Only peddlers. Sifters, hmm. We Sifters!"

"See! They deny being *goblins*, Gilly. But not *murderers*, though, because *that's* fine!" Titha gritted through her teeth.

"Yess, yess! Not goblinses, right, rights! We Sifters, *hmm*? And Sifters always shows you ways out of the Wicks for simple shiny'ss, yess? What you gots, hmm?"

"What you gots? Hmm? what you gots?" the others all echoed in round.

"Nothing of value, I'm afraid," Titha responded, her hand mindfully slipping over her satchel. "We travel light, friends. No good traveler is ever caught in the muck with treasures in their pockets!"

"Fine, fine…" the shifty Sifter croaked. "Then we *skins you*."

"… Skins… us?" Titha echoed.

"*Skinsss…*" they all hissed together, knives appearing out of nowhere.

"Well that certainly narrows our options, doesn't it?" She smiled to her sister. "*What did I tell you*?"

Gilly was already panic-fumbling through her satchel atop Paw. Yet all she could muster was crumbled cake and spoiling fruits. Desperate, she pulled a handful of berries out, accidentally mushing them as she displayed her fist to the Sifters.

"Heartsss!" their leader replied. "Heartses, she hass! See how they bleeds? Yess, yess, we take! We take heartses!"

"Hearts!?" Gilly squealed. She looked to her hand as red and purple berry'juice oozed from between each finger. Another "Eek!" left her lips before she flung the squished fruit onto the cobblestone.

"Oh. No heartses. Just squissh."

"Squissh, hmm..." another peddler added.

"Squissh, yes, squishesss only, hmm..." they debated back and forth. "Squissh won't do."

As they moved inward Gilly wiped her hands into Paws fur, much to his chagrin. Cleaner hands revealed her amethyst ring, and *my* did it shine. Gilly's mind clicked to its potential in such a situation; but before she could do anything Titha caught her wrist.

"Don't you dare," she scolded, looking to the silver ring round her sister's finger.

"Mother would want us alive *without* her jewelry if the alternative is being *dead with* it!" Gilly exclaimed.

"Not an option," Titha ordered. She flung Gilly's hand away from their mother's amethyst as she dove into her own belongings. She found her circlet first, thumbing the spiral amid its gemstone before placing it below everything else (as to not let it's shine escape accidentally). Paw grumbled and murmured below, growing tired of the demanding strangers. "No, we're not doing that," his Luna-sister responded, still searching. "They've done us no harm, pal. We can't just mow them over. But I like where your head's at, fuzzy-butt—Wait! *Aha*!" she blurted. "How about... *this*?"

From her bag Titha flung a huge riverstone high into the air. She meant to hold on to it, of course, but instead shot its gleaming, beautiful shininess straight into the surrounding smog. The Sifters eyes all followed it up and over their huts before it disappeared into the foggy bogs outside. Paw let loose a massive groan.

"Gone! Gones. Won't do at alls, hmm. What else you gotss?" the lot inquired, each more impatient by the moment.

"Hunterss wait for no oness, *yesss*?" the shiftiest of the bunch mocked, squinching his eyes at Titha.

As it did, Haldor galloped center. Audun threw his entire satchel on the ground; its leather trappings full of precious drawings, mappings, and supplies.

"Take it," he spoke sternly. "All of it. It is yours."

Like vultures the Sifters descended onto the bag, ripping into it before they even knew what it held. Gleeful gasps and gargles broke out as they pulled shiny bits of coal and colored pigments from the bottom. Some took to marking the bare parchments and stones of their walkway, others each other.

"Magics?" one cried out. "Magicks!" another corrected, teeth chattering with the ancient sound of the extra 'k' on the end.

The eldest and first peddler they met stepped forward, its reddish irises wide within dim, yellowed eyes. "Deal?" it smiled generously, extending a wrinkled grey hand.

"Under one condition," Audun responded.

The peddler turned back to his gang, each of which was now cackling and screeching as they drew colors and shapes onto each other's faces, arms, and… everything else.

"Names it," it grinned.

"You must help us find our friend, Kernos. He is lost within your Wick as well, and he is gravely wounded."

"Kernos, Kernos!" it shouted back, the others all copying.

"Kernos, Kernos, yesss," they all quipped. "Old Wickerrr, hmm? Big hornses?"

"Yes! That's him!" Titha shouted "You've seen him?"

"Oh yess, yess, no stranger to the Wicks, is him, hmmm. And *stronggg* Satyr. He lives!"

"Did you hear that?" Audun chirped gleefully.

"But—your work, Audun. Your precious things. I We—I—could never—" Titha stopped herself. Her dear friend's masterful etchings laid ruined and muddied amidst a frenzy of ecstatic creatures drawing on rocks. "No. No! Don't do this. We can still save your maps if—"

"—It's okay," Audun smiled gently. "I promise. We owe Kernos our lives, and I really want to leave this place. I can always make more drawings, Titha. It's time to go home."

Titha lit up, completely renewed. "Audun, you're a wonderful human being," she lulled, placing her hand on her dearest friend's shoulder.

"I know," he grinned back.

"Thanks, Audun. Sincerely," Gilly echoed. "We will help you recreate each one. I promise."

"Well! That settles that!" Titha decreed. "You must take us to Kernos at once, you creepy little Sifters!"

"Yess, yess, to Kernos, to exitss, to Wickless landsss with new magick sticksss!" the Sifter melodied, waving its hands happily as its mates did the same with newfound treasures.

"*Magick sticksss!*" they all chorused, before breaking out into a raucous song:

Magick sticks, magick sticks
Mark the stones with turns of color
Magick sticks, magick sticks
New friends give so we don't murder!

Signs and symbols, draw together
Paths and ways and holes they conjur
Out and thru and off they go
To land where no fog holds them so!
Magick sticks, magick sticks
Vulture loses, you will see
Magick sticks, magick sticks
Free from Queen we soon will be!

The Young Companions laughed together for the first time in hours as the horrid singing voices of the Sifters rang through their ancient village like—well, like Audun's chalk on the stones below. Their leader offered its hand once more to Audun, its comrades still a'light in lyric; and with the official handshake of a peddler the deal was struck, and hope renewed.

Yet darker things echoed from the Sifter's song; its words steeped in the plight of far fouler fates. Audun wrapped his arms around Haldor's neck, his oblivious heart singing along, but Titha *felt it*. She felt the whirling pieces of everything falling together. Or were they falling apart? Something powerful, deep within the ancient stone village resonated with her. As if she should know it. She could *feel* it—in the beady red eyes of these wrinkled, forgotten beings that there was much more to the Breaking of Time than harsh words in Celtica and the murder of Calluna Mint. It was more than a feeling. It was the fear she could still picture stretched across Clover's face, now irrevocably tangible.

CHAPTER FOURTEEN

The Aurora's End

"By Craga's breath, there it is!" Nech shouted into the wind. "The Aurora's End! Oh, to be greeted by victory after such shivering trials! Let us hope we have made it to our destination at last!"

Indeed, they had made it. Sigrid's glorious red form soared over open skies. The Elder Companions had arrived with no time to spare, as morning's first light now tickled the Horizon; the golden glow of Day greatly inhibited the Aurora's emerald glows. Its brilliance had given way to a thin, wispy trail hours ago, yet remained just visible enough to show their destination. And that's all they needed.

The Western Svell Mountains sloped down into Svellvanyon: the legendary canyon that held Igdrasil's might just seasons ago was now beneath them. Nech swelled with joy, his imagination vividly painting what he'd hoped to find in wake of the Tree of Life. But nothing came. As they neared, the landscape became shockingly barren: browner, drier, and void of anything remarkable at all.

"Are we sure this is it?" Sigrid cried out from her golden beak. "Surely there is more to signal an arrival if so? My eyes see nothing but scorched earth."

"You were there with me!" Maya squawked in return. "We witnessed the pure devastation that was the *Breaking of the Horizon*, Shieldmaiden. I would not expect anything more than… this."

"Oh, how dreadfully disappointing," Nech murmured, finally putting his maps away.

A massive, bowl-shaped crater awaited them at the northernmost end of Svellvanyon. Even the Svells were carved by the *Breaking*, its calamitous energy leaving nothing spared of scars.

Nech looked behind as the fading violet of Night took the greens of vegetation with it. Nothing but waste awaited. Or so they thought.

"Nothing stirs," Maya confirmed, to no one's surprise. "It should be safe to land. Ready?"

"As we shall ever be," Nech echoed. "My Shieldmaiden, what say you?"

"We land," Sigrid spoke sternly.

And with her words they dove. Down, down, into the vast expanses of the soil-filled crater they went, its earthen hues overtaking all else. Yet as they drew nearer, the browns became more varied; their textures differentiating.

"Roots!" Sigrid cried out. "She has laid new roots! Igdrasil lives!"

Giant talons rushed to the ground. Sigrid threw Nech into the air as she transformed, feathers giving way to her natural form. Nech landed firmly in her arms, his eyes wide but his laughter welcome.

Maya landed onto a gigantic root beside them. Quickly she became upset as her talons tapped the bark. She scraped at it frantically, as if she'd become wild.

"Maya, my dear, what in Gaela's name are you doing!? These are sacred! Hallowed roots, they are! Certainly such a vast education as your own leaves for a wanting of preservation, not annihilation!?"

But she did not listen. The Peregrine was utterly consumed, flapping from one root to the next, clawing each as deep as her strength would allow.

"Maya! What is the meaning of this?" Sigrid yelled.

"They're dead!" she shouted back, heartbroken as she scraped still. "Every single one! All of these roots… They are dry and barren. Dead!"

"But they still hold a tinge of green to my eyes. Do they not to yours?" Sigrid responded, walking to Maya's root. "They are giant, yes… but these are not the roots of an adult. These are sapling roots! So young, they are! Young, but… dry. Bone-dry! As if someone has cut them from their very heart not but days ago! Who would do such a thing?"

"That we know full well," Maya soured. "Look, here, closer to the ground. My markings are not the first. Many shovels and axes have hit wood. These roots may not have been attacked directly, but rather are victims of a search gone awry."

"Yes… I see it now. An astute, yet astoundingly gloom'ridden observation, my dear," Nech agreed. "And there are more. Over this way, many smaller but equally dry roots bare the markings of brutish diggers. Such reckless, boorish hacking!" The old Scribe walked along the length of the giant root, sorrow growing with each cut he found. "Yes, yes... Pawns were surely sent here before us, of this we should not be surprised... Yet their tenacity does suggest a keen urgency, which in turn envokes knowledge they must possess, but we do not ourselves! How, I ask?"

"It is all for this Lifestone Ugar demands of us," Sigrid added, walking to him. "An artifact of which we Companions have never heard hide nor hair. And that demon now beckons us to retrieve it? To do what his own could not, at the command of some new 'master' he stands loyal to?" She withdrew her axe, the mighty Autumnbringer of her late husband, and looked to its shape. "They wish for us to succeed where others have failed..." She drove its blade into the earth, shattering a mighty mound of soil. "A wise judge of character on their part—" *THWACK!* She drove its heft into the ground again. "—For we shall not fail!" *CRRSH!* "But our victory—" *SCRUSH!* "—Shall not be shared with the corrupt—" *THRONG!* "—Or the *wicked*!"

Her final swing landed with such heft it shook the crater from the bottom out. Dirt and ash unclogged from a thousand crags. Previously unknown nooks and divots appeared, and Sigrid's companions took to digging.

But it was Autumnbringer that bested the lands. The Shieldmaiden wielded it with a wrathful fury—one so hot it could only have been stoked by the conceited demands of evil's kin. She wielded such burning fury with keen mastery, and from its blows the ground quaked.

"Over here, I say!" Nech finally cried out. He stood

further in, nearest to the crater's center. "A light!" he shouted again. "A shining light breaks forth from the soil! It is deep, but it is ever-present! And it glows with the emerald of the Aurora! This must be the center, yes? The heart! The center cluster from which the roots have grown! You have done it, my Shieldmaiden! You have done it, indeed!"

"Let's not count our eggs before they hatch," Maya scoffed, ever the skeptic. She flew to Nech's shoulder to get a better look, and there the soil brimmed with a gorgeous green light below their feet. Nech took to his knees, shoveling with knobby fingers, their yellow skin thick from years of similar field research.

"Are you enjoying yourself, my dear?" he joked to Maya who sat still atop him.

"I have always wondered what it would be like to watch while *you* do all the hard work," Maya smiled.

"Pip'pip, you curmudgeon! Though I must admit, it is wonderful to be excavating an artifact firmly planted in Gaela's ground once more. Even if—my bones are—entirely too old for the trade these days... *Oh my...*"

His hands hit a cluster. Its wood was spoiling, and from each crack came the blazing emerald sheen.

"Her heart..." Nech whispered. "It is rotting away... Without her many roots, the offspring of Igdrasil shall shrivel... into nothingness..." The old Craglin sniffled, placing his yellow hand onto the heart as it pulsated light.

"The Aurora... It was a cry for help," Sigrid added, standing tall. She looked into the sky, and as the yellow Sun brought Morning's light, the borealis died out completely. "She is dying."

"What do we do?" Maya asked. "What *can* we do?"

"Exactly what we came here to," Sigrid decreed. "I know not why it—*she*—chose me. But if the consequences in my dreams are as real as all else they have shown, then we must not fail her. We will not fail her!"

She stepped before them and raised Autumnbringer above her head, its twin blades gleaming in Morning's first light.

"Sire? My Shieldmaiden? Perhaps brute strength is not the—" Nech stumbled before Maya grabbed his vest, pulling him out of the way in an impressive, split-second decision.

Sigrid's axe struck true and deep, and for the briefest moment all was quiet. Then, it split.

With all the fury of Life and Death themselves, the rotting wood exploded into a blast of pure green energy. Soil and splintered wood flew the full length of the enormous crater. In a fit of instinct, Sigrid had transformed into the Glorious Red Eagle, her magnificent wings hardening to shield herself and her Companions like a wall of plated armor.

As the dust settled around them, the 'heart' was revealed. Its dying wood corpse laid open, only the bottom's cradle remaining; the entirety a'light with the same emerald green that had led them there. At its center, their purpose was finally in sight:

The "Lifestone".

"It... it is no *stone* at all!" Nech gasped as he laid eyes upon it. "It is... a *seed. The Seed of Igdrasil*!"

His scholarly mind was unable to resist the object and its pure glow. Slowly his knobby knees slid down into the crater, hands outstretched. Sigrid and Maya peered over the edge above, their eyes lit with green.

"It is magnificent," Sigrid whispered from her golden beak.

"That it is," Maya agreed from a much, much smaller beak. "Though, Nech, I doubt it is the best idea for you to touch—"

Another burst of light shot forth from the hole, and Nech was sent flying back out into the open. His hands smoked as if scolded, but no burns showed.

"...Gracious me..." he blurted, firmly planted on his arse. "Perhaps, yes! My theory is correct!"

"How is that your first thought right now? Are you alright?" Maya asked, flying to him.

"P-er-perfectly sound, my dear falcon! T-thank you," he pipped, his body quaking. "Apologies, my Companions. It would have been prudent of me to mention said theory first, but I have never been one to resist an artifact of such splendor. Yet, here I sit, scolded by the Lifestone—the seed's very luminescence, and all holds true. This artifact's beauty is rivaled only by the memory of the Moonstone and Sunstone!"

"Yes," Sigrid added. "I see them in its splendor."

"Which pertains precisely to my theory, Shieldmaiden. I, myself, a simple Craglin Scribe, do not possess that which is required to wield its majesty! But you, Sigrid Autumnsdottir, vessel of the first blood of Man— Former Wielder of the Sunstone—I believe *you* may."

"And when did you come up with this theory?" Maya asked.

"Somewhere between touching the seed and landing on my posterior, I believe. It is amazing the thoughts we have when one's life flashes before one's eyes," he chuckled back.

"My dreams..." Sigrid finally spoke.

"Exactly, Shieldmaiden. Does this revelation not bring you some sense of comfort?" Nech asked. "Or knowledge you have sought, at the very least?"

"It does," she replied. Her beak gave way to rose-tinted lips as glorious red feathers withdrew into armor. She leaned to the crater, making her way down into its glistening core. As she neared it, she took one last look at the seed. It appeared as one would expect the seed of a hardy tree to look, only much larger. Her mind's eye compared it to a walnut; an enormous, dark shelled husk protecting the precious glowing green seed'stone within.

As its glow met her hands, all hesitation ceased. She felt comforted by its presence, and in a strange way she felt her own presence comforting it. The nearer she drew, the fainter the pleading light became. Sigrid placed a hand down onto its core, and no torrential light nor burning came. Instead, she stood calmly as one with the Seed of Igdrasil, its warmth invigorating her touch just as the Sunstone had before it.

"It is a most precious thing," she said as she looked into its gleaming center. "And the wicked shall not have it."

Slowly she brought it out of the soil. As she did, its husk crumpled in her grasp, the walnut-like casing turning to the same ashen-soil that surrounded them. Only the glistening core—the Lifestone—remained.

Sigrid tore a swatch from her own Wolv's'fur cloak and wrapped the Seed tightly before handing it to Nech. "Hold her tight, my friend," she told him with a stern look, "for I must deliver a message of my own."

She flung her satchel around, retrieving the sharp

Runestone from it. "Maya, if you would, please, fetch some kindling."

"Shieldmaiden, we do not know how this magick works," Maya retorted. "For all we know this Rune's fire is a portal, and Ugar may then step straight through it. I felt as if he was close to doing so the first time he appeared."

"Good! Let him come."

"He will not be alone! Think, Sigrid. Now is not the time to, well, be a *Viking* about this!"

"What would you have me do, instead?"

"I would have *us* take it back to Celtica. Protect it from harm or foul influence."

"But the people, Maya. You must think of the innocents residing within Celtica!" Nech decreed.

"If I summon the demon here and now, I may face him in a land void of consequence," Sigrid clarified to Maya. "If he is to appear, and his aim is to claim the Seed for his own, then let it be here, in the shadow of our former victory."

"I suppose that is less risky," Maya pondered.

"The Elder Drakes are dead, and the only other Great Avian, to my knowledge, is our dear Theole," Sigrid added. "Unless Ugar appears to us in a far larger form, I do not fear any threat he may pose. Kindling, please."

"Are we doing this?" Maya turned to Nech.

"It would be most unwise to attempt a commune with Ugar in Celtica, my dear, or to simply return with the Seed and await his arrival. I believe, if we are to stay one step ahead, our current territory and situation would be one to take advantage of."

"Fine," she replied, hesitant. "But let's not make a habit out of having the small bird gather sticks, no?" She huffed as she began to gather what remnants of the dead roots she could.

"We are going to help you, Maya. Do not fret," Sigrid said as she joined in. Slowly, then, as Maya became busy, she turned to Nech. "Do you think she will mind if I send her for Celtica after we are done gathering?"

"I can hear you and yes I mind," Maya squawked back, throwing her sticks into the pile. "I have a home and an Order to return to, as do you both. I am not some tool to be used as seen fit!"

"Maya, please, I meant no offense," Sigrid sighed. "You are the fastest being in all of Gaela. I simply find it wise to alert Theole to what we have discovered and allow him as much time to ready our homesteads for potential threats as possible. Do you not agree?"

"I think that would be smart, yes. But I also planned to finally return home after this. I have fulfilled my end of our bargain."

"Does this not trouble you greatly?" Sigrid asked. "Does nothing outside our bargain matter to you?"

"Of course not! I'm just gathering sticks like a nesting songbird at the whims of a plundering human for the sake of it!"

"My fellows, please! Please!" Nech interjected. "Too much is at stake for our small band to splinter now! Let us think on this as we light a fire, then contemplate our course of action one step at a time."

"Great," Maya snuffed. "I'll be here. On standby for those who really matter."

Nech rolled his eyes, wagging his finger as he dropped a

few more slivers of splintered wood into their pile.

"It would mean a lot to us both if you did stay, Maya," Sigrid replied. "And if I am granted the chance to separate Ugar's head from his body, I am fairly certain you will not want to miss it."

Maya grinned. "... I'll consider it."

Sigrid returned the falcon's smirk, then took to their small pile. She still held the Cragoan Runestone, flicking it up into the air before catching it. It looked as plain as any blade'tip. Wielding it like a flint, she pulled her axe forward and *SHUCK*! She struck its blade with the Rune many times, sparks flying into the kindling. Nech bowed to blow into the fire, his lungs conjuring all the hot air a timeworn Craglin could muster. Before long a smoke escaped their stack. The Runestone lit up, and a tiny flame began to dance below.

Within seconds the tiny flame burst to life and became a roaring inferno. The Companions fell backward, singed by its fury. A familiar, sinister face billowed upward into the fire; two red eyes rising amidst charred black skin.

"Good. You have it," Ugar growled through, embers spewing from his visage. "Bring it to me as we agreed, and my Master will spare your peoples from further harm. No more need die in Celtica."

"We agreed to no such thing, demon," Sigrid replied. She whirled her axe, guarding Nech and Maya with it as they stood behind her. "We will be keeping the Lifestone. It is under our protection now. If you wish to have it, it will be over my corpse."

Ugar laughed, each vile chortle rippling the fire's intensity. "We thought you would say this. Predictable as ever. I ask one final time—and urge you to caution."

"Peck off, Ugar! She said no, so come and get it if you can, you coward!" Maya screeched.

"What the Peregrite said," Sigrid smiled.

"That is an unfortunate answer. For you. Allow me to show you something. The alternative, if you will."

Ugar's face subsided into smoke, and the flames gave way to a vision of three people walking, their small party surrounded by short creatures with a known bear and hound in tow.

"Titha?" Nech asked, squinting into the flames. The vision became clearer, and there burned the faces of those they loved most.

"Audun! My son!" Sigrid shouted, her fist clenched to Autumnbringer. "Where are they? Where have you taken my son? Where have you taken them? Hear me now, devil, if one scratch is laid upon those children, I will reign a fury on you and your kin the likes of which this world has never seen!"

Ugar's laugh could be heard again, but the vision in the flames stood firm as his voice rumbled through.

"No harm has fallen them. Yet. Our minions have the younglings firmly in their grasp—and lead them straight to the Ruins. Bring us the Lifestone, Shieldmaiden, or the Ruins shall be the last place your son, their beasts, and the daughters of Theole, ever breathe."

Sigrid burst forth screaming, her axe cutting through the flames. She grabbed at their heat as Ugar's laugh echoed, but as suddenly as the inferno had erupted—it vanished.

Nech held his mouth, his eyes wide with disbelief. Maya landed on his shoulder, her head bowed. Before them, Sigrid fell to her knees. A horrible scream left her body, her fists clenched tighter than stone. Her fear and rage echoed through the crater, then into all of Svellvanyon. Her Companions moved to her, placing hand and wing on her shoulder as she came to terms with what they had been shown.

"What in Gaela's name are the children doing so near the Ruins of Byle?" Nech thought aloud. "Were they captured? Have we truly been gone so long as for such a fate to have transpired?"

"They were not in bindings, nor did their faces look of fear," Maya replied. "My instincts tell me, though, that Ugar is not bluffing. He knows where they are, and if those little *things* they travel with lead them to the Ruins, as he said, then—"

"Do not say it," Sigrid spat, her words broken. "We will bring Ugar his prize—this Lifestone. No object, spawn of Igdrasil or no, is worth those lives to this world. None. But know this; if the villains aim to *keep* the Seed, then it will cost my life. I will save our children first, but I will not leave the Ruins behind *without* the Seed of Igdrasil, or the *heads* of those who torment us so."

"Nor will I," Nech replied. "If our nemesis aims to hurt those we love most, then, I dare say these old bones still have plenty of fight left in them. Curse that wicked monster! Never would I have imagined this turn of events."

Sigrid placed a hand on the Craglin's shoulder, looking to him, and then Maya.

"Maya," she began, "You must—"

"—I know, I know," she replied. "I will tell Theole everything I ca—"

"No. There is no time," Sigrid interrupted. "I do not know the way to these Ruins. Our top priority now is saving the children from whatever fate awaits them. Can you lead us there? Now?"

"Yes," Maya replied hesitantly. "Though I must warn you, the last I saw of that wretched place, it was shrouded in a mist so thick I could barely make out the lands below."

"Then we breach it upon arrival," Sigrid spoke. "Nothing else matters."

"I concur," Nech added.

"And hope for the best," Maya spoke as she flapped her wings to get their blood pumping. "Once we spot the spires of the Ruins, I will leave you for Yythengrey and tell Theole all that has transpired. We will need all the help we can get."

"Thank you," Sigrid said.

"Don't thank me yet, Shieldmaiden. Secure that shrouded Seed and let's prepare to fly like we've never flown before."

"Oh, again? So soon?" Nech mumbled, adjusting his breeches.

Sigrid took on her Avian form with haste, and the massive wings of the Glorious Red Eagle shimmered in the morning Sun. The Northern half of the Companions flew back into the South as such; the faces of Titha, Audun, and Gilly giving a speed to their wings the likes of which Gaela had never seen before.

CHAPTER FIFTEEN

Runes & Ruin

If the Sifters had told Titha their exit from the Wick would be entirely uphill, she wouldn't have believed them.

"Only way outs," their leader reassured her, its long fingers gripping to rocks like hooks. "Climbings is almost over, yess?"

"Yess," the hooded Sifter replied. "Less wheeze now. Air is crisps. Much easier to be breathings." It came over the edge of their gradual climb first, then stood with an outstretched hand to help those along who still struggled. A rare patch of kindness, Titha observed.

Meanwhile, Paw fumbled up the incline with all the grace of a mammoth below her.

"Just a few more steps, pal," Titha encouraged, Gilly holding on for dear life. To their right, Haldor careened up the rocks, nimble as ever, with Audun grinning astride. Paw roared and shook his shoulders before leaping with all the energy he had left. He landed with a *plop*, his nose just ahead of the hound, and a great smirk took his muzzle. Haldor barked, then raised his chin while trotting past the flattened bear. They had all made it out of the Wick. Alive.

The Sifters were delighted. They took to skipping and singing again, with one particular verse repeating:

Out of Wicks, Out of Wicks
Vulture loses, you will see
Out of Wicks, Out of Wicks
Free from Queen we soon will be!

"Boy do they like their songs," Audun said, trilling along with them. "Even more than you Lunas!"

"About these songs..." Titha replied. She nudged Gilly, prompting them both to slide off Paw to give him some semblance of rest. "Your people have a Queen you're not overly fond of?" She asked the head Sifter as they caught up to it. "I'm definitely sensing a pattern in your lyrics, here."

"Horrible iss new Queen, yess. Horrible..." it replied. "No leavings Wicks for Sifterss, hmm. Queen keeps all her thingss forever."

"Glad we stumbled across you and not this Queen, then,"

Titha replied with a finger on her chin.

"Hmmhmm! Yess, Queen not nice like Sifters, hmm. She skinss princesses without askings first, hmmhmm… Sifters always ask first."

"A charming trait, really," Gilly groaned.

"But all can changess, hmm? Sifters not be trapped for long!"

"And how's that?" Titha questioned.

"You will sees. We all sees. Sifters help, yess? Sifters helped so good things come for Sifters, *hmmhmm*?"

"If only that were the way it worked," Titha replied. "Still, you've stayed true to your word so far, which is a start. And as soon as we have Kernos back, we'll be on our way home and out of your hair forever."

"Satyr, Satyr, yess, Satyr," the others chirped in round. "Soon, yess? *To him soon we soon will be,"*

Tis good we passed on meals of late
Where lesser beings would stew and ate
Not us, ho ho! Our mucky muds
Did save the Satyr steeped in bloods

"Okay that is enough singing for now, thank you," Titha grumbled. "I'll believe those… interesting lyrics… when we see him alive for ourselves."

To him soon we soon will be!

"We believe you!" Gilly shouted. "Please, *please* just stop."

"Aw, it was really beginning to grow on me," Audun replied with a frown. "Save the Satyr steeped in blood—To him soon we soon will be—"

Gilly whipped around. "I will hit a boy," she threatened.

"Sssh! Both of you," Titha shushed, her head hung low beside Paw's. "Look, they're splitting up. Anyone hear them mumble why?"

Haldor shook his head 'no', followed by Audun. Paw looked to the left, where half the Sifters waddled—then right, where the rest of their compatriots trotted off into the distance.

With the pitter'patter of their tiny feet the fog began to clear. An enormous stone wall stood behind its curtain, each stone older than the last. Moss, lichen, mushrooms—all what'have'you's expected to grow on forgotten things—grew here. Vines trailed up from unruly weeds, wrapping themselves around a great doorway that had partially collapsed.

Paw stopped. Titha's eyes rose slowly, but she could not find the top of the structure. Wherever it ended was lost to the mist. As the Young Companions stared into the opening all else fell silent.

"Okay goodbyes," the lead Sifter croaked.

"And just where are you all running off to?" Titha questioned, alerting Paw. The big bear harrumphed backward, cutting off their path from his side of the doorway.

"Satyrs is in here," their leader replied. "Our services are kaputs. Goodbyes, princesses."

"I don't think so!" Titha shouted. "You expect me to walk into this dark, dank old place and just trust that Kernos is in there?"

"Yessirs."

"Not a chance. It's horrifying. What is this place, anyway?"

"Uh—Titha," Audun stuttered. He sat still as a statue above Haldor, his finger pointed above the stone entrance. "Does that symbol mean anything to you?"

Titha placed her hand over her mouth. Gilly gasped behind her; chills shooting up their limbs. As the mists dissipated, an enormous sigil revealed itself above the doorway: It was an entrance stone, just like the one on their ancestral Cairn in Ythengrey—Tri-Spiral and all.

"Oh boy," Titha exhaled, nervous energy twitching her feet. "That's not good."

"What is it? It's fascinating," Audun pondered. He reached around to grab sketching supplies, but then, sadly, remembered what had become of them.

"Well, it's *us*," Titha responded. "It's an ancient Lunish symbol father just recently showed us on an old burial site at home. So either the Sifters are *way* good and we're back in Ythengrey, or—"

"—Or what?" Audun gulped.

"Or things just got a lot more complicated," Gilly answered. She let go of Titha and slid down Paw's side; her gaze locked onto the Tri-Spiral. As she approached the old stones, she could feel their... something. Energy, perhaps. They radiated history to her. A familiar one.

"Where are we?" Gilly questioned, slowly turning back to the leader of the Sifters. "Where have you taken us?"

All Sifters stared to the ground, as if they were not to look upon the great symbol or its gate.

"To the Satyr, hmm? Inside, you will sees," one replied.

"That's not what I asked you, you freakish little creature!" Gilly growled. She approached the leader with heavy footsteps. "Answer me."

"Sifters tell truths! Princesses asks for safe passages out of Wicks, but first to fetch Satyrs! Satyrs is here, hmm? At Ruins!"

"Of course," Titha exhaled. "The Ruins. We're here, guys. We're here. We made it after all."

"You put him… in *there*… to *heal*?" Gillian scoffed. All her mind had conjured of these fabled Ruins did not paint it as a place of healing, nor as a place she wanted to be at all. Ever. As such, her fury only grew. "What are you not telling us, you little rat'fink?"

"Sifters tell alls! Ruins shelter here!" Their leader quivered as Gilly held it off the ground by its collar. "Wicks no good for healing outsiders. Took Satyrs here to rest, hmm? Needed much rest, yes, hmmhmm!"

"Well this is just grand, isn't it?" Titha yelled, flapping her arms into the air. "We get to where we were going only by trying to run away from it."

"Ruins of B…" Audun muttered, remembering his torn map and the single letter denoting its true name.

Titha turned back to Gilly, who leaned onto Paw, rubbing her temples.

"I can't even begin to process this right now," Gilly said as all the recent back-and-forth between sisters rung in her head. "Do we go in there now? That has to be a tremendously terrible idea, right?"

"Maybe, maybe not?" Titha replied coyly. "One step at a time. You there, leader. Come here. You're coming with me."

Titha snatched the lead Sifter's hood and walked it forward as she motioned for Paw to walk with.

"What are you doing, Titha?" Gilly asked, mortified. "Titha. Titha! Titha Lilly Mae don't you even think about walking in there!"

Her request, as expected, fell on deaf ears. Titha careened into the foreign catacombs, and couldn't help but let out a sincere "wow..."

The Ruins were even more breathtaking on the inside than she'd ever have imagined. Ancient stonework, far more gentle and intricate that any in Autumnhill, crafted a monument to the skill of whoever had built it. It was beyond too much to take in. Mere Nights ago she'd never even heard of this place, yet here she stood amidst its splendor, like she'd been before and never left.

"Go get Kernos, please," Titha commanded, flinging the leader forward. "You promised us our friend. I expect you to retrieve him. No tricks."

"No tricks, no tricksss..."

"That's what I said, no tricks. So what's the holdup?"

"No hold'ups, none, hmhmm. Nothing to holds, see? We, we left hims here, on moss'bed. Here—" It scuttled over to a corner, running its hands along the clear impression of an absent body. A burnt-out torch and several ruined provisions were cobbled nearby.

"Gone! Satyr friend is gone, hmm? Sees? No tricks, no tricks. Just gone friend."

"*No...*" Titha whispered as she approached the moss. She leaned over, great disappointment filling her bones. "Then where is he?"

Paw whimpered, nudging the back of Titha. He was confused. He felt the hope leaving his Luna-sister's body to be replaced by anger.

"Where is the Satyr, Sifter? Where did you take him?"

"Nowheres! He has legs, he walks off with them, hmm?"

"I can't believe this. What do we do now?"

Paw grunted in response.

"I guess so, buddy," Titha replied, folding into defeat. "Let's go tell the others."

"Wheres you going, hmm?" the lead Sifter asked.

"Home. Kernos isn't here. You said you'd take us out of the Wick after we found him. Well now he isn't here, and we're still deep in this mess, so, want to know what's worse, little Sifter? All this journey has done is show me how I never should've left home in the first place… how I never should have let my sister, or my best friend, come with me, and how I've only made things worse, not better."

"Thingss get better. You will sees. You not in Wicks anymore. You in Ruins now."

"Titha! Get away from 'at creature!" A thick voice rang out from the depths of the room. The accent was unmistakable.

"Kernos!" Titha shouted, happiness swelling inside her like the budding of a Moonflower. She turned to run to him, only to find that he was sprinting toward her like the ghost of Vulduun himself chased from behind. Halfway to, he careened into the air, twirling his shepherd's staff once before sending it cracking across the lead Sifter's face. The tiny curmudgeon shot across the Ruins head-first, before splatting into a timeworn column with a *most* unpleasant sound.

"*Woah*!" Titha gulped. "What'd you do that for?"

"How long have ye been with these ghouls, lass? *Speak*!" His voice was harsh and urgent, and his tartans remained bloody.

"They—they led us out of the Wick! We traded them some supplies for safe passage, but—"

"But! *But* is right, aye, isn't it, lass? They led yins here, not ta safety! Rotten vermin! Where be its kin? I'll end the lot of 'em fer this!"

"It's okay, Kernos, it's okay! You, you can show us the way back now. Forget about them!"

"Ye donnae understand lass. Those creatures are as foul as teh Wick makes 'em! Yer sister and the Viking boy, where are 'ey? Why aren't they with ye?"

"They're just outside with the others."

"Other Sifters?"

"Yes…"

Kernos huffed and puffed, wasting no time in grabbing Titha's collar and flinging her atop Paw. The Satyr shot out the Ruins' entrance, his nimble hooves bounding from one fallen stone to the next.

"Titha Mae, ye daft little Luna!" Kernos cried. "No one's out here, lass! 'Ey're gone!"

"That's impossible," Titha replied astride Paw, his claws landing onto the soil behind Kernos. "They were just… right *here*…"

But gone they were. No Sifters. No sister... no Audun, Haldor… Not a single other loved one in sight.

"No, *no no no*, we can't split up!" Titha scurried about, her hands shaking. "Kernos where are they? Where is Audun? And

Gillian, oh Gods, where—*where is my sister!?"*

As panic filled Titha, so did the mist on the path before the Ruins.

"With me now, lads! No time t'waste if we are ta' save 'em," Kernos decreed, a great grimace taking his visage. Paw heeded, rolling into a hasty re-entrance behind their ally.

"Save them? From what? Tell me what's going on!" Titha yelled. "Where are my kin? We can't leave here without them! This is where we last saw them so we, we need to stop. Stop! *Stop*!"

"They've been taken, lass! Come ta' terms and get yer wits about ye! They've been taken by teh same dastardly maggots 'at tied me up in these ruins, an' fooled yins into trusting 'em!"

"The Sifters? They led us out of the Wick and straight to you—They earned our trust!"

"Earned it, did 'ey, now?" Kernos laughed before gritting his teeth. "Never trust a stranger that requires somethin' in return."

"Now you tell me this!"

"Oh, was I absent, lass? Fergive mine exit befar the Wick, aye? T'was simply struggin' *not ta bleed out* from throwin' me'self betwixt yer kin and three Dusklions! T'ink nothin' of'it!"

"It was sarcasm, Kernos! Relax, please—you get even harder to understand when you're upset."

"Upset?" Kernos huffed. "Ye haven't seen upset yet, lass. Stay close."

The shepherd rushed forward, leading them further into the darkness of the Ruins, shoulders and horns lowered as if to plow through a wall of stone if need be. Paw rumbled behind, dodging rocks and boulders that had fallen lifetimes ago. Periodically Titha would find her mind slipping from peril into the trance of the architecture, only to have the sharp *CLOPs* of Kernos' hooves hitting stone snap her out of it.

"How will we find them? Do you know where you're going?" she yelled ahead, juking left and right astride Paw.

"Aye."

"How?"

"I've been here befar'."

"What? You know what this place is?"

"Aye. Home of yer ancestors. Long dead, they are. Still kickin', am I."

Titha cocked her head. "*My* ancestors? I've never even heard of this place! And just *when* were you last here?"

"I'd wager it's been on several hundred years now, lass. Told ye I was old, dinn'I? Yer folk aren't the only ones lingerin' round long past death's call."

"You're not just a shepherd, are you?" Titha asked, ducking below a collapsed beam as Paw bounded on.

"Never told ye I was, lass. Never told ye I was."

"That's *all* you told me!"

"Ye ask the wrong questions, then. I am a shepherd now, t'ru and t'ru. Disnae mean that's all I've e'er been, now doessit?"

"Guess not."

"Ne'er judge a stranger by his cloak, lass, for we all need one from time ta' time."

Kernos slowed his gallop. He tossed his staff from one hand to the other, tapping one of his horns with it a few times. "Aye, it has been ages since mine horns graced these halls," he thought aloud. "Left, ar' right, was it now?"

"You said you knew where you were going," Titha quipped impatiently. "This isn't the time to forget! My sister and friends are in here somewhere!"

"Shh! Lardie'be. Not so loud, sprite. Ye think we're alone in here, babblin' on like 'at?"

"I have no idea! I know precisely squat because that's all you've deemed worthy of sharing!"

"*Lard'be'mighty* do ye ever stop flappin' yer gums?" Kernos groaned back. "Now's not teh time! Pipe down—wait—Ah, there we go, lads. On this way, then. *Silently.*"

"He says as he continues to yell at me," Titha whispered to Paw, earning a needed smile. "Hurry up, would you?" she poked the Satyr.

Before Kernos could offer any sort of witty retort, a great raucous broke out down the hallway. Great wisping flashes of light, followed by familiar poofings of black and purple smoke, engulfed their destination without warning.

"I'd wager that's a right negative sign 'at we're headin the right a'way… You ready, lass?

"Oh, now I can talk? That's good, because that smoke ahead looks an awful lot like what we were chasing before we met you."

"Ye were chasin' smoke? Tell me ye weren't chasin' smoke—"

"No, smartie'arse, we weren't. We were chasing the villains responsible for it."

Kernos took a deep breath. "No idea what lies ahead, lads, but I doubt yer kin and the wee Viking'lad will be the first we come 'cross… so keep yer horns and hooves sharp, aye?"

"Aye," Titha pipped as she thumbed Feathersword. Paw grumbled, flicking his claws against the old stones, flinting their sharp edges. Ahead of them Kernos began to gallop, his crown of thick, curved horns pointed directly for danger. This was not lost on Titha, as she added it to her long list of reasons why she was glad to have Kernos back, even if he was the only being she'd ever met more stubborn than her ('that wasn't a Mae').

"Ack!" the Satyr called out suddenly, his stride cut short.

Titha watched as the flashes overtook the end of the hallway again. With each brim of light she could see Kernos' silhouette in a different pose, his breath heavy as he swished and swung his staff back and forth, it's crook occasionally swatting objects—each hit ringing out like someone flinged a rat flat onto wet rocks.

"Run, Mae. *Run*!" he cried back into the flashing light and dark. But Titha could barely understand the warning amidst increasingly intense blasts of black ash and white light. Everything had happened so fast! Her senses became overwhelmed, as did Paw's, and it was too late.

"Kernos?" she shouted, but there was no reply.

The flash-booming continued—accented only by Kernos' distant grunts—and it became clear to Titha that her valiant friend was overwhelmed by something, or someone, in the darkness. She called his name once more as she clutched ever-tighter to Paw, but no answers came except for battle-hardened grunts, *humphs* and the biting of gargling, gnashing teeth worn by battle.

"*Kernos*!" she cried out one last time, before another flash of cold light revealed a sight worthy of bringing silence to her dry throat.

From the cracks and corners of the hallway tiny hands and feet crawled into the noise. Each explosion revealed another grey creature, their skin barely hanging from bones; pale eyes reflecting each bright blast. One's hand shot up from the ground, grabbing Titha's leg.

"Let go!" she screamed, drawing Feathersword instinctively, before swinging it down below. *SCHLOP*! The scraggly arm flew clean off its host, a gargling cry echoing out into the hall. Another bony hand took her as the blasts strobed on, but she was too fast for this one, too. *SHRICK*! The hand cartwheeled into the stone wall, splatting with a thick *THUD*.

Paw roared below her as he swatted back creature after creature, but more kept at it. More and more hobbled in from each direction, until the flashing explosions revealed nothing but their eyes glitting in the darkness.

A hand shot out of pitch black to the back of Titha's neck, squeezing as the breath of something foul lingered up from behind her. Another hand took her ankle. Then another. Another tugged at her tunic. Then two more grabbed her hair, and a horrible, shrill, shriek left her mouth.

"*Kernos*!" she screamed. "*Kernos*, please! *Help*!"

No answer came.

"Help me!" she cried. "Paw! Do something!"

The seedy things began to crawl atop Paw, overtaking him, too. Grunts and groans burst from the bear, but even he could not best their sheer numbers. In one last-ditch, panicked effort, Paw threw all his weight backward, thrusting himself onto his hind legs with a gigantic, brumbling GRR*ROAR*.

It worked! Dozens of the creatures were sent flying from

his fur—but so was Titha.

"*No*!" she shrieked, terrified. "*Paw*!" *PAW*!"

Wrinkled grey hands filled her eyesight entirely before the flashing stopped, and all was taken over by the muffled, hurried sound of a hundred foul things dragging her away from her friends, then down, down, down into a place she'd never have wished on even the worst of Lunas back home.

CHAPTER SIXTEEN

Prisoner of the Past

"**This isn't so bad,**" Titha frowned, her hands rubbing together in thick darkness. "I don't mind being alone. Suits me fine. A badge of character, father says it is."

She wouldn't have been fooling anyone, if there were anyone around to fool. Her words were non-chalant, but her mind was practically scrambling itself with worry over Paw, Audun, Haldor, and especially Gilly. "Kernos, though, he can take care of himself," she thought aloud, her voice fading into pitch black. "I hope."

She took a seat, cross-legged within a moldy stone dungeon; not a window in sight. Nervously she thumbed Feathersword's hilt, the silver losing its warmth in the dampness. Down there, which she was certain to be the underground sort of dungeon, was much cooler; crisper. Sopped. Murky. Nothing to keep the ears busy but the plopping of water droplets.

"I'm coming for you, family. I promise," she whispered into her cell. But acknowledging the plight of her loved ones a'loud, while in a similar situation, was entirely too heavy a burden, and her attempt at chippering up flickered out. Was Paw in a stone hole, too? All alone in the pitch dark? Was Audun? Haldor? No. Surely not. Who, or what, could be so cruel as to put that sweet boy and those sweeter beasts in a place like this?

"They don't deserve this," she thought to herself, her eyes dampening. "None of them do. And it is all my fault." Those last six words ran through her mind in the voice of her older sister, which proved too much. "I'm sorry, Gillian. I really am…" Titha finally cracked under her decision to pursue what turned out to be the most-dangerous of whims.

A sniffle escaped her cold, rosy nose, before green eyes swelled as wet as the floor. She flinched as a tear hit the puddle beneath her knees, then looked to it, and was met by her own reflection rippling in crystal clear water. "Wait a minute," she thought, cocking her head. "I can see? I can see!"

Jumping to her feet, she looked about, amazed as the dim features of her cavernous cell finally faded into view. Behind her, the faintest glimmer of light broke through the top of the back wall. Not even the size of a snail's eyeball, was it, but that's all her nocturnal eyes needed.

Ahead, the dome of a doorway hovered in her sight, its worn stones barely visible. So there was a way out! Titha snapped her fingers, a smirk topping her chin. Maybe this wouldn't be so hard, after all. With a pep restored to her step she careened for the archway, long feet splashing each cold puddle along the way. As she neared the doorway, she drew Feathersword, twirling it once before *CLANG*—she hit something hard, landing flat on her backside before she knew what had happened. Titha shook her head, opening her eyes to the glisten of Feathersword before her on the ground, its blade resting right against a series of coiled, ornate black'iron bars. There was, it turned out, a door in said prison doorway. Go figure.

She reached up to rub her forehead, her fingertips meeting her mother's crown. "This thing has multiple uses," she thought aloud, bringing her fingers down to check for blood. "No purple, no problem!" she exclaimed, having done such a check on herself a thousand times before. There may have been no Lunish blood, but the ringing betwixt her ears was enough to remind her that there was, in fact, an iron door closing her into this room. She leaned down to retrieve her sword from its base, and as she picked it up, she was reminded of its heft. Perhaps it had as many purposes as her crown?

Titha felt the doorway over, running Feathersword along the edges of the iron bars. Its blade tripped, making a great racket. "Oops," she pipped, before trying to remove the blade. But it was stuck! She wiggled it back and forth—no give. "Huh…" she exhaled, tapping her chin. She took a step back, spat in her hands, rubbed them together like an otter with somewhere to be, then snatched Feathersword's hilt before yanking it sideways with all the strength her sproutly muscles could muster. Several pebbles bounced from the stonewall's hold on the door, and from there it only took a few more hefty prying-movements before *CLINK… CLANK…. Tink.* Something iron dropped to the floor!

"It's working!" she whispered to herself gleefully. She grabbed a'hold again, bending her knees a few times for good measure before *CLAAMMN*! A great racket shook the space outside her own.

Her eyes squinted as her highly sensitive vision was flooded with a flash of bright light, its harsh rays bouncing from every ancient stone. She flew back from the doorway, splashing into a puddle as the sound of footsteps filled the air. Everything was fuzzy and awful. She could barely see before, but now her eyes were positively useless. The echoes, however, were long and many, and her mind painted a vision of a hallway outside the iron bars; not just another room. Then, she heard it:

"Grooooouunnnt!" a massive beast cried out.

"Paw!" Titha spat with every fiber of her being, recognizing the grunt instantly. "Paw, my baby bear!" She cried, tears and saliva flying from her face as she shot for the door.

"Garrounng!" he replied with a strong, bludgeoning roar.

"Are you hurt? Did they hurt you?"

"Grorooooaan," he mumbled, a solid bear'ish 'no' to her.

"You're—you're okay!" Titha screamed, her body trembling. "I'm coming for you, do you hear me, baby boy? I'm coming for you right now! Don't do anything stupid until I get there!"

"*Grrroooooouuuuummmmn*!" he called back to her, his roar and the many footsteps of those carrying him now farther down the hall.

"I love you, too!" she screamed to him, her knuckles white around the black bars. "I… I love you, too…" she collapsed, shaking.

Slowly the sorrow in her bones was pumped away by a growing determination. Her heart pounded as she jumped to the right of Feathersword, its blade still levered between the iron door and the stone archway. She let out a hard scream;

frustration spilling forth into strength. Fiercely she yanked her weapon toward her, then pushed it away, creating a terrible, cratchety racket that could've woken the dead. She yanked more, pushing harder, then wrenched harder, then pushing even harder; all of her might culminating into one final ferocious, guttural scream as she flipped her hands around to re-grip the hilt before snatching it t'ward her in a Viking'esque rage. And it worked! The iron-barred door flung loose, bouncing against the opposite side of the doorway before slamming hard into her cell floor.

"Haha!" she exclaimed, clenching her sword in mirth. "This place has definitely seen better days."

Her head rang loud still, but her eyes cleared up. At some point someone must've closed the source of all that blinding light; the hallway was as dark as her cell now. "Works for me," she said to herself as she took her first step out into the wider space. The vision before her, however, allowed for no further words.

She stood dumbfounded as the tiny bit of light remaining bounced from one cell door to the next. The hallway seemed endless, its deep corridor curving 'round to the right; each side populated by barred door after door after door. She walked silently, cautious footsteps guiding her down a path she did not like at all, ears'a'ringing. The further along she went, the narrower the passage got, as if it was wrapping back around into its own spiral.

Eventually the piercing ring in her head was replaced by low squabble, and as her senses sharpened back up the dungeon came to life. A sort of low babbling chatter mixed with the scuffing and scoffing of feet and hands filled the hall—the occasional bark or growl peppering in. One grunt in particular, though, sounded enough like Paw to flutter her heart, and she froze...

"Paw? Brother bear, is that you?"

The grunting began again, but this time was far more frantic, almost painful in tambour.

"I'm on my way, okay?" she spoke through her hand, fingers covering her mouth. "Let me know where you are! Give me a bit more to work with. The faster I get to you, the faster we can get sis and the boys out o—"

A massive hand shot from iron bars to her left, snatching her tunic. Titha flinched, a gasp accompanying her right hand shooting immediately to her sword.

"Little girl!" the voice attached to the hand whispered harshly. His skin was pale—human! "Little girl, you must get me out of here, little girl! Please!"

"Who—who are you?" Titha stammered, half-drawing her weapon.

"Please, please, little one! Let me out of this place! I—I can help you! I am not your enemy. The enemy—the enemy is above us!"

"What do you mean?" she asked. She could hear the fear in his voice, even if it was as deep as the grunts of a wooly rhino. "What is this place?"

"I do not know, little one. In morning I am making the fires of my forge, then Autumnhill is panic, and I wake up in this cell!"

"You're from the 'hill?" she gasped. "I am looking for Audun Angvarsson and—"

"By the Gods, no!" the Vikingman growled, loosening his hold on Titha. "The Shieldmaiden's tiny son, he is trapped here? We must go to him! He must be safe from this evil place!"

The man stepped forward, showing the full girth of himself. He was an enormous grizzly of a Viking, a full bushy black beard covering most of his face and all of his neck. Titha immediately wondered how this gigantic man was trapped in one of these old cells if she herself was able to get out. Yet as her eyes adjusted to his silhouette, she could see his left arm was completely limp and dripping what was more than likely not water.

"You're hurt!" she said, gripping the bars of his cell door. "What is your name?"

"Bjor, little girl. I am Bjor. Honored Blacksmith to Sigrid, sons, and Skaldhall," he replied.

"I remember you… You sound so different down here."

"It is the pain, little one. The pain is great. I killed many of their little black beasts. To this, they did not take kindly. I was punished."

"That's horrible," she replied. "I'm so sorry they hurt you. Was it those nasty little crawling things?"

"No… it was the *feathered* ones…" Bjor shook. "Stronger than they look. In great numbers, very strong they become."

"The crawly-ones dragged me and my forest-brother down here," she added. "There are more of my kin in here, and I'm going to get them out—and you, too, okay? But I'm going to need help to do it," she continued as she shook the iron door, but it would not budge. This cell, unlike hers, was in much better condition. "Don't go anywhere," she huffed. "Sorry, I didn't mean it like— like that. Not the time. Clearly you can't go anywhere so—so I'll be right back with my bear."

"You has bear?" Bjor asked. "In here? Not what I expect, but is good! Hurry, little one, hurry!"

Titha scampered off. "I'll be back soon, Bjor! I promise!"

Her ears readjusted to the hallway, but there was no hint of animalistic grunting now. "Paw!" she cried out. "Now is not the time to suddenly develop the ability to stay quiet!"

Her sarcasm was met with a deep snort of air in the distance, but it was entirely too gruff to be Paw, she thought. It was definitely bear'ish, though. "Poor human probably thinks this place is full of monsters," she huffed, following the heavy breathing, "when all it is is one big fuzzybutt."

As she grew closer, the breath of an enormous beast blasted onto her right side. It came from the cell right before her! Her nocturnal eyes focused, and in the deep two nostrils flared, attached to the maw of a bear.

"That creature is ferocious, tiny girl!" Bjor shouted from far behind. "Stay back! Is not worth my life, child!"

"… Fuzzybutt? Is… that you?" she asked. She stepped forward to grab the bars, and a massive mauve tongue began licking her hands furiously. Her hands reached in to pet the bear, but as her fingers ran through its hair, she found it far too long, and far too course, to be Paw's. Its face rose, and one brown eye glinted back at her, the other staring blank; glazed over with a scar running from top to bottom of its face.

She knew this battle-worn face, too. She knew it immediately.

"… Arbor?" Titha asked slowly, a chill running up her spine. "Arbor, is that you?"

The bear nodded, his greyed hair glinting in what little

light she could see amidst thick clumps of clotted hair and scars. He let out a grunt before pressing his wide forehead onto the bars to be closer to her touch.

"... What... *happened* to you?" she asked, running her hand down his snout, heartbroken. He whimpered in reply, then flinched as the sound of footsteps drummed up behind him.

"Get back, you *wench*," a gruff voice commanded from the pitch dark of the cell. "Do what you will with me, but you shall not lay another claw on this bea... *By the Moon and Gods above....*" the voice continued, its timeworn rasp all too familiar to Titha's ears. "Titha Mae? Is that... is that you? Could it be?"

Through the dominating shadows a strong, wide figure stepped forth, his head thick with white hair, the moustache below just as thick and white. Titha flinched, snatching her hands back as Arbor lumbered from view, revealing a faint face she hadn't seen in seasons, and didn't expect she'd ever see again.

"... *Cypress*?" she guffed. "What... *why*?"

"For Gaela's sake, child, does your mischief know no end?" the figure returned, stiff arms waving about. It was Cypress, indeed. "What in oblivion are you doing down here?" he continued. "Answer swiftly, you have not time for more."

"... I don't even know where to begin. You... you're here. *Here*, here. In the Ruins?"

This was all terribly confusing. The elder Luna was like family for her entire childhood, yet her left shoulder still bore the thick, tragic scar of his treachery.

"Titha, this is no place for you. You must believe me when I say you are in grave, terrible danger. A danger far too horrendous for idle chat in the spiral of this dungeon. You must leave. Now."

"Well I have way too many questions to do that. No one has seen or heard from you since—"

"Since my exile?" he interrupted. "Your curiosity will have to wait," Cypress shushed back, still dumbfounded. "I am in here of my own making. I do not wish to see you suffer the same fate."

"I... can't leave," she spoke softly, holding her left arm. "Not yet. Not until I find Gilly, Paw, and the others."

Cypress stomped to the front of the cell, slamming his hands onto the bars. "How many of you are in here?" he demanded. "It is worse than I feared... has your father been captured? What of our people?"

"No, just me and Gilly, and Paw. And Audun and his dog, Haldor."

Cypress said nothing, choosing to glare down at her instead. "I see," he finally muttered. "So the company you keep has not changed."

"Wow," she returned, wide-eyed. "Nice to hear you haven't changed, either... Pathetic. Really pathetic. And to think I was just... so happy to see you. To find you. I don't know why."

He settled, returning her still gaze.

"Because we are family, child. Regardless of our disagreements or beliefs, we will always be family."

"No. Family trusts each other, Cypress. Family doesn't betray one another. I'll never *trust you* again. Not after what you did to us. To father. He was heartbroken after you left. So was I. We *all* were. You betrayed us and our people."

"I am not the betrayer, young one, nor do we have time for this same tired argument!" His pointed ears began to twitch, followed by Titha's. "Footsteps," he whispered. "They're coming back! Quick, you must free us. It is the only way for you to survive what is coming without Paw! Arbor is too weak, he cannot break these bars! They have… hurt him, and others."

"Who has?" Titha asked.

"A discussion worth having once time allows! How many times must I say it, child? Now is not the time for—"

"Alright, alright! But we are not leaving this dungeon without my sister, Paw, and our friends. *Human* friends who are *also* suffering. Deal?"

"No further harm will come to your sister, nor any of our people trapped in here. That I can guarantee."

"Or the *humans,* Cypress. It's all or nothing. Unless you'd prefer I leave you where I found you."

"… Alright," he finally coughed under his breath.

"Alright what?"

"Alright, I will also help free your… *friends.*"

"That's a good boy," Titha smirked. "We'll need to retrieve Paw first, so he can hold you two accountable whenever you choose to stab us in the back. Again."

"Your sense of humor remains intact. Good," he groaned. "You'll need it."

"Uh huh," she mumbled as she drew Feathersword. "I was able to pry my door open, is yours loose enough to do the same?"

"I have had no weapon for many Moons, child," Cypress revealed, placing his hands on his wide, scruffy face. "If I had, would I still be in here, do you think?"

"Well, lucky for you," Titha smirked as she jutted her blade, jamming it between the iron and stone, "I have mine."

Cypress coughed, caught off guard, before stumbling backward onto Arbor. As Titha wedged her weapon betwixt iron and stone, the distant footsteps rang louder, then louder still from a'top of the winding hallway.

"Faster, child!" Cypress commanded.

"You are in no position to be making demands of me, like, ever. Step up or shut up," she hushed back, her arms prying as hard as they might.

"What are those markings? Here, on your father's feather?" Cypress asked, looking to the new hilt on her sword as he pulled at the bars in tandem.

"They're Celtican," she answered as she worked, her tongue flitting as busily as her sword.

"Those are not the marks of your mother," he retorted, pulling the bars harder.

"No—they're not!" She huffed one last time, before *CLAGSH*! The door flung from the stones and into Cypress' grasp.

"Celtica is a city. A lot of good things have happened in your absence," she replied, twirling the blade before placing it back in its equally dashing silver hilt. "Imagine that."

"Oh, I am *overly* aware of your little camp between Ythengrey and Autumnhill," Cypress scoffed as he threw the iron bars to the back of his cell, Arbor dodging them with a worn-down harrumph. "But I refuse to refer to it by the hallowed name of your mother—" He paused, his words cut short by the faint glint of the light purple stone on Titha's forehead. "That, treasure, however, is *undoubtedly* of your mother's grace…" He walked up to her in the archway, his stubby finger landing onto her forehead. "How… odd to see it again… *Here*. After all this time."

Titha, with all her thoughts gripped by the urge to rescue her kin, muffled by the shock of Cypress' presence, had completely forgotten what she wore on her brow. She swatted Cypress away, then jilted to the silver crown, the amethyst's single spiral swirling underneath her touch.

"Mother's circlet... Yes," she said. "Father gave it to me."

"Curious timing, indeed," Cypress replied, tapping his chin as he led his injured Bear-brother out the narrow doorway.

"Arbor, look at you. You poor thing," Titha frowned, looking him over as best she could. "You're limping!" She stroked his cheek, her heart breaking for him.

"He is as brave a warrior as any to ever suffer these dungeons," Cypress lamented. "He has suffered much for our cause."

"You mean your *mistakes*," Titha scoffed. "Hope whatever you've been up to down here was worth this. Look at him!"

"Keep your voice down, child. This way! Further into the spiral," Cypress replied, grabbing her arm as he led her away from still-approaching footsteps. They weren't particularly heavy or numerous, but remained unidentified which, in a dungeon, was cause for concern, nonetheless.

"There are many entrances to this place," he added, looking about. "But only one exit."

Titha scurried along with her old mentor, her mind foggy simply from his presence. Where to even start?

"You still haven't told me why you're down here," she asked. A solid place to begin questioning, surely.

"Do you wish for the simple answer, or the truth?" he offered, not breaking his stride or gaze.

"Both," she replied without hesitation.

"Very well," he frowned. "By now you must understand the origins of the Ruins you walk within, do you not?"

"I saw the spiral symbol upon our entrance, but our people do not build with stone, nor do they use that symbol anymore, and now you're also here, so it's a lot to take in."

"Lunish hands made marvels of quarry long before humans stole the source of said stone, the artform itself, and the *very air we breathe*. You are in the ruins of our people, Titha. The first kingdom of Lunas. This very ruin, in all its majesty, is the last remaining castle of our great ancestors. *My* ancestors, specifically. These are the Ruins of *Byle*, child, from the very beginning of the First Eon." He yanked her arm harder, hastening their pace. "Quickly now."

Titha grunted, keeping her ears perked for the sound of any other bears, but found it hard to hear over the heavy breathing of poor Arbor. As she looked into each cell, she found most empty (so far as she could tell, anyway). It wasn't hard to imagine others imprisoned here thinking they were all alone, like she did. The spiral went on, and on, and on still.

Cypress marched forth, dragging her as he spoke; unaffected by the possibility of any strangers being of consequence.

"In my exile I have returned to my roots, child," he continued to her, quietly. "It was not a hard decision to make after your father saw fit to toss an Eon's worth of progress to the wolves, banishing me from our forest home. Yet where this once brought me great anger, I soon found the purpose—great purpose—it presented within me. Your family's *desecration* of our people's hallowed haven allowed me to fully embrace the past; to reclaim our history, and to truly see unto the ends of all possible outcomes. That is, until I unleashed the *truth*." The heft in his voice cracked, and he cleared his throat as he looked straight ahead. "I wished to save our people from the greatest fallacy of the mortal world—from Gaela's gravest failing—*mortal death*. But that was before the awakening… before I saw… the *other side*. I met one who walks the *Otherworld*, Titha Mae; one that holds all the answers to which I sought."

"Riiiiight," Titha returned, rolling her eyes.

"Believe you me, I did not think it could be true at first, either. No more than you do now, child. But then… I was *shown*. I was shown horrible things."

"Elaborate, please," she exhaled, raising an eyebrow.

"I was right, Titha Mae. *I am right*. The Mae's—*your family's* dismantling of our ancient forest's shrouded Time is of terrible consequence. For I was shown, child, that Death is real. Life is finite. And its end now comes for all Lunas."

"Charming," Titha quipped in return, her feet slapping the wet pathway as she scanned for any other signs of life. "But no one lives forever… Not even Lunas. We know this already. So what are you leaving out?"

"That the fairy tales are indeed fairy tales, young one. Not all are born equal, and not all will share the same fate in Death, just as we do not in Life. And only those who know the way shall walk into the afterlife."

"And the way is?"

"Sacrifice."

"*So it was you*?" Titha jerked back, stopping abruptly. "*You are behind all of this*! How could you!?" she screamed.

"What?" he clapped. "Keep your voice down!" he

shushed, the footsteps behind now hastening.

"Sacrifice, huh?" she spat back. "Was she worth it? Was Calluna Mint worth it, you nasty, putrid slug of a—"

Her fists started flying, pounding the frayed white rags Cypress wore. Arbor grunted, bounding backward in confusion as Cypress defended himself.

"What—are you—*stop*, child! *Stop*! What of Calluna? What of her?"

"Her death was all for your noble cause, right? It's okay for Lunas to die if you *need* them to! Sacrifice? *Sacrifice*? You hypocrite! You fiend! You *villain*!"

"Calluna... is dead?" Cypress asked, his blood running cold.

"Oh, please. Drop the act! How could you? *How could you?*"

Cypress' eyes shot wide from behind brows that rarely revealed them. "Who did this? *How*?" He grabbed Titha's shoulders, his words now as frantic as her own. "*Tell me!*"

Titha's arms shot up, breaking her old mentor's grasp. "I can't believe I let you out of that cell!" she screamed. "I should have let you *rot* in there like you *deserve*!"

Behind them the pitter-patter grew to a fever-pitch, and the racket drew dangerously close. Arbor roared boarishly, nudging his old nose between the feuding Lunas. But it was of no use. Cypress fended off Titha's flickering fists, both oblivious to the approaching demons of the dark. Arbor, however, was gravely aware. He careened around, slamming his huge paws into the stone floor with all that was left within him. A great, gurgling roar spat forth from his maw; teeth and gums jutting. Suddenly, and appropriately, all pitter-pattering ceased. Soft, tiny chatter replaced it, followed by an inaudible shout. With it, the marching continued.

"They're here," Cypress decreed, turning about. "Do you know how to use that blade, little one?"

"So far," Titha replied, slashing Feathersword from its hilt. She ran to Arbor's side, brandishing the silver like a seasoned warrior. Those that approached, however, knew that she was not. Or they carried no fear. Either way, it was a fight they sought. And a fight they were granted.

Arbor lunged forward, his gigantic face biting into the crowd of hurried creatures. He flung them about, one mauled individual landing before Titha. She looked to it, then to its mobbing brethren—and the horror of being dragged down deep into the dungeon resurfaced. She could hear the defeated voice of Bjor in the back of her head, warning her of their strength in numbers—something she, too, had experience with. Yet this time, unlike before, they charged directly for her. She could see their faces! THUD! Another mauled grey figure landed before her—and as its lifeless face rolled over… *Sifters*! They weren't just horrid little crawling, grabby things—they were Sifters! Hundreds upon hundreds of them. Yet no life filled their eyes, not like the mischevious ones she'd met in the Wick. These creatures… it was as if they had crawled from their graves.

"If you're just going to stand there then toss me the bloody sword!" Cypress yelled, his trunk-like fists pounding the face of each Sifter that gnashed his way.

Titha shook off her shock. She jumped over the deceased, and before she knew it found herself screaming ferociously as she hacked and slashed her way through the onslaught.

"You"—*THWACK*—"Took"—*SCHLUMP*—"My"—

SHRIKT—"Sister!"—THRIMP!

The head of a particularly gangly Sifter flew clean off, flying up and over Arbor. "And *my brother bear*!" Another head flew. "And —my—*best—friend*!" *CLOP!* One more for good measure careened to Cypress' feet.

"By the Moon's Light I didn't think you had it in you, girl!" Cypress laughed as he lifted one Sifter to slam it into another. "Fight on, Titha Mae—*Fight on*!"

And fight she did. With every swing of her sword another foul Sifter fell, and in the shadows of her ancestor's dungeon she became the spitting image of her mother—circlet, ferocity, and all.

But it was not to last.

"There's too many of them!" Titha screamed, more making their way down the hall's curve than she could cut down. Amongst them small, black figures began to scratch through, their unexpected emergence tipping the scales in favor of the vile.

"What are these? More vermin?" Cypress cried out. Soon he, too, was overwhelmed. Yet as he pummeled these new threats, his fists became covered with down, not blood.

"Black feathers?" he cried out, tripping backward. "No! No! Not again!"

Arbor looked to his Lunish kin, the sudden fear in his brother's eyes shining within pitch black. Then back to the horde he turned, growling voraciously as he reared to his hind legs. Down he came, slamming his full weight into the foul beings, sending all manner of critters flying. Gargling yelps and cries erupted, but the great forest bear did not cease. Their screams only elevated his tenacity.

"With me, now!" Cypress trumpeted above the mess.

"No! We cannot leave him! Not like this!" Titha cried.

"He has made a choice, Titha Mae! One that is not ours to waste! If these gangly imps consume us all there will be no escape for *any*—we shall not get another chance!" Cypress shoved her away, making sure she was off and running before he turned from Arbor.

"This is not your last, my brother!" he shouted to his beloved bear. "Do unto them what they have wrought upon you! To their ends, mighty beast! To their ends!"

Arbor let loose another calamitous cry, then swatted the entire front line of creatures back from whence they came. A smile replaced his grimace; focus taking his rage. If this was to be his last stand, it was to be grand.

A silent "thank you" left Titha's lips, and the darkness of the dungeon consumed her once more as she barreled deeper into its bowels with the most unlikely of allies.

CHAPTER SEVENTEEN

Darker Things

"**Who's there?"** Gillian shouted. She, too, had found herself imprisoned in a dark stone cell. But not alone.

"What do you hear?" Audun asked, huddled close to Haldor. "Is someone coming?"

"I'm not sure yet. Whatever it is, I think it is close... maybe on the other side of the wall," Gilly replied. "I hear—it's like a knocking. I can almost make out a..."

"... A what?"

"A muffled voice! Someone's in there! There must be a room next to ours! Hello!?" Gilly screamed. A reply came, but she could not make it out.

"I can't hear anything!" Audun shouted.

"Here! The sound is coming from here!" Gilly exclaimed, her keen ear pressed against the stone wall. "Ugh, this wall is disgusting—I hate fungus and—Oh! This old, rock is loose! It's letting the sound through. Maybe if I push… on it…"

As she tried to shove the stone, a stronger force shoved back, and the slag shot straight from the wall in front of her face before shattering on the floor. Two long arms withdrew back through the hole before words accompanied them.

"Uh, uhm, hello?" a melodic voice asked, its pleasant tone bouncing into their cell. "I can't, lords I truly cannot see a thing down here with my, my old eyes. Can you, stranger whom I have so wondrously discovered?"

Gilly gave a sideways glance thru the opening. She knew that voice. It was another Luna! But it couldn't be who she thought it was. No harm in asking, though, right?

"Mister Fernbloom?"

"Ah! Correct, young lady, correct. And who, ah, who might you be? Could that be the sweet voice of Gillian Rose I hear?"

"Yes! Yes! It's me!" she chirped frantically.

"Fantastic!" the voice replied. "Simply fantastic. What are the odds, really?"

"Audun! I know him! It's Mister Fernbloom! From Yythengrey!"

"Woah!" he replied, flabbergasted with pretty much everything at this point. "Ask him if he can get us out of here."

"No, uh, no-can-do tiny fella, I'm afraid," Fernbloom responded, his voice downtrodden. "I seem to be just as stuck and, ah, hopeless as you twittling sprouts. Curse these ancient yet, if I may say so myself, finely made iron bars."

"Agreed. Uh huh. Listen, I will be right back, alright?"

Gilly offered into the high opening between their cells.

"Sure, sure, ah, take your time. I don't seem to be going anywhere, currently," Fernbloom replied, before waving himself down into the humming of a familiar Lunish melody.

"Who *is* this guy?" Audun asked Gilly as she stepped down to him. "What a weirdo."

"That's... that's Clover's father," she replied, dumbfounded.

"Oh no!" Audun chirped back. "Wait, that is bad, right? Is he a bad seed like Clover?"

"I don't know yet! Should I ask him about his son, y'know, helping murder our teacher?"

"Is that why he's in here, you think? Surely he knows?"

"I—I don't know, I don't know! Do I mention it to him?"

"Why are you asking me?"

"Because you're the smart one! That's your thing, right? You're super smart?"

"I am smart enough to know you are wasting time, Gillian! Please do *something*!" Audun frowned, waving her toward the hole in the wall.

"Titha's not here, Audun. You don't have to act all tough. I genuinely think you're smart."

"Thanks, but I'm being serious, too. You are stalling. And I know you think your sister bullies me, but she doesn't. She pushes me to do more, to see more, and to be more. I've learned a lot from Titha, and I think you could, too. Like right now she would be asking this guy questions so we could get out of here, not stalling because she's uncomfortable with the consequences."

"Wow..." Gilly blinked. "Okay then."

Haldor agreed, marked by a singular, sharp bark.

"Goodness gracious me, young wola! You, uhm, you seem to have a, a hound in there with you. How peculiar. And is that small voice human, or am I simply growing delirious among all this remarkably identical moss?"

"Great job, he is human. Remarkable. Mister Fernbloom, though, sir, may I ask why you're in here?" Gillian stumbled, struggling to find the right words.

"Now there's a fine question, young wola. Ah, yes. I've been pondering this myself, you see, with all the time I've had within these stone walls and, uhm, I must say—No. No, I have no idea. Though, hey! Yes, hey! I would ask you about my son, Clover. I seem to recall you two getting rather close, am I right? I am very, very worried about him and his demeanor as of late. Very gloomy, very non-committal, and such, and I would talk to him about it but blast if I did not wake up in a dungeon some evening past."

Gillian smacked her head. She leaned down to Audun. "He has no idea!" she whispered to him, rolling her eyes from the speech she just endured.

"Tell him!" Audun replied, his patience gone, too. "If he's lying it'll come out if you just tell the truth. This feels like a time to tell the truth!"

"Right. Yeah, okay," she stumbled again, rising back up to Fernbloom. "Listen, sir, Clover's been acting strangely because he's gotten into a really big mess. With the wrong people, and—"

"The truth, Gillian. The truth!" Audun clenched.

"Clover conspired with a human to help murder our teacher, Calluna Mint, then half-blew up Skaldhall before fleeing with said murderer into the Southlands," she spat out all at once before gasping for air. "There… that meet your approval, twerp?"

"Yes," Audun smiled from atop Haldor.

"Well that is, ah, definitely not what I expected to hear," Mister Fernbloom replied, rubbing his eyes beneath ancient, cracked glasses.

"Hi, I'm Audun," the young Viking added, popping up from Haldor's back into the hole as he shoved Gillian aside. "I'm friends with the Maes."

"Oh, ah, hello young Man—"

"—We do not know if your son, Clover, did the murdering, or if he was involved willingly, or if he was forced to partake, but now that I think of it this could explain why you are trapped inside this dungeon here, as well. In the Ruins."

"You think so?" Fernbloom pondered.

"I do. I think you may be here as—co-uhm-collateral."

"Ah, well, I see. That is… very unfortunate as well," the elder Luna replied, utterly defeated. He scratched the stubble on his face again. "But who would do such a thing to, to such a quiet one? To my only boy? To my, my pride and joy?"

"That's how we ended up here, sir. To find the answer to that question, too," Audun answered sincere. "But things took a turn for the worse."

"There's an understatement," Gilly added. "We think Clover is here somewhere, sir. He told us as much. He told us he had to come back here or he'd be killed, or worse."

"And the worse is probably *you* being killed. To make him do as he's told." Audun added.

"I wonder if the others in here, if they're all here as

collateral, too," Fernbloom added.

"The others?" Gilly asked. "Who else is in here? More of our people?"

"My people?" Audun pipped in.

"Both, both, I'm afraid. Something very large, and very, very *dark* is afoot, my younglings. Something foul, indeed."

"If it is any consolation, we really did try to get Clover out of it," Audun said, still peeking into the hole. "Or Titha did. We wanted to help, so, I hope your son is alright. Titha, too."

A great roar careened down the hallway with perfect timing. Its bellow was not threatening, however, but longing. Sad, almost.

"Ah, yes, see? What'd I tell you. Bad, very bad, scary things," Fernbloom stuttered.

"That sounds like a forest bear," Gilly said. She hopped down from the wall and ran to the iron bars, trying to make light of the darkness. Another curious roar bounded down the stonework; this one far too close for comfort.

"If it's a bear then it sure is moving fast!" Audun spoke with wide eyes. "Can you see anything?" he asked blindly. "I can't see a thing down he—"

A great blast of black fur shot past their doorway, its side rattling the bars, knocking Gillian clean into Haldor's snout. The pup whimpered, then nuzzled Gillian to her feet before darting for the iron, barking frantically.

"What is it, boy?" Audun asked.

Haldor returned even more frantic vocalizations, his howl nearly recognizable as Westlyn speech. As he continued, the bounding beast in the hallway came to a stop, returning several grunts and groans. Haldor's tail wagged wildly. A massive ball of fur slammed onto the door's gate, and there two beasts stood licking one another with reckless, loving abandon.

"Paw!" Gillian screamed, pushing Haldor aside. "Oh, Gaela, is that really you, you mush of a bear?" she cried. Paw nodded his head jovially, looking them over. "How did you escape? How did you find us? Wait… *where's Titha*? Is she not with you?"

Paw's head lowered, a heart-wrenching moan leaving his muzzle.

"She has to be alright," Gillian's hands shook as she spoke. "Tell me our sister is okay, Paw."

He gave a defeated shrug, as if to say he hoped so, but wanted to know the same. He grunted a few more bearish syllables, urging his trapped kin to join in his search for her.

"Get us out of here, now!" Gillian growled. "We are going to find her."

Her Bear-brother nodded, then took a few steps back.

"Paw, you might want to wait for us to get out of the way—" Gilly screamed before the bars came crashing in. Haldor snatched her from its path, placing her up against the wall. A faint "thanks" escaped her lips before a massive exhale.

Paw jumped into the cell, bounding and hopping about as his tiny stump of a tail wagged vigorously. Kisses for all, he brought, as well as a glimmer of hope.

"Fantastic!" Fernbloom spouted from his cell. "Absolutely so! Say, Bear-brother, care to, ah, free another Lunish prisoner?"

Paw cocked his head. He looked to Gilly for advice, and she didn't hesitate to give the signal. Paw thrusted his heft through the already-cracked wall, prompting thoughts that this place was built long before Luna's forged such strong bonds with such strong beasts.

Fernbloom dusted himself off, removing his glasses, de-smudging them.

"Really impressive, my bear friend, sincerely. Wow. Just wow," he added, shaking his head. Then he turned to them, not stepping through the gaping void. "Hey, kids, listen, about that thing you told me," he continued. "There's someone, ah, I definitely think you should meet," he hummed, glazed over.

From behind Fernbloom a figure approached, cloaked in absolute shadow. As the rotund form stepped forth into Lunish view, it took on the shape of someone Gillian could've sworn she recognized.

"You," she muttered. "You're him. You're the stranger from Celtica!"

Paw and Haldor both lunged down into pouncing position, growling angrily.

Audun was more frustrated now than ever before that he could barely see in such conditions, but he wasted no time. "Pin him to the floor, boy," he commanded of Haldor.

"Please, please! Let me speak!" the Stranger replied.

Gilly looked his unusually plain face over. Sparse facial hair dotted rosy, rounded cheeks, and made for just as non-intimidating of a visage now as it did the moment she first saw him—right after Mint's murder.

"I... am not... what you think I am," the Stranger said slowly, approaching with his hands up.

Gilly paused to hear him out, but the beasts were not having it. "Let him speak, boys," she demanded, waving them down. "Go on, stranger. But I warn you, one wrong word and these two get to do with you what they will."

"Ah, that's, uh, rather gruesome for a young lady," Fernbloom muddled in.

"It is alright, Lunish friend. It is alright," the round Man replied. "Listen to me carefully, you must. I did not murder your kin, the one called Calluna Mint. But I know the one who did. And he is here, in this very dungeon! We are all on the brink of sacrifice! By *his* hand!"

"Spare me the cryptics!" Gilly shouted. "Who murdered Calluna Mint?"

"It was… your old mentor," he continued, flinching as Paw and Haldor growled on. "Please, please! You must listen… For it was the master of these Ruins… The Ruins of Byle. *Cypress… Silvanus… Byle.*"

Gilly shuttered at the thought. "He wouldn't," she added, her mind at war with itself. "Killing one of our kin goes against everything he's ever said, believed, or done."

Yet as the Stranger drew nearer to Gilly, his expression changed. She raised her right hand to stop his advance, and a particular glistening stone caught his eye. A blank stare took him over. The worry of his words seemed to leave him completely as his focus shifted solely to Gillian's right hand.

"My, my…" he mumbled. "Such a… beautiful ring. Where, may I ask… *did you get that*?"

Gilly snatched her hand back, utterly creeped beyond her threshold.

"Now you can eat him, boys," she spat, waving the beasts forward.

"Wait, wait, wait!" the man screeched, his body recoiling. "I am but a blacksmith's apprentice! I sincerely wish to know! It is such a fine piece!"

"It was my mother's, you creep," Gillian replied. She looked to Audun, motioning that it was about time to make an abrupt exit.

"Ah, yes, Thea Celtica Mae," Fernbloom bustled in, musing of the past. "Boy, I tell you, if you think that ring is beautiful, fella, you should've seen her mother. What a sight, what a sight, what—a—sight—she was."

"Your… mother… is Thea?" the Stranger asked, head tilted and eyes glossed over.

"Was," Gilly stepped back. "She passed away."

"Oh yes, oh yes. Terrible tragedy, long ago," the Stranger replied.

"You didn't know my mother," she barked, grabbing a'hold of Paw's fur as he rumbled.

"On the contrary, little girl," the stranger hissed. "*I know her better than you.*"

With those words the man flung himself forward in a great blast of black smoke—his arms outstretched for Gillian as his jaw gaped to inhuman proportions; a ghastly scream leaving a beak-like mouth. Gilly shrieked as Paw lunged for the Stranger, but he passed straight through him as if he were smoke. The horrifying figure's eyes began to glow, illuminating the cell around them. Haldor pounced for the specter next, but *piffed* straight through, too, landing face first on Paw in the corner. Gilly let loose another hair-curling scream, but it was no use. The man, or what they had been led to believe was one, pinned her against the wall. She threw a knee directly into his stomach, proving that not all of him was smoke, before instinct had her sliding down and across the wet stone floor with nimble legs. She turned around to deliver a punch to the Stranger's unbearably hideous face, but as she did her fist was met with another poof of black smoke. Her hand passed through it, careening directly into the stone wall. An awful crack shook her knuckles, then the bones of her hand, before she grabbed it, screaming in pain. As her agony echoed through the chamber, the cold light of the specter's eyes left the room, and he vanished.

"I, uh, did *not* see that coming," Fernbloom gulped, firmly huddled into the opposite corner. "Are you alright, Gillian dear? Your hand, it, ah, it must be broken, you poor darling."

She snatched away as he reached for her. "I'll be fine," she said, her words as hard as the stone that shattered her right-hook. "Get up, Mister—what is your first name, anyway?"

"Marigold, dear. Marigold Fernbloom. And I thank you, sincerely, young lady. Thank you. I can see now, yes, why Clover speaks so highly of you."

"Sure. That's great. Now get up. We've got to find my sister before that *thing* does."

"Say, ah, here's a thought I'm having," he replied, waving his pointer finger to Audun and the boys. "Why don't you more, how do I say, appropriately suited fellows head on into the dangerous thing you just mentioned, and let me take a look about for my son, hm? If he's here I'd, well, I'd like to know that for myself."

"Go for it," Gilly scoffed, completely exhausted of the man's eccentric tone. She flinched, grabbing her right hand. "Definitely broken," she gritted.

"Let me help you with that," Audun offered. He reached over to Fernbloom, grabbing the ragged yellow scarf from his neck.

"That is pure dusk'worm silk!" he hocked. "My wife made, ah, made that for me, so—please, Lords alive, don't get blood on it! She will kill me."

"I think you've got bigger problems, guy," Audun pipped as he wrapped the truly nice scarf around Gilly's wrist and hand as best he could in darkness. "You are not exactly in our good graces right now, Mister Marigold," Audun said sternly, his little voice packing a punch. "So if you would like to change that, then please tell us anything you know—and start with any details that will lead us out of this dungeon so we can find our friend—before you run off to find your son."

"I, ah, have none of those details, unfortunately," Fernbloom replied, "But I am inclined to notice, my dear, that your, uhm, that precious ring you so valiantly defended is now gone from the hand your human friend is wrapping. Does that help?"

"What?" Gilly coughed. Her violet eyes shot to the ring finger on her right hand, and her heart dropped through her gut. "It's gone..." she murmured, pulling back the scarf. "He took it! That creep took it!"

"Moon's Light, that is, that is awful. Never can trust a ghoul, now can you?" Fernbloom twiddled.

Gillian threw her fists to her sides, screaming an awful sound that turned into a growl once her broken hand made contact with bony hip.

"Let's go, boys!" she shouted through her pain. "You, too, Marigold, and if we do find your son you can tell him that we are most definitely no longer a thing, because I am never speaking to that, that *rat'fink* again! This is *all* his fault!"

"Uh, ah—noted, young lady."

"So you *were* dating!" Audun pipped.

"I was thinking about it, okay? But I'm certainly not now!" she squealed as she stormed out the entrance to their cell, holding her wrapped hand. Audun felt his way onto Haldor, and as he had done many times before Paw led them out of the darkness, and into certain trouble.

CHAPTER EIGHTEEN

What Once Was

"**Let me get this straight,**" Titha soured, taking a breath as the dungeon finally quieted down. "Everything that has happened these past few Nights and Days in Celtica, you know nothing of what's going on? At all?"

"I do not," Cypress replied sincerely.

"And I am supposed to believe that you don't?" she followed.

"Indeed," he answered. "Though, from what you tell me it sounds rather… fitting. But I know nothing. I have been down here many more Moons than just those few of late, and far longer than I anticipated."

"Right. Well, I'm sure you understand my hesitance to believe you. Or take your word on anything. Ever again."

"Oh, my little Titha Mae. If only you knew the truth, it

would be *me* that you confided in, not your Companions. Not even your father, I am afraid. There is so much you do not know."

"Then tell me," Titha demanded. "This pit of a place is never-ending," she said as she flipped a flat rock down the hall, its echo vast. "We've got the time, unfortunately."

"That is not my place," Cypress returned.

"Right. Seems it is no one's. I'm learning that real fast."

"You will learn, in time, child, that *some things are better kept secret.*"

Suddenly the rock's ricocheting echo stopped. Titha's sharp tone was cut short, too, and the Lunas froze, looking to one another. Cypress held a finger up to his mouth, shushing Titha as they proceeded as quiet and as swift as Children of Night could ever be.

Light broke from the top of the hall in the opposite direction; the same cold light that had filled it before. Were they trapped?

"*Where is she*?" a thin but powerful voice shot down the hall. A deeper one replied, but Titha could only hear it as guttural mumbles, as deep and far off as they were. The gruff voice then turned to a very-human, painful scream.

"Bjor!" Titha cried out before immediately covering her mouth.

"Fool of a girl!" Cypress clenched.

Titha could feel the air shift as whatever tortured Bjor dropped his body. He was no longer its concern. Now it came for her.

Grey limbs began to ooze from the tiny offshoots of the

spiral hallway. One on top of the other, Sifters poured out of the stonework, their chattery, indistinct mutterings echoing downhill to wary ears.

Titha jumped to the middle of path, looking both directions in the faint but still illuminated dungeon hall.

"Is there another way out?" she questioned.

"No!" Cypress barked. "I told you as much! That entrance is the only way in or out unless you are one of *those* things!" He clamored about, rooting for a loose stone to use as a weapon as the Sifters grew closer. They carried with them a swift, terrible sound this time; like a hurricane battering rocky cliffs.

"You wished to know more, Titha Mae," Cypress said as he tossed a large stone from one hand to the other. "I believe you are to get your wish sooner than expected."

Swirling black smoke turned the round corners toward them, hundreds of tiny grey hands and feet flickering as they crawled the walls and floor in its foggy mass. At its center, a pale face marked by bright yellow and red eyes came for them faster than anything that had threatened either before.

A few particularly fast Sifters scraggled ahead, leaping for Cypress. He wielded his found-stone like a hammer, jamming it into the brittle bones of each that threatened their survival. Yet a familiar voice to his ears, a voice of smoke and fear, was enough to make him drop the stone altogether.

"*Give it to me*!" the black mass hissed, more purple wisps leaving its maw as it barreled toward them.

"No stone nor blade will piece that *thing*, Titha," Cypress shouted above swirling air.

"What—what does it want?" Titha questioned.

"Something that never should have been brought here."

"Give it to me!" it hissed again.

Its eyes were alarmingly terrifying in themselves; pitch black, tiny pupils scorched Titha's soul as their yellow irises expanded into blood red eyeballs. It was entirely unrecognizable to her as a lifeform, which made it all the more gruesome to behold.

"I have reasoned with it before," Cypress yelled to Titha above the storm the ghoul produced. "Perhaps I can do so again." He pushed Titha behind him, guarding her with one arm. The other arm snatched her mother's circlet clean off her head.

"What are you doing?" she screamed.

"Giving it what it wants," Cypress shouted, his moustache wavering in the oncoming winds. "So that you may live."

"No! Give it back, Cypress. *Give it back!*" Titha yelled, her voice hard and desperate as she fought his wide arm.

"There is no other way!" he cried, the ghoul's black smoke rolling faster and harder toward them. "It is the circlet or your life!"

With little effort he threw her further down into the spiraling hallway. She screamed again, jumping to her bare feet.

"You liar!" she scolded, spit flying from a furious jaw.

"Stop!" Cypress shouted, his circlet-wielding hand shooting forward. Like a great shield, it stopped the swirling smoke in its tracks. Sifters screeched as they bumbled over one another to halt with what plainly appeared to be their current 'master'.

"Give it… to me…" the mass thundered; repeating the only words it seemed capable of uttering in its guttural tongue.

"Cypress, please," Titha pleaded one last time. "That's all I have left of mother."

"*Give… it… now*!" the mass thundered.

Cypress turned to her. "If you are to free your sister and escape this place, child," he whispered to her, "Then you must trust me. You will see, when all the pieces have fallen, that I have always done my best to protect you."

"This isn't an option!" Titha shouted, despair filling her. She drew Feathersword, swinging its weight upward. She aimed its point to his throat, unwavering. Cypress stared into her green eyes, calling her bluff.

Its patience exhausted, the black mass whooshed upward as if a wave, its middle opening like the elongated mouth of a deep sea creature as its eyes shone brighter than ever.

Cypress smiled an uncomfortable smile. "I have always done my best…" he spoke again, a calm taking him over as the smoke engulfed him, "… to protect you."

The cloud and its pale face sucked violently inward as a great flash of light erupted. Stones of the walls, floor, and ceiling cracked from the pressure. Titha was sent flying backward, her head knocking against the cold ground.

Everything became a blur again. As she rose to her knees she could see what looked to be the Sifters dissipating into the cracks, leaving them to die in this foul place.

"… Cypress?" she called into the dark. But there was no answer. No "them". Cypress was gone, and so was her mother's circlet.

Madness took her. Fury blurred her vision as she stumbled into the dissipating smoke. She huffed and puffed, drawing Feathersword with a grunt. She sliced forward, but nothing remained, and her blade fell through thin purple air.

It dropped from her hand, and as the silver hit the stone floor below the blade clinked and clanged something horrible.

There she stood. Alone again. But she did not plan to stay that way for long.

"Cypress or no Cypress, help or no help," she said as she turned toe, "I am coming for you, family."

Titha drudged on, nothing to keep her company but the echo of her own footsteps. Cypress' reappearance into her life, and the brief time spent with him, felt like some sort of fever-dream. His words, though, stuck with her. Whatever plan had been set in motion by the murder of Calluna Mint was culminating there in the very dungeon she traversed.

Every dozen cells or so, she would come to find, were occupied. A handful of Lunas, humans, and even the odd Goblin were being kept against their will. None had the strength left to rise as Bjor did before them, though. Their fates laid captives to the shadows.

With each passing prisoner Titha could feel, more and more, that she was meant to come here. How many of these poor souls would've gone unaccounted for, or remained until it was too late? She had felt quite naïve, brazen, and foolhardy in the second half of their outing. Even if she was, she cared no longer. Her purpose only grew.

It proved to be an appropriate time for a renewed sense of vigor, too. The deeper she went, the narrower and darker it became, until she was fumbling over fallen walls and discarded remants of her people's past.

To her right stood the remains of a cell entrance; its ornate, spiraling bars bent and furled into a grotesque mess of iron. Chunks of stone were missing from the doorway, and her hand was drawn to them like moth to flame. Gently she brushed down the scene, finding unmistakable bear claw'marks among the wreckage. She followed them down, until:

"*Gwah*!" she cried, screaming as her hand stumbled onto the corpse of a Sifter… or what was left of it. "Ew, ew, ew ew *ewwww*!" she scuttled, flicking her hands furiously to rid them of gooey remnants.

Her outcry awoke… something. Deeper still into the dungeon a great growl erupted, and Titha did not hesitate to react. She had learned not to linger in this place.

Feathersword shot forward, Titha's elbows locked firm. "Get back from whence you came, demon, or I shall focus the energy of this sword *—of my people—* into a force you *will not survive*." She walked forward slowly, giving as much gravitas to her cobbled tall tale as she could.

Nothing answered in return.

"I will not repeat myself!" she declared, still marching firm. But no answer still.

Four shadows formed in her dim eyesight: two furry, one small, and one characteristically lanky. All were crouched, as if to avoid the very danger she herself wished to.

"Who's there?" Titha shouted into the dark. "Show yourself!"

"… Titha?" a shrieking voice cried out. "Titha, is that you?"

The voice of a sister was, and is forevermore, unmistakable. Titha ran into the uncertainty of her vision, ignoring it for the hope of embracing her older sibling. She was, at last, not disappointed.

Two long, warm arms wrapped around her as the eldest of Mae sisters collapsed into one another on the cold stone floor: Reunited at last.

Gilly wiped tears from Titha's face, brushing her matted hair back before bringing her into her chest.

"I thought I'd lost you," Gilly cried. "When Paw found us without you I, I thought the worst and—thank Gaela you're alright—"

"I thought I lost *you*!" Titha shouted through her tears. "I'll never ask you to go anywhere ever again, I promise. I'll—I'll never leave home again," she hiccuped, her faced pressed against her sister's neck.

"We both know that's not true," Gilly laughed, bringing Titha out to look into her green eyes.

Titha jilted to the movement behind her sister, and there sat Paw holding Haldor and Audun to his belly, gigantic bear-tears falling down his cheeks.

"My boys!" Titha squealed through her crackly throat, the words barely forming. She rushed into their hug, never wanting it to end. Paw nuzzled her so hard she thought her head was going to pop off as clean as a Sifter's. She shifted her embrace to Audun, picking him up into a strangling cuddle.

"Don't ever leave me again, okay?" she said.

"I won't," he smiled, his heart singing. "I'm sorry we lost you."

"Don't you dare apologize, either," Titha replied, hugging him tighter. "This is my fault. Not yours."

"Ah, wow. Such a touching, touching moment, truly," a voice interjected awkwardly from the shadows.

Titha's eyebrows cocked as she looked over Paw's shoulder. "Mister Fernbloom?" she asked.

"Correct, young lady, correct. So good to see you, and in one piece might I add, Titha Mae," he replied, walking to Gilly. "Your sister, well more aptly put your Bear-brother, was so kind as to free me from this, ah, dastardly place, and a rather peculiar cellmate."

"I knew you had it in you," Titha smiled, slapping Gilly's shoulder. "But, wait, oh Gods," she gulped. "He knows, right?"

"He knows," Gilly groaned, motioning to Fernbloom. "We're going to find Clover and pull him out of this mess, too."

"If none of us have seen him below ground, though," Titha added, "then he's above ground where all the exceptionally bad things keep coming from. Prepare yourself for that, okay?"

"I'm trying, thanks," Gilly exhaled.

"I was talking to Clover's *father*. Not his sort-of-girlfriend," Titha rolled her eyes.

Gilly grabbed her smart-aleck sister's face to chastise her but was quickly reminded of her broken right hand by severe, shooting pain. She gritted through it, then completely washed it aside as she searched Titha's dome.

"Uhm, sis? Are you alright, there?" Titha asked as Gilly's hands contorted her brow.

"Where is it?" Gilly scoffed. "Where's mother's circlet? You didn't lose it, did you? You lost it! I knew father shouldn't have given them to you and Beebee. You're just not ready, I tho—"

"—Cypress took it," Titha interrupted, knowing that the blunt truth was the only thing that could get her sister to shut up.

It took a while, and a couple of shakes, but eventually Gilly believed her, even if it did take Titha recounting the entire tale. Cypress was there, in those very Ruins and its Dungeons, and was abruptly back into their lives. Such a revelation only added to Gilly's anger, however.

"You have a sword, don't you!?" she erupted. "So why did you let him take it? *Are you stupid?"*

"I didn't have a choice!"

"Of course you did, brat!" Gilly screeched, back to her old self sooner than expected. "*See this*?" She flung the long fingers of her right hand into her sister's face. "Notice anything missing?"

"Gilly! Did you break your hand? It looks awful!" Titha yelped, readjusting the yellow silk around her sister's mangled hand.

"What? Yes, I punched a wall but that's not what I—*look closer, moron.* What's *missing*?"

"Mother's ring!" Titha shouted back. "What happened to it?"

"That *freakish stranger* from Celtica, the one that bloody *murdered* Calluna Mint, turned into a mortifying demon-thing and stole it from me!"

"Oh..." Titha exhaled. "Wait, that's what I was going to—"

"No, *you* wait, brat, 'cause it gets better, you stupid, *stupid* little girl!" Gilly slung, rumbling into a tirade as Audun stepped out of her way. "Right before the murderer took one of mother's three amethysts from my hand, he told me that your buddy and pal Cypress was behind all of this! *All of it*!"

"He did?" Titha asked.

"He did…" Audun piped in before Gilly flung her unbroken hand over his mouth.

"And now who has *two* of the total *three* stones, Titha? Hmm? Bloody *Cypress and his demon friend, could it be*?"

"Yes…" she mumbled.

"Yes is bloody correct, Titha Mae! Cypress, the Luna who betrayed the entirety of our family and peoples, now holds the majority of mother's precious history. So well done, hero. Bloody *well done*!" An earth-shattering "*UGH*" followed.

"You're upset, Gillian, I get it," Titha tiptoed. "I am, too. They were such amazing gifts to inherit, but… they're just jewelry, okay? We don't need them to remember mother! She'll… always be with us. And Cypress loved her, too, remember. I don't think he took my circlet to keep. I think he took it to save my life… Say what you will but my gut still tells me it's true, and that it was the right thing to do to let it go."

"*Eat* with your stomach, Titha. Stop *bloody thinking with it*," her sister spat back. "*Gods*, I cannot even *look* at you right now!"

"If we can stop shouting for a moment," Audun interjected carefully, "I think it is important to make note of a few things. For one, the demon thing we have all seen—we can agree that it is, in fact, the stranger from Celtica and the trial—yes?"

"Yes. It has to be, right?" Gilly fumbled.

"I think so, too. Okay. Good. Or, not good, rather, but agreed. Secondly," he continued, "we can then say that, since *he* took Gillian's ring, and then Titha's circlet *from* Cypress, that it is the ghoul alone that now holds two of the three. Correct?"

"You are sounding more like Nech every day," Titha observed. "And yes. Correct."

"So, we can then agree that it will go for the third piece next. Right? For whatever reason?"

Titha's stomach dropped.

"Oh, Gaela's grace," Gilly whimpered, her hands covering her mouth as she, too, came to the same conclusion before Audun could ask.

"So who has the third piece of jewelry?" he spoke up, catching on to the fact that he was missing a vital piece of information. "And why does this ghoul want them?"

"Beebee…" Titha spoke slowly. "Beebee has the third piece. It's a necklace."

Paw grunted, lowering his head and pushing his nose into Titha.

"Ah, if I may, children, please," Fernbloom interjected, "I'd like to offer a thought, here, to hopefully quell some of this unbearable shock and sadness. Your tiniest sister is back home and safe with your father, is she not?"

"Yes, of course," Titha replied. "But that only puts them *both* in danger, and not just her."

"We have to get home to them before it does!" Gilly added, shaking. "We have to warn them!"

"But how?" Audun asked as he rubbed Haldor's cheeks, comforting the beast. "We've all seen how fast this demon-thing is!"

"Well we know what we have to do first," Titha responded, tapping the silver at her hip. "And that is *get out of here*. But we're not alone in this dungeon. I don't know how everything has worked out the way it has, but I think we were meant to come here, and we're meant to free our people. We're not leaving anyone behind, just like in the Wick." She leaned to

Paw, stroking under his chin.

"About that," Gilly said, stepping to her little sister. "We were dumped about as far back in this hole as you can be... and on our way up we haven't seen Kernos in any of the cells."

"I know," Titha replied calmly. "I haven't either, and it may sound strange, but I didn't expect to. I know he's not your favorite, or anyone else's, but there's something about him... I don't think this place could hold him."

"Great, so he just up and broke out of here and left us?" Gilly spat back.

"Perhaps he has his hands as full as we do," Audun chirped, his own thoughts on the Satyr aligning with Titha's.

"What he said," Titha smiled. "And with that in mind we better get moving toward the top of the spiral. Paw, my precious loaf of fuzz, we're going to need all your strength to get out of here, okay?"

The big bear nodded, narrowing his chestnut eyes. Titha smiled, placing her forehead onto his.

"Your blacksmith is here, Audun," she added in an attempt to rally everyone else to her cause.

"Bjor?" the tiny Viking lit up. "Is he hurt?"

"Yes," Titha frowned, "As are others. So we must do everything we can to free them. I'm sure Haldor is up to the task as well, aren't you boy?"

"We get it, Titha," Gilly pipped. "We're with you."

Titha grinned, placing a hand on her sister's shoulder. She took a deep breath, then turned to a silent Fernbloom.

"I want to bring Clover home with us, too, sir. I really do, and of course I know you do, too," she added, noting the Luna's disposition. "But you need to know now, before we find him, before you see him again, that he is not the same boy he was in the forest."

Fernbloom's eyes misted, and his fluid mood ceased. "I, ah, just want my son back," he choked.

"We won't leave without him," Gilly reassured, rubbing his back.

"Now, have you your own Bear-brother, sir?" Titha interjected abruptly, feeling out the situation to come.

"Is now really the time?" Gilly scolded.

"What? I need to know if he can handle the ride before I plop him onto Paw!"

"You've never asked me before doing it! Not once!"

"That's because you're my sister," Titha offered, smirking. "He's not."

"I, ah, no, Titha Mae," Fernbloom replied. "I was not chosen for one. Not me, no, no. My eldest sibling was. Never, never, ah, have I ridden one before."

"Welp," Titha smiled, "you're going to ride one tonight."

Audun smiled, hurdling himself onto Haldor. They watched as three Lunas climbed aboard one forest bear, Titha being the only one to look a'natural.

"Get us out of here, brother," Titha declared, eliciting a determined '*harumph*' from Paw before he bounded into a stride.

Up they barreled out of the deep spiral toward its top, with every intention of freeing their fellow captives along the way.

"We're coming, Beebee," Titha whispered into the darkness of their path, Gilly huddled onto her. "We're coming…"

CHAPTER NINETEEN

Of Spawn & Stones

Above the Ruins, a thundering sky erupted. Lightning crashed through heavy clouds, revealing the silhouette of an enormous bird of prey atop the castle's highest pillar. There perched Sigrid, Shieldmaiden of Autumnhill, in the form of the Glorious Red Eagle; her golden talons piercing the stone's very make. Astride her sat Nech, strapped on for dear life as billowing winds and bouldering thunder threatened to sweep him off into the Night.

"This is your last chance to reconsider," Sigrid cawed into the storm. "You do not have to enter this foul place with me. I would never ask such a thing of a Scribe. Nor a friend."

"And what, my Shieldmaiden, miss Ugar being brought to the long overdue end he deserves? Not for the world, my Shieldmaiden. Not for the world!" Nech smiled.

"Very well," Sigrid returned, lowering her head to spot the entrance below them. "But you must promise me: whatever happens in these ruins, Nech, you will hold true to the plan. Our young are our top priority, but do not forsake the Lifestone, not even for our own lives, once the children are safe. The Seed of Igdrasil must not fall into the wrong hands."

"I shall guard it with my very flesh and being, Sire," he swore, his bag heavy with much more than maps. "Let us only hope my old horned friend follows through on his end of the bargain. Till the end."

"Till the end," she repeated. "Hold on tight."

"*How am I just now hearing of this?*" Theole thundered as he covered Beebee's ears, his voice shaking Roostwood with unbridled anger. "You should have come straight to me with this, Maya! Furious does not even begin to describe my current temperament!"

"I can see that," Maya replied, brushing off her beak with worn feathers. "We did not expect you to be thrilled with the circumstances of my arrival."

"And yet I am still the last to learn of my daughters' true whereabouts?" he replied, bouncing the youngest of the three in his arms, while his heart pounded with fear for the other two. "Rainer and I have exhausted all our resources in search, and meanwhile you know exactly where they are! Confirming my worst fears, no less!"

"Theole, we have held their safety as our utmost concern, just as you, this entire time," Maya returned, attempting to quell her own emotions. "Sigrid will be within the Ruins now and will stop at nothing to ensure the survival of our younglings. Navigating the entirety of Westlyn is not novice work. We did what we felt would best serve the situation, and now there is much more to be done, so I would ask that we focus on what can be helped, which is rarely decisions of the past."

Their confrontation only continued to escalate; temper-ridden elders butting heads like the fiercest of Rams. Beebee, though caught in the middle, was used to feuding within their home. She looked up to her father and patted his bushy cheek with one tiny hand.

"It's al'wight, father," she reassured him. "Sisters are okay, see?" From beneath her little purple dress she pulled her mother's long necklace chain, dangling its spiral amethyst for all to see. "My jewel is glowing," she added, smiling into its sheen.

Theole's eyes sparked with its reflection. "I... have never seen it do that before," he replied, gob-smacked. "What does this mean?" he muttered to himself.

"Theole, please!" Maya shouted from a sharp beak. "I highly doubt your daughter's necklace should be our top concern!"

The stone ebbed and flowed with a faint mauve light, its purple core glistening beneath the spiral like a tiny star looking for its kin.

Theole grabbed his brow, massaging it as Maya's squawking continued. He placed Beebee onto his throne as his impatience hit new heights.

A wet, small, and very welcomed frog popped onto the arm of Theole's throne from the mossy floor, plopping its green body right next to Beebee. She lit up as bright as her necklace, grinning as she scooted t'ward.

"See my neck-a-lace?" she said to the frog. "It tells me things," she smiled, lifting it to her cheek to feel its warmth. The frog's head rolled to the side; two beady black eyes blinking back at the littlest Luna. "It's my buddy, like a liiiittle purple firefly," she continued. "But you can't eat it," she chirped as she cradled it. "Hear it, little phrog? It says they're coming for us. So we be okay, right? Right."

The amethyst gave out a bit more light before a faint pop gurgled within its core, extinguishing the glow. The frog croaked in turn, hurriedly hopping from the sound.

"Sire!" a voice shot into the throne room, shattering Beebee's precious thoughts as two Cedarguard slammed open

Roostwood's entrance. There before them rushed another of Theole's most trusted personal guard, Hawthorn. And he looked as if he'd seen a ghost. A *real* ghost.

"Oh, thank Gaela you have returned," Theole exhaled. "Tell me you bring illuminating news?"

"Foxglove, sir," Hawthorn replied, folding over as he threw the silver helmet from his head. "He was taken! Taken by the black mist! We searched for him as well as your daughters, but they are not within the known perimeters of Celtica, nor Autumnhill, nor the Fields We cannot find them, nor the others!"

"The others?" Theole questioned.

"Our peoples in the Meadow, and in Celtica, report to us more disappearances, Sire. We—we cannot keep up—something very foul is a'foot!"

More Cedarguard rushed in, and with them came the heavy sounds of worry and panic in Ythengrey below.

"Where is my husband?" a particularly dainty voice screeched, its tone echoing all the way up the Grand Stairs. "Where is my son?" She cried out again, her voice ripe with terror. "*Why is this happening*?"

Sigrid's golden talons hit the soft ground; the Ruins of Byle shuttering at her entrance. She walked forward, her eagle eyes prying every inch of the chamber in which they'd landed. She sloped forward cautiously, letting Nech slide down onto the damp pathway.

"I do hope this storm lets up," he said, looking above. Half of the vaulted ceiling had collapsed long ago, its remnants resting a great distance below. Among them Nech scuttled, carrying a bundled cloth from which a familiar emerald glow escaped, lighting their way.

"Stay close to me," Sigrid replied, airing on the side of caution.

Yet Nech found himself entranced with their timeworn surroundings. A body of Ruins he had yet to enter? It was, regardless of circumstance, a potential paradise to his mind.

"My, my, would you look at this most sensational stonework," he gasped. "Nothing like the handiwork of Man, Goblin, nor any o'er maker. Simply breathtaking, isn't it?"

"Not when it holds my son and our Young Companions captive," Sigrid soured, her vision still darting for any sign of movement. Her red shoulders tensed with the anticipation of ambush, or at the very least, the reappearance of Ugar himself, as promised.

Above them the skies still churned, lightning cracking as viciously as the torrential winds. Their nasty howling filled the Ruins from behind them, shelter only offered on the far end they had yet to reach.

"What could have possibly separated Lunas from such a sensational sense of stone masonry?" Nech asked, still dumbfounded.

As they neared the inner core of the cathedral-like space, its far, massive wall filled their gaze; the towering slab'work entangled with vines both living and dead. Their foliage covered exquisite carvings—endless spirals and knotwork surrounding deities of old. At the center of it all rested a marvelous rendering of an Elder-Dragon; undoubtedly Meriduun, whom the Lunas of such an age had come to worship as their one true Goddess. Her wings hovered over all the wall had to offer; their billowing shapes outstretched as to mark a splendor none could ever match.

Beneath her timeworn silhouette sat three large stone thrones on a gigantic raised slab of natural rock. From each seat an intricate pathway spiraled out, forming three distinct branches. But the center throne was the most grandiose of the three, by far. Nech's keen eyes marked where gemstones were once encrusted within— every inch of the high-seat decorated with spirals and intricate knotwork to surround them. The old Scribe became enamored with this throne, even moreso than the 'splendiforous' wall behind. He could hear the howling winds outside sweeping into, then around, the chamber, culminating behind this particular seat as if Nature herself still held it in high esteem.

"Careful, Nech!" Sigrid whispered, her enormous eagles'feet slowing before the thrones. "There is another entrance behind the thrones," she noted with keen eagle eyes. "It no doubt leads to more sacred chambers, the most convenient of holdings for those who take claim over this place." She whisked a wing beside him, urging him backward. "We go no further. It is always best to let your enemy come to you, not the other way around."

"Quite right, Shieldmaiden," a deep, sinister voice replied. Its heinous, gruff tambor echoed from the very hallway Sigrid eyed.

Nech stammered and gasped, clutching his bundled shroud as he stumbled into Sigrid's wing, tripping on an overturned stone in the spiral path.

From behind the three thrones Ugar stepped forward, and lightning struck fierce in the dark heavens above.

Sigrid hissed, her golden beak sharp with anticipation. Their true meeting had finally come: Face to face. "Where are our children?" she cawed, wasting no time.

"In the dungeons," Ugar bellowed with a smirk. "You shall have them when we have the Lifestone, as we agreed."

"Show me they are safe, first," Sigrid replied. "I want to see my son, and the Mae'kin."

"In time, Shieldmaiden, in time. He will be returned to you, as will the forest sprites. All when we have the Stone. I feel your intentions. I know you wish to strike me down as soon as the Stone is turned over to me. As such, the children remain imprisoned for their eventual sacrifice, until the stone is *ours*."

Sigrid exhaled deeply, her nostrils shooting hot, powerful breath into their enemy's face. "Fine," she stated hesitantly, looking to Nech. "We will hand it over. But know this, demon, if one scratch has come to our young by your hand, you will suffer the wrath of a thousand Valkyrie for it."

"My master does not wish to sacrifice your young. Yet," he replied snarkily, stepping forward. "So if it is done, it will be by your hands. Not ours."

Nech stumbled backward, barely holding onto the shrouded, glowing object within his grasp as Ugar approached.

"I proposed we end their miserable little lives either way," the foul Ugar continued. "But luck is with you, as my master sees greater purpose in them." He stopped, his enormous silhouette hanging over Nech as lightning cracked the sky. "The Lifestone, worm. Now."

Nech swallowed an enormous amount of saliva coupled

with just as much fear and doubt. He looked to the artifact he held as it glistened emerald beams from beneath olive'wool fabric. Slowly he lifted it, his old, bony arms shaking. Ugar snatched it without hesitation, growling as he did. A great, nasty laugh escaped his maw as jagged teeth flared into another flash from the storm above.

"At last, my master will have its glory!" Ugar growled triumphantly. "And I, my own prize for it."

"What prize, Ugar the Terrible, could possibly be worth two lifetimes wasted in the servitude of evil?" Nech spat from Ugar's shadow.

"Your head," the demon seethed back. The singe of his defeat, and loss of his once-glorious crown of horns to Nech and his allies during the end of Vulduun's Ever-war, burned forever still.

"Koree'makth!" Ugar gargled, the ancient words sending embers of brimstone from his maw into heavy air as he lifted the shrouded Stone. With this came a wave of black smoke and equally dark creatures scampering from the hall behind the thrones. Impenetrable purple mist coiled from betwixt the ancient seats of royal Lunas long gone; a central black mass slithering toward Sigrid and Nech like a gigantic, hungry serpent surrounded by its own tiny minions. Soon Ugar was flanked by countless Sifters scratching and clawing at one another as small black-feathered, flightless birds scuttled at their feet.

As their foul ranks settled, a hissing voice slithered through the swirling smoke, making itself known to Ugar, then to Sigrid and Nech. Ugar froze in place and lowered his prize.

"My master wishes to thank you for honoring the bargain," Ugar spoke in a muted tone. "Do not move, nor even think of moving, or you will be ended."

Nech crawled up onto his feet, running back to Sigrid's guard. She lifted one enormous leg in front of him as her red feathers hardened with an ambered, steel-like resolve; her stare unwavering as she awaited this *'master'*—the imprisoner of her youngest son and most cherished Young Companions—the carver of their path and thief of her destinies.

Slowly the billowing black parted, and a stout frame stepped forward. Shoulders near as wide as Ugar's approached astride bare, broad footsteps.

"By Craga's fury… it *is* you!" Nech cried out in shock as his eyes beheld a familiar round face. "But why?"

"Welcome… to my home," the figure replied. Arms outstretched into the vast stonework of the Ruins of Byle. Smoke cleared as they did, and in their absence the face of Cypress Sylvanus Byle was revealed. Behind him two cloaked disciples stepped out of the smog, each clad in silver laced midnight robes.

"How could you?" Sigrid screeched immediately. "To stoop so low from where you have come?" she cried. "Have you fallen so far as to relish in the imprisonment of those you once loved like family?" Her heart broke for Titha, Paw, and Gilly at the sight. A dear mentor, uncle-like in their reverence, now stood as an heir to Vulduun and his madness. It struck her so that she was still not able to fully accept what her eyes beheld. Something was… *off*.

Cypress brushed soot from the shoulders of his ensemble: a white robe every bit as intricately knotted in silver as the ancestral thrones behind him. He walked to Ugar, his approach eliciting a hasty bow from the demon. To his master Ugar offered up the Lifestone, its majesty bound and tied. The very glow of the

Stone seemed to ebb away with Cypress' presence. He smiled, stopping just short of taking it from his servant. Ugar remained kneeling, holding the artifact in place like an altar.

"Is it safe to unravel, I wonder? To touch with my own flesh?" Cypress asked plainly, his brow rising to Sigrid as he tapped the shrouded Stone with one finger. "I seem to recall no others than the blood'kin of Theole being able to touch the Moonstone, and yours to your Sunstone, Shieldmaiden. Has this Stone proven the same?"

"I will tell you nothing until I see that my son and the daughters of Theole are safe," Sigrid spat. Her feathers perked like the quills of a porcupine. She flickered her wings in anticipation as she thought of how easy it would be to dispatch them both, here and now, if not for the safety of the children.

"Patience, my Avian friend. First things first. I want to see it for myself," Cypress smirked, his eyes twinkling with emerald.

"That would be unwise!" Nech shouted abruptly, popping up. "Its immense power will surely overwhelm any who are not of the First'blood!"

"Hah!" Cypress scoffed. "A curious thing, isn't it? You stand in the halls of my great kin, *maggot* of a Goblin. *My* blood is as pure as has ever flowed a'top Gaela's soils!"

"But it is not the oldest nor first of your Lunish kin, is it?" Nech decreed, knowing this would push Cypress further into vanity's rage. "It is not First'blood! That prestige belongs to Theole and the Maes. Not you. Perhaps you have sought the Lifestone in vain!"

Cypress did not bite, as if he tired of upholding such a charade. His true focus was the Stone. Ugar began to quake beneath it as he felt his master step directly overhead, both disciples coming out of the shadows and flanking him. One by one the cloaked figures unfolded wraps of heavy wool from a round, glass-like body as green light brimmed out onto their master's face. Cypress laughed as Ugar's shaking intensified. His disciples, however, continued as they were commanded in complete, silent obedience.

"What do we do?" Nech whispered up to Sigrid who remained hunched and ready to pounce.

"I have waited a long time for this moment…" Cypress spoke as he lifted the last shroud. "And here we are… seasons on, and my most trusted servant has delivered to me… *this*."

Ugar flinched below as he felt the cold object in his bare hands. He awaited the eternal burning of his flesh from its holy nature… but nothing came.

Cypress laughed again. Then once more, louder. "This… is a jar of fireflies!" he gritted, lifting it from Ugar's palms.

No sooner could Ugar look up into his master's eyes then did his head leave his shoulders. Nech gasped as it plopped from body to floor, flinching as the face of his most hated enemy rolled over to scowl at him one last time.

"A jar of bugs!" Cypress cackled, throwing the glass to shatter across ancient stonework before sheathing bladed, unnatural fingers. "Ingenious, really," he added as he grabbed the decapitated body of Ugar before him, wrenching it to the ground. "But I *despise* being lied to."

As lightning continued to plague the skies above, thunder crashed down into the chamber as Cypress' disciples, one thin and one stout as their master, stepped aside to make way for their minions. Sifters flanked the three, the small black birds hobbling from beneath the creature's bony ankles. They formed a wave of glistening dark feathers as each scuttled to the corpse of the fallen Ugar. Like vultures they crabbled a'top his lifeless husk, picking it clean until nothing but a barrel-chested skeleton remained on the cold stone floor.

"You are next, Companions, as are your children, if you do not cease with the such deceit," Cypress spat, projecting a calm fury the likes of which they'd never seen. He approached Sigrid, stepping onto the bones of Ugar. She flinched at the cruelty of every crack underneath his heels, watching as the Sifters and disciples marched in tow.

In that moment, Sigrid felt defeated. She had counted on the brash arrogance of Ugar, and in turn of his master, to render them vulnerable—but had not foreseen such ravenous and plentiful minions. In moments past, as the jar of fireflies was revealed, they were to take their enemies by surprise and strike down all that stood between them and the children. Yet reality conjured a worser fate, as it always does, presenting a far greater mob to overcome. They were grossly outmatched by the sheer volume of things waiting for them in the black mist. And as it all approached her, Sigrid felt herself cave.

"We mustn't hand it over!" Nech cried, scrambling atop her. "We must only buy time! Remember your words, *our* words, mighty Shieldmaiden! The true Lifestone shall not fall into the hands of evil!"

"Evil?" Cypress laughed. "Evil is prizing an artifact over the lives of your own children, is it not? You have taken a great gamble with their souls, here, with this trickery… with this miscalculation. I have but to snap my fingers and they will disappear in the halls of my dungeon. Unless you hand… over the Stone… to *me*."

"Do it," Sigrid exhaled. "Give it to him."

"Shieldmaiden, no!" Nech cried.

"Time runs thin," she retorted with great loss in her voice. "Do as I say, and we shall see our young once more."

Nech bowed, his eyes swelling as he rooted betwixt their belongings strapped to the giant eagle's back. From them he pulled another woolen bundle. This one's emerald sheen, though, even as it remained shrouded, was magnificent enough to blind a Great Drake.

"There she is..." Cypress whispered into the light it produced. "The Stone... the Seed... the Answer."

Sigrid bowed her head to lower Nech. He looked away as he handed the prize over to a Luna he had sworn would never be capable of such ends. Yet as he placed it in Cypress' hands, a great wind rushed in from the storm outside. It pressed his old bones forward, forcing his hands harder onto the fabric surrounding the Seed. To it his fingers clasped, and in a split-second decision Nech ripped the woolen'cloth from the Lifestone, leaving it bare in Cypress' unwitting hands.

Immediately it seared his flesh, black smoke escaping from the bubbling wounds of the Luna's palms. Everything in the Ruins, for that moment, became emerald.

"*What have you done?*" Cypress screamed in pain amidst the pulsating energy of the Seed of Igdrasil.

Sigrid blurted out an eagle's cry in pure shock.

"I believe this answers your question, foul Luna!" Nech decreed, jutting back astride Sigrid's feathers. "It would indeed seem that you need be of the First'blood to wield such a mighty Spawn of Galea! Now may *it take you*!"

Cypress let loose another horrendous scream, his voice

gurgling and burning away in tandem with his very flesh. Battle-hardened indigo skin singed into ash as his silver-spiraled robes burst into white flames. His disciples fell back in dreadful fear, emerald light washing over them. Their master's head shot back, purple smoke pouring from his mouth. Ash piled all around his silhouette as his stout frame peeled off from its core, falling to the ground. Cypress now laid at the feet of himself, unconscious and unmoving as a vision of his former stance continued to burn in the Seed's glory—for it was not truly *he* who *burned.*

As flames continued to peel away at the curious anatomy still locked onto the Seed, ashes of deceit fell, revealing the visage of a human equally as stout as Cypress. The Man's limbs contorted as he bent unto the mercy of the cleansing emerald energy. Swiftly his face shot 'round, locking eyes with Sigrid as his visage melted into place: the Stranger from Celtica! The rotund man now stared back at her, grotesque gargling bubbled from between his teeth—but he, too, fell to the wayside of the inferno's purpose—his body collapsing to the floor as Cypress' form had done before it.

In his wake, a third form peeled from the ashen shape, its plump body wasting no time in hitting the ground to the right of whatever still stood, completing a triumvirate of fallen souls. There was no fight, no life left in this last discharged mortal… but her form was unmistakable.

Sigrid stumbled backward. "*Calluna…*" she whispered, astonished as the third and final body rolled over toward her. Mint's body was as lifeless and forlorn as it was when staked to the center of Celtica.

But the inferno still raged. The Seed had more to show them.

In its ethereal conquest it burned ever-brighter, not letting go of whoever, or whatever now held it. Slowly the emerald energy created an absolving flame of the same color, one that washed over its captor entirely, from palms to heels. As it burned away final false skins and visages, the Seed revealed a pale white figure, fresh as a nightmare and thin as a forgotten mare. With one last screech, the figure dropped the Seed, the weight of it cracking the slate below. Hundreds of the tiny black bird creatures rushed from the shadows to its white skin, crawling up and around it in a great swirling manner before manifesting into a husky cloak made entirely of their black feathers. As they did, the white figure brought her hands in, licking her burnt palms before bringing the cloak to a hasty close 'round.

Sigrid, Nech, and the two hooded disciples stood in complete, dread-like awe. Before them harrowed a being unlike any they had ever beheld: her pure white skin as bright as the center of a star. She… it… whatever it was, ran her hands through a head full of remarkable dust orange hair, its feathery length as wild and striped as a tiger's hide. Such a striking mane careened backward from an oddly-pretty visage, marked by red eyes with bright yellow irises, each set deep into black sockets that brushed wide over into sharp cheeks.

The figure's vision adjusted, her pitch black pupils finally beholding Sigrid, the Glorious Red Eagle, with her own eyes. She then turned to the disciples behind her, her black cloak flanked to the left, right, and back by three fallen souls; each a martyr of their own peoples. A nervous tick compelled her to speak.

"…Let me be the first to say I did not expect that to happen," she spoke from dark lips, her voice unusual, almost alien to both the Companions and the disciples. "You look shocked," she continued to those standing closest to her. "Allow me to explain—"

Whether her words were to be trickery or truth, the room was swiftly interrupted by an abrupt *BOOM* stemming from the far westwardly expanse of the chamber. *BRUNG*! The same bolstering sound rung again. It was if something—something rather large—was attempting to break in. Or break *out*.

One final *BAROOSH* shook the entirety of the Ruins, and Sigrid, Nech, both disciples, and the feather-cloaked figure all stumbled back from the sound. In the shadows of the far reaches of the chamber rushed a large band of individuals, each more different than the last. Sifters cackled and screeched as they watched boisterous beings jump forth from what *they* knew to be the once-locked entrance to the Dungeons of Byle.

Leading the pack was none other than Paw of Yythengrey, and his ever-rambunctious Luna-sister sat astride him, with her big sis' holding on tight.

Titha gave a distinct holler marking her arrival, her green eyes burning as brightly as the Seed of Igdrasil at the center of the hall. Paw followed suit with an excited roar, identical howls shooting forth from both Audun and Haldor. Their calls careened straight up into the exposed, raging sky, and a great cheer erupted behind them as fellow prisoners felt the rush of Gaela's winds for the first time in what felt like an eternity.

Finally, the Young Companions were free from the dungeon. And they brought company.

CHAPTER TWENTY
Falora Fomora

Not a Sifter stood dormant, hundreds of grimy feet shuffling in discontent. Their prisoners were upon them; they had escaped! This was a most grave failing on their part, made much worse by being the *only* task their master had bestowed upon them. Each of the knobby, exhausted little beings shivered at the thought of their master's consequences. Perhaps that "long-overdue death" they were promised was now at hand. Such a thought did their worn minds in, and their ranks took to a frantic, clanging chatter.

Titha perceived their shifty nature as threatening, however, not marking their *fear* for what it was. She yanked on Paw's fur, bringing him to a halt just as they came upon the gravity of the Sifter's sheer numbers. Behind her Gilly called out to a dozen silhouettes—some Man, some Luna, all freed prisoners; each rallying to form a line behind them.

The sisters took in their surroundings, walking slowly uphill into the center of the immensely tall space. Most of the ebbing crowd awaiting them in this throne chamber blended in with their surroundings. Save for two silver-clad cloaks and a giant red eagle, that is.

"Sigrid!" Titha shouted.

"Mother!" Audun yelled in tandem, both overjoyed. "I knew you'd come," he smiled, driving his heels into Haldor. "We have so much you need to hear!"

"*Children, stop*!" Sigrid shouted from her golden beak, fear shattering her usual tambour.

With her warning came the slow turn of another cloaked figure, one that had gone unnoticed to the Young Companions as it stood cloaked in black. As her body of purple-sheened feathers came about, Titha's eyes locked onto a face not far off in features from Gilly's—if Gilly were the pale fuel of Men's nightmares.

"Who's *this* witch?" Titha spat, Sigrid's warning ringing sincere. "And what... is *that*?"

The pale lady gave a smile under a strong nose. "It is a most precious thing, isn't it?" she replied softly, swooning over the Lifestone. Her yellow gaze rose to Titha. She stepped away from the Stone, and the crumbled bones of Ugar, to approach the Luna addressing her. Sigrid's enormous wing shot out, stopping her as swiftly as a boulder would a newt.

"You have what you willed of me, spirit," Sigrid hissed to her. "And I see that you have been true to your word, our young now before us. But that is the last step you will ever take towards them."

"Sigrid?" Titha spoke out again. "Could it be? Is that another Eternal Stone?" Her green eyes locked to it, their emerald light giving and receiving.

"Not exactly, if I may be so bold," a well-known voice replied from behind Sigrid. Nech walked out beside her, not letting go of her shielding.

"Nech, what are you doing here?" Titha asked, looking to Audun and Gilly behind her, each befuzzled by his presence.

"Gracious, if I am not surrounded by those who doubt my century's experience with dangerous delves!" he snorted, hands on his hips. "I am here to help, brave Titha. As I assume you are? The glowing beauty before you, we have been told, is the Lifestone."

"Though let us all drop the charade and acknowledge it for what we know it to be, shall we?" The pale lady interjected, taking a step back from Sigrid's wing. "The legends were wrong, as they so very often are. It is no stone at all! It is the Seed of Igdrasil, young Luna, and it is the key to the salvation of my dying world."

Titha's brow lowered. Sigrid and Nech treated this new being with great malice, but her voice did not ring a'foul to the young ones. It bit at her attention with the same charisma and determination that she liked to see in herself.

"Do not speak to her as if she is your guest, here," Sigrid cawed, knowing Titha's openness.

"Let her speak," Titha retorted. "Please."

Gilly groaned, leaning up into her sister's ear. "In no way is that a good idea," she added.

"A dying world?" Titha repeated. "I want to hear what she has to say first. Don't you?"

"Not as badly as I want to live!" Gilly whispered. "And that requires escaping, not *blossoming conversations*."

"*Sssh*!" Titha hushed. "I'm pulling a Rainer!"

"A what?" Gilly and Audun whispered back-to-back.

"A Rainer! I'm *stalling* her," Titha smirked. "I don't think escape is possible at the moment. Not yet, anway—so do you see those two cloaks, sis? The two monk-looking figures standing out like silver thumbs?"

"Yeah?" Gilly answered.

"I think the skinny one is Clover. Look how he's standing. Let me keep this suspiciously attractive ghoul lady busy, and you and Mr. Fernbloom can maybe figure out if that is his son over there?"

Gilly nodded, sliding down from Paw and back into the crowd of escapees.

"Can I ask you a question, Miss... uhm... ghoul lady?" Titha asked, turning back to the pale figure, fully prepared to capture her attention. "Well, two questions, actually. Though it could be a hundred, if you'd allow."

"Please don't," the pale lady grimaced. "I am absolutely *plagued* with exhaustion."

"Right. That's fair. So two questions? Two it is. Firstly, and I think most importantly, where do you come from that is in such great need of this thing that you would imprison us all, then maybe sacrifice us, for it? A dying world, you said? Where in Gaela is the land so far gone?"

"Not Gaela, child," her dark purple lips curled. "*Oathera...*" she whispered, its sound shooting like a hushed arrow into Titha's ear.

"Oathera... the Otherworld?" Titha replied. "You're from the Otherworld?"

"I am..."

"Wow. Okay. That is heavy, if true. So, secondly then—well, I lied because this is definitely the more important question—we've seen what you can do, assuming all the smoking about and nasty giant ghoul-facing was you... What is it going to take for me and all my friends to walk out of here alive?"

"What makes you think I am standing in the way of that?" The lady replied coyly.

"Oh, just the three corpses and pile of bones at your feet," Titha replied.

The thick black and purple smoke surrounding such forms was wafting away with the commotion, and the trio of fallen souls resurfaced. At first, Titha only saw them as an astute observation of hers; casualties of battle, perhaps. Then, as the smoke rolled back entirely, the three figures became less corpses, and more the bodies of people she knew.

"Cypress!" Titha screamed, the first fallen face coming into view. Paw growled as Titha jumped from her. She ran to Cypress, his limp body pointed directly toward her. As she approached, the form behind the pale lady was revealed, too.

"The... Stranger..." Titha continued, her hands moving to cradle Cypress' head. Then, as the smoke finally dissipated, the third soul came into view.

"... *Mrs. Mint*?" she asked in shock. "That's... impossible," Titha cried. "We buried... we buried her..."

"In a tomb to the Otherworld," the pale lady smiled. "Curious, then, is it not? I thought I may need her services again, but oh, how useful others of your kind have proven in her stead."

As Titha looked to the bodies, holding Cypress still, her stomach dropped. A lump swelled in her throat as her head creaked up to the pale lady standing directly behind her.

"*You…*" Titha said. "It was *you*. The whispering in Celtica. The riots, the fighting, the *murder*… All of this… has been done by *you*."

The lady's smile disappeared as her gaze lowered to Titha. Their eyes locked.

"Who are you?" Titha asked.

A deep breath filled the foreign lungs of the pale lady. Sigrid crouched again, readying herself to pounce at the slightest hint of discord from her or her minions. But nothing came (for the moment) as the pale figure lowered herself to Titha on the stone floor, her cloak of feathers billowing out like the smoke that surrounded everything else.

"I am *Falora*," she revealed softly, wind sweeping the chamber. "*Falora Fomora*, heir to the Fomorrigan, granddaughter to the Great Drakes; And I am the *reckoning of your realm*."

Titha could not speak, nor blink. She knew of the Fomorrigan, of course, from their people's songs. But wasn't such a being just a fairy tale? A myth? One told to children to keep them from straying into the mist and shadows, to keep them on the path of the Moon's Light? So many things rung familiar about this new being, yet every fiber of Titha knew they'd never met. Was she really who she said she was? *Meriduun and Vulduun's Granddaughter*? Really? And the heir of a Goddess? Whoever she was, staring into her eyes was like staring into the Oblivions Vulduun once threatened upon them all.

"Falora… Fomora," Titha spoke, the name rolling off her tongue. "Why… why do you feel… so familiar?"

"Because I have been there all along, little Luna. You just don't know it yet," Falora replied, squinting her pitch black eyelids. "You have not heard my name, but you know my mother's, don't you? Your illustrious Fomorrigan; The one and only! Who she was, what she has done, what she stood for—" Her words ceased as she caught Gilly skulking in the background. "It's okay, girl. Go to them. They are no longer needed," she offered to Gilly, a long white finger pointing to Cypress' two disciples.

Gilly didn't hesitate. She sprinted for the two cloaks, Mr. Fernbloom in tow. One hood flipped back, and the air of a familiar 'freckle-faced sprite' exhaled as if he'd been holding in the darkest of things all his life.

In that moment she embraced Clover, holding him as the entirety of the Luna boy shook. The chamber fell still as she held him in silence, his body convulsed'ly sobbing.

He wanted to apologize. He wanted to so bady. For everything. But there were no words to convey how immensely sad he was at it all, and how deeply entombed in regret he'd become.

"Is that you, my son?" Fernbloom wept as he stepped out of the shadow behind Gilly. Clover collapsed at the sound of his father's voice, a deep wail of emotion leaving him. Fernbloom careened for him, but found himself stopped cold by the smack of a large Lunish hand. His jaw slammed shut as his head shot back from the hit; ancient glasses crashing to the ground.

"Back, fool!" the much larger, other cloaked disciple shouted. "You are a *pawn*, Merigold. A pawn in a prophecy that has not yet been fulfilled! But the boy is a *disciple*. And he belongs to us, now!"

Fernbloom spat purple from his mouth, tasting his own blood again sooner than he'd expected. "Now, ah, se here, fella'," he started, wiping his face clean. "This is my only boy, my only, so very precious son. And I will not lose him, or any of our kin, to you—you and your dastardly cultist'y ways!"

The enormous disciple growled, his body wailing into a fit as his arm arched upward again. Though before he could strike twice, Falora gripped his wrist, twisting it 'round till it snapped.

"Your prophecy was a lie," she stated plainly, "And your misguided Luna master lies before you, defeated. Poor stooge... Of what use are you now?"

Her eyes began to glow wildly. Titha, Audun, and Gilly watched as Falora's gaze burned exactly as Theole or Sigrid's did when they summoned the almighty power of their Avian selves.

"Don't!" Gilly shouted into the grapple. "Don't kill him! He made mistakes, yes, but he is still kin! A Luna! Aren't you, Birch?"

The stocky Luna's eyes darted as he looked to the many Companions in the room.

"Or has your cousin Cypress poisoned your mind so thoroughly that you would choose his folly over your own life?" Gilly asked. "Birch... please. Don't."

Birch spat to her feet, wrenching his broken wrist from Falora as he turned to run. The Sifters gargled as an angry mob before him, and Falora did not wave them down.

"They will pass judgement on him," she stated, turning to Gilly. "He has played his part."

The Companions watched as one of the few living Byle's fled deep into the shadows of his ancestral home, in awe of Falora's seeming-mercy. The Sifters, perhaps undecided on his fate, eyed Birch in a most scrutinous way.

"The truth is, girl, that the Luna whose head you cradle deserves death, not that boy," Falora said as she looked down to Titha, her arms still holding Cypress' head.

Titha's eyes swelled. "Is he... is he dead? Did you kill him, too?" she shivered.

"No," Falora answered. "Not yet."

Titha looked to the others: the fallen Stranger and the horrid husk of Calluna Mint.

"The others are very dead, though," Falora continued, "So, apologies for that, and what'not. They didn't have the strength this chestnut of a mortal possesses. He was, if nothing else, useful in his time."

"What have you done?" Titha asked, a tear escaping her eye.

Falora did not answer. Instead, she turned to the Seed of Igdrasil, its glow less prominent than in moments past. She parted her cloak, dipping a long white leg from it. Daintily she placed one toe onto the Seed, and as she expected... it accepted her touch. No singing nor searing of her skin came. Not now that she stood in her true form. Her rightful flesh and blood.

"When I still inhabited your friend Cypress, here," she said as she bent over to embrace the Seed, "The small Craglin fellow threatened me. He told me I could not wield this beautiful thing! As if I was not of the First'blood of my people. Cypress is certainly not, much to his own displeasure, so I grant the Goblin that. But as you can see... I am so much more than that bigot could ever be. And *I am*, as you now plainly behold—like your father—like the Glorious Red Eagle before us—*very much of the First'blood.*"

Falora lifted the Seed over her head, its emerald glow

reigniting into a furious burst of energy. It danced with the beauty of the Northern Aurora within the Ruins, lightning crashing above it.

"*Behold, the rightful Fomorrigan*!" she cried, fingers gripped to the Seed, "Heir to my mother's cause! Carrier of my grandmother's might! And I shall bring *salvation*!"

The sight was awe-inspiring, yet dreadful to behold. Gilly, Clover, and his father darted to the band of freed prisoners, huddling behind Paw. Audun shouted for Titha as he rode Haldor to his mother; his wits as muddled as all the others. But Titha could not bring herself to leave Cypress to this Falora Fomora, this Fomorrigan, and tired arms clung to her old mentor still.

"You cradle Cypress, little one, but he is responsible for *all of this*!" Falora said looking down to Titha again. "From the windows of fog and mist and shadow have I watched your world—your precious Gaela— flourish under Igdrasil's life-giving might. But now she is gone, and her Seed glows ready to bestow such prosperity on another realm—*my* realm! And your dear Cypress made it all possible. He wounded your world, your *entire realm,* by bypassing the old windows between us, and finding instead—a door. A *door to Oathera*! His ignorance *started* this Calamity, you see. I simply aim to *finish it*."

"Finish what?" Titha screamed, her white hair flowing back from the unbridled energy on display. "Tell me!" she shouted harder, then harder still. "*Tell me*!"

"I will *annihilate Celtica,* child!" Falora decreed, her fiery eyes filled with disgust. "I will utterly *obliterate* its existence, and all connected to it! We were hanging—*gripping* to existence by a thread—already doomed to disappear into the dark nothings of

Oathera—barely surviving in our Gods-forsaken realm... then you... and your *Companions*... have the *audacity* to bring about the hand-holding and flowerswapping of that dreadfully *boring* city, bringing our already crumbling foundation in the Otherworld to its very knees! Everything, child—*everything* I have inherited crumbles to dust because of *you*. Your lust for peace and prosperity has robbed Oathera of the energies—the *souls* —that are our *right*! Our only source of *life*! And you have *broken the natural order of things*! All so you can 'make home' with one another, forfeiting the necessities of *war* for *what*? *Playtime*?" Falora screeched feverishly as the Seed's light came to a fever-pitch, shaking the stones of the throne chamber around them all. "The naïvety on display sickens me! It *burns* at me. Therefore I, the Fomorrigan inherent, will bring about the Dusk of Celtica as swiftly as its Dawn—and I will break every single bond Lunas, Men, and Goblins have built so that the cauldrons of Oathera may ring *full* with the souls of those who perish in natural, unavoidalbe conflict!" She brought the stone down to her chest, staring into it as she spat the most riveting truth of all:

"And I will bring this most precious Seed home to Oathera, girl, so that *our* realm—*not* yours—will finally be a *cradle of life*—a fertile land of blossoming souls and prospering peoples! I will breathe *growth* into a world *long overdue* for a champion to avenge the *death of my mothers, and the endless suffering of our peoples*! *Long live the Fomorrigana, Mothers of Eternity!*"

Hard black feathers shot out from her cloak. Falora cawed and cackled as her formerly blasé demeanor shattered under the reality of her true intent. Wings as dark as her wrappings broke free from her arms, their length tripling as they transformed. White talons cracked and spread from her feet, ensnaring the Seed of Igdrasil in their grasp. Her sharp nose tweaked in a most nasty way, revealing itself a curved black beak. Pale cheeks gave way to the harsh plumage of a *Vulture,* the pitch dark markings around her eyes growing evermore prominent betwixt a bone-white face. Her mane of frantic orange hair billowed into a dusty, feathered crown…

And she was *reborn.*

"You are *Avian…*" Sigrid cried into the commotion, guarding Nech from the onslaught of old magick.

Sigrid beheld a being of her equal now, its black-feathered wings lifting a massive, threatening Vulture into the heights of the throne chamber. And as Falora engulfed the air above them, the Seed's Emerald Aurora dancing behind, Sigrid's mind exploded with the fear of her nightmares all over again.

"It wasn't my own darkness I feared," she cried out into swirling currents, her eyes now locked with the same Black Avian from her dreams. "*… It was you.*"

The beast smiled much as it had in Falora's form, and with a great *CAW* the Ghastly Black Vulture motioned for her minions to *consume.*

Sigrid let loose a trumpeting cry from her golden beak, the majesty of the Glorious Red Eagle rising to meet her Avian adversary of equal size and potential.

From the shadows, hundreds of Sifters did as they did best, their bony bodies taking to every surface in attempt to surround the Companions as ordered. Paw slammed his front feet into the floor, shattering stone as he roared in defiance.

"We can't leave him!" Titha cried to her Bear-brother, her arms heavy with the fate of Cypress.

Paw grunted, shaking his head as he stared his Luna-sister down. He was not having it.

"Come get him, Paw! Please!" she shouted back. "And take him out of here with the others!"

"*Garrrounnnphh*?" Paw grumbled back in Bearish.

"No, I'm not coming! I'm going to fight," Titha answered. She laid her fallen mentor onto the cold slab in waiting, rising to the Sifters and their malice with the sheen of Feathersword.

"For Celtica..." she spoke, looking back to the prisoners they'd freed. Her eyes met with Audun's, and the confidence they always restored in one another was reignited.

"For Celtica," Audun replied, smiling.

"For Celtica!" Bjor the Blacksmith replied behind him.

"Yeah, wow, absolutely!" Fernbloom rejoiced, lifting a rock to arm himself. "Absolutely! For Celtica!"

Sifters descended swiftly, as they had on each of them in the past. Some, like Gilly and Bjor, fought on bravely with grave injuries. Even Nech and Clover put every ounce of life they had left into the fray for this last stand in the Ruins of Byle.

Sigrid did the same above them. Golden talons grappled with bone white claws; the two Avians locked in mortal combat.

"*You will not win this*!" Sigrid cawed out, her left wing swooping across Falora's beak with a hardy *CRACK*.

"But I have already beaten you," Falora cringed back, her free talon ripping into Sigrid's other wing. "For like my mother before me, Eagle, I am to be all things that spell the doom of my enemies. I am the *fog*. I am the *soul-taker*. I am the *Vulture Queen*."

Falora dove like a spear into Sigrid, driving her beak into her red chest. Great, squawking pain erupted before Sigrid retaliated. She slashed back, closing each of her taloned feet deep into Falora's leg that held the Seed.

"I have seen what you will do," Sigrid cried, grappling with her enemy. "You have shown me plainly, in the nightmares I have been plagued with. But know this, as I do, that such a time will only come shall I fail. And I will not fail."

Sigrid ripped down with her claws, searing the flesh from the Vulture's right leg, loosening her grip on the Seed. Falora gritted her beak, jutting her enormous head back for one more pass at the Eagle. Powerful as she was, though, she would soon learn that Sigrid spoke true, and that there were few women, in any realm, as versed in battle or strength as she.

The Glorious Red Eagle flipped her weight backward, taking Falora with her as all of her weight flung the Vulture to the ground. A mighty *THUD* shook the Ruins as the self-proclaimed Fomorrigan crashed into ancient stones, shattering them with the weight of her bones.

The Seed, for a moment, floated within the air. Sigrid snatched it in her talons, swooping over her fallen foe.

"*Give it back*!" Falora cackled like a child, her demeanor flipping as fast as she had from the sky. "Your realm prospers! You have no need for such a prize! Give it back to me and there will be no more bloodshed!"

With this offer, Sigrid looked down to her son and his Young Companions as they held off the Sifters as best they could. But she knew, in her heart of hearts, that no matter the cost she could not let this Oatherian being, one who had shown such lack of a respect for *Life*, in any form, take the Seed of Igdrasil into a realm that spawned such vile beings as she.

"I cannot," Sigrid replied in fury. "I will not!"

"*Give it*!" Falora spat from the ghastly maw of the Vulture Queen. "Or watch your children pay the price!"

"*No*."

"You do not see the wrath my ghouls bring upon them? My Sifters are numb and ruthless, Eagle, like me! And they will not stop until *they get what they want*—which just so happens to be *whatever I want*."

"I do not doubt that," Sigrid replied. "But I finally hear it."

Falora's head cocked. "Hear it? Hear what?"

Vulturian eyes darted about frantically as her façade cracked further under panic. "What do you hear!?" she cawed.

"The sound we Companions have awaited since our arrival," Sigrid smiled. "It is the sound of your undoing."

Titha's ears perked up below on the ground. "I know that rabble," she said to herself excitedly as she hacked down another Sifter.

"Just more thunder, isn't it?" Gilly replied as she wrestled back an equally-statured imp alongside Clover.

"That's no thunder," Titha smiled. "It's hooves!"

From outside the throne chamber a great rolling herd of Rams approached. Their huge horns sliced through thick fog and rain, their own thundering competing with the storm's symphony above. Astride the most impressive of the herd rode the only Satyr Titha Mae had ever come to know: Kernos had returned, and with him came liberation.

"Now, Shieldmaiden!" the shepherd shouted, his plaid cloak waving in fierce winds. "And brace yerselves, lads!" he followed with a laugh. "Mine Rams come a' knockin' fer an ol' fashioned reckoning!"

Like the hammer of a God through thin flint, Kernos and his Rams shattered the front wall of the chamber. Sigrid heeded his call, hardening her feathers into steel-like amber as she spread wings over the Young Companions and their freed kin.

Waves of Bighorn Rams tore into the Sifters, tossing them aside; pulverizing their weak frames into the timeworn surroundings.

"Hoorah!" Titha cried out as she beheld the rambunctious site, cheers erupting from her sister, Bear-brother, best friend, and all their kin.

"*What magick!? What feat of sorcery is this*?" Falora squealed as she stumbled to her talons then back onto her tail, dodging the charge of a particularly massive Ram. "*What spell have you cast, Eagle*?"

"No spells," Nech smirked from below Sigrid, the Seed shining bright above him. "Just an old shepherd. And his goats."

"*Sheep*!" Kernos yelled. "They are *Sheep*, yah pointy-eared knob'lin! Do none of ye know a Bighorn when ye lay eyes?" he chortled as the weighted crook of his staff came 'round, swiping an entire wave of Sifters into the wall. He finished its twirl, sending its curve slamming down into the floor, shattering the stonework into a mightily impressive crater before Falora.

"Mornin', lass," he winked to her, staring straight into the Vulture's eyes. "I'd advise ye keep yer arse firmly planted where it be, less ye wanna lose that beautiful black beak o' yers." He gave one more twirl to his shepherd's staff for flare before slamming its end into the ground beside his hooves; the lightning above curiously aligning with his stroke. "Ah, there she be, the wee lass. Titha Mae, with all yer fingers an' toes about ye, I presume?"

Titha jumped to him, wrapping her arms around his wooly neck as his Rams continued to fight back the Sifters.

"We've no time fer mushin', wean. Got to get ye and yer kin as far from 'ere as possible. Ye donnae know who yer dealin' with. Not yet."

"Is that so?" Titha replied, still overjoyed to see him. "But how? How did you—"

"T'ese villains aren't t'first to try an' imprison this ol' shepherd, lass. I knew I'd be needin' help ta free yeh, so I called upon the glory o' me bride, the *glory* bein' we're both still *alive* t'help. As fer *ye*, Oatherian," he continued, lifting his staff to point it directly at Falora's face. "Donnae expect to stay the same... Mine particularly strong an' feisty bride be waitin' fer ye right outside this here collapsed wall o' stone, fer not but ta make sure mine friends leave all safe and sound'like. So no tryin' somet'in funny as they go, aye?"

Falora rolled her eyes. Her minions were all but depleted, as was her resolve, as the Rams tore through her ranks. She contemplated taking another form, one she had used to consume the efforts of several Companions on Nights before, but too much was at stake. For her. For her home. For the entirety of the Otherworld. So, no. Her wits it would have to be.

"Well played, all. Well played. Truly," she muttered, flickering her broad black wings to her in anger. "A mighty showing. Impressive, to the last. Look at all of you. Each so different, yet happily laying down lives for one another. And with such spunk. Touching. I am almost honored. But I must be *counting wrong...*" She stepped back from the crater of Kernos' making, her eyes looking to Titha, then Gilly. "Yes, I am now outnumbered, and yes the Seed is protected—for now— but... do I only see *two* Mae sisters here total? In all this rabble? Is there not a *third to show*?"

Titha and Gilly's ears burned at the threat. Both Cypress and the Stranger from Celtica laid unconscious in the Ruins... There was no longer any room to doubt who now wielded both stolen pieces of their mother's jewelry.

Falora reached into her downy bosom, retrieving two trinkets of the finest silver from her keepings: a ring... and a circlet.

"Two Mae sisters here... two pieces of the Tri-Spiral Runestone brought straight to me," she smiled, dangling both possessions at the tip of her sharpest feather. "So where... oh where... could the third piece be?"

Titha's eyes grew wide as time slowed around her; Falora's words bouncing hard between her ears. "Pieces?" she thought. "Tri-Spiral? Runestone?" she heard over, and over again. Were these simple spiraled amethysts, such precious gifts from their late mother, not simply mere jewels set in silver? Were they *pieces*, as Falora said? Three spiral pieces of a whole? This Tri-Spiral *Runestone*?

"I think I know where the last spiral is..." Falora continued. "For my mother was begotten three daughters, so yours must've been, as well, right? The Rule of Three, as we know, is a sacred rule, isn't it? Especially in *our families. First'blood* families. And if I were to keep my *youngest* sister safe... why, I think it'd be nowhere other than *with her father*."

Titha spat to the ground, wiping her mouth with her sword-wielding arm. "My father is the Watcher of Ythengrey. He sees all that enters and leaves our forest. You'll *never* get to them," she scolded, her knuckles white around the hilt of Feathersword.

"*Watch me.*" Falora swept out her wings, lifting into the air with a fury great enough to knock Sigrid aside.

"Won't be the first time I slip in unnoticed, then right out again, will it?" Falora smiled, looking over to the lifeless body of Calluna Mint. "So if you will not surrender the Seed of Igdrasil to me here and now, then I suppose I shall have to *open another door*!"

In a flash of blinding white light Falora turned for the opening in the ceiling, her wings giving off plumes of searing black smoke as she took for the swirling skies. Soot and wet ash dropped from her exit, falling from feather after feather until it covered the slain husks of those she had manipulated entirely. In the center of such smoking cinders laid Calluna Mint, once ever-a-friend and ally to the Maes of Ythengrey. As the ash consumed her entirely, her body faded into Falora's smoke, never to be seen in Gaela's realm again.

"Guard the children with your life, shepherd!" Sigrid commanded as she turned tail. "And thank you," she offered before shooting up into the storm in hot pursuit of the Vulture Queen.

Paw lumbered through the battlefield below her exit, stepping over countless lifeless Sifters as he made his way to Titha and Gilly, Bighorns bleeting triumphantly around them. The worn-out bear groaned a weary sigh, licking any scrapes he could find on his Luna-sisters.

"We have to beat her there," Titha exclaimed, fists shaking as she sheathed Feathersword to mount Paw. "Waste no more time! We have to save our little sister!"

"Aye, lass, ye do," Kernos replied as he tended to his herd. "An' in that lies the last wee bit o' Sigrid, Nech and I's plan."

"Good, great, a plan. I love plans," Titha quipped as she shoved Paw backward. "Get Cypress onto your back, brother," she commanded.

"*Grounnnp*!" Paw sputtered in definance.

"I don't care what he did a year ago, you overgrown raccoon!" his Luna-sis' spat back. "It's Cypress! He saved my life in the Dungeon, okay? Perhaps all of our lives, and even if he didn't, we're not leaving him, or anyone alive, behind. Now lift!"

Paw begrudgingly did as he was told, lifting their old mentor up across his broad back.

"Do we tie him down, or…" Gilly groaned as she climbed a'top Paw, her face contorted at the sight of the unconscious old Luna.

"Oh my Gods both of you shush!" Titha yelped as she slung her leg over Paw's neck. "Kernos! What's this plan? Because we're leaving."

"Aye," the Satyr replied immediately. "Listen up, lads!" Kernos swirled his staff to shepherd both folk and Ram to him. "Every soul here, standin' 'er not, is to mount a Ram as swiftly as their feet'll take 'em. Help those who need a'hand, and leave no fallen behind, as the Maes have decreed. Nech, yer with me, ye old traveller. Fer Celtica, lambs, we ride!"

CHAPTER TWENTY-ONE

The Battle for Celtica

"How much farther?" Titha shouted ahead, one hand shielding her eyes from continuous, pelting rain.

"T'ere is no faster way to traverse mine lands, lass," Kernos yelled without turning. "Patience, Mae!"

"I don't have that," she gritted, "especially not when my family is under attack." Paw grunted in agreeance, trying his hardest to match pace with the many mighty Rams galloping 'round them.

However tedious it seemed to her in such tense moments, galloping down from the Ruins' ridgetop proved vastly easier than climbing up out of the sludgy Wick. Such sloppy bits of their journey seemed like an age past; a 'once upon a time' of sorts. But the fresh stirring in Titha's gut told her that was not the case.

"The Vulture shall not beat us 'ere by much, if by any at'all," Kernos continued, shouting back over the thundering of both sky and herd.

"We wonnae let a hair be touched a'top her bonnie head, wee one," a much fairer voice replied from his right. Brigid, his 'better half', had finally been able to join them in conquest, and the Young Companions felt beyond grateful for it. Her bow, laced with golden trimmings, was the most beautiful weapon Titha had ever seen, and the arrows that accompanied it (within a similarly-laden quiver) looked thick enough to pierce a mammoth.

As Kernos rallied their flock beside her, the pointed visage of Nech peered 'round to the shepherd's side, his face much more green than yellow as he rode behind Kernos on the heartiest Ram Westlyn had ever birthed.

"May I request a substituting of stallions Kernos, my heartiest sir of sirs?" he shouted, finger pointed. "As wonderful as it has been to become reacquainted, my old bones cannot survive much more of this creature's cantankerous careening."

"Aye, Scribe," Kernos laughed. Without much more than a thought and a breath, he thwapped the old Craglin from his seat behind him with the curve of his staff and tossed him through the air over onto Paw's broad back. Unfortunately for Nech, such a switch-up meant landing directly onto the unconscious body of Cypress.

"Careful what you wish for," Gilly smirked from in front of him, her legs locked onto her Bear-brother as she attempted to settle Nech into a more comfortable position. She tried to keep the tartan shroud Kernos had given her between her hair and the storm whilst doing so, but it proved nigh' impossible; what with the handful of mentors bounding behind her, and all.

"This is taking too long!" she yelled, pulling the plaid tight like a bonnet with one hand while attempting to hold Cypress' unconscious (and beyond robust) body a'top Paw's backside with the other. "There is no way we traveled all this ground before. The sheeps aren't lost, are they?"

"I do not believe the beasts are at fault for what you are experiencing, master Gillian!" Nech decreed, his jowls bobbling.

"What does he mean, Titha?" she asked her sister, knowing full well that if she asked Nech himself to clarify it'd be days before she got a straight answer.

Titha's brow furrowed. Their journey—each hard corner and even harsher reality—rushed along with her. "He means Time," she offered back after a rough silence. "Before the trial, before Mrs. Mint's murder, before all of this, Paw lifted Audun and I up to the window outside Cypress' study as we listened to father, Sigrid, Maya, and our pal Nech, here, discuss everything."

Gilly looked to their northwestern side as Haldor led the way. There Audun rode astride as the hound's speed matched that of the fastest Rams. Their young friend clutched the Seed of Igdrasil tightly in his arms as both girls looked to him, but all Titha could see was her journey with him one year ago, when his fair hands had been thrust the fate of the Sunstone in such a similar way. What heavy burdens his youth had bared.

"Father spoke of everything as if it were far past the point of repair," Titha continued without looking back. "Time is breaking. *Has* broken. And we're simply along for the ride."

"Though like all parts of nature it will surely right itself," Nech added from behind them.

"You *think*," Gilly spat back. "Where was I during all this?"

"With Clover," Titha answered firm.

"Ah. Right," her sister replied, hiding her eyes. She turned back, staring over Nech's head as she spotted Mr. Fernbloom galloping astride a Ram with the worn-down body of his misguided son—the only boy she'd ever felt more than friendship for—straddled between his legs.

"But—*broken*?" Gilly continued. "That is a tad dramatic, isn't it?" Her instincts told her the opposite, but the eldest Mae sister never missed a chance to talk herself out of worry. "Meriduun's mist has been gone for a long time, Titha. Father and the elders—you included, Nech—are just reacting to the removing of the shroud. We're all caught up in change, and it's getting the better of us."

"I'd agree with you," Titha said as she ducked into Paw's speed, "If we hadn't just seen all we've seen, or if it were actually possible to experience what we have in the short time we *think* it's been. But it's not, is it? It isn't possible. Everything's changed, Gilly. Forever. Should we really expect anything to stay the same in a new Eon? One with the Great Drakes gone from Gaela for good?"

She almost ate her words as she spoke. Lightning struck something fierce before their path, igniting the clouds and all before them. In its ferocity the Tower of Celtica finally flashed into view, but it was accompanied by a sight fit for the tapestries of history:

Two gigantic Avians unfurled their wings within the lightning's glow—hooked beaks and talons ripping into one another's very being.

It was far from the homecoming they wished for.

"Perhaps the presence of the Great Drakes has not been eradicated," Nech bellowed, flabbergasted. "It would appear their divine roles were simply vacated, not vanquished—and such a void will not go unfilled. Not when Avians of equal splendor now claim our skies. It is a new Eon, indeed."

"Mother!" Audun shouted from a'far into the sideways deluge. Others gasped as they beheld Sigrid's plight upon the far horizon.

"—And the Vulture," Titha added from gritted teeth. "Falora has no idea who she's messing with."

"We must go to her!" Audun decreed, Haldor barking in tandem. "Mother needs our help!"

"We can't!" Titha retorted. "You know your mother can take care of herself—That gangly buzzard could never take her! We must protect the ones that do not know what comes for them! If we can see Falora then she hasn't gotten to Beebee or her necklace, and Time is still on our side—So first, father and my people must be warned!"

"Aye, 'at may be true, Mae," Kernos interrupted from the front ranks, "But the lad carries the Lifestone. P'raps a splitting o' the company would do well fer our cause?"

"Understood," Audun yelled abruptly. He lowered his chin to the top of Haldor's head. Four curly grey legs moved into a buzz-like rhythm, sending the hound into a sprint he was bred for.

"Donnae be daft, laddie!" Kernos shouted. "I didnae mean by yerself! Halt now! Halt, yeh wee dobber!"

"Audun, wait!" Titha added, but unlike Kernos, she knew he wouldn't turn back. The Viking'boy was off for the Tower of Celtica, Falora, and his Mother—the Seed of Igdrasil illuminating his path.

"He'll be offed! Killed dead, the poor dearie!" Brigid

screamed to Kernos. "After'em, or Falora will surely retrieve t'Stone from a lifeless lad!"

Kernos' eyes narrowed, several grim scenarios churning the meat o' his mind. He turned to take note of Titha's demeanor, looking to Nech for permission for what he was about to do.

"I donnae want t'leave ye again, lass," he yelled to her, the rain drenching his rust-colored fur, "But the lad leaves us no choice. Falora musn't take the Spawn of teh Tree o' Life into teh Otherworld!"

"Go, then!" Titha shouted back, "Nech and I will lead the others into Yythengrey."

Kernos looked to his bride. Brigid nodded, placing her bow at the ready as she drove her hooves into the side of her fierce Ewe.

"Stop staring and go!" Titha yelled.

Kernos heeded, and the last shepherds of their kind barreled up into Celtica with nothing but the protection of a tiny friend and his cargo on their minds.

Titha managed to send Bjor after them, too, with all other Vikings they'd liberated in tow. As they departed, she let loose a whistle only Audun and Haldor would recognize (aside from Paw, of course), its twirling notes splitting the hair in Nech's long ears. After a few agonizing moments, its melody returned to her from the distance; the twill perfectly replicated by her best friend. A smile lit the space between Titha's two chapped indigo cheeks, and with it she knew Audun would be alright. She *hoped* he would be alright.

Gilly placed her hands on her little sister's shoulders. "You've certainly rubbed off on that boy," she grinned softly. "Look at him go."

But Titha returned no such remarks. She rode still in that moment, praying to whatever forces Gaela controlled that her beloved friend survived this journey. "Just one more," she thought to herself. "Let him be okay through this last leg, and I'll never ask anything of him, or you, again."

"He will make it," Nech offered to them softly. "They all will, indeed, for that wretched witch messed with the *wrong* Companions."

Titha leaned back into Gilly and the Goblin as she ran her hand through Paw's thick coat. They headed westward as their party split in two, their rough band of Lunish survivors headed for Ythengrey. For *home.*

High above the muddied streets of Celtica, the fiercest of battles unfurled. Locked in combat Sigrid was, with a foe more cunning and dastardly than any she'd faced head-to-head. Falora Fomora, heir to the Fomorrigan, Vulture Queen of the Otherworld, dove and slashed tenaciously, relying on the power of Darkness to aid her. The weight of their combined wings doubled the strength of the storm churning around them, and all of Celtica fell into panic below their might.

"Did you expect a clean fight?" Falora cackled from a sharp black beak, the yellow around her irises gleaming in the blackness. She swooped below Sigrid, flipping her back toward the ground as two sets of bone-white talons ripped into the feathers of the Eagle's underside. Sigrid cawed in pain, her back careening backward into the Tower of Celtica with an awful shuttering of stone.

"We both know I would be dead by now if we fought on soil," Falora taunted from above, "but you're in the *skies* now, woman. And they are *my* territory."

Another gnashing wave of talons swept down into Sigrid, and more Avian cries mashed with thunder as she fell.

"I've been watching you, Shieldmaiden—Prying into your world and your mind from the windows of your dreams," she threatened as she smacked the falling Eagle's skull with a clubbed foot, sending Sigrid careening to the rocks below the Tower. "You wield the power of an Avian—of a *Goddess*! Yet you hide from it like a weakling—a coward—an heir running from the All-mighty they wish not to become—afraid to wield the power your very *blood* promises you! I expected so, so much more."

Sigrid's heft shattered the rock of the courtyard below, another crack of lightning illuminating the Tower over her.

"Once you're dead, I'll fill my mother's cauldrons with the mist of *every soul* you cherish, and take the Seed of Igdrasil for my own, and Oathera *will* prosper aga—"

CRACK! A massive stone shattered the words within Falora's beak, her head flinging back into her wing. "*Gaah*!" she cawed in shock before—*THRACK*— another enormous chunk of rock caught her underside, knocking the breath from her lungs.

A gasping inhale took her. "*Who dares*!?" she shrieked, absolutely astounded.

Sigrid rose slowly from her cratered surroundings to find all who remained in Celtica rallying around her. To her side they huddled: not just Vikingmen and women, but Lunas, too. Lumen, wolas, and their Goblin friends formed a perimeter, each wielding the largest projectile they could muster.

"*Rocks*!?" Falora screeched, flapping a mighty gust from ghastly black wings. "*Really*?"

A spear then pierced the primary feathers of her left wing, scraping just enough skin from the meat of her to send shockwaves through her body. The Vultress scrambled upward, wailing as she clawed her way behind the point of the Tower's top. She slammed her talons into its stone work, using it as a shield mere moments before dozens more projectiles crashed into the side opposite her. Panic, then, seemed an appropriate reaction, and her hateful eyes bulged.

"You may have me bested as an Avian, Falora," Sigrid cried out, finally standing to her golden feet, "but you shall never know the victory that unity brings. Try as you might to tear us apart from the shadows—for you shall only make us *stronger*."

Another wave of weapons crashed into the Tower of Celtica, the cries of its peoples echoing with the same veracity. Yet as powerful as their show for Sigrid was, greater was the will of Darkness. Their pelting of the Tower left many scars in its stone, and as Falora huddled behind its mass she felt its integrity begin to *shift*.

The cunning Vultress let loose a hissing caw, her black wings spitting outward as lightning dressed her in spectacle. *CRUCK!* She kicked, thousands of pebbles stumbling from the wounded Tower. But the projectiles still came. CROCK! She kicked again, then again; swift talon'hammering sending chunks of the Tower's stonework down into the crowd.

"*Oh no,*" Sigrid cried under her breath as her mind's eye

saw what was about to be. "Everyone back!" she screeched, but it was too late. Falora twirled the entirety of her Vulturian form as her feathers hardened into black obsidian. Like an axe through butter they crashed through, and the entire top half of the Tower broke free from its base; its heft falling with all the force of Gaela's great gravity. Sigrid's feathers hardened to amber as her wings shot out with enormous size, their brazen length forming a shield over every citizen beneath her. Lightning struck as Falora cackled above, her black soul taking great pleasure in watching such a symbol of unity come crashing down upon everything that had, in her eyes, cost her her own family.

The Tower's top shattered across Sigrid's red feathers as every inch of her shuttered to protect those she was sworn to. Awful cries of three races billowed from beneath as the slabs pummeled their Eagle guardian, but no such cries came from her. Her golden beak fell silent. Sigrid became pinned to the earth, her still body the only thing shielding Celtica's citizens from being crushed into Oblivion.

As her body shivered, a shrieking cry erupted from the far southern fields, followed by a bright emerald light and the thundering of not thunder itself, but one hundred and eight hooves initiating the beginning of the end of the Battle for Celtica.

Audun shrieked again, screaming for his mother as the sight of her crushed Eagalian body became clearer to him in the Seed's light. Haldor howled with him, rushing winds pelting his wet nose as he darted for the debris at the foot of the Tower.

"What fortune!" Falora cawed unexpectedly. The Vultress crept out of the shadow of the broken monument, her eyes glistening within the glow of the Lifestone. Haldor threw his paws into the mud, sliding them to a hasty halt at a safe distance.

"Is every treasure of this world entrusted to dim-witted children? How blissfully naïve you all are!" she cackled. Her head creaked down as her neck arched; the dusty orange feathers of her mane flickering rainwater wildly. "Bring it here, little boy! Pip'pip! Bring the Seed here, yes? Bring it to me, and I will not rip the gullet from your mother's neck right before your tiny, innocent eyes," she smiled.

Audun lowered his gaze. Haldor looked up to him as his master slid down his side; the Seed shining ever-brighter in his arms.

"That's a good boy," Falora cawed, her beak contorting into an even more crooked smile.

But the sound of thundering hooves behind Audun did not cease, nor did his grip on the prize.

"I may be small," he said, little feet plopping among enormous raindrops, "but I am Audun Angvarsson, Son of Angvar the Bold and Sigrid the Glorious Red Eagle, and I will not bend to evil!"

He had friends to back up such a show of strength, too. A breath of relief escaped him as Kernos, Brigid, and their herd boomed onto the landscape behind him, with Bjor the Blacksmith leading the next flank.

The smirk dropped from Falora's face immediately. A graceless murmur blasted from her beak before she stomped her talons further into the shattered Tower, her fiery eyes scowling down at all who now rose to oppose her. She had faced greater odds, however. Her life had been spent in a world of decay—and she was made all the fiercer for it. She blamed such a hard life on everyone currently surrounding her, too. There was no scenario she hadn't prepared for, and this one in-particular was a vision she had prayed would come to fruition. She yearned for it, ever since she first infiltrated the mist of Sigrid's dreams. Her feathers shimmered as she leapt from her perch, enormous talons unfurling as she slammed into a hard stance on the ground. Slowly her head lowered parallel to the mud; each gangly foot retracting then stomping as she crept toward Sigrid's exposed head, her eyes locked onto those that threatened her destiny.

"Do not touch her!" Audun spat, Haldor growling behind him.

"Or what?" Falora cackled, gnashing her beak. Her right talons flittered out, clasping a'hold of Sigrid's feathered neck. The Shieldmaiden's eyes shot open in pain, the ice blue of her natural irises coming through her Eagalian amber.

As Audun's eyes met his mothers, the entirety of their relationship flashed before his mind and heart. He felt her sturdy arms cradling his infantile body as she sang tales of grand halls and Great Drakes. He could see his beloved father and brother approaching from the doors of their home as he played with stuffed animals and wooden warriors atop the pelted rugs of Skaldhall. Sunny skies then swirled over his vision, the golden hills of their lands breaking through as Sigrid took his small hands into her own, forming a mound of soil with them. At its center rested a sapling in their precious garden.

"Now it will grow big and strong, my son," she said to him, her smile worth more than all the gold in the world. A single sprout flickered before him, its two tiny leaves dancing in kind. "Tend to our earth, and it will always tend to you in return," his mother spoke before leaning down to kiss his forehead.

Audun jolted back to life as he felt her love. The Seed of Igdrasil creaked in return, jittering in his hands.

"What are you doing, boy?" Falora spat, glaring down at him. Her eyes darted along with every movement the Seed made. "Is this another trick? What do you truly hold there?"

Audun's feet were already sinking into the wet, worn soils of Celtica below, and the wiggling of the Seed only intensified it. Before he could struggle to free himself, a single root burst forth from the Seed, shattering an opening like a living vine through green glass. Its tendrilous form shot deep into the earth, and with it Audun's purpose became clear.

"Tend to our earth," the littlest Viking heard within, "and it will always tend to you in return."

That single, tiny sapling from his childhood danced in his mind's eye once more, and for a moment nothing else mattered.

Audun arched the Seed up into the air with a mighty cry from worn lungs. With one fell swoop he drove it down into the coarse mud, using every inch of his body to bury it deep within.

"Stop! *No*!" Falora cackled and cawed. She let loose of Sigrid's throat as she dashed for the Seed.

One after the other, roots broke from its emerald casing; each larger than the last. Twisting and turning, they became one with the wet soil of Celtica, the roots pulling the fallen stones of the Tower down into the dirt as Gaela's very earth shone with all the radiance of an Emerald Aurora.

"*Ckrrraaaawwww*!" Falora screeched. The Vulture Queen pointed her body like the shaft of a spear behind a beak of a blade as she shot directly for Audun and his treacherous act. But Gaela would not have it. From the soil a seedling erupted, its top pointed like the Tower of Celtica before it. The living sapling speared Falora's breast as she erupted into blood-curdling cries and black feathers. Hastily the sapling rocketed into the sky above with the Vultress staked a'top it, knotted roots solidifying its presence there all the while. The Vultress clawed at the forming trunk as it coiled upward, but there was no escape. The Spawn of the Seed of Igdrasil grew ever-taller and ever-mightier, taking the fallen stones of the Tower of Celtica into its very bark as it formed the makings of Igdrasil's Daughter. Just as it reached a height any creature would bow to, the sapling burst with emerald light, sending the Ghastly Black Vulture flailing into the storm above.

"Aye, pure brilliance, lad!" Kernos cried, his staff high above his head. He hooked it forward, pulling Audun and Haldor back to him as the wounded bird fell from the sky. Before them Falora tumbled down the sapling's budding branches, each taking a chunk of feathers with it. *PLOP* she went as her bruised white form splatted into the mud at the sapling's roots; Avian no more.

Audun pushed Kernos' staff from his front, bursting for his mother. She remained still and strong, though the life was leaving her eyes. Every ounce of her held only one purpose—one that was unclear to her son until he came upon her. Faint calls for help escaped from beneath stones and giant feathers, but they fell on deaf ears. All Audun cared about, in that moment, was his beloved mother.

"Mother?" he cried, placing both tiny hands on her golden beak. "Mother, can you hear me?"

Slowly her eyes looked to him, and a smile took her. "My son," she shuttered. "I am so very proud of you." She attempted to lean her beak toward him, but flinched to a pause as massive stones shifted a'top her back.

"Do not struggle, mother, please," he offered, stroking the

feathers of her enormous red cheek. "Kernos and Brigid are here with us. We are going to get these boulders off you."

Sigrid's smile slid into an exhale, and her head fell to the mud below.

"Mother? *Mother*!" Audun screamed, taking her beak again. But she did not budge.

"*Help*!" he cried into the rain. "*Come help her!*"

Every set of hooves present galloped to their aid, each with the intent of lifting mighty stones with mightier horns. Yet before they could pry any loose, the soil beneath Sigrid began to stir. From Gaela herself the roots of the sapling arched upward, lifting each piece of the Tower from the Shieldmaiden's body. One by one the debris was removed, finally freeing Sigrid from her plight. Calls of joy rung out from below her as the roots settled into a natural state.

"Woah," Audun whispered. From beneath his mother's wings the people of Celtica emerged—battered, muddy, and bloody—but alive.

Sigrid rolled over as her chest instinctively gasped for air. Slowly the amber of her feathers left her, and she returned to a woman; a warrior bathed in the shadows of those she had sacrificed her body to protect. The rain cooled her face as she laid upon her back, and for the first time her eyes beheld the glory of the Sapling.

"*By the Gods,*" she exhaled, tears leaving her eyes. "She has returned to us… a Daughter. The *Daughter of Igdrasil.*"

Celtica's citizens looked up into the continuing storm as the most massive sapling since the creation of Time stood mightily before them: its roots taking into the very soil they shared. A gentle emerald glow glistened from its top, placing a glimmer of green hope in the eyes of all who basked in her splendor.

"*Why?*" a broken voice muttered from distant mud. "*Why would you do this to us?*" it continued.

Falora reappeared, her broken body crawling across the ground as sparse feathers covered a form half-person and half-Avian. "*You did not need another Tree!*" she spat before hacking up an awful black substance. "*You do not need her might* to prosper! *Cretons! Gluttons! Greedy, selfish, conceited filth! All of you!*" She stood to crooked legs, a cloak of purple smoke slowly covering her wretched form. "You have doomed Oathera! You have *doomed* the shadow, the *sister* of your own world! *You have doomed us all!*"

Audun looked up from his mother as Haldor licked her wounds. Brigid drew her bow as a flickering Falora stumbled for them, but the threat of arrows loosening apparently wasn't enough to halt her. Not in such a state, where retribution was a'kin to air or water. *THWIP*! The first arrow fired anyway—and Falora deflected it with all the swiftness and accuracy of a seasoned ranger. *THRAP—THWONG!* Two more arrows left Brigid's bow, but none could pierce the white hide below black smoke.

"You may have just deprived me of my world's greatest hope," Falora spat as she crept toward Audun, "But know now, boy, that the war is just beginning."

Kernos yelled a furious war'cry as he leapt for her, his staff aiming to cut her down. Despite all his swiftness, she dodged his attack with little effort, sliding directly for Audun on a fog of deceit. From her bosom she pulled Titha's circlet and Gilly's ring, clutching them tight within crooked fingers as she dangled them before him.

"Only one piece left," she grinned as the black of her cloak swirled wildly. "If I can no longer bring the Tree of Life to Oathera," she screeched, *"Then I shall bring Oathera to the Tree."*

One bony finger rose up, its black nail twitching across Audun's forehead, tearing his skin. Haldor lashed out from behind Sigrid, but he, too, was bested by her smoke. From afar Brigid shot one last arrow t'ward Falora's trajectory—but it found no target.

In a flash of cold light and mist the Vulture Queen vanished westward—the echoes of her cackling laugh raining ash onto the surrounding people. As her soot swirled it transformed, unleashing the full fury of her feathered minions onto what remained of Celtica.

"Where did she go?" Audun yelled, flanked by ensuing chaos once more; a single drop of blood trickling down the cut on his brow.

"Fer the reckoning of the Mae clan, lad!" Kernos cried, his staff swatting an entire wave of the gangly black birds away. "May Gaela have mercy on 'eir souls."

CHAPTER TWENTY-TWO

Entombed

"Tell me to calm down *one more time*, please!" Titha screamed as she charged atop Paw, his barreling bounds leading them alongside the Great Daenu River and far into the Duskridge; into home.

"I'm scared for her, too, Titha! But—I am trying to prepare you for any possible outcome!" Gilly shouted from behind, her fists clenched onto her middle sister's tunic. "And no, before you say it, I'm not just trying to start an argument."

"Coulda' fooled me!" Titha spat, ducking into Paw's drift. "There is no way this ends other than saving Beebee and sending that *witch* back into the *hole* she crawled out of."

"We're all on the same page with that," Gilly replied,

shielding her eyes. "But if you barge into this all over-confident you're going to get someone else hurt! Again! Now is not the time to be impulsive. *Again*! We need a plan!"

Titha let loose a guttural exhale. "Turn around, then, and tell Clover, and his father, then all the others that we freed from certain death—or worse, from some sick *Otherworld sacrifice*—that we should've just stayed home," she scowled, infuriated. "Look back and tell your lover'boy that they'd all be better off if I was a perfect little angel-baby and they were all forgotten and rotting in some ruins in the South! *Go on*, I'll wait!" she spat, wiping her mouth clean of the taste of her sister's pessimism. "I have a plan, and it's called 'kill the buzzard and save our little sister'. If you've got a better one, I'm all ears."

Gilly's face was scrunched as tight as it would scrunch, both from the bustling winds and the smacking of Titha's words. She turned around, her eyes glaring over to Nech, who now steadied Cypress' still-unconscious body astride his own mighty Ram, before her vision darted to the Fernblooms aboard another Bighorn. Perhaps if she stared hard enough, Clover would make eye contact with her—but no such gratification came. The Luna boy hung his head in shame, his disciple's hood still covering his brow as his father steered their sheep into Yythengrey. He may have been spared from a worser fate in Titha's view, but nothing about his demeanor implied he shared that sentiment.

Gilly may have finally gone silent, but Titha tried within every flinching motion to ward off her harmful words. Every sight, every sound, and every adorable Duskridge creature leaping from their thundering path reminded her more and more of Beebee, and how every turn in their twisting journey had, somehow, managed to put the tiniest Mae in mortal danger. For all the good they'd accomplished, it seemed mightily unfair.

Behind them, Nech began to sway atop his Ram, a shrieking "Gracious me!" catching the attention of all. The sisters turned back in tandem with his trademark phrase, precisely in time to see his body flying upward atop his Bighorn. Right beneath, the much greater body of Cypress shot upright in a panic, flinging the poor Goblin fully off and onto the riverbank.

"*Not again*!" Cypress shouted just as Nech hit the ground. Titha pulled Paw's fur until he halted, and their party came to an abrupt stop aside the rushing waters of the revered Daenu.

Nech stumbled fast, scoffing as he finally fumbled to a stop on the riverbank. He grabbed his bony knees, hissing as his hands met pebble-filled scrapes.

"Don't move," Titha spouted to Gilly as she shot down from their Bear-brother.

Gilly scolded her. "I'm getting pretty tired of you thinking you can order me around, little—"

—Titha shot 'round with a glare so sharp it cut Gilly's sentence in two.

"Cypress, it's us!" Titha shouted, furious with any waste of time. But she sucked it up, turned about, and tended to Nech's Ram, gently placing her hands on his muzzle as she proved once again what a way she had with animals. Cypress, though, was not to be calmed. He thrashed about, his mind taken by a fever dream so great that he was convinced he was reliving every ounce of trauma Falora inflicted upon him. Paw whipped around, the hair standing up on his neck as he hunched toward their old mentor, waiting for him to betray them again, as his Luna-sisters warned he might.

"Cypress, please! Listen to my voice—It is me! It's

Titha—"

But his thrashing would not cease. Paw growled, rolling his lips as a fierce spit left his clenched teeth.

"Stand down, brother," Titha commanded. She saw the same fright and anger in Cypress' own frothing mood, and in this, thankfully, a solution clicked. Gently she reached out, just as she did to the Ram, placing her hands upon Cypress'. He flinched, and one arm shot round like a tumbling log—yet just before it struck her into the river—it ceased; his fever melting into a calm that mimicked the flowing waters beside them.

"*Where*... where am I?" he stammered. Clear-mindedness still eluded him, but the sounds of the streaming, life-giving waters of the Daenu River were unmistakable to his ears.

"Am I... *home*?" Cypress whimpered, still and wet'eyed.

"You are," Titha squinted, watching him like a hawk.

"*Why*..." he retorted, enormous fists retreating to him. The fog of his exile slowly drifted from the corners of his vision, and familiar foliage greeted the complicated Luna. He sunk to his knees in disbelief as the smell of the Daenu, the trees, and the soil, filled his nostrils. "Why..." he whimpered again. "Why did you bring me here?"

"Because the alternative was leaving you to die," Titha answered. "But make no mistake, we're not here for *you*. Get up, now. Beebee is in danger. All of our people are. *Because* of you."

"The Oatherian... Falora, she has left the Ruins?" he stammered. "I should have foreseen this... It... *She*... is far more dangerous than anything from our world," he clenched. "I was foolish to ever assume an alliance could be formed between our realms."

"I don't care what your plan was, or what your intentions

were," Titha soured. "Everything you've done has led to that twisted *wench* threatening the life of my—*of my baby sister*!" She drew Feathersword instinctively, and without so much as a flinch swung the blade up to Cypress' throat. "So you are going to get your enormous arse back up on that beautiful sheep and ride it until you stand directly between Falora and the safety of Begonia Bee Mae!"

Nech hobbled to her, placing a gentle hand on her back. "Easy, easy, my dearest. I, nor our company, wish to see you stoop to this betrayer's depths of boorish depravity."

Cypress muttered something, grinding his teeth at the sight of this stooge-of-a-Goblin that took his place beside Theole. "You know not of what you speak, *maggot*," he roared from his throat.

Titha didn't like what she heard, nor Cypress' incessant lingering, and pressed Feathersword into the indigo flesh of his gullet, silencing him.

"That *maggot* has been the only thing stopping your unconscious body from flailing off the back of this sweet Ram," she threatened, turning her blade slightly.

Cypress flinched, but no smile or emotion escaped.

"Get. On. The sheep," Titha commanded.

"You still assume I am your enemy in this, my child?" Cypress retorted, pressing his finger against the flat of the sword, removing it from a primed position. "I assure you once more, whether you are to believe me or not, that all I have ever done has been to protect you, your sisters, and our people."

Titha jerked back Feathersword, sending it across Cypress' shoulder. *THWAP*! A great tear flapped from his ragged attire, and purple dripped from the edge of her blade. Nech and the Fernblooms stumbled away from her tenacious display. Gilly's hand shot to her mouth as Paw's gaped open.

"I'm not going to ask you again," Titha commanded, pointing her sword into Cypress' chest, then to the awaiting Ram.

The old Luna raised his hands in defeat, walking for the Bighorn before assisting Nech's re-saddling as Titha instructed. As the two opposite beings settled on, she held her weapon still, marching to Gilly and Paw with zero remorse.

"We ride for Roostwood immediately," she peppered, stone-hard. But to her great aggravation, Cypress did not comply.

"None will be there," he replied sternly. "If Falora has gathered enough strength to finally leave the mists of the Ruins—and she is indeed headed here—then she aims to complete the Tri-Spiral Runestone. And then *use* it. Thus, there is only one place such an artifact will prove useful to her within our hallowed walls."

"—The Tomb," Titha blurted instinctively.

"Yes, child," Cypress confirmed. "And although you have brought us along the riverbank as opposed to our forest's front gate, you know as well as I do that here, in Yythengrey, your father sees *all*. As soon as he catches sight of my presence he will flock to wherever we linger. I suggest we go to the location where Falora is most likely to appear, as I now sense we have not time for nor the luxury of second chances. It is best we aim for two birds with one stone."

"Why are you stalling then, Cypress?" a meek voice added to the fray, breaking its own silence. Clover lowered his hood, raising his gaze for the first time since returning home, if only to lay eyes on the master who had led him so far astray. "The girls are right," he continued, his father and their Ram behind him. "This is your fault. Our fault. *My* fault. And you weren't given a second chance so we could stand by the river and suffer listening to you enjoy the sound of your own voice."

Gilly's eyes glinted at the resurgence of her former fling's vigor. Cypress, though, did not reply. He found the hostile tone of his former disciple beyond disrespectful in such a moment. But he was no longer in control. Not here. Titha, her blade, and the company she bore, were. It was her footsteps he followed now.

"To the Tomb," Titha decreed, her knuckles still white around Feathersword's Celtican hilt. "And mark my words, Cypress, if we are too late, and my little sister has paid the price for whatever game you've been playing, I will make sure your fate is *far* worse than hers."

Paw flinched as his *very* angry sister climbed atop his shoulders. "Ride," she decreed, and off they went up the riverbank with even more haste than before. Tunnels were carved through brush; new paths made beneath thick canopies. No bramble nor thicket slowed their advance, and Titha's bristling determination only grew wilder with every passing landmark.

Yet they would not find their people's ancient tomb unattended. As old trees parted and the company finally arrived, a great bustle of Bear-brothers lumbered at the Tomb's entrance. Each beast heaved massive new boulders over its opening as if they expected Dragons themselves to resurrect from its bowels. Yet there their tiny sister rocked: Titha exhaled a sigh strong enough to down an ox as she beheld Begonia Bee Mae, cool as a cucumber amidst her father's hysteria. Theole cradled her tightly in his arms; his gaze locked onto the Tri-Spiral of the Tomb's entrance stone as it let out a faint glow.

"More!" the Watcher commanded, waving his hand over

to the outcrop of stone each bear pulled from. "We take no more chances. We risk no more lives! Seal this Cairn as if forever, and if such a pathway truly rests within, it shall haunt us ne'er again!"

Titha jolted backward amid Paw's stride. She felt her father's watchful eyes break from the Tomb and lock onto her from a distance. He not only knew they were coming—he expected them.

With a great, star-like burst of blue his Ozark staff materialized. Pure, ancient Moonlit magick shimmered down from the heavens as he waved the staff in a circle, cloaking the Tomb and its grounds in a protective sphere of sapphire light. Its wall greeted Titha abruptly as she barged straight for her kin with Paw and Gilly; their eyes closed and braced for impact. But the luminous blue let them pass through unhindered. So, too, did Clover and his father careen through, their faces lit with pure shock. Nech charged forth in their example, guiding his Ram toward the sapphire sheen with Cypress holding on behind. He closed his wrinkled eyelids tight and took a deep breath. With bubbled-up cheeks he, and his Bighorn, charged through unscathed, but not without flinching from the grave "*Gyah*!" that erupted from the seat behind him. Nech turned about to find Cypress flat on his back, the air knocked from his chest as the sphere's wall stood firm between him and the rest of his company. The old Luna grabbed his thick head, sitting up as he began to brim with his own sort of magick. The once illustrious white and silver of his exile's cloak sparked back to life upon him as he stood; its fabrics crackling forth from thin air as he shed the appearance of a broken prisoner with time to lose.

"Let down your guard, Theole!" he shouted, readily preparing for what would come next. "You have no idea what now heads our way!" He rose in splendor, revealing a Luna unshackled by Falora's torment. "I, too, wished for our reunion to be under different circumstances, but you must trust that I have not returned home as your enemy, and let me pass!"

"I know not what role you play in this—and in spirit of such you shall *not* be welcomed here!" Theole trumpeted, his tiniest daughter buried into his robes. Titha leapt from Paw as she ran for her father and sister, with Gilly and Nech right behind. The family embraced, but each knew there was not time for more.

"*No*!" Cypress spat furiously as he barged for the sapphire barrier again. Then again. Its cleansing energy seared into his cloaken-flesh every time, sending him careening back. "You do not understand!" he cried.

"You are correct, I do not!" Theole shouted back. "And until I *do*, you shall not set foot anywhere near this hallowed place, nor breathe the same air as my daughters e'er again!"

"*She* is coming, Theole!" Cypress cried out. "The heir to the Fomorrigan is upon us! And if you do not let me pass, she will break through this thinly veiled spell and take you all into the foulest reaches of the Otherworld through the very Tomb you cling to!"

"More lies!" Nech shouted from beside the Maes, his hands twitching beneath the billowing energies that encased them. "Do not listen to a single, malicious word he utters, Sire! For it was *he* who summoned her, this Falora Fomora! It was *Cypress* who unleashed the Vulture Queen upon us all!"

"*Shut your wretched mouth, imp*!" Cypress frothed in reply, his heft quaking. His hands shot out, spreading wide into the forest as a similar light to Theole's began to bristle at his fingertips—but of a bright purple. "*How*?" he muttered, stunned as he stared to his own hands. Yet as the light gathered enough energy to crackle, it burst like lightning, and Cypress gave into its command. With great purpose he drove his hands together and a deafening clap rung out, equaled only by the sky's own thunder. From this he gestured a spiral shape, carving the thin air with purple electricity, and a smile ignited beneath his moustache. Each of his arms jutted forward like the fiercest of boars as he pushed, driving the spiral through Theole's sapphire conjuration—and as much to his own amazement as Theole's—a pathway shattered through the sapphire wall. Slowly Cypress sauntered in, his brow heavy as violet lightning danced betwixt thick fingers.

Theole darted forward, brushing his family behind him, but Titha would not have it. This was the exact moment she'd been waiting for. She knew Cypress was hiding something, and this had to be it! Purple lightning? Self-materializing, pearly white robes? Where was the broken, weakened Luna who sat stranded in his family's own ancient dungeon? Whoever approached her now was not him. Whatever granted him such gaudy powers was not to be trusted, either.

Furious, Titha shoved her father's guard away, brandishing the sword she'd never sheathed in anticipation of Cypress' betrayal. Together they stood, father and daughter, wielding their familiar weapons against a familiar friend turned foe. Cypress, though, did not poise himself to attack in turn. Nor did he see himself in the same villainous light.

"Falora will be upon us any moment," he offered instead, fingertips crackling. Several bears dropped their stones by the Tomb, turning to snarl and advance on Cypress, but a quick blast of violet kept them at bay. "We can either continue to squabble over the past, rendering ourselves defenseless, or you can *stand down* and let me do what I came here to do!" he spoke sincere.

"Go away!" Beebee shouted, pawing her tiny hand at Cypress. "Shoo! Shoo!" she cried out from her father's chest.

"You heard the lady," Titha replied, her sword between Cypress and her little sister. The three Mae girls shared a glance before turning it on the aggressor.

"We've seen too much to ever trust you again," Titha declared.

"I cannot back down, littlest Luna," Cypress returned to Beebee, the light of his hands growing ever-fiercer. "For if I do, you shall surely perish."

For a brief moment Cypress locked still-eyes with the Lunas he once considered family. Theole pointed the Ozark staff firm; he could feel the hearts of his daughters slipping toward their kin's words. And just as they wished to lower their guard to him, Cypress lunged for Beebee, his hands curved like the tusks of a Dusklion. But Titha was faster. Feathersword slashed outward, meeting Cypress's wrist before he could capture Beebee. To the disbelief of all present—*SCHLOP*—Cypress' right hand schlepped clean off, landing amid the moss below.

Horribly he cried out as Titha held firm, but the gesture only proved enough to distract the Maes from his *left* hand. With it, he snatched not Beebee, but the necklace dangling beneath her chin.

The chain had been made of the finest silver Lunas could conjur—yet no material in all of Gaela's bosom could've stopped Cypress from this deed. He knew, unlike his old family, that the Tri-Spiral Runestone had to be made whole again for *their* survival—not Falora's.

Beebee shrieked in pain as the silver chain left a mark behind her neck, its amethyst firmly in Cypress' grasp. He jerked his handless wrist back from Titha, shoving it into his cloak as his blood turned it from white to purple. Before he could compose himself, the shining end of the Ozark staff cracked into his jaw, sending the crippled Luna down hard into the earth. Beebee clutched Theole's neck as she continued to cry. "My neck-a-lace, my neck-a-lace!" she shouted, and with each of her teeny tears Theole's rage grew tenfold.

"To hear her cry at the hand of *your* treachery!" he shouted. "*You*, Cypress! To think I should have killed you when I had the chance one year ago!"

Cypress rose silently, clutching the spiraled amethyst tightly as he lifted his cloak to his mouth, biting down on it. With one swoop he ripped a large, bloodied swatch from it, wrapping his severed wrist as he stumbled from the loss of life-giving blood. Slowly his eyes drifted downward from Theole and Beebee. Tears swelled in Titha's eyes as she pointed her sword to him again, his blood still dripping from it. Slowly his gaze locked to her own.

"In this and all else, my child," the battered Luna swore to her one last time, "*I have always done my best to protect you.*"

With the fury of a thousand harpies a whirling force of destruction ripped through the tree'line from the east, shattering the composure of all. Splintering Eons-old tree'trunks as if they were twigs, the butchering force of black smoke screeched and cawed as it made itself known by crashing through Theole's sapphire spell like fine glass.

Gilly screamed as she snatched Nech up, throwing him

between her and her father, whose robes had risen to protect Beebee and all others—the feathers of his Grand Silver Owl'en form forming along its edge—each acting as a shield for his kin. Fernbloom and his son stood frozen adjacent to the boulder-filled entrance to the Tomb, Clover's joints locked in terror.

"She's here," Clover cried, shivering to his father.

Falora burst into her Vulturian shape above the Cairn, her horrid cry stabbing the ears of every Luna beneath her smoking talons. But she was not to be met with cowardice.

The first to attack were Kernos' Rams, each unrelenting and non-hesitant in their charge, just as they had been upon entering Ythengrey. Great bleets left their maws as they darted into the air, horns first. Falora cackled as she cut them down one by one, their bodies falling in pieces. Titha screamed in dread as she brandished her sword to avenge the fallen beasts. Theole's staff shot out before her, stopping her from a most unnecessary death.

Cypress turned to meet Falora—his wrapped stub of a wrist dripping with thick, timeworn blood. As he let go of it, the violet light of the last piece of the Tri-Spiral amethyst escaped his remaining hand, and Falora swept into a grotesque display of pleasure as she landed atop the Tomb bearing its same symbol.

"I am beyond pleased!" she cawed brazenly, a twisted smile shaping her black beak as the creaking sound of her voice escaped it. *"It seems that you shall not fail me in the end, Luna."*

"Never, my master," Cypress decreed, bowing before her.

Slowly he walked toward her presence; into the Moonlit shadow of the massive Vulture perched overhead.

"Traitor!" Titha screamed, the word and its weight scratching her throat. But Cypress did not turn back. He only

marched t'ward the entrance of the Tomb.

Above him Falora spread her wing out, revealing Thea's circlet and ring with her sharp feathers, just as she had in the Ruins. Her other wing spread in kind, lowering to Cypress as if he knew what to do next.

"The soil," he replied to her gesture. "The hallowed soil of this place is required to rejoin the Tri-Spiral."

Falora twitched. "*So be it,*" she splintered. Her talons let loose of the Tomb as she leapt down onto the ground, her grandeur shattering the stance of all in her presence. The bears of the forest began to growl and grunt behind Paw's lead, each ready to rip the meat from the buzzard's bones when the moment presented itself. Cypress stepped to his proclaimed master amidst their grizzling, then lifted the last piece of his people's sacred Runestone to Falora. The Vulture inhaled deeply as the moment she had coveted came to fruition. Her massive, outstretched feathers slowly molted as she held the three pieces of jewelry together, the form of the Vulture Queen giving way to her true self. Her beak retreated into silky black lips, but the fire in her eyes remained; burning ever-fiercer.

With her bare hands she laid the artifacts into the mossy soil at the entrance to the Tomb. There, in that ghastly moment did Titha, Gilly, and Beebee finally see the shape their mother's amethyst once held before it became three pieces of jewelry.

Falora pressed their silver into the peat, leaving only the spiraled fragments exposed. The ground began to quake as their bulk was buried, and a familiar light began to glow from each piece. Behind them, the Tri-Spiral of the Tomb suddenly ignited, its entrance stone vibrating with the power of the symbol. Theole's eyes locked onto it once more as its faint, Moon-like glow erupted into a visceral display of violet light the likes of which he'd never seen here.

Titha gripped Feathersword with both hands as she looked to Paw, each waiting for the right moment to strike. Theole kept shaking his head 'no' at her, but she was far past the advice of others. She was not about to let Falora's revenge take hold, not in this sacred place nor any other.

Just before she felt herself pouncing, the ground around the amethysts erupted further, sending its moss into a burst of purple flames. Slowly the amethysts pulled toward each other, the spirals itching to join as if magnetized. The violet flames grew higher and higher as Falora cackled in their flickering light.

"The humans may have stolen the Lifestone from me, but *oh*, how much better this will be," she cried. "Here, quite poetically, will you witness the coming of Oathera, as the mist of *my* lands *takes you for its own*!"

A burst of awful cold escaped the mound of amethysts, and with it they were rejoined. Their silver holdings melted into the earth, and behind them the boulders blocking the Tomb's entrance began to tremble in tandem. One by one they cracked under the quaking, before a terrible force began sucking them inward.

"What is this?" Theole thought aloud, Ozark staff still poised. He awaited the right moment to strike, but could not sacrifice the safety of his daughters, nor Nech, that clung to him so.

The bears began roaring and clawing onto their hind legs as the boulders they had moved with their own might began slugging inward, like a great force was ripping them into the tomb. A light as violet as the Tri-Spirals ignited from behind, and with it an explosion completely shattered the entrance. Each boulder flew into a hundred pieces, pelting Falora and Cypress back as an all-consuming, swirling purple vortex enveloped the inside of the Cairn. Falora stared into it, obsessed with its majesty as she erupted into more laughter.

"Now *my* people shall prosper at the behest of *yours*!" she screeched, black nails pointed to the Maes. "Oh, how *pleased* my ancestos shall be."

Yet as she spoke, the force of the vortex became too much, and she hiccuped as she felt her clawed toes sliding inward. Her demeanor flipped immediately, the fire in her eyes turning to panic. Many foul words left her lips, and her crooked form hunched over as she planted the claws of her toes and fingers deep into the earth, wrenching herself backward to grab the Tri-Spiral Runestone in its whole form.

Before the Tomb, Cypress stumbled into the consuming pull of the purple portal. He looked over his shoulder to see Theole holding Beebee and Gilly tight. Titha's gaze was locked onto him, her blade still wet with his blood as she pointed it to him still, protecting Nech behind her. To the south stood a youth he had found companionship in: Clover, who removed his disciple's cloak, letting it be sucked into the torrenting pull of the vortex as he turned to his father's embrace. They stood firm, holding each other, neither thinking for a second of ever letting the other go.

A faint smile lit the space beneath Cypress' thick, curled mustache as he turned back to Falora. He watched as her arm jutted up, a great cackle leaving her lips as she wielded her prize. She clutched the Runestone with all her might, wielding it over her head as she turned to Cypress, returning his smile.

"Quickly!" she shouted. "Stabilize the portal, my sweet pawn, *or*— "

Cypress grabbed her wrist mid-air, squeezing it hard enough to shatter bone. "—*Or* we'll be sucked in with the Runestone?" he hissed, cutting her words short as he ripped her wrist toward the vortex.

"*What are you doing*!?" Falora cried hysterically.

"What I should have done the moment you stepped foot into the land of my kin!" he shouted above the swirling Night air. With a great display of grunting strength he flung her gangly form t'ward the vortex; frantic screams leaving her lips.

Titha's green eyes burst to life at the unexpected sight. Feathersword shot into the air as she cheered for Cypress, but it was in vain. Falora's claws latched to the remaining entryway, her legs dangling into the portal's vacuum. She drove her fingers into Cypress' arm, pulling him in with her. There they remained, locked in combat as Cypress clung to her with his remaining hand, slogging at her feathered cloak with all his might in a last attempt to rid Gaela of Falora Fomora and her meddling.

His injured state, however, made it clear to those around him that he was not going to win this last struggle. Falora hinged herself to stone with one clawed hand as she slashed at Cypress with the other, opening wound after wound on his already worn body. He jumped, clinging as tightly as he could to the other side of the entrance, but with only one hand he could do nothing but suffer her wrath as he fought the pull of the vortex.

There before her, Titha saw the broken, imprisoned Luna once more. No purple magic existed in his eyes. Only sadness and defeat.

"*Stop it*!" she cried as she drove her sword into the soil, the portal's pull intensifying. "*You're going to kill him*!" she shouted, tears welling in her eyes. As the vortex began to pull each driplet from her gaze, a great swell of anger and sorrow rose within her. She began lifting and stabbing Feathersword into the earth a foot at a time, screaming as she worked her way inward to the portal.

"Titha, don't!" Gilly screeched from behind, but she could not budge from her father's own strength.

"Sissy! Come back!" Beebee yelled, but Titha could not hear them. She could only see Cypress' very life being sucked into the vortex to protect them all.

"Titha, *please*!" Gilly screamed. "It will take you, too! Titha! *Titha*!" she shouted so hard it turned into a cough, and she collapsed.

Theole's own fearful grip became so great it shattered the Ozark staff in his hand, and their footing became unstable.

"To the ground!" he cried, pushing Nech and his girls into the moss as his own body pulled toward Titha. His enormous feet drudged up dirt as he slid for her. "Give me your hand!" he cried to his precious daughter.

Titha looked to Cypress, his body bloody and gaping with wounds as Falora continued to slice at him in order to free herself, but the old Luna fought with his injured arm, his legs, and every fiber of his being to keep her from escaping.

Titha then looked back to her father.

"*Give me your hand*!" he cried, his beard pulling into the vacuum that threatened to rip his daughter from her sword.

"I can't let him go!" she shouted to her father, her words broken amidst her sobbing. "I can't let him go. Not again. Not forever."

"Titha, it is time," a voice rang in her head.

She turned back to Cypress, screaming horribly as she heard such words. Gilly screeched for her sister, her body convulsing in the dirt as she wailed into the howling, sucking winds. As she did, a familiar face floated through her vision. It was the most fair and freckled face to ever grace a boy of Ythengrey. In an instant she knew the lines of his face, and her screams intensified.

Clover had pushing himself away from his father, letting go into the vortex. His body careened through the tunneling force of its pull—past Paw, Nech, Beebee, and every other he could not bare to watch disappear by Falora's evil.

Time, then, slowed. But only for a moment. A moment long enough to allow Clover's eyes to meet with Gillian's.

"I'm sorry," he said to her as he careened by; before the pull became too much. One last smile lit his face before he exhaled, and with it his body was dragged from her sight.

His long silhouette flew past Theole, then Titha, then turned from them all with great purpose reflected in his gaze, his freckled face gone from Gillian's view.

Falora's eyes burned, and her mouth opened like the gaping maw of the Tomb's portal. Gillian's gurgling howls reached a fever-pitch. But just before they were all lost to the strength of the vortex, Clover gave completely into its pull, aiming himself directly for Falora. Like an arrow pointed for death itself he struck her, his hands driving deep into her torso as the weight of his sacrifice slingshotted her into the portal with him.

But Falora refused to give up her prize, even as she swirled into the Tomb's purple hell with Clover. She clutched ever-tighter to the Tri-Spiral Runestone, carrying it with her deep into the bowels of the vortex. As she sunk into the Otherworld's pull, the relic's light extinguished, and to her dismay—so did the portal's. Around them the opening's light vanished, its vacuum pulling the remaining stonework of the entrance in on itself. She clawed for Cypress in the distance one last time—but could not reach him. Darkness took her. Then, as if Gaela herself had snuffed out the last of evil's flame, the Tomb's Tri-Spiraled entrance stone fell, landing with an unrivaled *THUD* as it blocked off the opening once and for all.

Lunas and bears fell forward as the vortex's pull finally disappeared. Theole's arms tumbled for his brave daughter, and to him Titha leapt as they held each other before crumbled stone. Behind them, Gilly sobbed on her knees as she held Beebee as tightly as she could; her tiny angel of a sister petting her cheeks, trying as hard as she might to comfort her. Nech's worn body stood slowly as he placed his hands onto his arched, sorrowful young master.

"*... My boy...*" a broken voice whispered from the back of the Tomb's grounds. "My only... precious boy," it continued.

Fernbloom collapsed, his body trembling as the Tomb stood as lifeless and ancient as ever... his only begotten son now on the other side.

"Mister Merigold," Titha offered as his sorrow met her ears. "Clover, I... *No...*"

Neither could comprehend what just happened to the beloved son. None, in their age, could.

"We tried so hard to bring him back—to get him out of this mess," Titha wept as she stepped from Theole. "But in the end—" She couldn't finish the words aloud.

"He… he, ah, he sacrificed himself," Fernbloom finally muttered. "He told me he had to make it—to *make it right*, he said—just before he pushed away. I—I could not hold onto him. I could not hold on. And now he is gone."

Titha walked to him slowly before her older sister brushed her side, approaching him first. She fell to her knees before him, collapsing onto him as they wept for Clover together.

"He saved us all," Titha spoke over the lump in her throat. "Not just us here, but all of us. All of Gaela." She bowed her head next to her family.

"Merigold, my dear boy, his sacrifice was of the highest any could offer," Theole decreed over them. "Our banners shall bear his name for eternity… And no Luna shall bud without learning *to heart* the courageous tale of Clover Crocus Fernbloom—"

"*Stop it*!" Gillian shouted. "*All of you*! Stop talking about him as if he's *dead*! He's not dead, is he? He's something worse, *right*? He's in *that* place," she screeched, pointing to the Tomb. "He's in the *Otherworld*! With that souless, *putrid witch*!"

"*She's right*—" a weak voice croaked out from the rubble'd Tomb. The bloodied form of a hefty Luna attempted to rise, but held no such strength.

"By the Great Drakes—*Cypress*!" Theole gasped. "You—you're *alive*!"

A hearty soul clung to a lashed mortal body; the entirety of his white robes turned to purple with blood, and his ankles black from the ash of Falora. As his old family rushed to his broken form, Gillian froze. Never had she felt such an anger—such vibrant disgust—for another being.

"*It should have been you*," she hissed, utterly ferocious with hate. "You *let* Clover make that sacrifice—you *let* him—a *boy*—do what you were too cowardly to do yourself. How dare you. *How dare you* still breathe the air of this forest while he—*he*—" Anguish outwilled the air within her, but she fought for breath. "*His father does not get to bury his son,* and I do not get to say *goodbye,* but we must look *you* in the eyes!"

She turned around to her family, showing them a face they hadn't seen since Thea left their lives.

"And you!" she cried to her father. "You stand here and preach as if this is just another death!" Gilly shouted. "But it's not. It's *not*! It is something so, so much worse."

Her disgust grew as Theole discarded his own outer robing to wrap Cypress' bleeding body. Titha commissioned several Bear-brothers to help, and gently they lifted him to be carried up to Roostwood for tending. Nech attempted to shield Beebee's eyes from the most gruesome sight, but she had inherited too much curiosity from Titha, and forced her fingers through the Craglin's so she could behold all that happened around her.

Clover's father, though, still could not move from the spot he last held his son.

"Master Gillian, if I may," Nech said as he stepped to her with Beebee. "Young Clover saved an immeasurable amount of lives—"

"*Do not touch me,*" she spurted as she broke away from Nech's touch. Beebee began to sob for her eldest sister in his arms, but Gilly was deep into shock. Her violet eyes darted about: to the discarded horns of mighty Rams, then the slain hand of Cypress beneath broken trees, to his swaddled body astride a forest bear, then to the cold Tomb and its crumbled entrance behind a stone bearing a symbol she now wished she'd never seen: one that had shattered her understanding of the world, and worse—had taken the only boy to ever make her feel the stirrings of young love.

"Gilly, wait—" Titha shouted, but there was no stopping her. Her family watched as she rushed for home, dashing past the bears that hurried Cypress' now unconscious body for the healers atop Mt. Meri.

"Our poor, poor Master Gillian," Nech spoke softly as he walked up behind Titha. "And the Fernblooms. Dear, oh dear. My heart aches."

Theole nodded, bringing Beebee into his neck. "Come, Titha. Let us tend to the healing and recouperation of Cypress and Merigold. I will have the Cedarguard doubled for any aftermath here at the Tomb. No more despair shall befall my daughters this Night."

"You go on ahead, father," Titha replied, her words tired. "Audun is… He and the others… Paw and I have to see that they are alright with our own eyes."

"By the Moon's Light! Are they?" Theole cried—their own plight so tremendous his thoughts had yet to leave his forest. "Maya and my Crows flew for Celtica but have yet to return."

"I'll let you know as soon as I do," she offered with sad eyes. "Please," she added before he attempted to stop her. "I won't be able to rest until I know they are all okay."

"My brave daughter," Theole smiled beneath a bushy beard. "How you've grown. I will see you at Dawn."

"Yes you will," she nodded back. And she meant it this time.

Titha watched as Nech and her father lifted the

heartbroken shell of Mr. Fernbloom up from the soil, two tall Lunas and a hobbled old Goblin making their way for the climb to Roostwood. Before they could leave the Tomb's clearing, Theole squirmed a bit before stopping, and his tiniest daughter popped loose from his arms.

Beebee ran as fast as her little legs could carry her and leapt into Titha's arms, just before her older sister could mount their Bear-brother.

"Thank you, big sister," Beebee pipped into Titha's ear as her chubby arms squeezed Titha's neck. They rocked each other back and forth in a moment Titha would never forget; their loving embrace holding Time itself still as Paw nuzzled in behind them.

"I love you very much," Beebee then added before dropping down.

"I love you, too, Weebee," Titha smiled, wiping a solitary tear from beneath green eyes. "And I'll always be here to protect you. Always."

"I know," Beebee smiled as she placed her round hand on Titha's battered cheek. As she did, two big brown chestnut eyes rose over Titha's shoulder to lick her tiny hands. "Thank you too Paw," Beebee wiggled. "You're my favo'wite, too," she declared as she popped down, kissing his big wet nose. Then, as quickly as she had arrived, she pipped off, back to the open arms of their father.

Titha turned to the mighty beast behind her, the black fur of her Bear-brother singed from such eventful Nights. All Paw cared about, though, was the tiny kiss he could still feel on his nose, and the unbreakable bond he shared with the Luna-sister resting on his maw. Titha embraced him as he continued to nuzzle, both beyond grateful their Nights together were to continue.

The presence of her people's desecrated Tomb lingered heavy behind them, however. The entrance stone and its Tri-Spiral stood perfectly upright; a towering testament to an event that would forever leave a scar on her and her family. On all of Gaela, for that matter.

Though as heavy as such revelations proved, they were no match for the constant buzzing worry of "are my friends, my *family*, alright?"

"Come on, fuzzybutt," Titha sighed as they turned eastward, her hand tussling his fur. "We've got one last journey before we can finally take that nap."

"*Grrount*," Paw rumbled in the hasty, bearish equivalent of 'deal'.

With Falora Fomora banished, Titha and Paw set out to learn of their beloved Celtica's fate. So much had happened, after all.

CHAPTER TWENTY-THREE
Daughters of Gaela

Celtica awaited in shambles. Paw lumbered into its borders heavy-footed and silent, an awful frown sagging his maw. Titha couldn't help but clench her hands as she beheld Celtican banners charred and blackened with Falora's ash; their brilliant greens and golds reduced to tattered greys. With every sight of a wrecked peddler's hut or decimated Viking workshop her anguish grew tenfold, her limbs coiling into Paw until her body had almost vanished into his fur. It wasn't just the city's fate that broke her heart. No. It was the fate of those souls either in or near such horrible destruction as it was wrought.

Right as all hope was leaving their hearts, Titha spotted a lone, sturdy Ram watching their every move as they neared the center of town. His brazen gold eyes shone with the intensity of Kernos himself as the Field's long amber waved around his hooves. He gave a bow of mighty horns as he turned southward, no doubt trotting off to reassure his reclusive masters of Titha's survival.

A faint, glinting smile lit her face, one that would soon turn into wide-eyed astonishment. As they turned themselves back to the center of Celtica, they were struck not by the absence of its titular Tower—but what now stood in its place, instead. As they drew nearer, an unmistakable aura radiated unto them. Warm, pleasant light of an emerald green called them forward, and in its center stood an enormous sapling unlike anything their world had seen since the Dawn of Time.

There stood the Daughter of Igdrasil, her bark twisting upward to near the same height as the Tower before it. Sparse leaves sprouted from her trunk, leading up to a hollowed knot near the tip-top that held the heart of her emerald energy. The very presence of the giant sapling erased any sorrowful thoughts from their minds. That is, until the remnants of the Tower's stonework were spotted cratered into the ground at its roots.

Titha drove her heels into her Bear-brother, and they rushed for the stones to search for life. But what they found was not panic nor the grizzly remains of a costly battle, but jovial Celtican citizens surrounding the base of the Daughter in celebration. There, at her base stood Audun, Haldor, and Sigrid; Maya perched a'top the Shieldmaiden's shoulder as they tended to all those who stayed behind to stand against Falora's maleficense.

Paw let loose a harrowing *baroo* as he bolted for their friends. Titha couldn't help but squeal, too, and the citizens began parting as they beheld the incoming duo.

"Titha!" Audun shouted, hands waving. "Paw! Is everyone else alright?" he asked as Haldor brushed past him to race for Paw.

Titha jumped from her brother as she tackled her best friend to the ground, each erupting with laughter and rosy bliss.

"You're not surprised *I'm* alive?" she joked, hugging him.

"Not one bit," he cackled. "I never doubted you for a second."

She squeezed him as tightly as she could, and they both burst into laughter again as Paw and Haldor wrestled and licked each other beside them.

Slowly the crowd at the Daughter's roots began to thin, and a shadow loomed over the younglings. They looked up to see the kind, ice blue eyes of Sigrid smiling down; Maya still perched proudly on her shoulder. Without a word she leaned down to them, embracing them both as they melted into her arms.

"My heart sings to see you safe, Titha," Sigrid said with a loving gaze, "and to hear from your father's Crows that all has ended. Please tell me your family shares your fortune?"

"We are all okay… but we lost Clover," she replied. "He sacrificed himself to save us all."

"So we were told," Maya replied as she motioned to more of Theole's Crows flying for the forest. "And Cypress lives in his stead. A shame."

"That's what Gilly said, too," Titha added. "But Cypress fought as hard as he could to banish her. He may have been able to finish the deed if I hadn't cut one of his hands off… so there's that..."

Sigrid and Maya chortled, taken a'back at her matter'o'factness, and the deed itself.

"I am sure you did what needed to be done," Sigrid told

her as she looked to Feathersword sheathed at Titha's hip. "But should you not be with your kin now?"

"I had to see you were alright with my own eyes," Titha said. "I am—I am just so happy you all are." She pulled Audun into her, locking her arm around him as he hugged her. "And this!" she cried, one arm jutting up toward the majesty of the Sapling. "Can it be?"

"The Daughter of Igdrasil," Maya replied as they all gazed upward to her. "She is what Falora was after. Everything else was only a means to an end, it seems. And she nearly succeeded, too, if not for Audun. He buried the Seed just as Falora had turned the tide in her favor."

"It was nothing," Audun smiled.

"It was *everything*," Sigrid retorted proudly.

As the Companions continued to fill each other in on their sides of the perilous tale, a familiar bustle returned to the town around them. It didn't take long for the grateful Celtican folk to get back to work—to rebuilding their city. Lunas, Humans, and Goblins toiled together once more—but would now forever do so beneath the shadow of the Daughter of Igdrasil—a sight that would've warmed even the stone heart of a Druid.

Audun looked to Titha during this tremendously happy moment, grinning as Maya flew off overhead. But the sparkle in his amber eyes struck Titha's heart in a peculiar way. Guilt washed over her as she looked to the soul of her best friend. For as easy as it was to come find him alive, it could've been just as easy to wander into Celtica and find him dead.

"Audun..." she muttered, her throat tight. "I need to apologize to you. I... I am so, so sorry."

"For what?" he replied, staring into green eyes.

"For... everything," she choked. "I never should have asked for—"

"—I'll stop you there," he interrupted. "Because I would not change any of it. Not a single thing."

Titha's indigo face ignited with a bright, loving pink. Her head fell over onto the tiny Viking's shoulder, and there they sat under the splendor of the Daughter's shadow, undisturbed for a brief moment in Time.

But she could not shake her guilt.

"Are you alright, little ones?" Sigrid asked, brushing a few well-earned tangles from Titha's hair before readjusting her son's curls.

"I messed up," Titha replied, choking on her words. "I put Audun and Gilly, Paw and Haldor; all of us in awful danger and I shouldn't have."

Sigrid sighed. She could feel the churning of Titha's mind. She lowered herself to their level, and in doing so opened Titha up like a floodgate.

"And on top of that," Titha continued, "all we wanted to do was bring Clover home... and in the end we did, sure, but now he's gone, and I just can't let it go. I wanted to do more. I still do. I wanted to help. I *had* to. It feels like something burning in my gut. Sometimes it burns so hot that I know it has to be a part of me. Like... a purpose. But I still feel so guilty... for putting Audun, my sisters, the boys, all of us in such horrible situations, and it... It was irresponsible, to say the least..."

"Breathe, my child," Sigrid smiled as she sat down beside them. "To cherish life as you do is as noble a belief as there will ever be. To wield the courage to *protect* life is no small feat, either. Rare is the person who harbors bravery and empathy together.

These are traits to be polished, not regretted. We may have lost a precious few, but it was to save hundreds more. We could not have done so without the actions of you two."

"But where does that leave us?" Titha asked, still gutted. "Do I just step aside and go back to posture and decorum lessons for another year—" her eyes fluttered as the face of Calluna Mint rushed into her mind, and she held her tongue from further disrespect. For the first time in her young life, she would have gladly sat for one of Mint's lectures. But none would ever have the honor of doing so again. And in that moment, perhaps, Titha felt her worst.

"I just don't... I don't know what to do if I'm—if I'm not *out here*," she exclaimed, her arms flopping onto her lap. "Father was made to be the Watcher. Gilly was *born* to be next, to follow in his footsteps. Not just because she's the eldest, but because she's *perfect* for it. If tradition holds and I, well, *do what I'm told*... What does that leave for me? What do I do with my life in Yythengrey? Is my destiny to be the little sister of the Watchress? Someone's lady in waiting? Is Audun's to be the little brother of the Jarl? Nothing more? We... I want to do so much more," she grimaced, the thought leaving a tangible, sorrowful taste in her mouth. "But I—I couldn't even save Clover, so, of what use am I, really?"

Sigrid exhaled as she leaned in to the children. "Clover chose his own fate, the Crows tell. In the end, he sacrificed himself to make right his wrongs, and to save you all from sharing his fate. This is not your burden to bear, child. Nor is it yours, my son," she said to Audun. "You both carry enough weight—and have tasted what it is like to change the world—but have also suffered such terrible losses. To know both how precious life is, and to accomplish the *meaningful* within it, is something few achieve—let alone those of your young years. I, and your father, Titha, believe that the two of you are destined for great things. But you must learn patience. It will come with time. Until then, we must practice in the present what we wish to be in the future."

"Yes, mother," Audun replied, his head low.

"This is not a criticism, my beloved," she said as she lifted his chin. "I am beyond proud, and in awe, of you both." She kissed his head before lifting him to his feet. "Fetch your brother for me, littlest, will you?"

Another "Yes, mother," left Audun's lips before he turned to Titha, embracing her again. "Love you, Luna," he chirped, before turning eastward for home.

"Love you more, squirt," she pipped back as she watched him run off with a whistle to Haldor and a mission to find Rainer.

Sigrid exhaled. A heavy brow now accompanied her smile as she lifted Titha to her feet.

"Uh oh," Titha blurted. "I'm in trouble, aren't I?"

"Not at all," Sigrid laughed, breaking her stoic demeanor. "I can feel your angst, child. I wish to speak to you before returning you to your family."

"Oh. Okay. What about?"

"Titha… I did not know your mother. I never had the chance to meet her, nor any other Luna before I met you. But from what you have told me, and what I have learned, I think we are two spirits from the same well. Theole sees much of her spark in you. I believe he sees it in me, too, at times."

"He does. And so do I. It's a wonderful thing, a good thing. I promise," Titha smiled.

"It must be, from what I have heard. And in this, I believe, lies the answers to the questions you burden yourself with, little one. Can I be more forward, and much more bold, with you?"

"Always," Titha squinted.

"Good to hear, as I was going to be regardless of your answer," Sigrid grinned. "Titha... You are surrounded by those who were born to—or handed, rather— a special title or place in this life; a purpose, per'say. And without one yourself, I see it wearing on you. It is hard to know your own place when everyone you love is so consumed with their own. We two understand this more than most. But in this, I want you to remember your mother. Theole has told me little of her, but I know she was not born unto royalty. She was a *wanderer*. He *found* her, did he not? He brought her into your world and through this a love blossomed. Thea Celtica Mae was not born to be what she became, and yet here you are: born of the very life she carved for herself. Do you understand?"

"I do…" Titha sniffed.

"Are you alright, dear?" Sigrid asked.

"Yes… it's just… I feel much closer to her right now—here, with you speaking of her in such a way—than I have in a long time."

"My sweet sprite," Sigrid offered, pulling her in. "I say this not to sadden you, but to show you that you should not fear for your future. I wish for you, instead, to covet it, and make it your own. I believe your desire to help, and the purity of your heart, wields the power to change our world forever. With this, you could learn to lead change not as Watcher or Queen, but as *warrior*. As *poet*. *Healer*. *Sage*. As a *mother yourself*, if you wish, someday. Whatever your heart desires."

"Really?" Titha smiled up at her. "But aren't those just other titles?"

"Titles are not to be feared," Sigrid chuckled. "They are to be wielded, and once you find one you feel is worth wielding, you will find the balance—the *belonging*— that you crave."

"See! *Gah*!" Titha scoffed, hopping to her feet. "No one talks to me like this! Like you are right now! No one… not even father. Gods, why—*how* am I so angry and so happy at the same time? I really want to believe you, to do and be *everything* you say I can be, but I know once I leave here and go back home it'll all return to the way it was, and father will continue to be who he is, as will all the others. But I don't want to fight with my family anymore. It's exhausting. I just don't think they'll ever understand the way you do... The way mother would have, too."

"Perhaps your elder sister will understand, now that she has seen more of the world?" Sigrid offered.

"Maybe.... We have been through a lot together. I think we're as close now as we're ever going to be because of it, but... Gilly always has something else on her mind."

"We all do. She holds great strength. But you wield *both,* Titha Mae: strength and *compassion.* This is the mark of a truly great luminary."

"So... *I should* become Watcher? *Not* Gilly?"

Sigrid looked to the bandages wrapping her hands, then pulled her late husband's axe from her side to hold it flat in front of them. "No. Do not tell your father I said this, but... I do not believe that 'watching' is enough during times such as these." She twirled Autumnbringer, showing its other side, where one enormous gash scarred an otherwise impressive luster. "People must be watched to be protected, yes, and they must be loved in turn, as your father does in spades—but they must also be *inspired.* Roused. Motivated. *Galvanized* to do more. To *become* more. I see the power to do all of this—in *you.*"

Titha's eyes swelled with the happiest of tears. Her heart sung, fluttered—practically flipping with joy in her indigo chest. "Thank you," she finally replied.

"You are welcome. And I believe—again, do not tell your father I said this—but such potential is wasted if it is trapped within the forest. I think you long to be a part of the *world,* Titha. And to the world should your talents be free."

"No pressure, huh?" Titha smirked, placing a hand on her head.

Sigrid laughed. "It is a lot to bear, but so far, you do it well. My husband did, too. And so I try, every day, to do the same in his footsteps—though much has changed since his passing."

"Your people miss him, but they love you more than anything," Titha exclaimed. "You must know that. I think some of my own kin are starting to love you more than anything, too," she grinned. "I don't know if Celtica would be possible without you. You've shown us all how easy it can be, how easy it *should* be to live with one another, regardless of where we're from or the color of our skins. And now, thanks to you and Audun, it's become clear that Igdrasil herself agrees."

The young Daughter of Igdrasil swayed tall and proud behind them, the core of its top letting loose its beautiful emerald sheen still. Sigrid stood, turning as she closed her eyes, letting the light of the Daughter caress her face. It was soothing to her, almost as if the sapling sought to heal the wounds Sigrid had sustained in protecting her; in saving her.

"If such kind words are true of me, child," Sigrid continued, "Then they are truer of you in the purest of ways."

"Trust me, it is true of you," Titha returned. "And I... I won't tell father what you said if you don't tell him that I said I... I want to be just like you."

Sigrid smiled again, placing her axe on the ground before wrapping an arm around her young Companion. "I think, if Celtica is to survive, and the Daughter with her, that we will all need you, Titha Mae. Now, yes, but in the future—if this city is to grow and flourish and blossom as The Daughter of Igdrasil wishes to above us now, we, and she, will need you. She will need all that burns within you. She will need your heart, your mind. And she will need your sword."

Titha's fingers grazed Feathersword's hilt at her side. "Can you teach me?" she asked sincere.

"Teach you what?" Sigrid grinned.

"All of it. All of this. To lead. To fight. To be like a Shieldmaiden. To be like you."

"So a path does burn within you?" Sigrid ignited, thrilled. "I think I may be able to teach you how to swing that blade properly, yes," she grinned, pulling Titha in tightly. "But know that I say all of this not to pressure you, child, but to let you know you are not alone in your heart's desire to find your place, and to see Celtica thrive."

"I know. And it will. I can feel it."

"I do not doubt that you can. But know that if life calls you upon a different path, for whatever reason, that you are free to walk it. Always. Let no one tell you otherwise."

"Deal," Titha replied. "This is where I want to be, though… Out here. This is where I belong."

"Hold that truth in your heart," Sigrid told her, "But remember the balance I spoke of. Never forget from whence you have come."

"How could I?" Titha smirked as she took the hint. "I'll see you tomorrow?"

Slowly the Night sky behind them gave way to a faint warm glow. Dawn's majesty approached, lighting a path of red and gold up to the silhouette of the Sapling.

"It would seem that tomorrow has already come," Sigrid offered in return, rubbing Titha's back. "Off you go, little one."

Titha turned about, taking one last look at Sigrid and the Daughter as beautiful blond braids and bright leaves flowed in the gentle breeze of tomorrow; Dawn's light breaking over the Horizon.

"A moment, Titha!" a fresh voice called to her from the East, its first light revealing two young Men astride a brilliant white horse. It was Rainer, smiling as wide as his chisled cheekbones would allow, his hand gripped to a gorgeous bouquet of wildflowers as he caught up to her. An "oh no" left Titha's lips before she sauntered over to the brothers, knowing full well whom those flowers were intended for.

"Ah! I am glad we caught you," Rainer grinned, passing his mother and the beasts. "Is your sister about?"

"Listen, Rainer, before you get your hopes up, now is not the time."

"That is where you are wrong!" he replied galliantly, his teeth glinting in the rising Sun as Audun placed his face in his palms. Rainer lifted the bouquet proudly, as if it would cheer up even the most distraught of damsels.

"Let me rephrase this for you so you understand," Titha groaned. "There will never be a time for you to hand her flowers. Not like that."

"But you told me—"

"I did, yes. I did tell you she loves fresh flowers. And she does love fresh flowers. Fresh *living* flowers. But I knew you'd go and pick them and hand my sister a clump of dying things and boy, let me tell you how sorry I am this didn't happen sooner, but—just don't, okay? She's been through enough."

"Ah. I see," Rainer replied, still processing. "Is Gilly going to be alright?" the young Jarl asked sincere, each flower already wilting in his grasp.

"We'll see," Titha shrugged gently, before Paw whisked them off for home. "We'll see…"

CHAPTER TWENTY-FOUR

Truth Be Told

In short; Gilly was *not* okay.

"*Unbelievable*!" she spat as she paced Roostwood's throne room, locked within a furious state. Her father stood before her, shielding his youngest daughter from the pointed words of his eldest. Beebee shifted down out of Theole's palms, drifting down into his throne before an impossibly-adorable sigh escaped from frazzled hair.

"So did you, or did you not, know how dangerous these shards were?" Gilly continued, her footsteps echoing with every word. "How could you just hand such perilous things over to us? To your daughters? And then have the *audacity* to act shocked when everything goes horribly wrong?"

"Gillian, please! Your tone! When have you ever known me to act in your disinterest, my daughter?" Theole replied. He fought hard not to show it, but the pain Gilly's disposition inflicted on him seeped through. "I am shocked at your sharp words! To mock me, your father, for handing over what I understood to be the precious jewelry of your mother!" he clarified, hopeful he could get through to her. "Their beauty, and the memories they held, were to be as precious to you three as they were to her!"

"Spare me your half-truths!" Gilly screeched before she could catch herself. "I—I am sorry, father," she added, "but I do not, I *cannot* believe that in all your vast knowledge, you knew nothing of their place as a Runestone."

"*Half-truths*? Why, I—Do you forget to whom you speak, young wola? I am your father! And it is *you* who is to be chastised for decisions of late, not myself! To foster your sister's habit of galavanting—I—I am beyond disappointed! In both of you!"

"I tried to stop her!" Gilly shouted back. "I *always* try to stop her! But does she listen? No! She listens to no one but the Gaela-forsaken *voice in her head*!"

From the doorway a deep clatter rang out. Father and daughter looked to Roostwood's entrance as an enormous bear attempted to squeeze himself through unnoticed—provision after provision clanking and clopping onto the floor around him. Faint mumbling broke out from under a thick, fuzzy backside, before the hobbled old body of Nech plopped into view; Paw and his Luna-sister landing atop. Titha tried to shove the bear off, but couldn't move until he saw fit. Paw finally bumbled upward, and she shushed then shoo'ed him into further chambers, her hands immediately flipping down to Nech.

"I am so terribly sorry, Sire," the old Goblin fumbled, brushing the dust form his pointy knees. "I—I tried to stop them, citing your current and pressingly private conversation with

Master Gillian—but Titha Mae proves as strong-willed as ever!"

"Case and point," Gilly replied, flinging an open palm in her little sister's direction.

"Hi..." Titha blurted, raising one hand. "Am I... interrupting something?"

"Aren't you always?" Gilly retorted, rolling her eyes.

"Again, please forgive our intrusion, masters," Nech bowed politely, grabbing Titha's arm.

"It's alright, Nech. Come, Titha, join us and rest," Theole motioned, his hand brushing the soft moss of the stoop before his throne, its wide seat hosting Beebee as she snoozed ever-so-peacefully.

"Look at that sweet, sweet angel baby," Titha smiled, tiptoeing for her Weebee.

"No—No!" Gilly slapped her hands away. "Let her sleep! You two will not use her to distract us from what is happening like you always do!" She smacked her fingers onto Titha's shoulders, plopping her down onto the stoop. "Sit and shush. Father was just about to tell me why he thought it appropriate to give his daughters three pieces of a rock that creates portals to the vulture-infested Realm of the Dead."

"Those are definitely your words, not his," Titha retorted before suffering a swift smack on the back from Gillian. But no matter how hard she tried, her sister, nor even her father, would break their somber demeanor.

"If... I am not needed, I... believe I shall see myself out," Nech added. Three glaring sets of Lunish eyes shot to him.

"Oh no you don't," Gilly replied in tow, motioning for Nech to step within their quarrel. He grinned nervously, inching to a stooled-seat just behind Theole.

"Can't this wait?" Titha asked impatiently. "We have all been through enough this past Moon."

"It cannot," Theole pointed, downtrodden. "Nor shall you escape punishment for your actions."

"*What*?" Titha scoffed. "*Seriously*?" she asked, absolutely flabbergasted. "We all witnessed what just happened, but we're going to treat this like I got in trouble in class—"

She stopped short, her words conjuring the face of Mint again—and in that moment, she understood where her father was coming from. Nech caught the sadness in her young eyes, hopping forth.

"Bless your gentle hearts, my young masters," he stated, making sure he still stood one step behind Theole. "I cannot fathom how either of you even begin to process such events within such youthful minds… but I must echo our Watcher's sentiments. Though you have succeeded in aiding our peoples and our world, we mustn't lose sight of the 'hows' and 'whys', must we?" He paused, looking to Theole before continuing.

"Mortality is never the concern of the youthful. When we are young, anything is possible because we have all the time in the world to accomplish it. But we mustn't forget that Time is, by definition, infinitely fleeting, and in this we must do our best to remember our duties to those who choose to devote their *own* time to our well-beings."

"I understand," Titha replied somberly, her head bowed. "And I am truly sorry for putting myself and everyone else in danger. It won't happen again. That I promise."

Nech flinched, taken a'back. He looked up to his Sire, who echoed such astonishment. Gilly, however, was not satisfied. Not in the slightest.

"That's it?" she coughed, her face crooked. "That is all you're going to say? Or ask? Not too long ago the Otherworld was a fairy tale we told each other to be less afraid of death! Wasn't it, father?" she asked before turning back to Titha. "Now all of a sudden it's *real*—and you're just going to *apologize* instead of bombarding us with a thousand annoying questions like you do about every other little thing?"

"Well of course I *want* to," Titha said as she leaned back, "But right now I'm just glad we're all here. Together."

"Nope! Not buying it," Gilly cringed again as she scolded her little sister. "I want to know! I want to know why you feign ignorance whenever we ask you more about our history, father. I want to know more about these amethysts! Their symbols—the symbols of our past! Our *mother*. I want to know the *truth*," she commanded of their father. "So tell us, please... *Tell us*!" she shouted again in defiance of his silence.

Theole did not stir. He hesitated instead. And in this Titha felt her first ping of true concern over what her father had and had not told them.

"I did, at the time, what I felt to be right," Theole offered on the brink of defeat. "A righteous leader must always strive for what they feel to be best for their people." He paused again as memories of his past—*their* past—became overwhelming. "My girls... my precious daughters," he continued, "There is so much you will not understand."

Titha felt the breath leave her. Suddenly the air changed around her family, as if a fog of falsities now existed, only to be ripped back at any moment. She looked to Gillian, then Nech, then over her shoulder to a curled-up Beebee.

"Perhaps it is time to fix that," she finally replied to her father.

Theole kept wishing to speak, but most words were replaced by sighs. "I agree," he finally said, and in truth he meant it. But it was not possible to tell them everything. Not without hurting them.

"With all that has happened just this past season," he finally began, "and how much the two of you have grown before me... I do agree that it is time." He walked to his throne to join Beebee, but as he turned back 'round to his eldest children there wasn't a hint of eagerness on his face, but a grimace bearing great concern.

"Your mother... she was not of this place. Of our Yythengrey," he began. "I cannot explain exactly where she came from. Nor can Nech, so please, do not ask him. Lunish, yes, she was, I would say, but so much more. When I gave your mother the Moonstone, I did not do it as a love-struck fool. Lovestruck I was, but *hopeful*, also. Beholden. *Humbled*. Truly humbled. Thea was everything we needed. Not just as a caring mother, but as a true guiding light, a savior. Meriduun had all but forsaken her children—all creatures of Night. She had become distant and her violet light cold. The less connected we Lunas felt to her embrace, the more comforted we were by Thea's presence among us. Her grace, her kindness. Her tranquility. She was everything Meriduun was no longer, and, as we discovered, would never be again. If any could lead our people to believe and prosper once more, it was your mother, and the three stones she wore. So I gave her one more—the Moonstone—not just as a symbol of our trust in her... but for a purpose."

Theole halted. His eyes were heavy with the past, but his brow firm. Nech attempted to step forth but was promptly waved down. Slowly, their father began again:

"Your mother was not to keep the Moonstone for herself. This was never our intention. That is fallacy. A lie born of jealousy. No, our most precious Stone was no simple gift for Thea to keep. She was to *deliver* it. To take it far away from the Horizon. She was to do what no other could: She was to save our people."

"From Meriduun?" Titha asked, sure as Night. And she was right.

Theole nodded with a heavy heart. "A great mist loomed as I stood watch those last fateful Nights, each spent with the Moonstone atop Mount Meri... during the last nights of Meriduun's life. At first, I feared an outside threat, some sort of darkness unbeknownst and creeping in; its foul fog thickening our own within the Duskridge. But the source was all-too-familiar, come to find. Upon the last Full Moon of Winter, the mists grew so thick they blocked out our Moon herself. In her place I looked up to see an eye—an eye so vibrant and violet that it could only be our Duskmother's. Yet as soon as my gaze met her's, the eye closed and vanished into a thick Night. This continued for some time before I knew what the Duskmother was plotting... before I realized the sinking feeling that formed within me was right. Meriduun did not eye me. She eyed the *Moonstone.*"

Titha and Gilly looked to one another amid their father's words.

"Something, or *someone* as we now know, had turned her gaze back to its power. Whether by the will of the Fomorrigan, or her professed daughter Falora, I do not know, Meriduun had grown to desire her precious Eternal Stone once more; to wield its power and to claim its light. I believe now that this, and all that followed, was a plan of the most ingenius sort—a riling of the Elder Drakes—so that our realm would be left weak and unguarded to eventual onslaught from Oathera…"

"Either way we couldn't let Meriduun wield that power again," Titha agreed, entranced with the tale.

"He could not," Nech agreed.

"Indeed, for we know what happened once its power was reclaimed," Theole replied. "Your mother and I knew no good would ever come of Meriduun retaking her stone, even before the Otherworld made itself known, so I did what I had sworn to the Duskmother—to all in the Three Families that I would never do—and I forfeited the stone to Thea. It was to be taken away—far away from Meriduun's mists. But she was watching. And she was cunning. The Moonstone in Thea's hands ignited a rage in our Duskmother the likes of which existence had never seen before. There was no time, no chance for the intended delivery to take place. Everything you know to follow ignighted right after this moment; the great destruction of the once-forested Barren Fields, the Ever-war… all of it started in that instance. With that one mistake."

"It wasn't a mistake. It was the right thing to do. Meriduun's actions are not your fault," Titha added, her eyes glassy.

"Father's bloodline, *our* bloodline, Titha, swore to protect the Moonstone," Gilly retorted. "We were—we *are*—tied to its protection. He was never to give it up. Not even in the face of Meriduun's betrayal. No other, not even the one father chose to take as his love, could ever claim it as their own."

"And yet she could," Theole added solemnly. "Your

mother held the stone unburnt, unsinged, and unaltered… and she did it whilst wearing the very circlet, ring, and necklace I gifted to you, my daughters. I have given it all much thought these past Moons; how our history may have played out if Thea had, in fact, escaped from Yythengrey with the Moonstone. Perhaps then Meriduun never would have perished, nor your mother, and Vulduun would have never been driven to the same madness as his love. Perhaps he could have brought Meriduun out of her own darkness. We may have lived now in an Eon still filled with the embrace of our land's Shapers. But we do not. And all for one moment… for one decision I was so unwaveringly sure was the right one. Perhaps that is what makes the past so painful; it will forever be a part of us that we cannot change."

"You still haven't told us where mother was to take the Moonstone," Gilly reminded harshly, "Or where the Tri-Spiral Runestone came from. Or what it means. Or where mother herself actually came from!"

Titha elbowed her sister's ribs. Theole was visibly distraught, but Gilly was not. She was angry.

"Where was she to take the stone, father?" Gilly asked once more. "Where is our mother actually from, if not here? *Answer me*!" she shouted, tears filling her eyes.

"I do not mean to upset you by telling you any of this, my child," Theole responded. "Or, rather, not telling you in the past—"

"—You haven't told us anything we do not know already!" Gilly interrupted. "I will not take your place as the Watcher… The *first Watchress of Yythengrey* someday if I am to sit upon a throne of *lies*!" she exclaimed, her voice cracking with hurt.

"Master Gillian!" Nech shouted in defense of his Sire, but she would not be pacified.

"This is *not* your place!" Gillian retorted harshly. "Please, father. No more half-truths... No more *lies*. Not to us."

"Oh, my eldest, my Gillian Rose… I have never lied to you. I have only told you what would not hurt you, for I could not bare to do so."

"Father," Titha butted-in softly, "That's kind of the same thing. Come on. We can take it. It's time to let it out. We should have, if nothing else, your *trust*."

Theole's hands grasped to his throne as he sat his weary form upright. "If I tell you, you must promise me one thing," he finally spoke, his voice frail.

"What could that possibly be, in the face of all this?" Gilly retorted.

"You must promise me you will leave it at *this* —*here*—in our halls. That you will never seek out what must not be sought. No more intrepid journeys into lands beyond your years. You must not go of where I speak."

"Because…" Titha waited.

"Because you will not like what you find there," a rough voice interjected from the far hall. There, in its shadows emerged Cypress, thickly bandaged and robed.

"Cypress, are you daft?" Titha exclaimed. "You should be resting."

"Not now, not in this moment," he decreed. "You must know the truth. And Theole will tell it," he retorted, on the verge of frustration. "We have been here before, your father and I… And I will not see you girls, and our future kin, robbed of the truth again. Too much is at stake."

"Sire!" Nech blurted, absolutely disgusted with Cypress' unannounced presence. "Shall I have this… treasonous *cretin* removed from our chambers?"

Cypress' reamining fist balled so tight that the air between his fingers snapped. "I saw to the very *construction* of these magnificent chambers before the first *ten generations* of your decrepit kind ever *began* to crawl out from the bowels of Cragoa, you feeble *simpleton.*"

"Why, I never!" Nech decreed, stumbling back. "To stand and be insulted by such a—"

"Nechalech, it may be best if you take your leave, my friend," Theole interjected.

"I—as you wish, Sire," he replied, rubbing his horns. The old Craglin looked to Titha before he left, conveying both a caring smile and mentor'ish protection with one glance. "I shall be in waiting, if I am needed."

"Thank you, Theole," Cypress added over Nech's slow exit. "I thought the imp would never lea—"

"Let me make one thing crystal clear for you, my old Squire," Theole interrupted, his voice as sharp as a wolf's bite. "You are not here as my guest. You are not here as ally, nor friend, nor council. You are here so that I may keep watch over you *every second*—of *every Night*—until your scheming proves inconsequential to the survival of my daughters, and my people. Are we clear?"

"Crystal, as you said, my old friend," Cypress chewed.

"Good," Theole retorted. Slowly he turned to his daughters, their eyes glassy and weighted. "The truth, my daughters, is deeply complicated, as are all things worth keeping close to the chest. To simply unfurl such cavernous wounds would be… irresponsible. It would *break* you, my children. And I could not bear it," Theole shuttered, breaking away from Cypress' stare and back into their state of affairs. His daughters, though, fell silent as he leaned over onto his throne's tall side. "I will tell you, if I must. But promise me. Promise me now, my daughters, that you will never seek it out."

"*Seek out what?*" Gilly spat. "We lost Clover! *I lost Clover* because of this mess! Because of *him*!" she screamed at Cypress. "Now he's here, being nursed back to health under the roof of a house he *forsook*—but you cannot even find the strength to tell your own *daughters* the truth?"

"The *Spring*– " Theole interrupted, his voice crumpling into a wheeze. "*The Spring holds... the truth…*" He coughed under the weight of his own words, his arms barely holding him upright. Something was horribly wrong.

"Father!" Titha shouted, attempting to prop him up. Cypress stepped to their side, helping his old friend lean backward into his throne where Beebee still laid swaddled and sleeping. There they placed the Watcher beside her as Dawn's final light breaking through the foliaged roof above. Beebee yawned, wiggling herself into Theole's robes before falling right back asleep.

"What's wrong with him?" Titha asked Cypress desperately.

Cypress exhaled. "What you ask of your father is not as simple, nor as easy, to convey as you two wish for it to be. He is old now, children. Far older than you see him with your own eyes. Rest now, Watcher," he uttered, waving his hands back as Theole drifted into a relaxed state. He melted into his usual resting place, his old body utterly and emotionally spent. Cypress stepped down, gripping the bandaged wrist where his right hand once resided. Looking to Titha, he took his place amidst the girls' quest for answers.

"Will he be alright?" Gilly asked softly, still frowning rather firmly.

"Yes," Cypress replied, "and it seems we must forgive your father's weakness on this particular subject, sproutlings; and my presence here, as well. It absolutely was, at one time, in your best interests to be shielded from the truth. By *all* your elders. Myself included. Yet here we stand, reunited by the very fallout of these lies..." he spoke as he lowered himself to sit on the stoop of Theole's throne. "So now you must know the *whole* truth. The truth of *who we are*."

Titha and Gilly left their father's side, stepping down to join their old mentor; each pointed ear perked as gazes widened.

"The best place to start, I believe, is with myself. I must apologize, for I had a hand in making this all far worse."

"We know," Gilly spat. "Falora was very forthcoming with that. It was you who brought her upon us."

"Oh no, child. She was already well on her way. My mistakes simply wrenched open a creaking door."

"How?" Titha asked.

Cypress leaned forward, tightening the bandage around his severed wrist as he looked again to the Luna responsible. "After your father saw fit to... *banish* me from all we had built together, I returned to my ancestral home; to the Ruins of Byle. This is where you found me, Titha, where we all became imprisoned by the Vulture Queen. Those were the dungeons of my family's building. My bloodline, the Byles, set that magnificent castle as the first stronghold of Lunish kind. It is the very beginning of our royal legacy. From it, we controlled all the Duskridge had to offer. All of Westlyn was ours, as Meriduun intended. We thrived in it, and in the midst of her bosom. As a banished soul I went southward to reclaim this past, and through it our future; our *rights.* I aimed, with every strand of me, to stop your father—to stop *you,* Titha Mae—from defiling our hallowed ways with the corrupted, weak hearts of lesser races and dooming us to the brevity of their fleeting, meaningless lives. I returned to our ancestral home to *save us from Celtica—from the Breaking of Time.*"

"So what stopped you, then?" Titha asked.

"The very ancestral lands I returned to," Cypress replied, his head meeting his hand.

The girls flittered, perplexed.

"These past seasons, experienced in solitude, allowed me to study, to *reclaim* skills my bloodline once posessed—those of a *Sage.* You have witnessed me use such clumsy power now... But the magick I wield is not of this world...not of our realm... and because of this, I discovered, it is wholly unreliable. To this end, I soon came to realize I could not achieve the heights of my ancestors, as the magick they wielded faded long ago, and was as your father's is - it was blood'born. Mine is not. As such... I resigned to defeat, knowing I could not achieve the rebalancing of Time *alone.* So I sought help. I sought it in the only place I knew such seedy help could come from... The Wicklands. You came to know them—the Wick—on your own journey, I take it. And in all that has transpired since—you have come to know its *people.*"

"... The Sifters, yes," Titha said, an eyebrow raised. "Treacherous little imps. What about them?"

"You did not see it?" Cypress asked, lit up with both knowledge and terror. "Grey in complexion, pointed in features, kin to both mist, Night, and Nature?"

"Speak plainly," Gilly commanded.

"They are *us*, girls. They… the Sifters… are ancestors. My ancestors. Byles. *Lunas* who chose to cling to what remained of Meriduun's dark Time-magick for fear of death. Lunas who should have met a natural end half an Eon ago—yet in the Wick's mist they have stowed away, their own Nights long past—each of their lives unended by the hard passings of *true* Time outside…" Cypress' eyes rose to the girls, his gaze glassy, reddened by defeat. "They achieved it. What all mortals seek; immortality. But look at what they have become... It is a fate worse than death."

"*What*?" Titha gasped. She looked to her sister who did not return her astonished look. Both sat in shock, expressing it in opposite ways (as they did all things).

"Falora only had but to take advantage of their desire to live-on, at whatever cost, to enlist their services. And in such, they were lost to the mists further still…"

"So that is what stopped you?" Titha asked, astonished. "That fate… Their fate… is the reason you stopped fighting Falora? Fighting us? And Celtica?"

"As if I had a choice," Cypress scoffed. "No. I am afraid it is far more complicated than that. Once my… *attempted* understanding of magick hit its heights, and Falora was given passage from the Otherworld, it became painfully clear to me that she knew everything there was to know of our history and its powerful artifacts… and that it was *she* who allowed my use of magick to take hold. She had been… *toying* with me. *Mocking me* from the shadows every step of the way… so that she could be freed. For a time I believed I could persuade her into cooperation, for the longevity of our Lunas as in the olden Nights, but there is no path that matters to Falora Fomora but her own. In the end, I was imprisoned for not giving her what she wanted: for refusing her the location of the Tri-Spiral Runestone. Once she pried its newfound existence as jewelry out of me, I understood the extent of her malice. So I sat in a cell, and that was where you found me, Titha. That is where your pieces of the Runestone found me, too, no doubt by Falora's design."

Titha didn't know what to say. Neither did Gilly. Never had they seen Cypress like this. Not even the anger born in the face of his banishment remained. He was truly broken. Shattered. Defeated.

"I thought I would find that place—the Ruins of my royal ancestors—*empty*; a hollow shell of a past I could rebuild... But Falora, for all her evil, opened my eyes. She showed me the ultimate destiny of our people here in Gaela, and it is of the *Sifters*. She relished in the pain this truth caused me..." He grabbed his forehead, wobbling from both injury and disdain. "They should not be alive. But they are, and it is all of Time's doing."

"But what does this have to do with mother?" Titha asked. "What does *your* failure—no offense—have to do with *our* mother?"

"*Everything,* child. It has *everything* to do with her —and the Moonstone, our people's history, and Meriduun's betrayal." Cypress rose to his feet, huffing. "We have been *played*."

"And still you refuse to tell us the whole truth, just like father," Gilly clenched.

"Because I do not know it, Gillian!" Cypress shouted in

retort. "What, do you think Falora sat me down in a chair and told me all her family had been scheming for centuries? Don't be a fool. Once I learned the truth—the truth of the *mists*, of our people's ultimate fate, and of immortality's cruel reality—I *refused* to help her or be her errand-boy. And she tossed me into that cell with the *rats*, stripping me of my powers and never uttering so much as another word to me."

"So you just gave up?" Gilly asked. "You expect us to believe all of this is true, and that you forfeited your holy crusade to keep our people locked into the slow mists of Time, just like that?"

"Yes."

"I don't buy it! I don't buy it at all," Gilly bellowed to Titha, her insides bubbling.

"Cypress, please," Titha asked as she gently cradled her sister's broken hand, "if you are hiding anything else, I won't stop until I find out what it is. Neither will she. If there is a 'whole truth', now is the time to tell us—*before* we get into more trouble trying to find it ourselves."

"I stand to let you girls down time and time again, as I do not wield such all-encompassing truth," the old Luna replied sincere, before turning slowly to them both. Shadow covered half his visage, just as it had in the dungeons of Byle, and from that dark state he uttered the words Titha didn't know she was waiting for:

"... But I do know where we can find it..."

The girls shuttered at his words; at the thought.

"I don't like that look," Titha frowned, her older sister's

lilac eyes burning a fierce purple beside her. "You know *more*. You know something father doesn't. That none of us do. Don't you, Cypress?"

He said nothing, all of him silent but his eyes. Instead he stepped forward, his blunt footsteps echoing around the still sleeping Theole and Beebee. From them the sisters followed Cypress—out of their lavish throne quarters and into the Southwing. Gilly took Titha's shoulders, attempting to comfort them both as they followed a Cypress who was far more frightening now in his silent ambition. As they neared the end of the hall he finally turned, and Titha knew exactly where he was leading them.

An intimate setting awaited, one neither sister had spent much time in, if Gilly had spent any at all. But there Titha was in Cypress' old study again—this time with his overwhelming presence, though, and not the calming light of their father.

The walls remained lined with branched bookcases; each full of tomes, scrolls, and parchments dustier than the last—except for those Theole had tossed aside in recent, frantic studies of his own. Amid the room's Moonlit center rested the aftermath of his panic: the table stood littered with parchments. Cypress stepped to its side, his bold frame ignited by the Moon shimmering down from one solitary, broken round window. Quickly he flung his hand out, sweeping everything from the wooden table with one motion. Titha coughed, fanning the dust and cobwebs from their faces before stepping into the light with their old mentor.

"What are you doing?" Titha asked as his eyes caught her attention.

Cypress coughed. "Nothing, I'm afraid, unless this

works," he replied half sincere. As his thick eyebrows bent inward a strange, contorting manner overtook him. He had done it at the Tomb, he thought, so there must be a path to summoning his ancestor's magick without Falora's blessing. But nothing came. Not yet.

"Nothing it is," Titha mumbled, disappointed.

"Quiet, child!" Cypress barked back—and within that flicker of anger he felt it. Magick!

To his hand a purple light was summoned, just as it had been in his rage at the Tomb. Slowly his splayed fingers crackled with energy, and a grin followed. But he said nothing, choosing instead to *show* the sisters why he had brought them there (now that he could).

The wooden table was no mere table, as they each knew. It was a *map*: an enormous, ancient carving that showed all of their known lands: from the corners of the Horizon, to Gaela Falls at the edge of the Highlands, and the expanses of Eastlyn below. Cypress placed a firm finger down onto the wooden surface's etchings, following a path that led straight south from their Duskridge home into places far, far below. What was usually labeled there as "Unknown Lands" on every map Titha Mae had ever seen, was instead alight with locales she had only recently learned of: *The Wick*, *The Ruins of Byle*, and everything inbetween. But the edge of such southern lands, as with all other maps, was where the knowledge ceased. Until Cypress placed his one hand on the blank, far side of the table.

He pressed firmly into the timeworn wood, feeling its own pulsating center before slowly raising his hand; the blood of his sorcerous ancestors returning within him. As his hand ascended, the rings of the wooden table responded—each bending to his sage-like will. Violet energy shot between his fingertips and the carved surface as symbols burst forth in a blue magick, their shapes dancing in the shadows of his hands as his own purple cancelled out whatever spell had surpressed them. Places the girls had never known nor heard of appeared, each as if they had always been there. The names of trees, plateaus, and rivers broke forth from the foggy illustrations of the Wick, expanding southward to an enormous, world-ending cliffside.

Cypress' finger dropped at the cliff's furthest edge. The energy he conjured popped as it lingered on into a twirl, the motion summoning artwork that depicted a vast sea. Spirals popped up within it, each representing an island. Once he was satisfied with the etchings unlocked, he stopped, the violet glow of his finger pointing to a specific shape: an intricate, dominant spiral betwixt all others.

"What is it?" Titha asked, her green eyes a'light with its spherical call.

Gilly took her sister's hand, and together they approached it. Cypress clenched his fist, ridding it of tremendous energy as he blew forth, banishing an Eon's worth of residue from the newly-restored surface. There rested the heart of what he had summoned—the etching of the islands still crackling with violet.

Titha squinted at them, then the writing just below, as they bristled in tandem.

"What is this place?" she asked, looking up to the shadowed, weary eyes below Cypress' tuffed brow. No response came. Instead, he nodded toward the sparkling text upon the table—its lettering burning away at the ancient wood; its visage nearly complete. Impatiently the sisters leaned in, batting away the tiny flakes of ash that floated from the map's embered etchings like newborn fireflies.

And there they stood: thirteen mystical letters flickering wildly—their majesty growing all-the-more enchanting with each spark. Amid such splendor, three simple words came to light, their influence vast amid a dense sea of spirals: each representing a speck of land more unknown to them than the last.

Titha reached out, extending a hand to feel through the unfurled, coiling brilliance on display. Her fingers flickered off from the lettering's end, sending burnt cobwebs up into dense air. Dust then gave way to the Moon's intense light, Cypress breathing a deep sigh as the air cleared. The beams overhead breathed with him, and in their glow the map was given life. To them its vision sang: three simple words glistening with intent—as if they promised to alter these Lunas' fates, and those of everyone they loved, for the rest of Time.

Tired lungs wisped cold breath from Titha's mouth. Slowly she read the three words aloud, and a strange melody filled her voice as if she'd known it all her life…

Titha and her Companions will return in:

Titha Mae and the Soul in the Lost Spring

Glossary:

Henceforth you'll find, hopefully, all terms you may wish to have help in defining, pronouncing, or just want to see one more time.

The Abyss: A deep, swallowing system of caverns and caves underneath the Fells—the furthest depths of which are completely unknown. Many had ventured in never to return.

Amethyst: A violet, purple-colored form of quartz, considered incredibly rare and precious to Gaela's peoples.

Angvar the Bold: (pronounced Yarl Ang-var, with 'Ang' as in angle and 'var' as in 'jar') Angvar was ruler of Autumnhill alongside his wife, Sigrid, before his death at the hands of Vulduun during the events of *The Ballad*. He was a steady and hardy Jarl (king amongst Vikingmen) whose skill in battle was only matched by Sigrid herself.

Apprentice: An assistant and/or inheritant appointed to a master in order to learn their craft.

Arbor: An elder, grizzly-looking forest bear with shaggy, long greyed fur and many scars. He was Bear-brother of Cypress Byle, and son of Aldin, Cypress' first Bear-kin.

Aspen: Once Captain of the Cedarguard and a long-trusted friend of Cypress and Theole. She was swift and gifted, and her word was greatly respected in Yythengrey, right up to her valiant death, wrought in effort to aid the Companion's cause in Mydlan during the events of ***The Ballad***.

<u>**Audun Angvarsson:**</u> (pronounced Aw-dune, as in 'aw' isn't he cute, and dune like a sand dune) The youngest son of Sigrid and Angvar, Audun was an avidly curious reader and very intelligent Young Companion who became inseparable from Titha during the events of The Ballad. Aftewards, he continued into a lively obsession with drawing, documenting, and mapping, earning an official apprenticeship with his beloved mentor, Nech. It was by his hands, too, that the Daughter of Igdrasil became planted within her Celtican home.

<u>**Aurora Borealis:**</u> A magical light produced by beings of great power, both its shapes and colors holding deep meaning. When such a display is present, it is only viewable by those able to behold the Horizons above the far North or South skies upon clear nights.

<u>**Autumnbringer:**</u> The axe crafted for Angvar the Bold when he was crowned Jarl of Autumnhill alongside his wife and Shieldmaiden, Sigrid Autumnsdottir. She wielded it after his death at the hands of Vulduun.

<u>**Autumnhill:**</u> The first and largest homestead of the Viking-men, Autumnhill was an impressive stone stronghold housed by the Boulderwall, a massive wall built from ancient stones seemingly too large to move. At the center of the many houses, workshops, and stables was Skaldhall, ancestral home of the Jarl and Shieldmaiden.

<u>**Bairn:**</u> A Highlander term of old origins, meaning child or baby.

<u>**Ballad**</u>**:** An epic, lyrical story passed down from one generation to the next as part of a land's folklore.

<u>**Barren Fields:**</u> The expansive fields and prairies that made up these barren lands were mostly void of trees and covered by thick golden grasses, wheats, and weeds instead. Despite much of the land being scarred from battles long ago, large grazing animals such as Buffalo, Rams, and Wooly Rhinos happily made homes there.

<u>**Bear-brother:**</u> The oldest companions of the Lunas of Yythengrey, these bears were all of the Forest Bear race, also referred to as Black Bears or Forest Black Bears. It was the bear who chose their Luna during the Festivals of Dawn, not the other way around.

<u>**Begonia Bee Mae**</u>: The youngest (and most adorable) Mae sister, Begonia was born during the final days of Thea's life, just before she met Meriduun in battle one last time. Called Beebee by her sisters, she was a sweet and tenacious youngling of four forest-years at the time of *Dawn of Celtica*.

<u>**Birch Botanus Byle:**</u> Cypress' younger cousin and a staunch supporter of his cause, Birch was one of two disciples chosen to carry out Cypress' plan before it all fell apart at the hands of Falora Fomora.

<u>**Blacksmith:**</u> A maker and craftor, skilled in creating objects of iron and other strong metals; from weapons and accessories to armor and jewelry.

<u>**Bjor the Blacksmith:**</u> An enormous black-haired bear of a man that oversaw the Royal Forge of Skaldhall, his family having done so for generations.

<u>**Boldin:**</u> The first and only Bear-brother of Theole the Watcher, and brother to Aldin, who perished during the early days of the Ever-war. After Boldin's passing, Theole could not suffer losing another Bear-kin, never seeking another.

<u>**Bonnie:**</u> a loving Highlander term meaning beautiful or sweet.

<u>**Breaking of the Horizon**</u>: The catastrophic ending of the First Eon, brought on by the treacherous Vulduun wishing to reclaim his Sunstone. It took place on the Horizon at the edge of the known lands of Gaela as the Companions successfully summoned the Elk Kings. Their divine power combined with both Eternal Stones and Igdrasil's mercy, broke the Horizon as it was known, and it was never the same again; ushering in the Second Eon.

Brigid the Faun: A mighty and ancient Faun, born of the first days of Westlyn. She, alongside her betrothed Satyr, Kernos, were known as Highlanders to those who respected them, and goat-people to the ignorant. She and Kernos watched over the southern mountains and lands of the Westlyn province as shepherds to its Rams. Brigid was master of their hearth and home, as well as proficient with bow and arrow in battle.

Cairn: A tomb, monument, or temple built as a mound of natural stones and earth. They are only found in places of great meaning and power.

Calluna Angelonia Mint: Once a respected, staunch historian and teacher of Lunish ettiquete and decorum, Mint served a short tenure as tutor to the Mae sisters before proving… incompatible… with Titha. Due to her old-fashioned beliefs, it is believed she was in league with Cypress Byle in attempt to overthrow Celtica and preserve the Old Ways, before Falora Fomora's interference. Considering her untimely death, we may never know.

Cedarguard: (Or Cedar Guard) Protectors of Yythengrey since the beginning of the First Eon, all were under the command of Cypress Byle before his exile. They stood guard at the Wood Gate still during the events of ***Dawn of Celtica***, with Sprucewill Foxglove serving as their Commander.

Celtica: (spoken with the traditional hard C, or K sound, as is the academic pronunciation of Celtic, i.e. Keltic-ah) A tradepost city built in the Barren Fields between Yythengrey and Autumnhill, Celtica was founded by the Companions as an attempt to end the conflictbearing Old Ways and join the worlds of Night and Day. It is heralded as the first territory to be shared by both Lunas and Men, signaling the very beginning of their peaceful relationship. The year of its creation was marked as the start of the Second Eon. The name Celtica itself was the name many races gave to Thea Mae upon her rising during the First Eon. It was then used by her daughter, Titha, to christen the new city in honor of Thea's sacrifice during the Ever-war.

Clover Crocus Fernbloom: Son of Yythengrey's Master of Music, Clover considered himself an intellectual and traditionalist young Luna, traits that landed him in considerable trouble on more than one occasion. Falling under the influence of Cypress's misguided teachings before the old Luna's exile, Clover became entangled within Falora Fomora's horrible plot to destroy Celtica and the alliances of Night & Day later on. Seeking to right his wrongs, Clover sacrificed himself to save his family and friends, his fate remaining uncertain after the events of The *Dawn of Celtica*.

The Companions: The band of heroes who came to Gaela's aid at the end of the First Eon. They are comprised of Titha Mae and Paw, Audun and Haldor, Nech and Maya, and Theole and Sigrid. Their bond in servitude to their peoples continues well on into the beginnings of the Second Eon.

Craga: The Goddess of the Craglins and their homeland of Cragoa. She is said to be one with Mt. Crag and all surrounding lands, her mood being the temperament of the volcano itself.

Craglin: A short, yellow-skinned race of Goblins originating in Cragoa. Males sport two small bony horns on their foreheads and long, pointed ears.

Craglands: Home to the Craglin Goblins, situated around Mt. Crag in its immense crater and comprised of dense clay huts.

Cragoa: A northern region of Mydlan covered in huge, dangerous craters and enormous pine trees.

Cragoan Runestone: An ancient Runestone tied to the lands of its namesake. The symbol upon it was said to represent an aerial view of Mt. Crag, its shape radiating with an intensem fire-like orange glow. An illustration of this Runestone can be found in Chapter Ten: ***Frost & Flames***.

Crown of Elk Kings: A crown only spoken of in the oldest known lore, said to be made up of the very Crown of the mightiest Elk King's skull and antlers. If said antlers were made to house the Moonstone and

Sunstone, whoever possessed the united Crown would wield control over the rise and fall of the Sun, Moon, and Time itself. It perished with the Elk Kings during the ***Breaking of the Horizon***.

Cypress Sylvanus Byle: (pronounced Sy-press, like the cypress tree) A Luna descended from the Line of Byle (one of the three original Lunish bloodlines), Cypress grew to prominence after his impressive victories over Vulduun's forces during the early Ever-war as Commander of the Cedarguard. He became like a brother to Theole whilst serving as his Squire and most trusted confidante, and was considered an uncle to the Mae sisters before being banished from Ythengrey for dangerous, violently-bigoted viewpoints. In his exile, he returned to his ancestral roots within the Ruins of Byle, discovering that his ancient bloodline held the power of Sages. Tapping into his own potential with such arcane magicks proved harsh and unpredictable, leading to the unexpected, and much maligned, summoning of Falora Fomora from the Otherworld.

Grandfather Dagdus: Theole's grandfather, one of the most ancient of known Lunas. He built the Tri-Spiral Tomb on the outskirts of Yyythengrey toward the beginning of the First Eon, in a time when the Great Drakes allowed for the worship of other deities alongside them.

Daughter of Igdrasil: An enormous, luminous sapling birthed from the Seed of Igdrasil, also thought to be an Eternal Stone: the Lifestone of legend. The sole seed left by the demise of the first Tree of Life, Igdrasil, this Daughter first attempted to spread roots in its mother's decimated lands, but was uprooted by foul beings attracted to its glorious emerald auroras. A nefarious plot hatched by Falora Fomora saw Sigrid Autumnsdottir manipulated into fetching the Seed, eventually leading to her son, Angvar, planting it beneath the Tower of Celtica—where it was reborn for the Second Eon.

Dawnfather: The Lunish name for Vulduun, the Elder Drake of the Sun and one of two shapers of the lands of Gaela before the First Eon.

Druidunes: Large, cavernous holes that extend into the deepest bowels of Gaela in areas of great importance. Each race has different names for them, such as The Abyss for the Vikingmen.

Druids: Beings that bridged the gap between the land and life, these ancient mystics were both part of the living and of the soil, rock, and roots of Gaela. They were said to know all the secrets She (Gaela) had to offer, but guarded them well, only passing on their vast wisdom to those who sought it with pure intentions. They would only become more reclusive as Time went on into the Second Eon.

Duskmother: The Lunish name for Meriduun, Great Drake of the Moon and Mother of Night.

Duskridge: The Duskridge is the oldest mountain range in Gaela, its peaks rounded by the erosion of time. It once formed the western-most border of the known lands of Gaela, and held a deep connection with the Lunas that called it home.

Eastlyn: The furthest land East in the known parts of Gaela. The Svells form its border with Mydlan.

The Elk Kings: The first Children of Mother Nature, and the reigning rulers of her kingdom. They were said to protect all that is sacred to Gaela and her daughter Igdrasil, the Tree of Life, before becoming one with the Horizon after their battle with Vulduun at the end of the First Eon.

Eon: A vast expanse of time, only defined by those who record it.

Eternal Stones: Used to refer to the Orbs of Power, such as the Moonstone and Sunstone, and later the supposed Lifestone, or Seed of Igdrasil.

Ever-war: The scholarly name for the secret war Vulduun raged against the people of Gaela during the First Eon. It ended with the Breaking of the Horizon, when both Vulduun and the Elk Kings, the last remaining natural deities of the First Eon, were undone in the Companions quest for peace.

Falora Fomora: The Vulture Queen of Oathera, she was also known as the Fomorrigan, a title inherited from her mother, both claiming to descend from Meriduun herself. Other ancient legends tell of Falora the Fallen, The Scavengeress, Queen of the Slain, or a full name of Falorrigannah Fomorrigan. Her family's role in their dark realm seems to have rested on taking the energies (souls) of any who fell in war (or any unnatural, conflict-born way) within Gaela into the Otherworld, regaling them to a less than desirable fate. It is said she did so in the form of the Ghastly Black Vulture, making her another of the Great Avians.

Faun: The female half of a deeply-ancient race of horned, hooved, wool-covered beings a'kin to both the earliest days of Men and Beast. Thought to have once inhabited the 'Unknown Highlands', these Ram-like people's origins remain a mystery to the learn'ed, as their kind were all but extinct by Titha's time. The male counterparts to Fauns were called Satyrs.

Feathersword: A single, sharp-edged feather from Theole's Grand Silver Owl form that Titha took as her weapon of choice during ***The Ballad.*** It was further modified into a proper short-sword and given a Celtican sheath during the Dawn of the city, at the hands of its finest craftsmen.

Fell River: This winding river is given life by the waters of the Northfjord, and runs through the Fells all the way to Mydlan. It formed the basis of the first stronghold of Westlyn's humans, the ***Vikingmen***.

The Fells: The dominant mountain range of the West, the Fells were harshly steep and rocky mountains covered by sparse, dry vegetation. They formed the east border of Westlyn. Their enormous presence across the landscape was deeply rooted in the legends and lore of many peoples, but none moreso than the Vikingmen of Autumnhill that made their homes in their foothills.

Festival of Dawn: A Yythengrey festival once held on the Summer Solstice (longest day of the year) to celebrate the Dawnfather and the life his Sun gave to the plants and animals of the world during sleeping Day. Needless to say, it was not celebrated any longer by the time of the ***Dawn of Celtica***.

First Eon: The first period of recorded history in Galea, accounted for by Scribes and scholars such as Nech and Maya, and their predecessors. The First Eon began with civilization, and ended with the ***Breaking of the Horizon***, marked by the founding of Celtica.

Fomorrigan: An ancient, nigh-forgotten (at the time of ***Dawn of Celtica***) deity of Lunish mythology closely associated with Death and the path to it. The most ancient tomb in all of Yythengrey, when rediscovered, was thought to have direct ties to the legacy of the Fomorrigan and her cauldron, an artifact used to collect fallen souls in Gaela to be taken into the Otherworld. Some of the Luna's earliest songs sing of this mysterious deity.

Frorora: An ancient, mysterious civilization carved from ice by its Frororian inhabitants. Known as a terrible land of Frost Giants to the Vikingmen, Frorora remains largely unexplored by other races due to the hostile nature of its people.

Frororans: Known as Frost-kin to some and Frost Giants to others, the Frororans were not of Man nor Luna, their origins tied mysteriously to another realm. Only one population of these fiercely-territorial giants was known to Gaela, and how they came to claim the Snowly Fells is completely unknown.

Gaela: (pronounced Gay-lah) The name used to describe all that is, was, and will be of the land, earth, and sky in the realm of the Companions.

Gaela Falls: The massive waterfall that flowed forth from the Great Svell River into the Unknown Lands.

Gaffer: A human term for old men, and coincidentally the name of an Autumnhill wiseman during the time of ***Dawn*** who was, in fact, so old he may or may not have remembered if Gaffer wass his actual name or not.

Gates of Igdrasil: Ancient gates said to have led to the Tree of Life herself, built upon the sacrifice of the Svell Mammoths before the First Eon.

Gillian Rose Mae: (pronounced Gill-ian, like the gill of a fish, and you know the rest) Titha's older, lankier, and supposedly more "mature" sister of seventeen forest-years at the time of ***Dawn of Celtica***. Poised to inherit the mantle of Watcher after her father's time, Gilly was to become the first female to inhabit the position, therefor becoming the first Watchress of Yythengrey. Her beauty was the subject of many'a suiter's affection, promising a long and dramatic string of courtships before she ever chose a life-partner.

Grand Avian(s): A legendary form connected to the Firstbloods, a.k.a. the first families of each race of peoples. Their existence is said to have been heavily tied to the power of the Eternal Stones. At the time of the Dawn of Celtica, only three Grand Avians were known: Theole the ***Grand Silver Owl***, Sigrid the ***Glorious Red Eagle***, and Falora the ***Ghastly Black Vulture.*** After the demise of the Great Drakes, many saw the Grand Avians as the natural successors to such deities, much to the chagrin of Theole and Sigrid.

Haldor the Wolfhound: (pronounced Hal-door, with 'Hal' as in hallelujah and door like a front door) Audun's fiercely loyal, unusually large, and prone-to-face-licking best friend. His breed was fostered by Vikingmen from their earliest days of companionship with wolves, before the last remaining natural canines fled deep into uninhabited wildernesses.

Hawthorn: One of Theole's trusted personal guard, and a veteran of Yythengrey's Cedarguard. He fought in the Ever-war alongside Theole and Cypress both, remaining loyal to his watcher forever after.

The Horizon: The edge of the known world of Gaela, where the lands of Westlyn, Mydlan, and Eastlyn end. It holds great importance to the people below its influence, as it rose and settled both the Sun and Moon, and nothing beyond it had been explored by the beginning of the ***Dawn of Celtica***.

Igdrasil: The Tree of Life herself; an indescribably large tree of Legend said to have resembled an Oak tree of many colors. The vast waters of Svellvanyon and Mydlan flowed both in and out of her enormous roots. She existed before any other Nature in Gaela, and was regarded as the

Daughter of Gaela (the world) herself. Igdrasil became one with the Horizon after the ***Breaking***, bearing a single seed that would eventually be planted in Celtica to give rise to the Daughter of Igdrasil.

Imp: A small creature most consider to be demonic in nature, marked by a seeded desire to do others harm.

Invertebrateà: A most-modern scientific term coined by Nech in attempt to begin classifying the various known creatures of Gaela during his later days. It means "without vertebrae", which is an animal without a backbone—like a worm, crab, or insect. To us, in modern times, the word is **invertebrate**.

Jarl: The ruler of Vikingmen, holding a similar position to a King or Emperor, but equal in power to the ***Shieldmaiden*** counterpart, unlike the traditional relationship between a King and subservient Queen.

Kelliah: (pronounced Kell-I-ah) The most brilliant white mare (female horse) ever born of Autumnhill's stables, and the noble steed of Rainer Angvarsson during his greatest days.

Kernos the Satyr: A mysterious and ancient shepherd of the Satyr/Faun race, whose history was deeply connected to the lands he once guided Westlyn's Rams across. Some whispered beliefs that Kernos wielded a great and terrible power, one he may have chosen to leave in his secretive, and troubled, past.

Kriggoth: The former Emperor of Cragoa, betrayed and murdered by Ugar the Terrible during the events of ***The Ballad.***

Lass / Lassie: Terms of endearment used by Highlanders, lass meaning boy, and lassie meaning girl.

Lifestone: Also called the Stone of Life or Seed of Igdrasil, this entity was born a seed of Igdrasil's last breath, among the dying light of the Sun and Moonstones (the Elderstones) upon the ***Breaking of the Horzion***.

Lumen: Luna men, a'la males of the Lunish race.

Luminary: An important person; leader or ruler.

Luna: The oldest known Children of the Night in Gaela's realm, and once Meriduun's most devoted kin. Their skin is a pale indigo and their hair white, grey, or silver. They harbored a deep connection with their mountainous Duskridge and forest home, Yythengrey, during Titha's time, and formed lifelong relationships with the Forest Bears that shared their lands. Eventually, they would branch out into a much, much wider world to the delight of some and the horror of others.

Luneralle: A funeral held for Lunas in Yythengrey.

Mammoth's Respite: The ancient wetlands where the winding Lesser Svell River meets the Great Svell River. Mammoths used it as a watering hole during the Time before the First Eon.

Maple: The family name and nickname of a small, spectacled and shy Luna girl that was one of Titha's only friends growing up in Yythengrey. Her full name was **Ashley Aster Maple**.

Maya the Peregrine Falcon: (pronounced Mai-ah, like the traditional name Maya) Head of the Peregrine Order and Nech's oldest friend & colleague, she was fiercely smart and independent to a fault. Her history was marked by tragedy, including the loss of all her kin to a foreign flock of Eagles. She continued to be of great service to her fellow Companions well into the beginning of the Second Eon, and was instrumental in securing a safer fate for the Daughter of Igdrasil.

Melvinnious Maple: An old friend of Theole's and an elder councilor of Yythengrey, whos youngest daughter was one of Titha's only childhood friends. He was a known sympethizor to the Old Ways, and may have conspired with Cypress Byle and Calluna Mint before her untimely death.

Meriduun: (pronounced 'Merih', followed by dune like a sand dune) One of the two Great Drakes responsible for shaping the lands of Gaela. She was the Duskmother to the Lunas and former love and light of

Vulduun. Her glory was worshipped by all creatures of Night before the time of Titha Mae. The events of ***Dawn of Celtica*** shed new light on her origins and intentions, revealing a malicious connection to the Other-world, and the villainous Fomorrigans.

Merigold Fernbloom: Father to Clover Fernbloom and a peculiar character in his own right, Merigold resided as Ythengrey's Master of Music through his entire service as an elder, and wrote many of the songs the later generations of Lunas cherished.

Mince Pie: a rich pie filled with a mixture of spices and fruits. The fruit is typically dried and spiced with said spices. Such a concotion was born of the joining of Lunish and Human cuisines in Celtica's earliest days.

Moonflower Bed(s): Giant white flowers that only grew in Ythengrey, and only bloomed at night by light of the Moon. It is said their growth was directly tied to the lives of each Luna that slept within them—from infancy until death.

Moonstone: One of two orbs older than time that were deeply connected to the origin of the Great Drakes and the ***Moon*** herself, who was seen as a deity by the Lunas. The Moonstone was trusted to Theole's bloodline after Meriduun forfeited its power, then seized by Vulduun in an effort to eliminate Night forever. Fortunately for all of Gaela, Titha and the Compan-ions were able to thward such malicious plans, sacrificing both the Sun and Moonstone during the Breaking of the Horizon.

Monk: A devoted follower of a practice or religion, typically robed or cloaked in a covered manner.

Mount Meri: The highest peak of the Duskridge Mountains that formed the center of Ythengrey. Also written as Mt. Meri.

Mount Crag: A dormant volcano, the largest in all of Gaela. It slumbered in the middle of Cragoa, adorned with the carvings of beasts revered by the Craglins. Its heart was said to be ruled by a Goddess, one unchained to the whims of the Great Drakes—that answered only to Gaela herself…

Mouth of Mydlan: An enormous cliff that dropped South from the Pine Forests of Mydlan. At its bottom rested a lake sharing the same name.

Mydlan: The great expanse of land between the Fells and Svells, populated by Craglins, Gnomes, and countless fantastical species. Its principle northern territory, Cragoa, began to decay as another power-struggle consumed it during the aftermath of Vulduun's treachery, far into the Second Eon.

Nechalec (Nech) the Scribe (Nech pronounced like the Scottish 'Loch') A well-learned and once-prosperous Craglin Scribe from the Craglands, Nech suffered a most violent exile at the hands of Ugar the Terrible when his homeland was overthrown. He found solace and companionship in Titha Mae during the events of ***The Ballad***, replacing Cypress as Theole's Squire and confidante afterward. He was instrumental in securing a far-more pleasant fate for the Daughter of Igdrasil, and in the cultivation of Celtica as a whole.

Northern Lights: Another term used by the races of Northern Gaela to describe an Aurora Borealis, or a most magical and colorful display of lights in the North skies.

Northfjord: A mighty fjord* that created the border between the Duskridge and the mighty Fell mountains, the Northfjord served as a port for seafaring Vikingmen since the dawn of civilization.
*Geologically, a **fjord** (pronounced fiord) is a long, narrow inlet with steep sides marked by cliffs or mountains, created by a glacier.

Oathera: Another realm that exists alongside Gaela, the two intertwined by the magics of mist and shadow. Every race has/had their own name for this place, those in Galea long believing it was where all or part of their people traveled upon Death. It is also referred to as the Otherworld, Otherdeath, or the Oblivion.

Ogre: A massive, brutish race covered in sparse, greasy hair and inclined to not-so-nice deeds.

Old Ways: The term used by Lunas to refer to their once near-immortal nature due to a close relationship with the Dusk-ridge and its slowing of Time. All of this, it turned out, was of Meriddun's design, and most unnatural. Once discovered, this led more progressive-thinking Lunas to an alliance with the Day Kin in effort to finally be free of the curse of Meriduun's deceitful Old Ways.

Otherworld: The name Lunas gave to Oathera, a realm existing on the other side of Gaela's heavy mists and natural magicks. Falora Fomora hailed from this place, being the first being of Oatherian origin to surface in the lifetime of those living during ***Dawn of Celtica***. Until her presence was made known, the Otherworld had largely fallen into obscurity and the forgetfulness of Time among Lunas and Man, its name and meaning only surviving throught the oldest of thier songs and verse.

Ozark Staff: Theole's staff made from the splintered spear of Thea and the Moonstone itself. The origina was destroyed by Vulduun during his invasion of Yythengrey. He created another, Moonstone-less Ozark Staff after the events of the Ballad, one he still used across the Second Eon.

Paw the Black Bear: (pronounced like the paw of a bear) Titha's Bear-brother, Paw was a rambunctious (and enormous) young forest black bear that chose Titha during her fifth Festival of Dawn. They were inseparable forever-after, growing up together as if they were born of the same womb. He bore a fierce love of and strength for Titha, one that saw her through even the most treacherous of obstacles.

Peony Ponderosa: A well-groomed and vibrantly-dressed baker who owned Celtica's most visited baked goods stand. He specialized in mushroom cakes, such as his famous Portobello Surprise.

Pine Forests: Usually refers to the dense forests of harsh pines that dominated Mydlan's mid-landscape.

Rainer Angvarsson (pronounced Rain-ehr, with 'Rain' as in water falling from the sky) The oldest son of Jarl Angvar and Shieldmaiden Sigrid of Autumnhill. Commander of the Houndsmen and devilishly handsome, Rainer inherited the title of Jarl from his father after Angvar's death at the hands of Vulduun.

Reeks: A race of semi-intelligent lizard people whos devotion to Vulduun twisted their scaly appearance into something foul and putrid during the Ever-war.

Reginald the Porcupine: A friendly yet somber porcupine that resided in Yythengrey. He was known for his affinity for Lunas, and the openness in which he shared his quills for tasks such as needlepoint and knitting.

The River Daenu: This mighty river flowed southward from Loch Daenu straight through the heart of Yythengrey. Its waters gave life to all creatures who lived there.

Riverstone: The currency used by Lunas of Yythengrey. The shinier, prettier, and flatter the stone, the more it was worth.

Roostwood: The home of Theole and his daughters that sat atop Mt. Meri in Yythengrey. It was of the finest wooden craftsmanship and only accessible from the Grand Steps that led up from the Meadow.

Ruins of Byle: A timeworn place with origins dating before the First Eon, this ancestral land of the Byle family hosted a magnificent castle during the early days of the First Eon, its splendor lost to the internal struggles of the Lunas long before the Ever-war. Afterward, it remained untouched for centuries until Cypress Sylvanus Byle returned to the Ruins after his exile from Yythengrey. Once there, he sought to rebuild a sanctuary for Lunas wishing to thrive in the Old Ways, using what remained of his ancient ancestral home.

Rune: An ancient symbol bearing great meaning.

Runestone: A stone holding great power, marked with a rune that is specific to its purpose and nature. Mydlan's Runestone was the first to have surfaced at the time of ***Dawn of Celtica***, alongside the fragmented Tri-Spiral Runestone of Titha Mae's family.

Sage: An individual who is highly skilled with an artform, typically one that is inherited or blood-born. In Cypress' instance, it is magic, making him inherently gifted with the arcane arts. Though he referred to himself as a proper Sage during the events of ***Dawn of Celtica***, his immense blunderous summoning of Falora Fomora proved he still had much to learn.

Satyr: A vastly-ancient being born of the earliest days of Men and Beast, distinguished by huge curved horns and hard, sturdy hooves like that of a Bighorn Sheep, or Ram. The females of this wool-covered race were known as Fauns, each revered by the ancestors of Man for their mastery over the mountains of Gaela.

Scribe: An ancient writer, keeper, and recorder of events, things, and persons important to history.

Second Eon: Marked by the Breaking of the Horizon and Dawn of Celtica in the same year, the Second Eon began with great promise as the worlds of Day and Night joined together for the first time, evening out Time's influence over the mortals of Gaela.

Shaman: A master of the magic, mystical, and dark arts who serves as a spiritual guide for their society.

Sifters: A gangly, grey and wide-faced peoples only found within the ancient, cursed mists of the Wick, where they capitalized on the misfortunes of those unlucky enough to be stranded there. The events of ***Dawn of Celtica*** revealed that Sifters were once Lunas themselves long ago, in a time before the power-struggles of the First Eon conned them into a fate worse than Death.

Sigrid Autumnsdóttir: (pronounced See-grid, as in look, 'see'! A 'grid'!) Shieldmaiden of and ruler over Autumnhill alongside her firstborn son, Jarl Rainer Angvarsson. A stoic yet gracefully beautiful warrior of fair hair, Sigrid inherited the mantle and power of her bloodline's Great

Avian: The Glorious Red Eagle. Being of the Firstblood, it is her family that originally settled Westlyn for the Men of Gaela, and her direct ancestors whom where bestowed the responsibility of the Sunstone after the Shaping of the Lands by Vulduun. It was a difficult and perilous journey for her to relinquish faith in Vulduun after his falling, her people's once revered and worshipped Great Drake still ever-present in their minds. She and her youngest son, Angvar, were directly responsible for securing a far-safer fate for the Daughter of Igdrasil in Celtica.

Skaldhall: The ancient home of Sigrid's Vikingmen ancestors, made to house the Sunstone and those in power within Autumnhill.

Smelting: The process in which metal is extracted from its natural ore casing, requiring immense, extreme heat.

Smithing: The artform of crafting objects from metals, such as weapons, armor, and building materials. It is one of the oldest, and proudest trades of all peoples.

Snowy Fells: The snow-covered mountains that made up the northernmost portion of the Fells.

Snowy Lands & Snowy Svells: The northernmost, snow-covered lands at the end of the Svells.

Sprucewill Foxglove: The younger brother and successor to Captain Aspen, Sprucewill served as Captain and Commander of the Cedarguard after the events of ***The Ballad***. He was a careful and sensitive leader, similar qualities his beloved sister was remembered for.

Squire: An armor-bearing individual of high status, who is in service to a master, or ***sire***, and is considered second-in-command.

Sunstone: Also called the Skaldstone, it was one of two ancient Orbs known as the Elder Stones. The Sunstone was entrusted to Sigrid's bloodline after Vulduun forfeited its power and entrusted its keeping to the Vikingmen of Westlyn. Her son, Angvar, carried it all the way to the Gates of Igdrasil alongside Titha Mae, where the pair would sacrifice the two stones for peace. Its origins were deeply connected to the birth of the Great Drakes and the ***Sun*** itself.

Svells: The Great Svell Mountains; harsh peaks that form the border between Mydlan and Eastlyn. It is said that the 'V' in their name came from the V-shape they form around Svellvanyon, the vast canyon in-between.

Svell Valley: A large valley in the Western Svells that houses the Winding Wundi River down out of Cragoa into Mamm-oth's Respite.

Svellvanyon: The massive, deep canyon in the 'V' of the Svells that dominated the landscape of Northern Eastlyn. Legend tells that Svellvanyon held the Gates of Igdrasil that led to the Tree of Life herself, before the Breaking of the Horizon.

Tartan: A wool fabric bearing criss-crossed horizontal and vertical bands, also known as a plaid pattern. At the time of ***Dawn of Celtica,*** it had only been seen as part of the clothing made by Highlanders. It is said that the colors used in its patterning and making represent the clans and families of which the wearer originates.

Thea Celtica Mae: Mother of Gilly, Titha, and Beebee, and the fallen Lady of Yythengrey. She was said to have been unmatched in her beauty and shared a peculiar kinship with Gaela. None miss her more than her daughters and the betrothed soulmate she left behind, Theole. Not much else is known of Thea, a point of contention for her oldest daughter, Gillian.

Theole the Watcher: (pronounced The-Ohl, with 'The' as in Theodore) Father of Titha, Gilly, and Beebee Mae and the great protector of Yythengrey. His betrothed, Thea, perished alongside Meriduun, marking the beginning of the Ever-war he fought tirelessly to end. Theole housed great, ancient power as inheritor of the Firstblood of the Maes, and thus was capable of taking the form of the ***Grand Silver Owl.*** It was his trust and love for both his middle daughter, Titha, and fellow captive Sigrid, that allowed Celtica to become a reality upon their return toward the end of ***The Ballad.***

Titha Lilly Mae: (pronounced Tih-tha Lilly May, with the 'Ti' sound as in 'tip', Lilly like the flower, and May like the month) Aged twelve forest-years at the time of ***Dawn of Celtica,*** Titha Mae is the adventurous middle child of Theole the Watcher and Thea Celtica Mae. She shares a deep love with all her forest home's kin, but none moreso than her Bear-brother, Paw. Her innate curiosity and protectiveness led to many perious journeys, both of which were retold for generations upon generations (and here we are!). Long story short, if not for her, Gaela and her peoples would have ceased to exist several times over.

Torai (pronounced Tor-eye) The largest member of the Peregrine Order and Maya's right-wing man. Also known as the Defiler of Ugar's Crown (of horns).

Torc: A type of thickly-crafted jewelry shaped like a C that is worn like a bracelet, but can also be crafted as a larger necklace/bangle type to be worn around the neck, as well.

Tower of Celtica: A monument built by the Vikingmen as a peace offering to the Lunas during the ***Dawn of Celtica***. It formed the centerpoint of the town before being destroyed and replaced by the sapling Daughter of Igdrasil.

Tri-Spiral: An ancient symbol thought to represent the three ruling families of the Lunish people. One being the Byles, another the Maes, and the last supposedly lost to the earliest days of history. An illustration of the Tri-Spiral can be found in Chapter Six, ***Fates Not Chosen***.

Tri-Spiral Amethysts: Three amethysts worn by Thea Celtica Mae in life, their origins unknown. These precious stones each bore a single spiral, and when rejoined would make the Tri-Spiral Runestone whole again. Before this, one piece resided in Thea's circlet, one in her ring, and one in her necklace. Each were given to her daughters Titha, Gillian, and Begonia respectively, years after her death.

Tri-Spiral Runestone: An ancient Runestone bearing the Tri-Spiral, a symbol with origins dating back to the very beginning of Lunish kind.

Tri-Spiral Tomb: A Lunish tomb built on the outskirts of Yythengrey by Theole's grandfather, Dagdus, as a resting place for Lunas who died in battle or in vain. Their bodies, and ashes of their Moonflowers, were to be taken here in tribute to the Fomorrigan, so she could watch over them in the Afterlife. The ancient cairn's true name has been lost to Time.

Ugar the Terrible: (pronounced Oo-gahr, with the 'Oo' as in tool, and 'gar' like the fang-toothed fish) A horrid foe who might as well have been the combination of all bad and ugly things in Gaela. His hideously scarred form shielded many secrets, up until the death of his first master, Vulduun. Once Vulduun was defeated, Ugar slinked form one evil master to the next, finding servitude under a deceitful and manipulative Oatherian called Falora Fomora, her influence growing from the shadows through him.

Unknown Lands: These are the lands… that were unknown… and have yet to be explored!

Vikingmen: The humans of Northern Gaela, their main stronghold being Autumnhill. Vulduun cherished them as the hardiest Children of Day before his betrayal.

Vulduun: (pronounced Vuhl-dune, with 'Vul' as in Vulcan and 'dune' like a sand dune) Vulduun was the last surviving Great Drake (Dragon, or ***Elderdrake)***. He was known by many names: Dawnfather to the Lunas, Great Day Drake, and Herald of the Sun. He was also shaper of the lands of Gaela alongside his fallen mate, Meriduun. Vulduun was driven mad by the death of Meriduun and turned on the very world he shaped before perishing during the ***Breaking of the Horizon.***

The Vulture Queen: The title ancient peoples of Gaela gave Falora Fomora when she first emerged from Oathera; the Otherworld.

Wargles: The fuzziest, most adorable little creatures to ever spawn from Gaela. They use their infamous cuteness to lure people into peculiar, magical places. Any who have seen them say they are tiny enough to wear an acorn cap on their head.

<u>**Waxing Moon:**</u> The stage of the Moon in which she is illuminated on her right side. When described as "sharp" or "crescent", the Moon is in a very thin C shape, often called a Crescent Moon.

<u>**The Watcher/Watchress:**</u> The ancient position of leadership in Yythengrey, in which a Luna was entrusted with watchful protection and guidance, rather than all-powerful rulership. Theole's eldest daughter, Gillian, will inherit the throne's title from him, bestowing her as the first female Watcher, or Watchress.

<u>**Welp:**</u> A hateful term used to describe smaller, weaker creatures in Cragoa.

<u>**Westlyn:**</u> The expanse of land west of the Fells that held everything from the Duskridge Mountains and Yythengrey to the Barren Fields and Autumnhill. It was home to the Cradle of Civilization, where the first great organizations of divine races came to be organized under banners and names in history. Or so they thought.

<u>**The Wick:**</u> Also known as the Wicklands, this murky swamp remained shrouded in a beyond-thick, smog-like mist that cursed all who lingered there. It was once a beautiful and prosperous part of the Duskridge before the power-struggles of the First Eon turned it into a most foul place. After such, it was only used as a place of refuge and hiding for ne're-do-well'ers and outcasts of society.

<u>**The Winding Wundi**</u>: A twisting, turning river that flowed through the Snowy Svells down into the Svell Valley; an offshoot of the Seas at the Horizon.

<u>**Wola:**</u> Lunish word for female or woman; a Luna lady.

<u>**Wooly Rhinoceros:**</u> Also known as Wooly Rhinos, these enormous rhinos were covered in long, thick hair and remained peaceful until challenged. They resided in the Barren Fields where they grazed on the tall, dry grasses.

Wundiberg: Home of the Gnomes in the North, comprised of intricate tunnels, hut-houses, and roads nestled into the Svell Mountains.

Ythengrey: **(pronounced Yee-thin-gray)** Home of the Lunas, Ythengrey was an ancient forest from the time of creation. Time passed slowly and peacefully there during the First Eon, before the joining of Day and Night during the ***Dawn of Celtica***. The center was formed by the Meadow, which led westward to the Duskridge's highest peak, Mt. Meri. Ythengrey housed many things seen nowhere else in Gaela, including enormous white Flowerbeds and a unique, powerful breed of black bears deeply connected to their Lunish kin.

About the Author

Jon and his siblings grew up in Knoxville, Tennessee in the foot-hills of the Great Smoky Mtns., the oldest mountain range in the world—and one every bit as full of magic as is present in Gaela. As an adult, Jon and his better half (see: *wife*, pictured left with Jon at the Giant's Causeway in Northern Ireland), Brandee, have made a habit of seeking out such magic around the globe, visiting historic lands and ruins everywhere from Iceland and Ireland to Japan and Israel. Their own Celtic, Norse, and American ancestry is present in every breath and page of this series, and continues to kindle flames of wonderment within them on a daily basis. Legends of dragons, gnomes, giants, and forest-kin are, after all, in their very *blood.*

When he's not toiling away in Titha's world, Jon is a writer by professon based in Nashville, TN. For much more on his work, visit **jonbdalvy.com** or **tithamae.com** anytime.

We cannot thank you enough for following along with Titha and her Companions. It quite literally means the world.

All the best,

Nechalec Press

www.ingramcontent.com/pod-product-compliance
Lightning Source LLC
Chambersburg PA
CBHW060758310726
48980CB00002B/138

* 9 7 8 0 5 7 8 4 8 6 4 5 1 *